THE TIME BOMB WAS SET
THIRTY YEARS AGO

Caine—An unbeatable wild card, the ex-CIA agent with hard green eyes and a dozen deadly talents.

C.J.—The California golden girl. Her suntanned body promised heaven, but her calculating heart would deliver Caine to hell.

Wasserman—An Auschwitz survivor, he built the biggest porn empire in America. Is he out to avenge the past—or to seize control of the future?

Dr. Mendoza—The world calls him saint. The natives at his jungle clinic call him a god. Does his noble presence conceal a history of sadism and terror?

Code name: Starfish—A sinister conspiracy composed of five deadly tentacles. Today it controls vast financial empires. Tomorrow, the world?

THE FUSE IS LIT. THE COUNTDOWN HAS BEGUN.
WHO WILL SURVIVE THE . . .
HOUR

HOUR
OF THE
ASSASSINS

Andrew Kaplan

A DELL BOOK

Published by
Dell Publishing Co., Inc.
1 Dag Hammarskjold Plaza
New York, New York 10017

Dell ® TM 681510, Dell Publishing Co., Inc.

ISBN 0-440-13530-3

Printed in the United States of America

First printing—December 1980

For Rose, Gilbert, Myron,
Maureen, and Anne

"Now is the hour of the assassins."

—*Arthur Rimbaud*

PROLOGUE

Most of the world thought of Dr. Felix Mendoza as something of a saint. Twice nominated for the Nobel peace prize, he was worshiped as a god by the Chama, Shipibo, and Yagua Indians who came to his jungle hospital. Yet the first time he heard of the Mendoza Institute, Caine somehow knew that he would have to murder the doctor.

Since the time of Hammurabi men have made a distinction between killing and murder. But this distinction has never been clear-cut, for every death is unique. Of course Caine was not the sort of man to be troubled by these speculations. If he had been, perhaps none of what came to be called "that damned Mendoza business" within the CIA, would have ever happened.

"Begin at the beginning," said the Red Queen to Alice, but where do you draw a line and say, This is where it all started. You could say it began in Austria, where Caine first heard Mendoza's name mentioned and felt that queer inevitability. But you could just as easily begin the story in Laos, where Caine looked down at what was left of the girl's body and decided to quit, or in Virginia where he was trained, or even in Germany before he was born. A million factors make up what we call *chance,* which as much as anything else determines our course. On the plane to Iquitos, Caine himself thought that the Mendoza business really began for him when an old man woke up in the middle of the night, shivering from the violence of a bad dream.

PART I

"O God, I could be bounded in a nutshell, and count myself a king of infinite space, were it not that I have bad dreams."

—*Hamlet, Act II, Scene 2*

CHAPTER 1

The heart of the porno district in Hollywood is the intersection of Western Avenue and Santa Monica Boulevard. Painted storefronts on Santa Monica advertise the massage parlors, adult bookstores, and skin flick movies that blanket the district. Along Western the come-on tends to be written in neon, until the parade of sex shops finally begins to give way to the eternal Halloween that is Hollywood Boulevard.

As the taxi turned up Western, Caine glanced past the driver at the brown hills. The letters of the HOLLYWOOD sign gleamed white as headstones in the late afternoon sun. High above the smog a few pale wisps of cirrus hung over the hills. He turned back to the street, looking for the address. Then he saw the sign, emblazoned across a drab two-story building in a flickering neon script. His eyes, invisible behind the sunglasses, glinted with amusement as he read:

"House of Oral Orgasm.
French Massage from our Luscious Hostesses.
BankAmericard Accepted."

A beautiful black girl, barely out of her teens, stood in the doorway, checking the street action. She wore a blond wig, high-heeled clogs, blue hot pants over red leotards, and a T-shirt that proclaimed: "There is no life east of Sepulveda!"

Hooray for Hollywood, Caine thought, as the cab pulled over to the curb. Out of habit he checked the side-door mirror before he got out of the cab, but he was clean. No reason for him not to be, but still, habits die hard. He remembered how his instructor at Langley used to say, "The day you stop going through the drill, no matter how irrelevant it seems, is the day you can forget about living to collect your pension."

He paid the driver and waited until the cab left before he walked up to the black girl, who tried to stifle a yawn and smile seductively at him at the same time. She looked at his boyish face, neat sandy hair, and well-tailored gray three-piece suit, and decided that he might be worth a very good tip, especially if he was kinky. She put her hand on his arm and purred, "I'm going to show you a special good time, baby."

"I'm here to see Mr. Wasserman."

"Ain't no Mr. Wasserman here, baby"—pouting her mouth. He didn't seem like a customer.

"Then take me to your leader," he said.

"My who?"

"Anybody who'll talk to those of us living east of Sepulveda," he grinned. She smiled back nervously. She had the Watts instinct for trouble and he looked like trouble.

"Hey, Freddie baby," she called over her shoulder. In a moment the doorway was filled by the massive bulk of a huge hairy white man, naked from the waist up, except for a Marine Corps tattoo on his arm and a single gold earring in his left ear, grinning like he ate middle linebackers for breakfast. He must have stood at least six foot six.

"What's the problem?" Freddie said.

"Take it easy, Freddie baby," Caine said, craning his neck to look up at him. "Tell Mr. Wasserman that Mr. Caine is here for our appointment. Of course, if he isn't here, then I'm going to turn around and walk out. Then Wasserman's your problem, not mine."

Freddie's smile disappeared. For a second it seemed to Caine that there was a flicker of fear in the giant's eyes, but then he dismissed the thought as too improbable. As he walked inside, Freddie mumbled something about waiting and quickly stepped behind a red curtain. Caine could feel the girl's eyes watching him intently as he looked around. The walls of the tiny reception room were covered with portraits of nude young girls in erotic poses. As he absentmindedly studied the photos, the girl relaxed enough to sit down and light a cigarette. After all he was just a man, like all the rest.

It doesn't make sense, Caine thought. None of it made any sense, that was why he had come. Not so much to find out why Wasserman wanted to see him, but how Wasserman had known that he existed. He remembered his surprise when the desk clerk at the Beverly Wilshire handed him the envelope as he was checking in. The envelope contained the three-word message: "Call me, Wasserman" and a phone number. It bothered him because he hadn't been back to L.A. in years and he had just landed at LAX that morning. He had made the call out of curiosity and because the whole thing was beginning to smell like Company business. That, and the fact that the message had been scrawled across the face of Benjamin Franklin on a hundred-dollar bill.

He heard the sound of heavy moaning from behind the red curtain. He pulled it aside and found himself in a tiny movie theater. On the screen a heavily-muscled black man was having sex with two women, a pretty blonde and a Chinese girl. For a terrible moment the Chinese girl reminded Caine of Lim, but he immediately quashed the memory. He turned at the sound of someone coming through the curtain. It was Freddie baby. He motioned for Caine to follow him through a side-door to a small well-lit corridor that ended at a solid steel door. Taped to the door was a small hand-lettered cardboard sign that read:

TRANSAMERICA NEWS, INC.

A closed-circuit television camera, mounted above the door, followed Caine's movements as he bent to read the sign. Freddie folded his arms and leered at Caine while they posed for the camera.

"Did you enjoy the movie?" he asked.

Caine shrugged.

"I think I liked the book better," he replied.

Freddie's eyes narrowed and Caine wondered if he hadn't put his foot in it. Just then the steel door noiselessly slid open. Freddie motioned Caine inside and took up his post beside the door.

Stepping through the doorway into Wasserman's office was like stepping through the looking glass. "Curiouser and curiouser," he thought, as the door closed silently behind him. The office was sumptuously furnished in authentic Chippendale. The delicacy and good taste of the furnishings seemed totally at odds with the setting and the large, beefy man behind the desk. Wasserman had a jowly red face, topped by a shock of white hair that contrasted nicely with the tan color of his velour leisure suit. He looked like one of those wealthy middle-aged men that beautiful young girls latch onto at the Candy Store in Beverly Hills, convinced they've just caught the brass ring.

Not that his appearance meant anything. Appearances could be fatally misleading, Caine thought. Like Smiley Gallagher, a short, pudgy man who looked like a cross between a nearsighted accountant and the Pillsbury Doughboy. Smiley had always seemed completely out of place in Nam, but in fact he was a pathological killer who had run the wet work in the Phoenix operation. He used to brag that he could get any prisoner, no matter how dedicated, to sell out his own mother inside of fifteen minutes.

Wasserman smiled and gestured for Caine to sit down. As he sat, Caine looked around the room wonderingly. The place was a museum. Against one wall stood a large armoire containing jade cat figurines that, he guessed, came from the Han period. The figurines were incongruously mixed with a dozen pre-Columbian *huacos*. Each of the *huacos* was a pottery vessel shaped like a feline and they all wore the strange Cheshire cat smile characteristic of the pre-Inca Andean cultures. The only modern note in the room was a Texas Instruments 700 computer terminal in a far corner, next to a separate telephone. Caine surmised that Wasserman used it to hook into a time-sharing service. If true, it meant that Wasserman's files were on disks on a local time-sharing service's computer. Only someone who knew which service he used, and Wasserman's user identification, password, and the data-set names could ever have access to those files.

Next to the terminal was a bank of four closed-circuit television screens. One of the screens showed a view of the street outside the front door. The next screen showed Freddie standing just beyond the steel door. The third screen was blank, while the last screen showed a nude girl slowly caressing a customer. Anyone with such an elaborate security system has got to have more than a couple of hookers to hide, Caine decided.

However the most interesting thing in the room was a bright painting hung on the wall opposite the armoire. Incredibly, there was no mistaking the warm yellows and greens of the field, the three slender trees, and the distant figure of the woman shading herself with an umbrella. He squinted at the signature in the lower right corner: "Claude Monet, 1887."

"You were wondering if it is genuine," Wasserman said, in a low, faintly German accent. "The first thing people usually ask is if it's real and then they wonder how much it cost. Am I right, Mr. Caine?" Wasserman smiled benignly, his round face radiating good humor.

"Actually, I was wondering how you ever got it from the Staatsgalerie in Stuttgart."

Wasserman nodded approvingly.

"That's quite a story. But I see that Harris was right about you."

"Did Harris set this up?" Caine asked. Bob Harris was an all-American boy in a Cardin suit who acted as the CIA liaison to various syndicate and union leaders. So that was how Wasserman had known how to find him, he thought. Just before he had left the Company, Harris had come over to say good-bye. He had been surprised at the time, because he and Harris weren't exactly close.

"Let's say that Bob owed me a favor," said Wasserman. Caine remembered Harris wishing him luck with a boyish smile that was as sincere as a deodorant commercial.

"Bob Harris wouldn't do a favor for his dying mother," Caine snapped.

"The favor cost me five thousand dollars cash."

"Oh, yes," Caine nodded. "He'd do that all right."

Wasserman nodded appreciatively and leaned forward, resting his elbows on the desk. "*Tochis afn tish*, as we say, Mr. Caine. Let's get down to business."

"All right," Caine said. He thought he might have the accent pinned down from the way Wasserman pronounced *tochis*. It sounded like *low German*, possibly Bavarian.

"What else do you know about me?"

"Quite a lot. For instance, I know that your name is John Caine. I also know that you were an extremely effective field operative, with excellent qualifications in geography, finance, linguistics, military and political science. Your best languages are German, Spanish, and Laotian and you have a black belt in karate. Although I don't have all the details, I believe that you were involved in certain dirty tricks in Europe, Asia, and the Middle East. I think the phrase is 'wet work,' isn't it? Now it seems you recently quit the CIA under somewhat unusual circumstances and I want to pay you one thousand dollars for exactly one hour of your time, beginning now."

That shit Harris must have peddled my file, Caine thought angrily, as Wasserman reached into his jacket pocket and brought out a thick wad of hundred-dollar bills. He counted out ten of them and laid them on the desk in front of Caine, replacing the wad back in his pocket.

"In exchange for what?"

"I want you to sit here and listen to a story." The two men looked at each other, measuring, testing the air with invisible antennae. What the hell, Caine thought, as he reached for the money.

"Sordid, isn't it?" Wasserman gestured at a customer getting an "X-rated" massage on the television monitor. He glanced at the screen, shook his head, then pressed a button on a desk console and the screen went blank.

"But don't knock it. I do over twenty million a year in business out of this office. I distribute films, magazines, newspapers, and sexual aids through a nationwide chain of adult bookstores and movie theaters. In addition, I do the biggest mail-order business in the country."

"Not to mention prostitution," Caine put in.

"Please, professional massage. After all I don't make the laws. I'm just a simple businessman who knows that boys will be boys, no matter what the law says," Wasserman said with a roguish wink, implying that he was just a man of the world, smiling at the harmless frailties of human nature.

"Still and all, despite these oppressive and unconstitutional laws, I've done all right for myself. I came to this country as a penniless immigrant after the war and America has been very good to me."

Jesus Christ, what comes next: a rousing chorus of "God Bless America"? Caine wondered. Something told him that he was going to earn that thousand.

"So what," he shrugged.

"So, I am a very wealthy man, who can afford to pay a great deal for what I want," Wasserman said, leaning back complacently.

"Which is?"

"I want you to kill a man."

Caine stood up, took the $1,000 out of his pocket, and dropped it on the desk.

"I don't know what Harris told you, but I've retired from the dirty tricks business," he snapped, and turned to leave.

"Sit down, Caine! I paid a thousand dollars for your time and you'll hear me out," Wasserman thundered. Then in a more conciliatory tone, "Hear me out, Caine. If, after we've spoken, you are still not interested, keep the money and we'll just forget the whole thing."

Caine hesitated for a moment. Then he picked up the money, put it back in his pocket, and sat down. Wasserman was beginning to arouse his curiosity.

For the first time, Wasserman appeared ill at ease, as if having come so far, he didn't know quite how to proceed. He offered Caine a cigar and when Caine declined, he lit one for himself with a solid gold Dunhill lighter. Then after a single puff, he made a wry face and stabbed the cigar out in an onyx ashtray. He looked around nervously, glanced at the television monitors, then pressed a few buttons and the other screens went blank. He stared at the blank screens for a moment and when he turned back to face Caine, his pale blue eyes had grown suddenly old.

"Do you do much dreaming, John?" asked Wasserman.

"Not much."

"Did you ever have the same dream, night after night?"

"No," Caine lied.

"Well, I do."

"It doesn't matter," Caine said. "Dreams aren't real."

"This one is," Wasserman replied, wiping his sweating face with a handkerchief. "Every night for the past three months, I have had the same horrible dream," began Wasserman. "Every night I put off sleep, because I know that as soon as I doze off, it will happen again. I've tried pills, sex, drugs, liquor; nothing works. How could it? Because every night, as soon as my eyes close, I am back there."

"There?" asked Caine.

"Auschwitz," Wasserman replied and, unbuttoning his sleeve, thrust his right arm at Caine. A number was tattooed on his forearm in faint blue characters.

"When I arrived in Auschwitz I was only twenty-six," Wasserman continued. "That was in 1941. By then my parents had already been taken. Before the Nazis came, I had worked with my father. We had the largest accounting firm in Leipzig. It was confiscated, of course. Later I managed to bribe a local Nazi party official and get a job as a laborer in a munitions factory. But it was all futile. They came for us one night and we were packed with hundreds of others into a boxcar. Myself, my wife, Hanna, and our baby son, Dieter. We were among the last Jews to leave Leipzig. She was so beautiful, my Hanna. Blond hair and gentle eyes—who would have thought there was so much strength in that slender body. And our baby, he was only fourteen months old."

It's always bad, Caine thought. Our generation

grew up with it. You'd have thought we'd have gotten used to it by now, that we'd have heard the worst by now. But it's always bad.

Wasserman's eyes were brimming wet, but he shook his head and went on.

"I don't understand how we survived that trip, standing crushed against the dead, the insane, and the dying for six days without food or water. But we did.

"When we arrived at Auschwitz, the *kapos* threw those of us who were still alive out of the boxcars and the guards marched us to the Birkenau railroad camp for our first selection. Hanna was clutching Dieter when they separated us. It was then that I caught my first glimpse of a short, swarthy SS officer. He was the camp doctor, SS *Hauptstürmführer* Josef Mengele. That was what the guards called him. We inmates had another name for him. We called him *malachos mavet*, in Hebrew it means the Angel of Death.

"Mengele selected those who were healthy enough to work for the labor barracks. All the others, and almost always the children, were sent to the gas chambers. Once, while standing in front of the crematorium, he stood with his hands on his hips and bragged, 'Here the Jews enter through the gate and leave through the chimney.' And all the while a small orchestra made up of inmates played Strauss waltzes. He wanted to make it *gemütlich*, don't you see?

"I never saw my son again. But Hanna I saw one more time, and God help me, I see her again now every night."

Wasserman rubbed his hands over his sweaty face, then he regained control and continued more calmly.

"Of all the Nazi criminals, Mengele was perhaps the most infamous. There is an open warrant for his arrest in West Germany and a fifteen-thousand-dollar reward. He is also wanted by Interpol, the U.S., Britain, France, Russia, and of course, the Israelis. He sentenced millions of people to death.

"I personally know of one instance when he threw a crying baby into an open fire before the horrified eyes of the mother. I once saw him bury a bayonet in a young girl's head. He would inject phenolic acid into children's eyes. You see, this monster was obsessed with breeding twins with blue eyes.

"But that isn't what I dream about, or why you are here. Because he did something much worse than all that to my Hanna."

Wasserman stared bleakly through Caine, as though he were seeing her face once more. It was coming now, Caine thought. In a reflex action Caine took out a cigarette and lit it. As he inhaled, he looked at Wasserman's empty blue eyes, lost in the dark night that never quite ends for survivors. But mixed with his pity was a sense of uneasiness. Something didn't fit, but he couldn't quite put his finger on it.

Wasserman took a deep breath and went on in a strangled, hoarse monotone, as the sweat poured down his face.

"Every night it starts the same way. The *kapos* come to rouse us and they march us through the fence into the women's compound for the first time. At first I don't recognize Hanna standing in front of the other women. Her head is shaved and she is so thin and ragged. But then she looks up for a moment and I see those gentle blue eyes filled with fear and courage and loathing and things I will never know. And then Mengele comes and stands on a platform to address us. As always, his black SS uniform is neatly pressed.

He was, like most vain men, a sharp dresser. I remember that he always wore clean white gloves.

"'Dogs,' he shouts. They always used to call the prisoners *dogs* and they called the guard dogs *men*. 'This Jewess has been elected by the other bitches in her barracks to bring a medical problem to my attention. It seems that the bitches in these barracks, like all bitches, are suffering from an infestation of lice. I want to thank this Jewess for bringing this medical problem to my attention and I've brought you all here to see that the New Order knows how to deal with lice. The barracks will be fumigated.' And then he smiled. A few of the women cheered and his smile grew broader. You see, he was no ordinary sadist.

"Then he marched the women, including Hanna, into the barracks. He ordered the doors sealed and then had the barracks fumigated—with mustard gas. . . . The women's screams seemed to go on for hours."

Wasserman slumped down in his chair, then after a time he looked up at Caine, as though seeing him from far away, from long ago.

"You want me to waste Mengele?" Caine asked.

"I'll pay you half a million dollars, if you can locate and kill Mengele within six months," said Wasserman.

"That's a lot of money."

"I need you, Caine. Ordinary hit men don't know how to work outside the country. Mercenaries don't have the brains or the resources to track him down and, even if they could, probably couldn't get close to him. Government agents and Israeli spies have tried and failed. I've gone over it from every angle. You're the man for the job. And I'll provide you with all the money and resources at my disposal to help you to do it."

Caine got up and walked over to the painting. He submitted himself to that pretty nineteenth-century scene as if to a baptism. Things were different then, he thought. They believed in things and fought for causes as if it mattered. The whole thing is crazy. Why had Wasserman waited thirty years for his revenge? Besides, he had come to Los Angeles to escape the past. He'd had enough of ghosts. Let the dead bury the dead, he decided, as he walked back to the chair and sat down.

"It won't wash, Wasserman," Caine said quietly. For a long moment the two men sat silently, then Wasserman shrugged helplessly.

"I can think of a dozen reasons why your story won't work," Caine continued. "For instance, you want me to believe that you want to pay me half a million to waste some old Nazi. That's all ancient history. Nobody cares about that crap anymore, including you. You go off and forget about this Mengele for thirty years, wake up one morning after a bad dream and say, My, my, I've waited long enough for my revenge, so I'll find some Company type, looking for a quick buck, to do in six months what half-a-dozen governments have been unable to accomplish in thirty years. And why, all of a sudden, are you having nightmares about the bad old days, after thirty years of pimping and indifference? Tell you what, why don't you wait a few years and the kraut bastard will drop dead from old age? And why me, Wasserman, why me?"

Wasserman slumped back in his chair, his eyes bleak and defeated. Then he sniffed, straightened up, and took out a cigar and lit it. In a way his gesture touched Caine more than anything he had said. In spite of everything, he had never quite given up. He puffed a few times and, exhaling the smoke, played his trump.

"All right, Caine, if I give you a satisfactory explanation, will you agree to consider my offer? Come with me to my beach house in Malibu. I have a dossier in my safe there that I've compiled on Mengele. I want you to see it and think it over. In the morning, if you still don't want the assignment, I'll pay you another thousand dollars for your trouble. Agreed?"

Despite himself, Caine was intrigued. Wasserman was no fool and he had clearly thought the whole thing out. Besides, it was an easy $1,000.

"Agreed," he replied.

"First of all, as to why I chose you," Wasserman began. "You know there's an ancient Afghani saying, that the Afghan wolf is hunted with an Afghan hound. I've bribed a lot of people to find out about you. There were favors exchanged through friends I have in the Syndicate. And money. I know you, Caine. You're a hunter. You're the Afghan hound I'm setting to kill the wolf."

"That won't do it," Caine said. "Why the six-month deadline, the thirty-year wait?"

"That's easy. I pushed it out of my mind. After the camp, nothing meant anything. Love, hate, joy, grief, these were only words. Morality had no meaning, so why not sell garbage to the swine? I was past caring. All I wanted was money, pleasure, power, so that I need never remember, never look back."

Listening to the story, Caine was reminded of something Yoshua had said the night they hit Abu Daud in Paris. That was back in the days when he was only a year out of training. Before Laos and Nam. Before it all fell apart. He was one of the Company's bright young men in those days. Then, it all went down the tubes in Asia and he spent a year shuffling paper in Langley, while heads rolled after the Chile fiasco and he knew he had to get out. Remembering that night in Paris was like eavesdropping on another era. He remembered that they were drinking in some nameless café off the Boulevard Saint-Michel and Yoshua, who was only a courier with the Mossad and had never done any wet work before, had pronounced in a drunken, maudlin tone:

"Which of us is not a Nazi in the end?"

"But you're a Jew," Caine had replied.

"Do you think that makes us any better? Listen, I come from a country where maybe a quarter of the population came from the camps. So I know. A few, a very few of the survivors were purified by their suffering and became true saints. But most of them are bastards. Do you understand? To survive they became just like the Nazis. Worse. They care for nothing."

So in a curious way, the fact that Wasserman was a tough son of a bitch made the whole thing believable.

"What happened three months ago?" Caine asked seriously. The job was starting to become real for him.

"I went to my doctor. I have an inoperable cancer of the lymph nodes." Wasserman nodded and smiled ironically. "You see, Caine, I have barely ten months left to live."

CHAPTER 2

The seagull hovered a few feet above the waves, his gray wings outstretched, unmoving. He seemed caught for eternity in the pool of light cast by the floodlights mounted on the restaurant's outside deck. Beyond the light there was only the immense blackness of the Pacific Ocean at night. With a quick movement the gull folded his wings and plummeted into a rising swell. Almost immediately he began to fly back up into the light, a slender silvery fish wiggling in his beak. Suddenly three loudly squawking gulls erupted out of the darkness and attacked the first gull, attempting to steal the fish. The first gull managed to swallow almost half the fish before the rest was stolen by one of the others. The gulls wheeled and shrieked and then they were gone. The floodlights lit only the incoming surf that shook the pilings on which the restaurant stood.

The Moonglow was one of those glass and wood restaurants, liberally sprinkled with hanging ferns and authentic-looking papier-mâché beams, that dot the California coast. On either side of the restaurant stretched a line of expensive beach houses that sold for upwards of $300,000 to buyers who wanted to live like beachcombers. A small group of rubberneckers stood on the restaurant's outside deck, sipping margaritas and congratulating each other on the view,

Roused by a change in the girl's tone of voice, Caine turned back to her, once more conscious of the undertone of conversation at the other tables. It seemed to him that he was looking at her from far away, as if through the wrong end of a telescope. Not that she was hard to look at. Her long blond hair was beautifully set off by her deep California tan, which made a striking contrast against her white T-shirt. She was braless and he could see her nipples clearly outlined against a fabric that bore the motto FOXY LADY. She had the healthy, scrubbed appearance of a surf bunny, the kind of long-legged blonde that they seemed to turn out on an assembly line down in Orange County. But it was her eyes that continually surprised him. They were incredibly blue, as blue as the Mediterranean, as blue as a turbulent Van Gogh sky.

Of course, Caine had seen more of her than that. He had seen her star in Wasserman's hard-core epic just before Freddie had taken him into Wasserman's office. C.J. smiled and repeated her question.

"How do you like Malibu?"

At the next table an attractive Beverly Hills woman wearing French jeans and dripping Gucci accessories wondered aloud about whether she should get a Jag or a Mercedes this year, raising her voice in case there was anyone in the restaurant who hadn't heard her.

"I like it fine," he said.

"The steaks are good here, aren't they," she said, dipping the meat into the teriyaki sauce.

"Terrific," he replied, chewing on his feedlot-raised beef, thinking it was pumped full of so many female hormones that it was no wonder America was turning into an androgynous culture.

The Gucci lady raised her voice again. It seemed that the quality of merchandise at Bullock's Westwood was deteriorating. Caine looked at C.J. and shook his head.

"Does everybody out here talk like that?"

"Like what?" she asked.

"Like they've all seen too much television," he replied. But then, everything that had happened to him since he arrived in L.A. seemed unreal. You have to remember that you're in Hollywood, the land of bumper-to-bumper freeways and plastic palm trees, he reminded himself.

After leaving Washington for good months ago, he had gone to New York to deposit a few things in the safety deposit box and to check out a line on a civilian job. The New York personnel manager referred him to their Los Angeles office and he had taken the red-eye flight to L.A., arriving just that morning. He had come to Los Angeles to start again, in a sunny world where everything is new and everyone is more interested in telling you their lies than in listening to your own. Instead he had received Wasserman's message and wound up spending the day rummaging in the past. But the job was real enough. It bothered him. Perhaps because Wasserman had too many reasons, had thought it out too well. Something smelled wrong, but it was just beyond him, the way you recognize the scent of a perfume you've smelled before, but can't quite remember which of the women in your past used to wear it.

Wasserman had laid it out for him during the drive

down to the beach. Wasserman drove a new beige Mercedes 450 SE, with enough dials on the dashboard to do everything but cook your breakfast, taking the curves along Sunset Boulevard in a nervous, jerky manner. They drove down the Strip and past the manicured estates of Beverly Hills and Bel-Air.

"I assume you'll want to put the money into a Swiss account," Wasserman remarked, adjusting his sunglasses. Caine automatically checked the mirrors, wondering why he still felt the need, but there was only the normal afternoon traffic behind them.

"You're also assuming I'll take the job," Caine replied.

"Oh, yes," Wasserman smiled. "You'll think about the money and you'll take the job."

"You know, you've been doing an awful lot of talking about money, but I haven't seen much besides talk, so far."

Wasserman reached into his jacket pocket, barely missing sideswiping a VW convertible as he did so. Two blond boys in the convertible, their surfboards sticking up in the air, gave Caine the finger as they swerved to avoid the Mercedes. Caine smiled broadly and nodded his head yes. Wasserman missed the entire episode and handed Caine a bulky envelope, addressed in an old-fashioned handwriting to a certain Thos. Jessom, Esq., care of the Bombay Auxiliary Bible Society, the Esplanade, Bombay. Caine counted fifty $500 bills inside the envelope.

"This is nowhere near the kind of money you've been talking about," Caine said.

"There's a lot more money there than you, or any customs agent in the world, will ever see. Look again," Wasserman said.

Caine reexamined the envelope, but there was nothing else in it but the money. He was about to hand it back to Wasserman and tell him that he was getting tired of his games, but something about the address bothered him. Why a Bible society in India and no return address? He looked at the stamp to see where it came from and then he saw it. He knew then that Wasserman was deadly serious. All at once he knew that he was holding the one chance everyone dreams about and that Wasserman was right, that he was going to do it. He was going to kill Mengele because one day in 1847, a missionary on the island of Mauritius in the Indian Ocean had sent a letter to the secretary of a Bombay Bible Society, thanking him for sending copies of the scriptures to help the mission. What made the letter so valuable were the two one-penny stamps issued by the post office at Port Louis, each bearing the profile of the young Queen Victoria.

"How many of them are there in the world?" Caine asked.

"There are fourteen known, but these two are the best. I purchased them at a New York auction in 1968 for three hundred eighty thousand dollars. They're worth well over half a million today," Wasserman replied.

They drove down the last curves of Pacific Palisades and Wasserman turned north, heading up the Pacific Coast Highway to Malibu. Caine glanced out at the ocean and then at the stamps again, knowing that he was going to take the job. This was what he'd been waiting for, without even knowing that he was waiting for it. It wasn't just the money, or the excitement. It wasn't because Mengele deserved to die. It was because Wasserman had been right about him.

He was the Afghan hound, the hunter. That was who he was.

"I work alone," he said.

"Harris told me," Wasserman replied. He turned into the driveway of a large glass-and-redwood beach house and shut off the engine.

"That means alone," Caine repeated. "Mengele has stayed alive all these years, so he must have friends. I'll need deep cover for when his friends come looking." He didn't mention the real cover he had in mind once the job was over, since it was the most important secret in his life. He had a safety-deposit box in a New York bank that contained a completely untraceable set of forged documents, as well as a few other interesting items that he retained from his Company days.

"How will I know what progress you're making?" Wasserman asked.

"I'll telex you every third or fourth day, more often when there's something to report. It'll be in standard commercial code."

"Suppose I have to get hold of you?"

"Don't call me, I'll call you," Caine said, trying out a casting director's tone of voice.

"How much in advance?" Wasserman asked, relaxing enough to lean back and light a cigar. This was the kind of negotiation he understood.

"I assume the twenty-five thousand dollars is for expenses," Caine said. Wasserman nodded affirmatively.

"Half up front. I take one stamp to Switzerland, you keep the other till the job's done."

"That's a lot of money, Caine."

"You're Jewish. You tell me what Mengele's death is worth."

"If I give you the stamp, how can I be sure you won't just disappear?" Wasserman asked.

"Common sense," Caine replied. "If you can afford this much for a single hit, you can afford to send troops after me. I intend to enjoy this money and I can't do that if I'm going to have to sleep with one eye open for the rest of my life."

"I'm glad we understand each other, Caine. If you try to cheat me, the second stamp buys your death."

"Suppose I can't locate him within the time limit."

"That's your problem," Wasserman snapped. "If you haven't completed the assignment within six months from today, you return the stamp or its equivalent in cash to me, or else every agent and thug in the world will be after your head."

"Fair enough." Caine nodded. "There's just one thing."

"What's that?"

"Suppose I waste him. How can I prove to you that he's dead and collect the other stamp?"

"I've thought that out too," Wasserman said. "When you've gone over the dossier I've compiled, you'll see that Mengele's fingerprints are on file with Interpol, and there's a copy of the prints in the dossier."

"So . . ."

"So, when you come to collect," Wasserman replied intently, "bring me his thumb."

He felt C.J.'s fingertips caressing his hand, sending little shivers up his palm. When he looked at her, she pouted slightly and said, "Karl told me to be nice to you. Don't you find me attractive?"

"Do you do everything Karl says?"

"We have an arrangement," she said, as the waiter came over and freshened their coffee.

"What arrangement?"

"We're not going together or anything like that." She smiled. "I'm a kind of social secretary *cum* mistress. I entertain for him, look pretty so he can show me off, kind of take care of things at the house."

"The work seems to agree with you."

"I do all right," she said pensively. "When this society talks about independence for women, what they really mean is you can be a glorified flunky, like a secretary or a waitress. Either that, or the corporate rat race. If I have to be a whore, at least let me be an honest and successful whore. Karl and I understand each other. He knows that I'm into making as much money as I can and that I'm my own woman. It's strictly a business relationship."

Relationship, that's our great twentieth-century word, he thought, with a vague sense of loss.

The waiter came over and asked if they wanted anything else. As Caine shook his head no, he looked at C.J.'s striking young beauty and wondered if the Wassermans of the world were right, if everything is for sale after all.

"How did you meet Wasserman?" Caine asked.

"When I came to work for him. I answered this ad in the paper for actresses. He had me fill out this form and it asked if I wanted a balling or non-balling role, so I put down non-balling"—smiling at her remembered innocence.

"Karl asked me, 'Why not?' and I told him that I didn't think I could get into it. Then I went back to this little closet of an apartment that I had in Hollywood and I thought about it."

"What made you change your mind?" Caine asked.

"Well, I thought it wasn't anything I hadn't done. I figured that it might be a way into movies and the worst it could be was a new experience. Besides, after I split from my old man, I was ready to try anything."

"What happened?"

"Oh, we were into drugs and then he started tripping on acid. We must have done a hundred tabs down in Mexico. Then we came back to Berkeley and he started getting really freaky. You know, whips and leather. The whole bit. One time he whipped me so bad, I had to go to the Free Clinic. He really did a number on me," she said softly. "So I split and came down to L.A. After I did the movie thing, Karl asked me to stay on at his place."

"How do you like it now?"

"He's very good to me. He protects me."

"That's what Jane said about Tarzan, but who wants to live in a tree?" Caine said.

"You saw the place. We live pretty well," she said, crossing her arms defensively.

"Yes, you do," he conceded.

That was true enough, Caine thought, remembering his first sight of her that afternoon. She had come to the door wearing nothing but a white bikini and a solid gold coke spoon on a chain around her neck. Wasserman wore a proud possessive smile as he gave her an affectionate peck on the cheek, but the effect was ruined by his roughly grabbing her bottom at the same time. C.J. just smiled and looked appraisingly over Wasserman's shoulder at Caine. Then her lips parted, the pink tip of her tongue peeking out between her lips, promising anything just for the hell of it.

She was looking at him the same way now, as if he was a fortune cookie she was dying to open. The lights along the Malibu shore were scattered like stars across the darkened restaurant window behind her, as Caine leaned back and smiled, imagining how she would look going down on him, feeling the first tingle in his groin. But he was really smiling at himself, he thought. After all they were both professionals. As she had said, it was strictly business. He had to keep reminding himself of that, because of the way his body had responded to her breathtaking sensuality from that first moment when he had arrived at the beach house with Wasserman.

The sun was unrolling an amber carpet across the sea, splashing gold light through the cathedral windows that looked out over the beach, as C.J. and Wasserman led him into the huge living room. The light reflected off a gas fire, dancing in a massive fireplace of Palos Verdes stone that might have just squeezed into the main hall at Windsor Castle. In the corner a soap opera droned on the tube. C.J. glanced at it out of the corner of her eye, as a doctor explained to the well-used blond heroine that she had to have the operation. She didn't want to face it, what with her husband running off with the sixteen-year-old baby-sitter, her son being busted for possession, her old lover running for the Senate, and her daughter about to get engaged to an African exchange student. The doctor tried to be sympathetic, but her ego began to crack like an egg as the music came up and the credit crawl began. With a shrug C.J. flicked the set off and invited them to sit down. Then completely unself-conscious, she sat cross-legged in a black Danica chair and offered Caine a joint. As he nodded no, Caine was aware of the contrast between the elegance of the surroundings and the raw assertiveness with which Wasserman displayed his possessions, including the girl. Once again, he was struck by the contradictions in Wasserman. The man furnished his office with antiques and his house in Danish Modern. He had an exquisite eye for beauty and seemed to delight in cheapening it. He was impossible to pin down.

For a moment Wasserman glanced at both of them and smiled. The girl had been one of his better investments.

"Pretty, isn't she?" he asked, as though she weren't there.

"Yes, very," Caine replied. Wasserman was pulling out all the stops, he decided, as he leaned back and crossed his legs, waiting for the hard sell.

"She has the best box in L.A. You ought to try it sometime," Wasserman bragged.

"Fringe benefits?" Caine asked.

"Beats Social Security," Wasserman laughed. He laughed a fraction longer than necessary at his own joke, then turned to the girl.

"Why don't you take a walk on the beach, dear?" It was not a question. Without a word she got up, shrugged, and walked out with a movement as rhythmic and fundamental as that of the sea. Conscious of their eyes upon her, she exaggerated her wiggle slightly as she went through the door.

"Do you want her?" Wasserman asked.

"Are you offering?"

"Sure. Take her. That's what she's for. That's what they're all for. Take what you like, only . . ."

"Only what?"

"Only get Mengele."

"Tell me about him."

"What do you want to know?"

"Everything," Caine replied, and lit a cigarette.

Wasserman got up and, motioning for Caine to remain where he was, left the room. The room was growing dark, the sunset a rosy blush over the darkening ocean. A sailboat was barely visible against the red embers of the horizon. Along the green fringe of the beach, palm trees glowed red, as though they were burning. It reminded him of the last time he had seen palm trees by a beach, the fronds blackened by smoke and smelling of cordite. Wasserman returned carrying a bulky folder. As he handed the folder to Caine, his features were caught in the flickering firelight. For a moment his eyes burned in his skull like candles in a jack-o'-lantern. As he took the folder, Caine felt an almost irresistible impulse to smash that greedy face, which seemed to flame with the fanaticism of a Torquemada in the dying light. Then Wasserman flicked the lamps on and the moment was gone. Caine paused to light a cigarette, then he opened the folder and began to read. At some time during the reading he heard the girl come back and there was the murmur of conversation between her and Wasserman in the bedroom. But he disregarded them and concentrated on the material.

The dossier, as Wasserman called it, was mostly a hodgepodge of newspaper and magazine clippings about Nazi war criminals. The bulk of the dossier were transcripts from Nuremberg based on unsubstantiated testimony. More interesting was a copy of a bill of indictment against Mengele issued by a court in Freiburg, dated June 5, 1959. The warrant listed

seventeen specific counts of murder. Even more useful were a copy of Mengele's Interpol file and a copy
of an application for an Argentinian identity card, made
out for a Dr. Gregor Schklastro on October 27, 1956.
There was a set of fingerprints in the Interpol file and
a second on the Argentinian application and it was
clear, even to Caine's untrained eye, that the fingerprints were strikingly similar. As Caine sifted through
the material, he began to get a vague picture of his
quarry.

As noted in the bill of indictment, Josef Mengele
was born to a wealthy manufacturer named Karl Mengele and his wife Walburga Mengele, *née* Hupfauer,
on March 16, 1911, in Günzburg, District of Swabia in
Bavaria. Karl Mengele had begun to manufacture
farm machinery in Günzburg, a quaint village situated
on the banks of the Danube, shortly after the Franco-
Prussian War. He had already established himself as
the town's leading citizen when he founded the firm
of Karl Mengele & Sons around the turn of the century. By the time Josef was born, more than half of
the men of Günzburg were employed by the Mengeles. As a child Josef was small and sickly. He was
spoiled by his mother, who couldn't understand why
her brilliant, dreamy son felt so frustrated at being
unable to keep up with his healthy blond schoolmates
in the rough and tumble of school sports. Small and
dark, with soft brown eyes, he suffered with envy of
those whom Thomas Mann, his favorite writer in
those idealistic days, had called "the blond-haired
and the blue-eyed." During the late 1920's Josef went
to Munich to study philosophy and medicine. Even at
that age he was already seeking some way to scientifi-
cally match the physical aspects of man to some per-

fect conception of man's metaphysical nature. Then one evening the lonely student heard Adolf Hitler speak in a beer hall, and his life was transformed. In a single evening the intoxicated and exhilarated Mengele became a fanatic and lifelong Nazi.

Shortly after Hitler invaded Poland, Mengele graduated and immediately enlisted as a medical officer in the Waffen SS. During the early years of the war Mengele served in France and later on the Russian front. It was during this time that he began to expound a theory that he had first formulated as a student. He believed that the only way Germany could succeed in ruling the world was to replace the *inferior races* with a multitude of pure Aryan babies. This could only be done, he decided, by producing multiple births as an ordinary occurrence. His early genetic research concentrated in two areas: the study of twins and an attempt to isolate the chromosome responsible for blue eyes. However, in the Waffen SS all he could do was theorize. He realized that he would need a supply of human guinea pigs and the right laboratory conditions in order to pursue his research. While on leave he petitioned SS Inspector General Glucks for the chance to do medical experiments at a concentration camp. In 1943, acting on a recommendation from Glucks, Heinrich Himmler appointed Mengele chief doctor at Auschwitz. As the surviving inmates of Auschwitz later attested, Himmler had made the perfect choice.

After the war Mengele returned home to Günzburg. His wife, family, and friends welcomed him as a good German who had done his duty during the war. Mengele started a successful medical practice and all went well until, in 1950, some of the SS small-fry being tried at Nuremberg began to mention Mengele's name.

By 1951 the outlines of his experiments and responsibilities at Auschwitz were becoming public knowledge. After a reporter from the *Frankfurter Allgemeine* tried to interview him, Mengele secretly began to liquidate his assets. Later that year a Bavarian police official received an inquiry from the American authorities in Nuremberg. The official was one of Mengele's patients, and his family had worked for the Mengeles for generations. He alerted the *Herr Doktor* and Mengele contacted some comrades in ODESSA.

According to a reprint of a *Der Spiegel* article in the dossier, ODESSA was a secret organization set up by certain high-ranking SS officers when it became apparent that the German defeat was inevitable. An acronym for *Organisation der SS—Angehörigen,* or Organization of SS Members, it was designed to help SS war criminals escape Allied retribution after the war. ODESSA apparently spirited Mengele out of Germany through an underground network called *die Spinne,* or the Spider. The Interpol file indicated that Mengele escaped to the Italian Tyrol via the Reschenpass-Merano route. From Genoa the comrades moved him to Madrid, where he contacted the "Special Assistance" department of the Falangista party. The Falangista arranged for Mengele's escape to Argentina. Except for the application for the Argentinian identity card in 1956, the Interpol entry was the last authoritative mention of Mengele's whereabouts contained in the dossier.

Caine dropped the folder in his lap, leaned back, and lit a cigarette. He could hear the timeless surf lapping at the beach, punctuated by the occasional cry of a gull. But the sea was hidden in darkness. He could barely make out the running lights of a freighter well off the coast. When he turned back, Wasserman was standing near his chair, studying him intently.

"What do you think?"

"Where's the girl?" Caine responded.

"She's in the bedroom getting dressed. I made dinner reservations for you two at the Moonglow," Wasserman said.

All this solicitude was beginning to make him nervous. What comes next, Caine wondered, cucumber sandwiches for Lady Bracknell?

"I don't want anyone to know anything about this," he said.

"Don't worry." Wasserman's expression implied that Caine was a fool even to raise the issue. "She thinks you're in the movie business."

"Worry is what keeps people like me alive, so let's get it straight. The next time I see you, it will be to collect the other stamp."

Wasserman's eyes gleamed with excitement.

"Then you think you can do it?" he prodded.

"I don't know. The goddamn trail has been cold for over twenty years and that's assuming that Interpol knows what it's talking about. And Interpol is notorious in the intelligence community for never having anything worth knowing."

"Then it's hopeless," Wasserman said dully.

"No, we have a few things going for us. First, after all this time Mengele might have let his guard down a little. He probably isn't expecting anyone to really come after him. Second, we have money to spend and that will open a few mouths anyway. Third, nobody knows anything about me. Anonymity is our strongest weapon. Fourth, whenever Interpol, the West Germans, or the Israelis went after Mengele, their primary objective was to extradite him to stand trial. Inevitably the legal maneuvering took time and gave Mengele the advance warning he needed to get away. This time we don't want to try him, just kill him. Finally, according to this dossier, the only people who have ever seriously gone after Mengele have been fanatic Jewish amateurs. This time you are sending a professional."

"What are you going to do now?"

"Now? I think I'll go with the girl and have myself a steak." Caine grinned.

"No, I mean how will you begin?"

"Oh, first I'll go to Vegas to launder the money and pick up a few things."

"So you still don't trust me." Wasserman smiled approvingly.

"Of course not." Caine smiled back. His eyes were emerald chips, glassy and empty of feeling. For the first time Wasserman suddenly realized what a dangerous man Caine really was.

"What are you going to pick up in Vegas?" Wasserman prompted.

"A dose of the clap."

"No, really. What things? Maybe I can help."

"Guns, things. The details are my business. I told you, I work alone," Caine snapped.

"Is that how you're going to do it. Shoot him?" Wasserman asked eagerly.

Caine stood up. He had had enough of this nonsense.

"I don't know. That depends on his setup, when and if I locate the son of a bitch."

"When are you leaving?"

"In the morning, after I've enjoyed the steak—and the girl," he added pointedly.

"I'm glad to see my employees enjoy their work," Wasserman said, trying to reassert his authority. Then he added, "Stay in touch, Caine. Do stay in touch." And Caine knew that what Cunningham had told him so long ago still applied. He would have to watch his back.

C.J. put her arm around his waist in the chill sea breeze outside the restaurant, clinging to him as if for warmth, while the Mexican parking lot attendant went to get her car. The Mexican brought the car, a silver Mercedes 450 SL hardtop, around to where they were standing. As they got in, two thoughts occurred to Caine: that the mistress business was still damn lucrative and that the Mercedes was the Chevy of West Los Angeles.

C.J. drove swiftly, surely, up the Pacific Coast Highway to the beach house. As she drove, she repeatedly glanced at Caine out of the corner of her eye. Although his face was shadowed, his green eyes seemed luminous in the reflected light of the dashboard dials. He caught her looking at him and they smiled, accomplices in the gentle urging of the California night.

"What did you discuss with Karl?" she asked.

"Business."

"What kind of business? What do you do, anyway?"

"I'm a PR man."

"What are you selling?"

"Hot air mostly," he replied and when she giggled, added, "Myself. That's what we all sell, isn't it?"

She looked at him sharply in response to the implied put-down.

"You think we're all so decadent, don't you? I think you have a touch of the Puritan in you. That wonderful self-righteousness of the solid citizen who goes to church on Sunday and then sneaks into the massage parlor on Monday," she said, contemptuously tossing back her hair.

"Perhaps you're right. I've been away a long time," Caine admitted.

"Then don't sit there making judgments about me. As Ivan Karamazov said, 'If God is dead, everything is permitted.'"

Caine looked at her curiously. Her erudition surprised him. She was beginning to interest him, much more than he would have ever admitted.

"How did you get hooked on Dostoevsky?" he asked.

"I majored in English Lit. at Berkeley. I'm really a very intellectual hooker," she said with a wry smile.

"We're all hookers, one way or another."

C.J. glanced at him with frank interest, green pinpoints of light from the dashboard reflected in her eyes. Then she smiled, as though he had passed some kind of test. The car slowed as they approached the beach house.

She turned into the driveway and they went into the house. Wasserman had gone. He had taken the dossier with him, and Caine quickly scanned the living room but found nothing to indicate that Wasserman had ever been there as C.J. put an album on the stereo. The man is as slippery as an eel, he thought. C.J. lit the fire and poured them snifters of Grand Marnier.

They sat before the fire and gently touched glasses, the brandy a molten orange gold in their hands. Her hair caught the firelight and tumbled down her cheeks like glowing streams of lava. For a brief moment they kissed, suddenly aware of each other, like two hyperbolas become tangent at a single point before being swept away in opposite directions for all eternity. She reached out and ran her fingers through his sandy hair, something she had been wanting to do all evening.

"What does C.J. stand for, anyway?" he asked.

"C for Carole, as in Lombard; J for Joan, as in Crawford. My mother was a fan," she shrugged.

"I'm glad my mother didn't feel the same way. Her favorite star was Lassie," he said, and she laughed.

Gold flecks of firelight flickered in her eyes. They gazed at each other with a strange sense of discovery.

"What do you want to do?" she said, her voice a drowsy whisper.

"You know what I want to do," he said, and smiled.

"I thought you'd never ask," she said with a throaty laugh and, taking his hand, led him into the bedroom.

CHAPTER 3

The French have a word for it. They call it the post-coital *tristesse*. It's a kind of vague sadness that comes sometimes when the act of love is over. Maybe because the reality of sex doesn't always measure up to the expectation. Maybe that was it, Caine mused as he lay next to C.J. in the darkness.

During his training in Virginia, his instructor had warned them that an agent was never more vulnerable than right after sex. Perhaps because the time after sex was a time for truth, Caine thought, remembering Lim.

"Tell me the truth, Tan Caine. Who are you really?" Lim had asked him that first time, her voice barely audible over the rain on the bamboo slats.

"Just a soldier," Caine replied, wondering if she was asking out of a woman's curiosity or whether she was really Pathet Lao.

"All men are soldiers now," she said. "Is that why you are fighting?"

"No," reaching for a cigarette. In the brief match flare her dark eyes searched his face, as though some answer might be written there.

"Then why do men make war?"

"Because the women are watching," he replied. And

then she had giggled, "Make love, not war. Isn't that what you Americans say?"

Well, he was no good at making love anymore either, Caine decided. C.J. certainly wouldn't disagree with that. They lay together in the soft California night, catching their breath and after a long silence she finally brought it out.

"You're a lousy lover, you know that," she said bitterly.

"Does it really matter?"

"Christ, that's a new one," she snapped. "You're the first guy I ever slept with who didn't want to know how good he was. You don't really care, do you? You just jerked off inside me, you bastard," bitterness eroding her anger.

"No, I guess I don't care very much. Is that what you felt?" Don't think about it, he told himself. This is the vulnerable time and you don't want to feel anything, just get it off so you can get some sleep.

"I felt that you wanted to get it over with as quickly as possible, like an unpleasant duty."

"Maybe you're right," he said. "I must be regressing."

"What are you talking about?"

"Nothing really. It's just that when you're young the object of sex is relief, not pleasure." Something in his tired voice plucked at her.

She leaned over him, her long blond hair tickling his face and said softly, "Boy, she really must have been something."

"Who?"

"The woman who did this to you," she replied. "But don't take it out on the rest of us. We've all been through the mill. You don't know what I went through with my old man. You think you've had it bad. Well you don't know what bad is."

"You're right," Caine said and then he lit a cigarette because there was no way to stop it now and sleep wouldn't come till morning. He rested his head on his arm and watched the smoke curl into the darkness.

The CIA, like most large corporations, does the bulk of its recruiting on college campuses. The Company, as it is called by the people who work there, looks for two types of recruits among the students it interviews: those with technical degrees in engineering, accounting, computer science, etc., to do "white" work at Agency headquarters in Langley, Virginia, and those with language skills and graduate majors in international-related studies to be enrolled in the Career Training Program. The CTP is a one-year course designed to prepare an agent in "black" work, which may involve hazardous assignments overseas.

John Caine had his first interview on a sunny spring morning at the Career Placement Center at UCLA, where he was completing his M.B.A. with a major in international finance. The recruiter was a shrewd, gregarious man in his early sixties with a ready smile and wit. Caine remembered with a wry smile that he had told the interviewer he was considering the CTP because he loved foreign travel and, besides, it sounded like fun. God, was I ever that young, he wondered. Shortly thereafter he sent in his application and medical history, similar to most job applications, except that it was much longer and more detailed, even requiring him to list every address he had ever stayed at for the past fifteen years. He then sat for a long three-part examination. The first part of the exam was a standard intelligence/knowledge test similar to the entrance exam for grad school. The second part was one of those psychological tests designed to determine which you would rather be: a lighthouse keeper or an insurance salesman. The last section was a test of the applicant's abilities in language acquisition. He was timed to see how quickly he learned an invented language. Since Caine claimed proficiency in German and Spanish, he was also given translation exercises.

When he passed the exam, a security check lasting nearly seven months was run on him. After he had been cleared by the Agency and the FBI, Caine was flown to Washington and interviewed again. A month later he received a verbal offer to join the CTP at a Civil Service Grade 9, which paid about eleven hundred dollars a month.

Twenty-nine months later Caine was on a jet to Laos.

He lay next to C.J., his bare arm touching hers, a world away, staring into darkness and listening to the occasional sounds of night traffic along the coast highway. From somewhere came the sound of a late newscast, muffled and indistinct—something about a kidnapping. Insomnia must be the major disease of the twentieth century, he thought. C.J. stirred restlessly beside him. After a long silence she snuggled against his shoulder and whispered,

"Are you asleep?"

"Yes," he said, and smiled.

"I'm sorry I snapped at you before. It's never really good the first time. Oh, hell, it's lonely lying here by myself. Put your arm around me," she said in a little girl voice.

"I'm never any good the first time, either. Nerves, I guess," putting his arm around her.

"Your bracelet is scratching me. What is it anyway? I've never seen one like it," she said, running her fingers along the dull metal ring around his wrist.

"It's from Asia," he yawned.

"Were you in Asia?"

"Weren't we all?"

"You're like a politician," she laughed. "You have a way of answering questions without saying anything. What kind of a bracelet is it?"

"It's a Meo bracelet," he replied, remembering Dao. "It's supposed to protect you against evil *tlan* spirits."

"You don't really believe in spirits, do you?" she asked, amused.

Wouldn't it be lovely if you could blame it all on the *tlan* the way the Meo did? he thought. What do we Westerners know about spirits anyway? Just the Bible. They knew about it all right. *The spirit of man will sustain his infirmity. But a wounded spirit, who can bear?* But then, no one with a white skin knew much about Asia.

"In a way," he said.

"What's a Meo?" she asked in a sleepy voice. "It sounds like a cat."

"They're a mountain tribe in Indochina," he said. That had been his first mistake. He remembered Dao correcting him the first time they met at Airstrip 256. As they ducked under the air blast from the helicopter blades and ran to the edge of the clearing, Caine had shouted something about being glad to be with the Meo force at last. The chopper pulled heavily into the sky with an incredible clatter as Dao remarked pedantically:

"We are not Meo. *Meo* means 'barbarians' and is a name the Chinese gave to us thousands of years ago. We call ourselves *Hmong,* which means 'free men.'"

"I'll remember," Caine said, shouldering his pack. Thorns tore at his fatigues as he stumbled through the dense undergrowth, following Dao's wiry body tirelessly scrambling up the trail. He quickened his pace as Dao's blue air force jumpsuit almost disappeared into the dense jungle shade. Cunningham was right, Caine thought. It's going to be tricky. He'd met Cunningham, a hard hawk-nosed Yankee, ten minutes after he had landed at Long Tieng Air Base, CIA headquarters in Laos. The fan in Cunningham's tiny office barely stirred the air, stifling in the dense noon heat. Cunningham handed Caine a lukewarm Coke, sizing him up in a brief speculative glance. He took in Caine's muscled shoulders, sandy hair, bright green eyes, and almost too-handsome features. He looked like what you like to think an American looks like.

"Relax," he said. "You've got twenty minutes till your chopper takes off. You'll rendezvous with General Dao at Strip two fifty-six in the Annam border sector. I suppose Washington briefed you."

"They told me you'd be my control," Caine replied.

"Sure. I'll have about as much authority over you as you'll have over Dao, which is to say, zilch. Officially your assignment is to advise Dao. He's got about three thousand tribesmen attached to the Royal Lao Army and paid by us. They operate in Sector Five against twenty thousand Pathet Lao guerrillas and one, maybe two, NVA regiments in the area."

"Then I'd advise him to surrender," Caine snapped. "What's my real assignment?"

Cunningham smiled briefly with approval, gulped down his Coke, and let out a loud belch.

"To keep the roof from caving in. Dao may not be much, but he's the only thing keeping Charley from moving down into the Plain of Jars. It's going to be damn tricky, Caine. The Meo are brutal and superstitious. If you offend a *tlan* spirit, they might kill you five minutes after you walk into camp. And Dao has his own ambitions. We're using each other right now, but don't put any bets down on this marriage. Come on, I'll walk you to the chopper."

They walked out to the chopper, eyes squinting against the intense glare of the tarmac. As Caine slung his pack and M-16 aboard, Cunningham shouted: "You'll be on your own, Caine, so watch your back. And one more thing"—his voice almost lost in the scream of the rotor—"whatever you do, don't let them take you alive."

They'd taken Chong alive, Caine thought. That had been his fault. So many things were his fault: Lim, the child— No, he didn't want to go on any more guilt trips. Emotion is wasted energy, Dao would say. He remembered Dao laughing, sitting around the fire and all of them drunk on the potent corn liquor passed around by the spirit doctor, the *tu-ua-neng*. Chong was playing those strange plaintive sounds on his *khene* and then all of them were laughing, because Caine had suggested taking a prisoner and getting information.

"Prisoners," Dao laughed. "There are no prisoners in this war."

Christ, how do you turn it off, he wondered. C.J. lay quietly beside him, her breathing deep and regu-

lar. He got up and, still naked, walked into the living
room and took some brandy from the bottle left on
the coffee table. Then he went out on the balcony
and stared out at the pale froth of surf crashing
against the deserted beach. Far to the south, he could
just make out the lights of the Palos Verdes shore. He
drank the brandy with a sudden gasp, shivering in the
cool sea breeze.

We just don't fit, he thought. Like the kiwi that belongs to the sky yet is born without wings. L.A. is
filled with refugees caught at land's end. The reason
the pioneers stopped in California wasn't because they
had found what they were seeking, but because they
ran out of land. They simply couldn't go any farther.
Well, what happens when you come to the end of
yourself? Do you just stop? he wondered. We lost our
cherry in Asia. We thought we were going to defeat
the enemy. Nobody told us we *were* the enemy.

He was really cold now and he stepped back inside,
closing the glass balcony door against the chill and
the tireless pounding of the surf. C.J. was sleeping on
her side, her long hair tangled on the pillow. He
looked down at her and gently stroked her hair away
from her face. Her skin tan, almost the same color as
Lim's and her body delicately made, like Lim. But
how could you explain C.J. to Lim or Lim to C.J.?
Poor C.J., he smiled. Trying so hard to be a liberated
lady. And Lim, for whom the concept didn't even exist. Christ, why don't you just drop it and get some
sleep, he thought.

He got back into bed and put his arm around C.J.
She lay curled away from him, her hair tickling his
lips. It would be easy to fall in love with someone as
bright and beautiful as C.J., but who could afford it,

he thought. We give our heart away for free, but it costs us so much to get it back. Like Lim. Was it really love with Lim, or pity? From the beginning the two emotions had been part of each other. Even that afternoon when she came to his hut, the monsoon rain clattering on the bamboo roof, the green hills hidden in gray clouds. Caine had been clumsily trying to sew a rip in his pants.

She stood before him, wearing the black shirt and trousers of the Meo women, a red sash about her slender waist. She wore a black turban and around her neck three heavy silver rings, her dowry. Her skin a light tan, oval eyes dark, and her only really oriental feature was her slightly wide nose. On her feet she wore plastic shower shoes made in Japan. At first he didn't think of her as being pretty, but later he learned to look at her the way he looked at white women and to see how beautiful she really was. She smiled shyly and said, "I am Lim, lord. My Uncle Chong has given me to you in exchange for the rifle you gave him."

Flustered, he dropped his sewing, then picked it up and threw it on his bunk.

"I don't understand. Tell your Uncle Chong that he doesn't owe me anything."

"But I belong to you, Tan Caine. I am your woman now."

"People don't belong to people," he snapped. "Go home to your uncle."

"Please," her voice trembling. "All is yours now," taking off her silver neck rings and holding them out to him. "I will do everything to please you."

"Christ," he said, running his hand through his hair. "I can't take you, Lim. I'm a soldier, an American.

Surely there's some other man, one of your own people."

"No, there is no one," she replied morosely. "Since the war there are few men, many women. If you do not take me, no man will. And besides"—pointing to the bracelet Dao had given him—"you are Hmong now. Or is it because you already own a woman? I have heard that Americans may have only one wife. Is it true?"

"Yes."

"Only one wife?" Lim asked, puzzled. "How can a man live with only one woman?"

"I don't know." Caine laughed. "We're not very good at it either."

She knelt before him and touched her forehead to his hand.

"I am yours for as long as you want me, Tan Caine. All men have many women and you have none. Please don't send me away," she pleaded.

Touched, he put his hand to her cheek and said softly, "You know that before the monsoon ends, I'll have to go back to the war."

"I know, lord."

"And don't call me lord," he shouted. "You're a free woman."

"Yes, lord," she cried happily, hugging him tightly.

They made love throughout the long rainy afternoon. Although she lacked the languorous sensuality of the Lao women, her body heaved against his with a dark and primitive intensity. Drowsy with lovemaking and the rain, he fell asleep. Some sound, something woke him suddenly. He grabbed his .45 automatic and stealthily got out of bed. As Lim began to stir, he crept to the door, threw it open, and found himself aiming at a ten-year-old girl sitting motionless under the eaves of the hut. Although her face was without expression, Caine remembered thinking that she was the most beautiful child he had ever seen. She didn't look at him, but continued staring into the rain. He scooped her up in his left arm and brought her into the hut. Lim was awake, her eyes wide with fear.

"Who is this?" he demanded angrily.

"My daughter, lord. I was afraid to tell you"—her voice trembling.

"Then tell me now. What's the matter with her?"

"She has a great sadness. Her three souls have been stolen by evil *tlan* and have left her body behind."

"Fine. Now tell me what happened to her," his eyes blazing.

"I cannot," she sobbed. "It is a great shame for me."

It was Dao who finally told him about it at dinner the next day. Lim had roasted a chicken, and as protocol demanded, Caine offered the head to Dao. Dao crunched noisily and sucked out the brain before he finally answered.

"The child has lost her mind. There is nothing to be done, Tan Caine."

"Damn it, I want to know what happened," Caine said, his voice soft and cold.

"Why?" Dao demanded. "It will not make you any happier to know."

"What are you afraid of, Dao?"—his voice challenging, mocking.

"Lim and the child were in Muong Ngom. She is such a pretty child, that was the problem."

"So what?" Caine put in.

"Muong Ngom was one of our villages. The Pathet Lao held it for over three months until we pushed them out. Some officer must have taken a fancy to her. For three months she was kept naked in a small cage for the use of all the troops. She was raped hundreds of times in the most brutal fashion. You see," he sighed. "There is nothing to be done."

"Where are the guerrillas who occupied Muong Ngom now?"

"We think they've moved north, near Nong Het."

"Well, there's still some killing to be done," Caine said quietly.

"There are NVA in that area as well. It's too dangerous. And besides, that won't help the girl. Nothing will, except perhaps death."

"We won't be doing it for the girl. We'll be doing it for ourselves," Caine replied.

As it turned out, it took them over a year of fighting before they reached Nong Het. Lim was pregnant then, with a son, she assured Caine proudly. And so that the son-to-be would be strong, she continued to labor in the poppy fields despite Caine's objections. Throughout the long hot days the women worked in the fields that were bright red patches in the sun, like splashes of blood on the green hills, harvesting the opium for shipment to the heroin factories in Vientiane, Bangkok, and Saigon.

That last night Caine came back to his hut from the radio shack to find Chong playing his *khene,* his thin oriental face almost drowsy, like that of an opium smoker. Caine had just been arguing with Cunningham, demanding a flight of B-52's from Thailand to hit Nong Het once the trap was sprung. The plan itself was quite simple. Chong would take Nong Het with a Meo company and, acting as bait, would draw the Pathet Lao into an attack on the village, while

Caine and Dao would take the rest of the Meo force and seal the valley. Chong would dig in and the bombers would then saturate-bomb the valley, leaving Caine and Dao to move in and mop up. Caine also wanted some bombing in the neighborhood of the camp in order to protect their base, which would be defenseless once he moved out. Cunningham, of course, was furious.

"Damn it, Caine. How in hell am I supposed to get you a flight of bombers when officially we don't exist in Laos?"

"The flight is checked out for a strike in Nam. They just hit the wrong target. Accidents happen all the time in war," he said.

"No go, buddy. You're not only exceeding orders, you're blowing us wide open."

"Bullshit, Cunningham. Stupidity is being unable to do anything other than follow orders," he had retorted angrily. "Fuck orders, because I'm going in and unless you support me, the Meo force will cease to exist."

He went back to his hut confident that Cunningham would come through. People will do anything in the name of military expediency. The one great advantage they had in Laos was that officially they didn't exist. Cunningham more than anyone else should appreciate that, he thought. Not like those poor bastards in Nam who had politicians running the army, fucking things up all the way down to the company level. When he got back to the hut, he was disquieted by Chong's fatalistic calm.

"You're sure you'll be able to handle it, Uncle Chong? We only have this one chance to trap them," he said as Chong finished playing. In the corner Lim's daughter sat like an icon, staring into the fire. Her eyes were flames, the only thing about her that was alive.

"Rest easy, Tan Caine. You will lead us to victory as you have before. We will destroy all of them, God help them."

How can Chong not hate them, he wondered. He remembered the time Chong had straightened the contorted limbs of a guerrilla they had killed in an ambush, so that his soul would rest more comfortably.

"Leave him alone," Dao demanded angrily. "He was a Communist."

"He was a man," Chong had answered simply.

But it was Dao who had been right, Caine thought. Compassion was weakness. Perhaps it was compassion that had made Chong hesitate that fraction of a second and led to his being captured. Death is nothing; it's dying that is so hard, he decided. And Chong's calm. He couldn't understand that either. Perhaps he'd had a premonition. Lim had a premonition and it made her anything but calm. He'd awakened in the middle of the night to find her trying to stifle her sobbing so as not to disturb him.

"I'm so afraid," the words bursting out of her. "When you are gone, who will look after us? Who will protect your son?"

He cradled her in his arms as though she were a child, gently stroking her long black hair. What the hell, he thought. What the hell.

"Perhaps you'll find another man, who will give you a dozen sons," he teased.

She shook her head wildly. "I'm yours forever," she cried desperately.

"Only death is forever," he said.

Nowhere in the record of propaganda called history

will one find any mention of the battle of Nong Het. The Communists never talked about their defeat, the Laotians publicly ignored it, and the Americans officially weren't involved. Sure, Caine thought. Tell that to Chong and the thousands who filled that valley with the stench of death. More than anything, he remembered the stench of blackened corpses when they finally took the village.

He had found Chong's naked body tied to a stake at the edge of the village, recognizable only by the necklace around his neck. The flesh below his knees had been beaten off with bicycle chains and bones gleaming white in the sun were all that was left of his legs. They had gouged out his eyes and cut off his ears, nose, lips, and genitals. The wounds were black with maggots and fat swarming flies. With a shudder, he cut Chong down and forced himself to straighten the limbs as Chong himself had done.

Lynhiavu came up to him, smiling, proudly holding up a severed head for Caine's approval. The dusty street was full of bodies and by the thorn fence dozens of bodies were piled in a loose tangle. Sporadic fire and grenade explosions still echoed in the remorseless heat as the mopping up went on.

"There are many prisoners in the big hut, Tan Caine. What should we do with them?" Lynhiavu asked, grinning.

"Don't waste ammunition," Caine replied tonelessly. "Secure the hut and set fire to it."

He was damp with sweat as he got out of bed to get another cigarette, lighting it from the still burning butt in his mouth. A gray misty dawn was breaking over the beach. He noted with satisfaction that his hand wasn't trembling as he lit up. When he turned around, he found that C.J. was awake. She regarded him seriously, a vague concern mirrored in her soft blue eyes.

"You smoke too much," she said quietly.

He found that wildly funny and let out a short harsh laugh. Nobody in Indochina ever figured that they'd live long enough to get cancer. What do they know anyway, he thought. He remembered telling the psychologist during his exit interview in Langley that he didn't want to burn down any more huts with screaming gooks inside.

"What else is bothering you?" the psychologist had asked, as if that wasn't enough.

If they couldn't understand that, how would they understand how he found Lim when he returned to base? The camp had been hit by a cluster bomb and most of her body was a festering blob of flesh and insects, indentifiable only by her plastic shower shoes. The stench was indescribable and he was retching with the salt taste of tears and sweat on his lips. Nothing was left of the little girl's body, except for a few tatters of rags and charred bones, and all he kept thinking was, we did it. It wasn't just the gooks or Charley, it was us, and he knew that he had to quit.

"I've been thinking about you while I was asleep," C.J. brought out tentatively. She patted the bed for him to sit beside her and then she began stroking his arm.

"You were in Vietnam, weren't you?" she asked.

"Yes, sort of."

"Did you ever kill anybody?"

"That's what war is all about, isn't it?" he snapped.

"What's it like to kill someone?"

That question always fascinated women, he thought. Maybe it's a turn-on for them. Maybe that's what war is all about, a turn-on for the spectators.

"It's easy," he said.

"God, sometimes you scare me."

He leaned over and kissed her brutally, his hands pressing her into the mattress, his tongue thrusting deep into her mouth. At first she responded, then she twisted away desperately, terrified at the sudden power and sheer savagery of his body. Abruptly he shoved her away and took a drag from his cigarette, his eyes bright and cold as green ice.

"How long have you been back?" she asked, surprising him. He hadn't given her credit for being so perceptive and tough-minded.

"It's been a while," he said, and suddenly tired, he lay back on the pillow and watched the smoke rise to the ceiling.

She thought a long time, then put her fingers hesitantly to his cheek.

"No," she said softly, sadly. "You never came back."

CHAPTER 4

Everything is for sale in Las Vegas. That's probably
true in most cities, but nowhere does money talk more
loudly and openly than in Vegas. In its own way Vegas is the unique embodiment of the American dream
carved in concrete, neon, and white stucco. It is the
Babylon of the middle class, the Monte Carlo for sales-
men and secretaries, the one place in America where
the term *working girl* means prostitute and where you
can indulge in any sin, so long as you pay for it in
cash.

Even before the Paiute Indians came, the sixteenth-
century Spaniards, who were building the Spanish
Trail between Sante Fe and the Camino Real, had discovered the fertile valley. Ringed by harsh treeless
mountains, the valley was an oasis of grass fields fed
by natural springs, and so the Spanish called their settlement Las Vegas, meaning "The Meadows." But if
Vegas got its name from the Spanish, it got its character from Bugsy Siegel, a gangster of the forties, who
understood, perhaps better than anyone else, that
what Americans really wanted was a gaudy cut-rate
merry-go-round where everyone gets a crack at the
brass ring and where even the losers can pay for their
sins on the installment plan. And that was why Caine

had come to Vegas. There were things he had to buy
and it would be easier in a town where money is as
sacred as the name of God to an orthodox Jew.

Or at least so Caine thought in the taxi from
McCarran International Airport to the Strip. The taxi
turned into the circular drive around a huge fountain
display and pulled up to the main entrance of Caesars
Palace. As the driver got Caine's suitcase out of the
trunk, he said, "There it is, pal. The biggest Italian car
wash in town," gesturing at the fountains spraying water at least a hundred feet into the air. Caine smiled
appreciatively, but his eyes behind his sunglasses
were not smiling. The tail in the brown sports jacket
he had first spotted at LAX was still with him. He
registered under the name Charles Hillary, the identity he had picked up in Hollywood the previous night.
The long-haired bellboy, who looked like a college
student except for his cynical expression and knowing
eyes, took Caine's suitcase up to the twelfth floor.
Caine barely glanced at the plaster Roman statues set
in niches along the corridor as he followed the bellboy
to his room. After the bellboy had put away the suitcase and fussed about the lavish suite a bit, Caine
gave him a five-dollar tip—adequate in case he
wanted to buy a little something extra later, but not
enough to make the boy remember him—and locked
the door as soon as he was alone.

He lit a cigarette and sat down in the large easy
chair opposite the bed. The room was opulently furnished, with oversized furniture on an ankle-deep gold
carpet. The living area was separated by arched divi-
ders from the bed that stood on a raised platform with
steps. Caine walked over to the window and looked
down at the city. The hotels and golf courses were

spread out below him like the toys of a giant. He turned away and looked at the immense raised bed again and grinned. The place was a standing invitation to debauchery.

Then his brow furrowed. He would have to flush the tail and find out who was after him and why. But he could take care of that later. He only planned to be in Vegas for a couple of days, so the Hillary cover should hold. But it was annoying that he had to worry about his cover so soon. After all, he had just acquired it a few hours ago.

The first thing C.J. had done yesterday morning was to take a snort of coke and go down on him. Then she straddled him, her sea-blue eyes fastened on his like a leech, as they bucked and heaved in a sweaty tangle. For the first time, he was truly aware of her, not of her body but of her, and he groaned as he came into her. Afterward she tenderly nuzzled his neck and ear.

"It was better this time," she said.

"Much."

"Karl said you have to leave. Will you be coming back?" she asked, and wouldn't look at him.

"I'll be back," he said and wondered if it was true. She smiled and snuggled against his shoulder.

After a leisurely brunch at Alice's on the Malibu pier C.J. had dropped him off at the airport. But instead of heading straight to Vegas, as he had indicated to Wasserman, he had doubled back and rented a car. He drove the freeways to Hollywood and checked into a cheap motel on Highland Avenue. He spent the rest of the day in his room, except for brief excursions to a stamp shop, a stationery store, and finally a costume store on Sunset, where he bought a curly black wig, a mustache, and a red silk shirt. On his way back to the motel he stopped at a photographer's studio and had half-a-dozen passport photos made, paying extra for immediate development.

Back in his room he wrote himself a meaningless business letter filled with buy-and-sell agricultural commodity quotations taken from *The Wall Street Journal*. He carefully glued the Mauritius one-penny stamp to the envelope and, next to it, two other canceled Mauritian stamps that had come in a two-dollar packet from the stamp store. He wrote a return address on the envelope from a nonexistent Mauritian company, but left the name of the addressee blank, since he didn't know what cover name he would be using. Then he burned the remaining stamps. He also burned the hundred-dollar bill that Wasserman had first sent him, using it to light a cigarette. He knew it was childish, but it was something he had always wanted to do, and besides, he had to destroy the bill in any case, since it had Wasserman's number on it and was the only physical link connecting them. The last thing he did before taking a nap was to ring the desk and instruct them to call him at 8:00 P.M.

He met Charles Hillary at the Peacock Lounge on Hollywood Boulevard, the second gay bar he had hit that evening. Hillary was just what he was looking for. He was the same height as Caine, although thinner, with wavy blond hair and fine even features. He squinted slightly, which indicated that he might be nearsighted, and he wore lipstick and just a touch of eye makeup. He would play the "fem" to Caine's "butch," and was probably used to a passive role, so he shouldn't be much trouble, Caine decided. After a few drinks, during which Hillary ran his fingers admiringly up Caine's arm, shivering slightly at the feel of the silk and the hard muscles underneath the shirt, they agreed that the noisy atmosphere of the bar, the queens screeching in noisy voices and cattily eyeing each other, was terribly crude and they left arm in arm. As they walked out, Hillary threw a triumphant glance at his fluttering friends. He had a dark-haired Adonis, oozing machismo, on his arm. Hillary drove them to his nearby apartment and, when they got inside, excused himself so he could slip into something more comfortable.

Hillary came out of the bedroom, wearing a flaming pink velvet robe and sat next to Caine on the couch. He nuzzled Caine's neck, then ran his lips down the silk shirt and breathed warmly on Caine's crotch. Caine spread his legs slightly and slid to the edge of the couch, as Hillary knelt before him and leaned forward. Suddenly, without any change in expression, Caine brought his knee up sharply into Hillary's chin, snapping the head back. Hillary crumpled to the floor, moaning through his shattered teeth. The blood trickled from his mouth and seeped into the carpet. He had almost completely bitten through his tongue. Caine considered kicking him again in the jaw, but the moaning stopped. He knelt and felt the erratic pulse of the unconscious man and was warmed by a vague sense of relief. After all, he hadn't wanted to kill the poor bastard. After a bit of searching, Caine found Hillary's wallet in a pants hip pocket in the bedroom and quickly scanned the driver's license and credit cards. He had been right. Hillary wore wire-rimmed glasses in the license photograph. He took the wallet and methodically rummaged through the apartment to make it look like an ordinary robbery. Not that he thought that Hillary would go to the police. Homosexuals usually avoided the police, from whom they could expect little sympathy. As he left the apartment, he heard Hillary beginning to groan. He quickly walked two blocks to Sunset. On the way he dropped the black wig and mustache in an apartment house trash bin. He caught a taxi outside Schwab's and took it to near where he had parked the car.

Caine briefly studied the license photograph in the car, then drove to an all-night drugstore, where he bought hair dye, a curling set, and a pair of Polaroid light-sensitive wire-rimmed glasses of the same type as in the photograph. Back in his motel room, he dyed his hair blond, set it in the style in the photograph, and practiced the signature on the license. He destroyed everything he had bought and put the shirt and the other things that couldn't be destroyed into the motel garbage can near the manager's office. Then he called and made a reservation for the morning flight to Vegas under his own name. He also called an all-night accommodation number and reserved a room at Caesars Palace under Hillary's name. Everything had gone perfectly, except for the tail he had spotted at LAX in the morning.

Caine stubbed out his cigarette in a large marble ashtray that stood on a coffee table modeled in the massive Roman style. He decided he would take care of the tail later that night. Meanwhile he had things to do that were innocent enough, so it didn't matter whether he was tailed or not. He found a telephone directory in a desk drawer and noted the address of the public library, a hardware store, a luggage shop, and several gun stores. Then he went down to the lobby, casually checking for the tail. He saw the arm of the brown jacket almost hidden behind a copy of the L.A. *Herald-Examiner*, then turned away and walked around until he found the Rent-a-Car booth, where he rented a Chevy Vega. He picked up a map of the city from the Rent-a-Car agency and followed it to the public library.

The librarian was a pretty young woman in jeans who proved very helpful. She directed him to the microfilm viewer, where he ran through back issues of the Las Vegas *Sun*. He was looking for the by-line of a reporter: someone who knew everything going on in town, but who was discreet enough not to mention names. After about an hour he decided on a reporter named Cassidy. He went outside the library to a pay booth and called the newspaper, asking for the reporter.

A twangy western voice answered and Caine suggested that they meet in Cleopatra's Barge that evening about eight thirty. He promised Cassidy the inside story on a hell of a scoop. Cassidy guardedly accepted his invitation, the cynicism and doubt heavy in his voice.

"How will I find you?" he asked.

"Don't worry, I'll find you," Caine replied and abruptly hung up.

Caine then bought hair color rinse and a large roll of plastic sheeting at a nearby supermarket. His next stop was the hardware store, where he picked up a hacksaw, a small vise, a trench shovel, flashlight, and a Smith & Wesson stainless steel folding knife. At the luggage shop he bought a large leather suitcase and a small vinyl airline-style shoulder bag. As he came out of the hardware store, he noted that the tail was in a gray Ford parked down the street. He placed the shovel and the plastic roll in the large suitcase and everything else into the airline bag. Then he drove downtown to the Greyhound bus station and put the large suitcase into a locker. Caine relaxed in the station for a few minutes till he made Brown Jacket again, then drove to the elaborate Boulevard Mall shopping center.

A large sign spread across the Sears window proclaimed, "Joy to the world, on earth peace and goodwill to men," and loudspeakers electronically carolled. For the first time, he was reminded that it was almost Christmas. The mall thronged with the bustle of holiday shoppers and he felt a sudden stab of loneliness. But wasn't it that same Christ who had said, "Foxes have dens, and birds of the air their nests; but the Son of man hath not where to lay his head," perhaps one of the loneliest sentences ever uttered? And Caine had no family or place to call his own, either. More than ever, he felt an alien in the crowd. He ambled along the bricked walk, peering at the shop windows stylishly dressed for Christmas and attractively enclosed with wrought-iron gates. After a while he went into the Broadway and purchased a pair of jeans and a cowboy shirt. Lastly, he stopped at a camera shop and purchased a Hasselblad, a cheap Polaroid camera, a Film Shield lead-coated pouch, and several rolls of film for both cameras. That was about all he could do with the tail on him, so he drove to the Desert Inn Country Club and played a challenging nine holes.

He completely forgot about the tail and concentrated totally on the game. In fact it was Caine's ability to dispassionately concentrate on something that made him so formidable. Just before making a chip shot on the seventh hole, he remembered that the psychologist at Langley had once asked him, "What is the most important thing in the world to you?"

With some surprise he had replied, "Whatever I happen to be doing at the time."

By the time Caine got back to the hotel, showered, and changed into his three-piece suit, it was almost six o'clock.

Caine began the evening with a steak dinner downstairs at the Bacchanale. While he was eating, Brown Jacket peered briefly into the restaurant. He was a burly man, about Caine's size, with deep-set eyes and unruly dark hair. Jesus, Caine thought, the dumb prick could use a few classes from Koenig, the Company's shadow and unarmed combat instructor. He explicitly ignored Brown Jacket and inwardly sighed. He would have to take him out right after dinner. The guy looked strong enough to be trouble, so he would have to do it quickly, he decided as he paid the pretty miniskirted waitress. Her eyes widened slightly as he peeled off one of the hundred-dollar bills from his roll. She smiled brightly, trying to expose her molars as she bent over to hand him his change, giving him the benefit of her cleavage all the way to the nipples. He raised his eyebrows and gave her a twenty-dollar tip. Maybe later, he told himself, and gave her saucy rump an affectionate pat as he got up to leave.

A spectacular rose-and-violet sunset splashed across the sky, like a giant reflection of the glittering neon that was lighting up all over the Strip, as he drove through the swarming evening traffic to the Pussy Cat A-Go-Go.

Catty-corner from the Pussy Cat, a white stucco chalet blazed with the neon invitation:

Wedding Chapel
Marriage License Information
Parking In Rear.

Next to the chapel was a storefront lawyer's office, with a large sign advertising, "Divorce. Uncontested Only $25." Caine grinned and headed into the Pussy Cat.

The large dark bar was relatively empty, since the band didn't come on till 10:00 P.M. It took a minute for Caine's eyes to become accustomed to the dim red light. He ordered a Coors from a red-cheeked bartender with a yellow bow tie and left the change on the bar.

Why is it bars are always dark? Caine wondered. Maybe people feel safer that way. Maybe it's so they can observe other people while they think that their own faces are safely hidden. While he waited, certain that Brown Jacket would have to come in to see if he was meeting anybody, he checked out the location of the men's room and the emergency exit.

At the other end of the bar two businessmen, the only other customers, were talking about how somebody named Roger didn't know a goddamned thing about the business. There was some discussion of Roger's connections. It couldn't be his brains, they agreed sagely, and argued over which of them should pay for the next round. Just then Brown Jacket came in, blinking blindly for a few seconds while his eyes adjusted to the gloom.

Brown Jacket sat at the other end of the bar, near the two businessmen, and ordered a bourbon and branch. When Caine was certain that Brown Jacket had made him, he glanced nervously at his watch a few times, as though he were waiting for someone, and headed for the men's room.

He stood waiting in front of the urinal, his hands in front of him. At last Brown Jacket stumbled in anxiously and, seeing Caine alone, quickly made for the urinal next to him.

"That beer just goes right through you," Caine drawled amiably. He noted the tail's shoulders relax a bit as he flushed the urinal.

"Yeah, I know what you—"

Brown Jacket never finished the sentence, for Caine, stepping quickly behind him, had thrown his right arm around the man's throat. As he leaned his weight against the back of Brown Jacket's knees, forcing him down, Caine shoved his left hand against the back of the head, smashing the startled face into the urinal. The sound of flushing water covered the man's gasp. Caine grabbed a fistful of hair and hauled the dazed man into one of the cubicles and slammed him onto the seat. He locked the door and unfolded the pocketknife. Brown Jacket sat there stunned, his nose broken and mouth bleeding. Caine grabbed the hair to keep the man's head still and pricked one of the half-closed eyelids with the knife point. Catching his breath, he said softly:

"I'm only going to ask you three times. If I don't get the answer I want the first time, I'm going to cut out your left eye. The second time I take the other eye. The third time I cut the carotid artery and you'll be unconscious in less than a minute and dead in less than five. And even if somebody somehow manages to save you, you'll be blind for life. Nod if you understand."

He felt a shudder run through the man and then the

weak, desperate nod. Brown Jacket's agonized gaze was desperately fixed on Caine's cold green eyes. Cat's eyes, Lim had called them once, Caine thought irrelevantly.

"Who are you?" he demanded quietly.

"Name's DePalma. Private investigator," Brown Jacket managed to gasp through his bloody mouth.

"Who sent you?"

"I don't know. Said his name was Smith."

"Say good-bye to your left eye," Caine said and began to press on the point.

"Wait, please!" he gasped desperately. "Jesus! Oh, God, that's what he told me. I just do what I'm paid for. He pointed you out at LAX and told me to stick. That's all I know, I swear."

"What did he look like?"

"He was a big guy. Hairy. You couldn't miss him. Oh, wait, he wore a gold earring," DePalma added eagerly.

Freddie, Caine thought ominously. What was that asshole Wasserman trying to do? Of course, he hadn't really expected Wasserman to trust him, but didn't Wasserman realize that a tail destroyed his anonymity and made him vulnerable? He frisked DePalma and removed a .38 revolver from a shoulder holster. Then he cracked open the cylinder and dropped the bullets into his jacket pocket and put the gun back in the holster.

"Listen to me very carefully," Caine said quietly. "If I ever see you again, that's the day you die. You catch the next plane to L.A. and tell the goon that hired you that I don't like company. Oh, yeah, and don't stop on your way to the airport."

Caine thought he saw a sudden hand movement

and, grabbing DePalma's throat so he couldn't scream, smashed his fist into the broken nose. DePalma started to slide to the floor, but Caine propped him against the side of the cubicle and left the bar by the emergency exit. He glanced at his watch as he got into the car. He just had time to get back to the hotel to meet Cassidy.

Cleopatra's Barge was a gaudy cocktail lounge, complete with oars, sails, waving ostrich feathers, and mini-togaed Nubian slave girls. The barge floated on a five-foot-deep Nile set beside a wide corridor just off the casino. At one end stood a lushly draped royal box, where the queen presumably entertained Antony. At the other end a baritone with capped teeth and an expensive toupee, fighting the battle of the bulge against his cumberbund, was standing on a small stage. He was holding a microphone in one hand, a cocktail in the other, and singing, "I Gotta Be Me."

Caine lurched aboard across a gangplank, feeling slightly seasick from the hydraulic mechanism that rocked the barge. He caught the eye of one of the older bartenders and asked for Cassidy. The bartender pointed out a thin, ruddy-cheeked man with short graying hair, wearing a rumpled green suit. Caine sat down at Cassidy's table and ordered "whatever my friend is having" from a busty blond waitress, her thigh-length toga swirling to show a flash of yellow panties.

"What's the story?" Cassidy asked, briefly glancing at Caine with indifferent eyes and then looking back to contemplate the bubbles in his drink.

"Money," Caine replied.

"That's what makes the world go round," Cassidy

said and finished his drink, wondering what Caine's hustle was.

"You sound like a cynic."

"So what?" Cassidy replied cynically.

"The trouble with a cynic is that he's just a disillusioned idealist."

"What's wrong with idealists, come to that?"

"They make mistakes," Caine said quietly, his voice almost obscured by the baritone crooning that he had done it his way. For the first time Cassidy looked directly at Caine, stirred by curiosity. The baggy folds under his eyes gave Cassidy the appearance of an intelligent cocker spaniel.

"What do you mean?" he asked.

"An idealist reasons that because roses smell better than onions, they must make better soup." The two men grinned at each other and for an instant they were almost friends.

"Okay, Mr. . . ." Cassidy hesitated.

"Hillary," Caine put in.

"Okay, Mr. Hillary. Are you buying or selling?"

"Buying. I want a name."

"What's in a name, speaking of roses," Cassidy remarked and signaled to the blonde for another drink.

"One thousand dollars," Caine replied. "Five hundred dollars now, five hundred dollars when I meet the name."

"That's a nice name. What are you looking for?"

"Suppose somebody wanted to buy a hundred-percent Grade A phony ID: passport, driver's license, the works. Top quality and satisfaction guaranteed not to be used in this town. Would you happen to know somebody who might have that kind of merchandise for sale?"

"Maybe," Cassidy said, sucking his teeth. Then he winked at the waitress bringing his drink. He took a quick gulp and when he put the glass down, he saw that it was resting on a five hundred-dollar bill that Caine had laid on the table.

"Merry Christmas," Caine said, but Cassidy made no move to touch the money.

"Are you with an organization, by any chance?"

"Relax. If I were with an organization, would I have to come to you for help?"

"No, I guess not," Cassidy said, rubbing his chin speculatively. After a moment he lifted the glass and took the money.

"The name," Caine prompted.

"There's this guy," Cassidy began. "Name is Hanratty. Pete Hanratty. He did a stretch at Folsom for counterfeiting. I hear he does some quality paperwork for a certain organization, which shall be nameless. He might be interested in a little private enterprise. It's okay to use my name. I've done him a few favors."

"Where do I find him?"

"He works nights as a dealer at Binion's Horseshoe in Glitter Gulch," using the term the locals have given to the central casino area on downtown Fremont.

"What's he look like?"

"Short fat guy. Mostly bald. Wears glasses too."

"Good enough," Caine said. "You wouldn't happen to know his address?"

"It's in the book," Cassidy said, finishing his drink. A burst of applause signaled the end of the baritone's lounge performance. As people started to get up, Caine touched Cassidy's arm.

"Just one more thing," Caine said. "Forget you ever

saw me. Remembering won't do either of us any good."

"What about the other five hundred dollars?" Cassidy asked.

"If Hanratty works out, you get the other five hundred dollars in the mail. If he doesn't," Caine added softly, "I'm coming back for my five hundred dollars."

"You're not threatening me, are you? Because I've been threatened before, by experts," Cassidy replied, suddenly straightening up.

"You seem like a nice guy, Cassidy. I'm not threatening you. I'm giving you the best advice you ever got. Believe me, you never want to see me again," Caine said, his cat's eyes glinting green and cold. Cassidy felt a shiver of uneasiness pass up his spine, and nodded. Caine put a ten-dollar bill down on the table. "For the drinks," he said, and left.

Caine went to a lobby phone and placed a call to Wasserman's number in Hollywood. An answering machine answered the phone and beeped. Caine spoke quickly to the machine.

"Your last associate botched the job. Send any more and the deal is off and I keep the down payment."

That should keep Wasserman off my back for a while, he thought as he hung up the phone. He checked his watch and decided that he had enough time to launder some of the money before he looked up Hanratty.

It was with a sense of wonder that Caine descended into the maelstrom of the hotel's sunken casino. The walls of the casino area were lined with plaster bas-reliefs of Roman gladiators, and the entire area was brilliantly lit by what was easily the largest crystal chandelier he had ever seen. The casino hummed with the noises of chips and machines and the exclamations of players begging whatever god they believed in to "Come on, baby." Perhaps the noisiest section was where the long banks of slot machines were situated—phalanxes of middle-aged women mechanically cranked coins into the machines with all the spontaneity of clockwork figures in an automated assembly line. This was the real essence of Vegas, Caine thought, its *raison d'être:* the money machine. He felt himself caught by the excitement and sternly reminded himself that he was there to launder the money and not to gamble.

It would have been simpler a few years ago, Caine mused, as he bought $10,000 worth of hundred-dollar chips. In those days chips from any casino were as good as cash anywhere in Vegas. All you had to do was buy chips in one casino, and cash them in at another. But in a classic example of Gresham's Law, that bad money drives out good, counterfeit chips had appeared and now each casino would only cash its own chips.

He went over to one of the crap tables, changed two of the hundred-dollar chips for ten-dollar chips and bet cautiously on the Don't Pass line. After about half an hour he was down $120. The dice passed to a middle-aged woman in a yellow print dress. She made a six point and on a hunch Caine bet a hundred on the hard eight. The woman rolled the two fours as though they were wired. Feeling that she was still good, Caine put five hundred of the thousand he had just won on the Come. She rolled an eleven and he put five hundred on the Pass line. She rolled a ten and after five excited rolls, she made her point. In less than a minute, he had won $2,000.

He collected his chips, tossing a few ten-dollar chips to the pit man, and went back to the cashier. He cashed them in, making sure he was paid in fifties so he wouldn't get Wasserman's hundred-dollar bills back again, and went to another cashier's window and bought $10,000 in $500 denomination American Express traveler's checks, keeping about $2,000 of the cashed-in chips in cash. Then, heading back to the parking area, he had the attendant bring the car and drove down to Glitter Gulch.

Entering Binion's Horseshoe, Caine was immediately struck, like any other gawking tourist, by the large glass display that contained one hundred $10,000 bills. The stern visage of Samuel Chase repeated itself across the felt like an Andy Warhol painting, and Caine tingled with the idea that he might soon be worth half of it. He was growing greedy, he thought. He would be willing to kill a hundred Mengeles for that kind of money.

Caine bought $10,000 in chips with the Wasserman money and wandered around the casino looking for Hanratty. The fat little man was dealing at a blackjack table. Hanratty dealt, with mechanical efficiency and all the excitement of an accountant doing a particularly boring audit, to two penny-ante customers, a middle-aged man and a young Japanese girl. Caine sat down at the table and began to play with ten-dollar chips. Hanratty had small black eyes set deep in rolls of fat. He wore a western string tie and a red vest bearing a tag that read, "Howdy, My name is Pete."

After a while the middle-aged man shrugged and walked away. The girl looked like she was there for the duration, but finally she went bust getting hit on a showing seven, while Hanratty showed only a six. As she turned away, Caine put down a hundred-dollar chip and said urgently,

"A reporter friend of mine named Cassidy suggested we get together."

"I'm off in twenty minutes," Hanratty replied tonelessly, scooping up the chip after hitting Caine with a king to his thirteen.

"Buy you a drink at the bar," Caine replied, and got up. He cashed in his chips and waited at one of the bar tables. Hanratty came over and ordered a J&B from the waitress.

"Cassidy sent you?" he asked. Caine nodded.

"Describe him," he said, and Caine did so. Then as Hanratty nervously watched him, Caine told him what he wanted.

"When do you need it?" Hanratty asked.

"Tomorrow."

"No can do. No, sir. No can do."

"Bullshit," Caine replied. "I never heard of a papermaker who didn't keep something stashed away for a special job. That's what I want, your special."

"You don't plan on using it here in Vegas?" Hanratty asked.

"No way," Caine said. Hanratty closed his eyes and considered for a minute.

"I might have something special," he admitted reluctantly. "But it'll cost you."

"Naturally."

"Three thousand in cash."

Caine pretended to think for a minute and then agreed. Hanratty was chagrined. He should have asked for more.

"What about photographs?"

Caine pulled out three of the passport photos he'd had made up in Hollywood and tucked them into Hanratty's vest pocket.

"I got a clean passport and Nevada driver's license made out for a William Foster. He was a straight nobody and he's been dead for less than a year. No family to speak of. I used it to get a vaccination record and an international driver's license from the Triple A. Let's see, put you down for a birthdate in '43, make you thirty-six. Height?"

"Five eleven, weight one seventy, green eyes, light brown hair, occupation lawyer, birthplace Los Angeles," Caine finished for him. Being a lawyer was one of those all-purpose covers that required just a bit of legal jargon to carry off and, like the law itself, it covered a multitude of sins. "All you have to do is fill in the blanks and seal the photographs. What else?"

"Do you want a different name?"

"How about Robert Redford?" Caine smiled and when Hanratty looked at him sharply, said, "William Foster is fine. Anything else?"

"Money," Hanratty said, biting his lower lip.

Caine counted out $1,500 and passed it under the table. Hanratty counted it as quickly as a bank teller and stuffed it into his hip pocket.

"Tomorrow night, this time," Caine added. "We'll make the switch in the john. If it looks good, you get the rest of the money."

"Fair enough." Hanratty smiled and started to get up. Caine stopped him by grabbing his sleeve.

"One more thing, Pete. After tomorrow night, you never heard of William Foster."

Hanratty looked aggrieved.

"What do you take me for? I'm a professional. I got a reputation," he protested and, yanking his arm away from Caine, waddled indignantly back to his blackjack table.

Caine laundered the rest of Wasserman's money at the Flamingo and walked back across the Strip to Caesars Palace. He debated between going to bed and catching Harry Belafonte's midnight show at the Circus Maximus. While he stood there indecisively, his waitress from the Bacchanale bumped into him and they decided to have sandwiches at the Noshorium.

He regarded her over the bagels and lox. She had long brown hair, dark eyes, a slim young figure with soft round breasts, and a pert uptilted Irish nose. He asked if she was a working girl.

"Part time," she murmured.

"A hundred do it?"

"Not for the whole night."

They finished their coffee and went up to his room. They undressed and she lay on the giant raised bed, a carnal offering to the gods. He played with her smooth round breasts, thinking not of Lim for the first time in a long time, but C.J. As he plunged into the girl, he remembered the feel of C.J.'s exquisite young skin, her gentle knowing touches, and was disturbed by the impact she had made on him. Something had passed between them all right, he thought.

Caine did all the things to the girl that he hadn't done to C.J., holding back his orgasm until after she had climaxed in a long series of shudders, moaning, "Oh, Daddy," over and over. Then he spurted into her and lay exhausted on her soft white body, like a castaway thrown up on a distant shore. She offered to stay the night with him anyway, but he shook his head. She dressed and came back to the bed to kiss him good night.

"By the way," she said. "My name is Nancy."

"Good night, Nancy," he said, thinking that he had to file away his feelings about C.J., that it was strictly business. He locked the door after the girl left and took a quick shower.

Before he slept, he called the desk and gave instructions for a 7:00 A.M. wake-up call.

The soft burring of the phone woke Caine out of a restless sleep. He methodically went through the morning ritual of exercise, shower, and shave, then dressed in jeans and the cowboy shirt. He again set his hair in the style affected by Hillary in the license photo. Hillary had been striving for a Byronic effect in the photo, but he hadn't quite brought it off. Caine practiced the prissy smile from the photo and spent another half hour practicing the signature. Then he went down to the Circus Maximus and enjoyed a lavish champagne breakfast.

After breakfast he used all the standard flushes, but he was clean. Caine knew that from now on he could no longer afford anything that even smelled like a tail.

He found Hanratty's address in the phone book and parked across the street from a small white tract house. A little boy was riding his tricycle on the sidewalk in front. Caine snapped a few Polaroids of the boy and when a thin woman in curlers and a red house dress came out and dragged the protesting child back into the house, he got a good picture of her as well.

He drove around town, like a tourist trying to get his bearings, then headed northwest on U.S. 95. After a while he turned west onto State Route 39 and drove into the sparse scrublands of Kyle Canyon, counting signposts from the turnoff. Just past the sixth signpost he spotted a clump of mesquite cactus about twenty yards off the road. He pulled over and shut off the engine. The canyon was deserted and silent except for the slight rustle of the wind through the Joshua trees. Satisfied, he turned the car around the way he had come. On the way back to town he stopped off at a plant shop, bought a knee-high mesquite cactus and put it in the backseat.

One of the reasons he had come to Vegas is that Nevada is a western state, proud of its frontier heritage, and as such, buying a gun in Nevada is almost as simple as buying a pack of cigarettes. At the first gun shop he went into, he purchased a tiny Bauer .25 caliber stainless steel automatic, two six-shot clips, and a box of standard Remington shells. Unfortunately the only legal .25 bullets were hard-nosed, which wouldn't stop a determined mosquito at twenty-five feet, the gun's maximum effective range, but he would take care of that later. As Caine handed the Hillary license to the amiable gum-chewing gun dealer and signed the purchase form with the practiced signature, he smiled the prissy smile. But the gun dealer didn't even glance up at him to check the license photo. Caine felt a slight sense of chagrin at the wasted effort. Still, better safe than sorry. What was it some Soviet general had once said, "Train hard, fight easy."

It was so easy, in fact, that he bought a Smith & Wesson .44 Magnum revolver with a six-and-a-half-inch barrel from the same dealer. After some discussion Caine bought a box of Remington 240 grain hollow head bullets to go with the S&W .44. He figured he could easily blow away anybody at a hundred yards with it. Before he left the shop, he also purchased an official-looking bronze badge that read, SPECIAL AGENT.

He next stopped at the bus station and retrieved the large suitcase from the locker. As he walked into another gun shop, on Charleston Boulevard, he reflected that he wasn't really sure what the job would ultimately require and he was simply trying to provide himself with the tools to use for any possible opportunity to make the hit that might present itself.

This time he bought a Winchester Model 70 bolt-action rifle and a Browning three-to-nine-power variable scope. For a moment he debated between the .300 and the .338, but decided that he wanted range over power and picked the .300 caliber model. He bought Magnum hollow-point shells and had the dealer mount the scope. Caine tried the gun out on a range behind the shop and made some minor adjustments to the scope. By the time he left the shop, he was confident that, with the scope, he could bring down a fucking elephant at twelve hundred yards. Any hit on a man, no matter on what part of the body, would almost certainly be fatal.

At another gun shop on Main Street he got a black Colt AR-15 rifle to give him some accurate firepower in case he needed it. The light .223 caliber rifle was a semiautomatic civilian version of the M-16. The gun came comfortably into his hand and for a moment it brought the feel of Indochina back to him. But he shook it off as he smiled the Hillary smile. He considered getting a three-power scope for the handle mount, but calculated that with the flip rear sight he could hit anything within 300 yards, and he already had the Winchester for long range. Lastly he bought five thirty-round clips and two boxes of Super X softpoint 5.56mm bullets. All told, he had spent about $1,600 for the guns and accessories, he calculated.

That done, he checked into the Star Motel on South Fourth, a concrete and plastic affair with a big neon sign shaped like a star. After he locked the door and made sure the windows were closed and shaded, he turned on the TV and got to work. As an afternoon game show came on the tube, a pretty curly-haired housewife was screaming in ecstasy as she embraced the fatuously smiling MC. The announcer's voice solemnly intoned the virtues of the refrigerator she had just won. Jesus, it made you wonder, Caine thought. Still, he was as much a whore as anybody, he admitted as he opened the large suitcase and began to tightly wrap the guns and bullets, except for the Bauer .25 automatic, in lengths of plastic cut from the roll. When he was finished, he tightly packed the guns, shovel, and flashlight into the suitcase.

Next he mounted the vise on a small table and dumdummed the .25 caliber bullets, making careful crisscross cuts with the hacksaw. The Bauer still wouldn't kill anybody, unless he got lucky with a head or a heart shot, but the dumdums would certainly make anyone hit with them pause and reconsider, he mused.

After going to the bathroom to wash the sweat off his hands and face, he loaded the clips and wrapped them and the Bauer in the lead-coated film pouch and inserted them, with handkerchiefs for padding, into the film compartment of the Hasselblad camera. It should pass any customs or airport inspection, he decided after critically inspecting the camera. Most airport magnetometers only picked up ferrous metals and would not detect the stainless steel automatic. The Wong magnetometer would pick it up, but the inspector would naturally assume that the camera itself was causing the bleep and the camera sheathing and the Film Shield pouch would screen the gun from X rays. It would do, Cain decided, and put the Hasselblad back into the airline bag and cleaned up the room. He deliberately rumpled the bed, wet one of the towels, and shut the TV, silencing a smiling salesman pitching the recreational joys of buying worthless desert land. No one noticed him as he locked the suitcase and bag in the car trunk and drove away.

As soon as it got dark, Caine drove out of the artificial electric noon of the Strip back to Kyle Canyon. It was as if the canyon were filled with the utter darkness and silence of death itself, once he had shut off the engine and the car lights. The only light to be seen came from myriad stars sprayed across the darkness like a distant city in the sky.

In spite of the desert chill that seemed to come from the endless night of outer space, he removed his jacket and shirt before he buried the large suitcase just to the right of the mesquite clump he had spotted that morning. Periodically he stopped and looked around, but there was nothing. Once he heard the sound of a car headed into town and clicked off the flashlight, waiting in the darkness until the car lights were long out of sight. He planted the cactus he had purchased at the plant shop on top of the layer of dirt covering the suitcase and then buried the shovel and flashlight in a shallow hole a few feet away. He wiped himself clean with a hotel towel and then used it to smooth away any evidence of digging or footprints. When he turned the headlights on, there was no indication that anyone had been there. The guns would keep until he came back for them, when and if he located Mengele.

Hanratty was anxiously waiting for him in the men's room at Binion's. Caine went into one of the cubicles and carefully examined the documents. Although he knew that they had been altered, he couldn't see any evidence of it. He was impressed—they were flawless. He counted out the $1,500 and handed it to Hanratty, who never took his eyes off the door. Then he added an extra $200 and the Polaroid pictures of Hanratty's wife and son. Hanratty blanched when he saw the pictures.

"What's that for?" he asked warily.

"The money's a little extra for a good job. The pictures are to remind you how vulnerable you are. You are never to mention anything about me or William Foster to anybody, including Cassidy."

"Even the Mob doesn't threaten a man's wife and kid. Besides, I got friends."

"Forget it, Pete. Your friends can't get at me. I'm not vulnerable. You are. And so are they"—indicating the pictures.

When he left the john, Hanratty was nervously attempting to comb his fringe of side hair across his large bald spot.

Caine spent the rest of the evening dining alone on the excellent escargots, followed by a tender filet mignon at the Top of the Mint. And he finally got to see Harry Belafonte at the Circus Maximus. Before he went upstairs, he told the desk clerk that he would be checking out in the morning. He put $500 in an envelope and mailed it to Cassidy, care of the Las Vegas Sun. Before going upstairs, he used a lobby phone to call and reserve a seat on the morning flight to New York under his own name.

Caine was tired by the time he finished a Scotch and soda in his room. Wearily he color-rinsed his hair in the shower, and after a final cigarette, he went to bed.

In the airport men's room the next morning he flushed Hillary's torn credit cards and driver's license down the toilet and put on his own wraparound sunglasses. He smoothed his hair into place, vaguely relieved to be even briefly back in his own identity. The envelope with the stamp on it, now addressed to William Foster, was in his jacket pocket. At the Western Union booth he sent a terse unsigned cable to Wasserman, telling him that he was flying to Switzerland to deal with the Zurich situation.

The sun was shining warm and clear over the tarmac as he boarded the plane for New York. The smiling stewardess took his boarding pass and asked him how he had done in Vegas, her blue eyes twinkling.

"Not bad." Caine smiled back boyishly. "Not bad at all."

CHAPTER 5

Suppose you wanted to find one person among all the billions of people on earth. Someone who might be anywhere in the world and under any name. Someone who had friends and money and who didn't want to be found. How would you do it?

That was the question that Caine asked himself as he finished the last of his lunch. The waiter, resplendent in a red jacket, wheeled over a multitiered serving cart crammed with the delicious pastries Kranzler's was famous for. Caine shook his head with an air of surrender and instead ordered a *Kirschwasser*.

He lit a cigarette and dropped the match into the remains of the broiled veal and potatoes. He watched the people at the tables in the crowded café. A blonde in a ski sweater descended a winding stairway from the upper floor of the café with a flutter of small movements, as if she were dancing down to meet Fred Astaire for the finale.

At the next table a stout Swiss or perhaps German businessman, with shiny pink skin, almost bursting out of his suit like a boiled sausage, paused for a moment to glance with satisfaction at his own reflection in one of the ornate wall mirrors, before resuming his greedy attack on a steaming *Bernerplatte*, piled high with boiled beef and sausages. For a moment Caine wondered what he had done during the war. Then he exhaled the smoke and brought his mind back to the issue.

The problem was complicated by the fact that he had to be very careful about using official channels. If any of the intelligence services were to get interested in what he was doing, it would queer the pitch for good. The waiter brought a glass of the clear white cherry brandy and Caine took a large sip, feeling the warmth of the brandy wash through his body. He was tired and probably suffering from jet lag, he decided. After all, he had been on the go since he had landed at Zurich's Kloten Airport late last night.

Using the William Foster cover, he had checked into the velour-upholstered comfort of the Baur au Lac Hotel. The plush luxury of his lakeside suite was a welcome relief from the cold, driving night rain, and he had gone straight to bed.

In the morning he strolled out of the hotel, shivering slightly against the winter chill. A steel-gray sky hung like an endless sheet of ice over the lake. After checking the lobby to flush any possible tail, he took a crowded blue-and-white tram on the Bahnhofstrasse. The elegant shops along the street were beautifully dressed with Christmas manger scenes and intricate doll displays. At Gübelin's a discreet red-and-white sign proclaimed *"Fröhliche Weihnachten"* over a display of diamond-studded Piaget watches. An exquisite mannequin stood against an Alpine landscape in the window of Grieder's, wearing a Dior throwaway on sale at a price that made Neiman-Marcus look like a Salvation Army giveaway. Caine hopped off the tram at the stop near the massive stone facade of the Union Bank of Switzerland.

As a serious young bank official ushered him into the manager's dark-paneled office, Herr Kröger came from behind his desk and briskly shook Caine's hand. Kröger was tall and slender, with a thatch of well-groomed white hair. He wore a three-piece Savile Row pinstripe suit and a silk Bond Street tie. He was the genuine gilt-edged article, Caine thought. No matter how you chipped away at him, you would find money.

Caine opened a numbered account with $5,000 in traveler's checks, which he countersigned in front of Kröger. Any further instructions from him would be by mail. He would sign his letters with only the account number, reversed on the right margin. Kröger nodded understandingly at what was, for him, a perfectly normal procedure.

Caine then changed another $5,000 in traveler's checks into Swiss francs. As they discussed the details of subsequent transactions, Caine found himself thinking wishfully that if he could get into the numbered accounts, he could probably find Mengele right there and then. But of course that was impossible. Still, that was something he had to remember. It was a prime rule of intelligence investigation—perhaps *the* prime rule: always follow the money.

He explained to Kröger that he anticipated selling a certain asset for something over a quarter of a million dollars and wanted the money immediately converted into Swiss francs at whatever the current rate was on the day of the transaction. Scenting a commission, Kröger delicately inquired if he might be of some assistance in the sale.

It was a difficult moment for Caine. Experience had taught him that the world was still a battlefield, that you could trust people or you could survive, but you couldn't do both. And he was a survivor. Still, he knew that Swiss banks were inviolable. He took the envelope out of his pocket and showed Kröger the stamp.

"Ingenious," Kröger remarked.

"The currency regulations," Caine began.

"Of course. That's why we are here: to deal with the inconveniences of business."

"Do you know someone?"

"Let me see," Kröger said, and spent a few minutes on the telephone. He replaced the receiver and smiled briefly at Caine. Kröger looked like he wanted to sell him a car, Caine thought.

"The firm of Beckmann *und* Schenck is highly recommended. I am told that Herr Beckmann is perhaps the leading stamp dealer in Europe. You'll find his office on the Uraniastrasse fifty-eight, near the Rudolf Brun Bridge. If you wish, I'll call and tell him to expect you. Once he has authenticated the stamp," Kröger said, raising his eyebrows slightly to indicate that a fraud would be unthinkable, "you can deposit the stamp in our vault and we can arrange to deliver the stamp to Beckmann when he has a buyer."

"That's very kind of you."

Kröger held up his hand as if to forestall any thanks.

"Our fee is five percent of the selling price."

"Of course," Caine responded.

Herr Beckmann was a stocky figure in a gray turtleneck sweater under a worn tweed blazer. His small deep-set eyes were magnified into owl's eyes by wire-rimmed glasses perched on his nose. The walls of his spartan office were lined with sheets of brightly colored stamps displayed in glass cases like butterflies. He smiled briefly at Caine and nodded in a perfunctory Prussian bow. But when Caine handed him the envelope and he saw the stamp, he began to blink rapidly. For a moment his eyes, like giant marbles behind the glass lenses, riveted on the stamp with the total concentration of a hawk spying a distant prey.

"Extraordinary," he murmured.

"I take it the stamp meets with your approval," Caine said softly.

"There is no question of its authenticity," Beckmann replied, his Swiss-German accent sibilant in English. "Where did you get it?"

"From the owner."

"*Ja*, of course," Beckmann murmured, almost to himself. "Where did he get it, *bitte?*"

"At a New York auction in 1968."

"*Ach*, the Teilman auction. But where is the other stamp?"

"I'm still negotiating for it. I expect to have it within six months." I wish, I wish, Caine thought. Beckmann began to blink again.

"I will find a buyer, or else I will buy it myself."

"What is it worth?"

Beckmann opened his hands in a bargaining gesture that might have predated Jacob's negotiation with Esau over a bowl of soup.

"The market is down these days and the stamp is by itself. Also, an item of this size is very difficult."

"What's it worth?" Caine repeated.

There was a long pause while Beckmann calculated.

He picked up the stamp again and examined it, like a doctor poking at a patient.

"I cannot guarantee you more than seven hundred seventy-five thousand francs." Caine tried to keep his face expressionless as he translated the sum. It was more than $310,000. "Of course," Beckmann added placatingly, "we may be able to get more. I will do my best for you."

"It's a deal," Caine replied and put the stamp back in his pocket. Beckmann's eyes followed the stamp, peering at Caine's jacket as if he could see the stamp through the fabric. "I shall deposit the stamp at the bank. When you have a cash buyer, you can make the arrangements through Herr Kröger."

Caine took a *Klein* taxi back to the bank and deposited the stamp with Kröger. Then he walked over to Kranzler's for a late lunch. So now all he had to do was find Mengele, Caine thought, sipping the *Kirschwasser*. There was nothing to it. All he had to do was get his junior James Bond secret agent kit, throw on his Burberry trench coat, and play a wild hunch. It always worked out in the movies.

He could start by eliminating Asia and Africa, where a white man stood out like a grain of salt in a pepper shaker, he thought. Except for the Middle East, where the Arabs had a penchant for German scientists with whom they could share a common dislike of Jews. Of course Mengele wasn't really a scientist. Still, it was a possibility. He could probably scratch Australia and North America, because the Jewish communities were too large and the climate for notorious Nazis too inhospitable. Europe was almost certainly out, except perhaps Spain. No, even Spain would have been too hot for the Angel of Death, and

Mengele wouldn't have gone east. If he had been picked up by the Communists, they wouldn't have bothered with the niceties of a public trial. Still, that was something to keep in mind. The Poles and the Russians still wanted Mengele and just might have some information on him. So that left South America at the top of the list, with the Middle East and Eastern Europe as places to be checked for information. According to the Interpol file Mengele was last heard of in Argentina, but that was in the days of Perón and long before the Eichmann snatch. It was hopeless, Caine thought as he motioned the waiter over for the check.

"*Rechnung, bitte,*" he said, shaking his head. The son of a bitch could be anywhere. He would have to play it by the book. His first targets would be information sources in the Middle East, Poland, and Germany. Then he could narrow it down to someplace in South America with a greater degree of certainty.

The Grill bar in the Baur au Lac is the place to be in Zurich. Long ago the action was at the Odeon Café, where Mata Hari danced for the officers and the young Mussolini played billiards; but since the war it's the Grill. That evening the bar was jammed with laughing businessmen and expensive women flashing jewelry from Meister's and conversation from the society pages. As Caine looked around, he thought he spotted agents from at least half-a-dozen intelligence services. It was like a spies' convention, he mused as he sipped a *marc*. Then he got lucky.

He saw a powerfully built man sitting at a corner table with a stunning blonde who was sensuously licking the cherry in her cocktail. He recognized Mahmoud Ibn Sallah from the briefing he'd had on the Abu Daud hit.

Ibn Sallah had dark curly hair and soft brown eyes nestled under long curling lashes. But the soft eyes that made him irresistible to women concealed a brain that could unravel Byzantine plots with the cunning ruthlessness of his Levantine forebears. His dark business suit did not disguise what was still an impressive body. In his youth he had been an Olympic wrestler.

At the moment Ibn Sallah was pouring champagne for the blonde, and from her reaction he appeared to be mouthing some extravagant courtesy. Caine thought that he looked like a high-class Armenian rug merchant, but in fact Ibn Sallah was the deputy director of the Moukhabarat, the Egyptian secret service.

As Caine looked around for shields, he wondered what Ibn Sallah was doing in Zurich. He grinned to himself as he thought that there must be more than a few men in the bar who would be wondering the same thing. But then why did anyone come to Zurich? There was an OPEC meeting in Geneva and Ibn Sallah probably stopped over in Zurich to do his banking, whether on his own account or somebody else's. Whatever else happened, Ibn Sallah wasn't the sort of man who was planning to retire just on a government pension. As for the blonde, Caine dismissed her. She was almost certainly just window dressing.

He had spotted two shields. One very dark skinned, leaning against a wall; the other more Semitic-looking, sitting at the bar. They were both beefy, powerful-looking men, like their master. Neither of them were drinking and Caine knew it wasn't because of anything written in the Koran. He knew them because he was cut from the same cloth. They were professionals.

Every few seconds they ran their eyes over the crowd near Ibn Sallah's table, like cops mentally frisking a suspect.

Caine finished the *marc* in a quick swallow. Should he try it? he wondered. A mistake could be fatal, but if it worked it could conceivably save him weeks. If he did it, it would have to be fast. He would have to make it a quick in-and-outer, before they had time to react. If he were still working for the Company, he would be signaling his case officer that he was going into the red zone. He got up and walked over to Ibn Sallah's table.

In a way it was an interesting tactical problem. And one that they had never covered at the Farm, because it wasn't supposed to happen. How do you approach a shielded member of the opposition and let him know that you have nothing more lethal on your mind than setting up a friendly r.d.v., without getting terminated? As he approached the table, Caine staggered slightly, hoping to buy a few seconds by convincing them that he was just a drunk civilian. He timed his approach so that he had to stumble against the table to avoid colliding with a waiter. The drink in his hand sloshed onto the table, startling the blonde.

"Excuse me, Fraulein," Caine said, slurring his words slightly and smiling his most ingratiating smile. Annoyed, her eyes blazed at him as Ibn Sallah calmly slid his hands out of sight under the table.

"*Bitte sehr*," she responded tartly.

"I hope you'll forgive me," Caine replied, turning to face the man. He kept his hands out in plain sight, feeling a ripple of fear trickle down his spine like a bead of sweat, anticipating the impact of a silenced slug slamming into his back.

"Not at all," Ibn Sallah replied, relaxing his shoulders. He was beginning to buy Caine's drunk act.

"It's important that we talk, monsieur," Caine replied. At that moment he felt something hard poke into his ribs and knew that the shields had come up. He was boxed in and there was nothing to do but brazen it out.

"Why is that?" Ibn Sallah asked quietly, his eyes hard and alert. Caine knew that if he couldn't convince Ibn Sallah now, that they would be sweeping him up with the morning garbage in some back alley off the Münstergasse.

"Because we're in the same business and it's to our mutual advantage," he replied.

Ibn Sallah paused, sizing Caine up. Then as if reminding himself of the shields, he nodded confidently.

"It had better be," he replied. He raised an eyebrow and the dark-skinned Arab bent over. Ibn Sallah whispered something to him briefly.

"It's been a pleasure meeting you, Fraulein," Caine responded, bowing slightly to the blonde, his eyebrow raised in a quizzical appraisal. She smiled back at Caine with a look that was equally appraising and disdainful. Then he and the dark-skinned Arab were walking arm in arm, like old business associates, out of the bar. When they reached the lobby, the Arab released Caine and whispered tonelessly in a heavily accented French,

"Tomorrow, the boat to Rapperswil."

"What time?"

"Eleven o'clock and, monsieur," the Arab added with an ominous hiss, "come alone, or else . . ."

The Arab turned and walked back toward the bar without finishing the threat. He didn't have to.

For a moment Caine considered going back to his room. He was tired and jumpy, and although he had been successful, he knew that he was pushing his luck with Ibn Sallah. He had to be careful. It was when you began cutting corners that you made mistakes. On an impulse he walked out of the lobby and down to the promenade by the lake.

The lake was as dark and endless as the sea and he couldn't see the black water as it lapped tirelessly at the shore. The promenade was deserted as the icy wind off the lake whipped across the darkness. Empty benches were lit by sporadic streetlamps glowing futilely, like the lost sentinels of a dead planet.

He felt cold and alone and wished he were back in Malibu, lying in front of a crackling fire against the warmth of C.J. Strange how he couldn't shake her from his thoughts. After all, she was just a pretty little pro with all the morals of a bitch in heat. Still, there was more to her than that, if only he could get at it. Somehow she had left an imprint on his mind, as faint and indelible as the trademark on a pat of butter.

He looked back at the twinkling lights of the city, climbing up the slopes of the Dolder into the night. And behind those lights lived the quiet ordinary lives he had rejected so long ago. But they belonged, all right. And he didn't belong anywhere. There were times, he thought, when he believed that loneliness was a word invented just for him.

He began to walk up the Bahnhofstrasse toward the Limmat River. Nearing a church, he heard the faint sounds of voices singing a German carol. He strained his ears and then he realized that they were singing,

"Silent Night." It was Christmas Eve. For a moment it brought back the Christmases of his childhood, the sense of awe in church before the adolescent doubts began, the odds and ends they used to decorate the tree, the colored electric lights strung outside the house. He remembered standing with his mother and piping the carols in his child's voice, all the while dreaming of snow and getting the bicycle that would make life perfect. And now he was plotting a murder this Christmas eve. Still, hadn't the first Christmas begun with thousands of murders, the Slaughter of the Innocents? Nothing really had changed since Herod's time, he decided. The innocents were still being slaughtered, only now we are better at it. The only difference was that then it was Herod's madness and now it was a political matter. The poet Rimbaud was right, he decided. "Now is the hour of the assassins." He turned away from the church and went back to the hotel.

Once in his room he got the Bauer automatic out of the Hasselblad and loaded it. Then he called room service and ordered a bottle of Scotch. When the bellboy came with the bottle, he kept his right hand in his pocket, gripped tightly around the Bauer. After the bellboy left, he carefully wedged a chair under the door handle, placed the Bauer under his pillow, and poured himself a drink. It took almost half a bottle before he managed to fall asleep.

Heavy white clouds full of snow scudded across the sky as Caine boarded the old-fashioned paddle-wheel steamboat to the Rapperswil side of the lake. The boat was crowded and noisy with the sounds of families on their Christmas day outing. He made his way to the promenade on the upper deck, where he had glimpsed the dark-skinned Arab just before boarding. But when he got there, the Arab was gone. He ignored the people around him, remembering the old CTP dictum that if you pay no attention to others, people are unlikely to pay attention to you. Instead he stood at the rail, looking out across the lake.

The sun peeked briefly through a rift in the clouds, casting shafts of white light onto the sparkling waves. Snow had fallen during the night, blanketing the hills around the lake with the shiny illusion of something clean and new. Quiet villages around the lake were scattered like miniatures in the snow. For a moment Switzerland was a Christmas card come to life. With a rumble the great paddle wheel began to turn and the boat throbbed with the vibration. The paddle wheel churned the gray water to a milky froth as the boat began to move. Caine suddenly felt a shiver slide up his spine, as though someone had stepped on his grave. Then out of the corner of his eye he saw the dark-skinned Arab gesture for him to follow.

He followed the Arab into the men's room, where the other shield stood in front of a mirror, painstakingly combing his hair. Without a word the dark-skinned Arab held out his hand. Caine briefly debated a bluff, then shrugged and handed over the Bauer. He put his hands on his head and the two men frisked him, quickly and expertly. Caine waited until the dark-skinned Arab grinned, before putting down his hands. For a second he was tempted to take them out just for the hell of it, but the Arab was still grinning as he turned and walked out the door.

Coming out on deck, Caine immediately spotted the massive bulk of Ibn Sallah at the rail, his curly brown hair fluttering in the chill wind. He was smoking a Havana cigar, and as Caine approached, Ibn Sallah impatiently checked his gold Patek-Philippe watch. There was plenty of room at the rail, since only a few of the holiday sailors stayed on deck to brave the wind and the choppy waves. Caine leaned against the rail about two feet from Ibn Sallah. For a while the two men looked out at the water, saying nothing. Ibn Sallah tossed his cigar into the water and turned slightly toward Caine.

"Why should I talk to you?" he asked.

"Because I'm the man who hit Abu Daud in Paris." Ibn Sallah's eyes narrowed, as though he were photographing Caine in his mind, then he seemed to relax. That was when he was most dangerous, Caine thought, like a lion who appeared to be reclining when he was really crouching.

"What makes you think I won't kill you?" Ibn Sallah murmured.

"Not here," Caine replied. "Besides, now that you Arabs are rich, you're becoming respectable."

A wide smile cracked Ibn Sallah's face open like a walnut and for a moment they were almost at ease with each other. Then his brow furrowed and he shook his head.

"Daud had a very pretty wife and three small children," he said.

"It was business," Caine replied.

"A sad business. They liked to live high. The best clubs, a big car, *vous comprenez*. They had no money put away. Now she's a prostitute."

"You can hear sadder stories from any life insurance salesman."

"Still, a sad business," Ibn Sallah said, jamming his hands into the pockets of his cashmere overcoat.

"Sure. Tell that to the Israelis the next time somebody decides to celebrate the Fourth of July on a crowded Tel Aviv bus. Like I said, it was strictly business, not personal."

"Speaking of business, what does the Company want from the Moukhabarat? No"—Ibn Sallah raised his hand mildly—"don't bother to deny that you're with the Company. Your accent in French is too American, not to mention your clothes and the typical American drunk act last night. You're from the Company." He shrugged with an expressive Levantine gesture and added speculatively, "So what does the Company want of me?"

"This isn't Company business."

"Then what is it?"

"Free enterprise."

"Of course." Ibn Sallah shook his head sagely. "I was forgetting how incredibly materialistic you Americans are."

"I don't remember us Americans taking out a patent on greed. Besides I read your dossier. I expected better of you than these clichés," Caine retorted sharply, looking directly at Ibn Sallah for the first time, his green eyes calm and still as the unfathomed depths of the lake. Ibn Sallah returned Caine's glance with his own dark serious gaze, then the corners of his eyes crinkled with amusement.

"You're not taping this, by any chance, with one of those marvelous little miniaturized things you Company types are so fond of?" Ibn Sallah remarked, dismissing the idea with a disdainful wave of his hand.

"I told you, this isn't Company business."

"*Vous comprenez,*" Ibn Sallah continued, "you Americans are always inventing the most incredible devices: poisoned fléchettes the size of phonograph needles, transmitters no bigger than a pinhead, VX nerve-gas cartridges concealed in clip-on ballpoint pens . . ."

"Not to mention frozen pizza and the banana daiquiri," Caine put in.

Ibn Sallah's booming laugh was almost lost in the hiss of spray whipped off the whitecaps by the wind. The sun was hidden behind the bleak clouds lowing over the lake. The boat plowed a widening triangle of ripples. A flock of gulls hovered over the wake of the boat, piercing the wind with cries that were almost human, as they waited to swoop down upon the garbage of the boat's passage. Ibn Sallah shook his head bemusedly.

"Americans," he said definitively. "What is one to make of such a people? So strong, so clever and sincere, and yet you are such children. Do you know what it is like to come from a land where half the people are starving and the other half don't care? No," he added with a sigh. "You are obsessed with your trinkets and your empire, worrying about calories and profits while the rest of the world struggles to survive."

"You don't exactly look like you're starving," Caine replied.

"Better and better." Ibn Sallah's laugh boomed again. "As you say, business is business."

"Then let's cut the shit and get to it."

Ibn Sallah looked at Caine with an air of appraisal mingled with a faint touch of approval. Caine took out a cigarette and lit it, cupping his hands around the match to protect it from the chill gray wind that flung the spray of the boat's passage across the deck.

"Then, down to business," Ibn Sallah said. "What is it you wish of me, monsieur?"

"I want an answer to a question. Just one word, yes or no. It won't compromise your position or have any effect on your country's politics. It has nothing to do with the Company or the Moukhabarat. I'll pay you five thousand dollars in Swiss francs for the one word and you'll never see or hear of me again. Not an unprofitable morning's work," Caine added dryly.

"Suppose I decide that it is official business and refuse to answer?" Ibn Sallah asked quietly.

"Then I'll take that as a yes and proceed accordingly."

"Suppose I simply lie and take the money?"

"You won't," Caine responded confidently. "Because first of all I'll find out that you lied fairly quickly and all you'll have done is cost me a slight delay. Perhaps a week or two." He shrugged.

"Time is usually of the essence in our business."

"Not in this case. Like I said, this isn't official business. And there's one more thing," Caine added.

"And that is?"

"If you lie to me, then it becomes personal."

Ibn Sallah studied Caine for a long moment. He saw the cheeks whipped red by the wind, the green eyes that were colder than the wind, and felt a slight uneasiness ripple through him. They were the eyes of a hunter.

"The money," Ibn Sallah replied, patting his overcoat pocket. "Here," and turned to look out at the water until he felt the bills being slipped into his pocket.

"I'm looking for a Nazi war criminal named Josef

Mengele. He was the camp doctor at Auschwitz. Do you know where he is?"

"So you're working for the Jews," Ibn Sallah sighed. "What a people. They are so much like us," he added, shaking his head sadly. "The sons of Isaac and the sons of Ishmael are both the sons of Abraham, *vous comprenez*. Ours is a family quarrel. Like us, they are very old and they never forget," he said, shivering inside his overcoat. "It's cold standing out here," he muttered, frowning at Caine.

"Do you know where he is?" Caine repeated.

"No," Ibn Sallah replied shortly and started to turn away. Caine put a hand on his arm and then removed it as Ibn Sallah looked back at him. The boat began to shudder as it slowed down to approach the Rapperswil dock. Along the shore, Caine could see a small crowd waiting to board.

"It's not so simple. You see, I know about the enclave of Nazi scientists you have at Helwân, outside Cairo," Caine prompted.

"Mengele was a madman, not a rocket scientist," Ibn Sallah retorted angrily.

"So he did try to stay in Egypt?" Caine said.

"You said only one question."

"When was he in Egypt?"

For a moment Ibn Sallah considered walking away, then he reconsidered. As Caine had said, it really wasn't anything to do with the Moukhabarat. If the Jews wanted to spend their money chasing after ghosts from the past, so much the better.

"I never met him, but I remember a memo from Nasser when it happened. That was back in 1961. I assume he got nervous after the Eichmann business in Argentina. He was in Alexandria for a few days. We told him he couldn't stay and the Germans slipped him out on a freighter. No." He held up his hand. "I don't know where the ship was going and I don't care. We didn't want him either. You're right. It isn't our affair. And now, monsieur, I believe our business is concluded," he said with finality.

"Good enough," Caine replied and, flipping his cigarette over the rail, turned and walked away. At the door to the salon he bumped against the dark-skinned Arab, who stood there unconcerned, watching Ibn Sallah. Caine put a quick back wristlock on the Arab as he reached into the Arab's pocket and retrieved the Bauer. As the Arab started to react, Caine stepped back and wagged a finger at the Arab. "Naughty, naughty," he said, smiling, and then the smile was gone. The two men looked at each other. It would be an interesting match, they seemed to say with a glance. Then the Arab went to join Ibn Sallah at the rail, while Caine went down and debarked. At the foot of the dock he caught a taxi that took him around the lake back to Zurich.

Back at the Baur au Lac, Caine called the local Orbis office, which stayed open on Christmas day to prove that they were good little Communists, and made a reservation on the morning LOT flight to Warsaw.

Caine felt a sense of excitement as he sat down to a late lunch of *raclette,* a potato dish made with Bagnes cheese, and a bottle of Dézalay Neuchâtel wine at the Mövenpick on Dreikonigstrasse. He was beginning to get a scent of his quarry, he thought as he watched the people around him munching as contentedly as cattle in a feedlot. He scanned the room, looking for tags that might have been sent by Ibn Sallah, but the restaurant was crowded with civilians. After all, he reasoned, his business with Ibn Sallah really was finished. Still, he couldn't take anything for granted. Ibn Sallah was a formidable man, he thought, and continued to look around the restaurant.

At a nearby table two blond Swiss girls were snickering at the antics of a pair of Italian men in flashy mod suits, who were trying to pick them up. One of the Italians kissed the girls' hands, while the other bantered and smiled hopefully. As the Italians sat down at the girls' table, a Swiss businessman, sitting with his family, glared balefully at them and muttered something into his fondue.

Caine sipped the wine as he rehashed his conversation with Ibn Sallah. Mengele was alive in 1961, that was the key thing, he thought excitedly. He had left South America and found that even Egypt was still too hot for him. So where could he go? After the Eichmann thing calmed down, he almost certainly would have gone back to South America. But probably not Argentina again, since that was where Eichmann had been picked up. He couldn't have gone east, but only after Caine went to Poland could he be sure of that. But he was still running scared in '61, that was the main thing.

Caine spent the afternoon in the Jelmoli department store, where he bought a heavy wool suit and a turtleneck sweater to wear in the Polish winter. After dinner he took a bottle of pear brandy back to his room and sipped at it while he packed. Then he took a long shower and went to bed.

Outside, the harsh night wind moaned around the corners of the hotel. He dreamed he was climbing up the frozen face of the Dolder. The wind was a cold implacable enemy that tore with icy fingers at his desperate hold on the mountain. He was clinging to a ledge, unable to pull himself up. To hang on was agony and to let go was death. He tried to shut out the terrible ache in his fingers, but mind disciplines wouldn't work and there was only the pain. A dark shadow above him kicked at his fingers and he fell screaming into a bottomless crevice in the glacier. He was still falling when he woke up, the morning light streaming brightly through the high hotel window.

CHAPTER 6

The snow-covered Silesian plain lay flat and white as a freshly laundered sheet under the wing of the Soviet-built Ilyushin. From his window seat Caine could see puffs of clouds floating like anti-aircraft bursts in the gray sky. Looking down at the white plains, he finally understood what Koenig had been talking about that time, during his Junior Officer Training at the Farm. The land was perfect tank country. It must have been a walk-through for the Wehrmacht, with the foolish, gallant Polish cavalry thrown against the panzers. The Poles might as well have used spitballs. Koenig had used the Polish cavalry to illustrate his point.

"This isn't a business for heroes," Koenig had said. "Guts stand about as much chance against brains and logistics as a rabbit in a tiger cage."

Caine ran over the story again in his mind. It wasn't great, but hopefully he wouldn't need it for long. Just until he made a quick snatch and got out. He was a lawyer coming to Warsaw to settle the estate of the late lamented Widow Wydobrowska. It was really a standard Company ploy: identify a scource, compromise him, scan the material, and get out, leaving him to take the fall. Caine didn't have to like it, and if he

wanted to worry about someone, he should be worrying about himself: because if the secret police didn't
buy his story, the only Polish hospitality they would
offer him would be a final cigarette as they stood him
against a blood-spattered wall.

But he didn't like it. Unbidden, a long-forgotten
line from Plutarch surfaced in his mind. Something
about frogs. That was it. "Though the boys throw
stones at frogs in sport, yet the frogs do not die in
sport but in earnest."

How many innocent bystanders had he already
hurt? Hillary; DePalma; Hanratty, whom he had
scared shitless; now some poor Pole he hadn't met yet.
And his hunt had barely begun. He'd do it all right,
because he was a hunter, but he didn't have to like it.

His ears began to pop as the Ilyushin began its descent to Okecie Airport. Through the window he
could see the glinting surface of the frozen Vistula,
twisting its tortured course across Warsaw like a vein
of ice. He had a bad moment as the wheels skidded
down the runway. He was a spy behind the Curtain,
and after all the mumbo jumbo about détente he
knew that if he made a mistake, they wouldn't just pat
him on the back and hand him the Order of Lenin.
With a final whine the jet turbines sighed into silence.

There was a hint of Magyar blood in the cheekbones of the young blond customs official. He had
the pug nose of the Polish peasantry and a touch of
the Teutonic in his blue eyes. No wonder they're paranoid, Caine thought. They've been raped often
enough. Then the knot in his stomach began to
tighten. He could control the rest as the fear shot
through him, but he couldn't stop the tightness as the
official began examining the Hasselblad with a more

than cursory interest. If he opened it and found the Bauer, Caine would be writing Wasserman a Dear John from a labor camp in the Urals, where they don't bother to put up a fence, since no one can make it across the snow without freezing to death anyway.

"Camera very good." The official smiled enthusiastically, for a moment reminding Caine how young he was. Caine handed the official his customs declaration form and passport. Let him chew on that instead of the camera, he thought.

And like a Pavlov-conditioned dog, the official began to scan Caine's documents, because this was a part of the world where papers mattered. Without them you had no identity, no right to breathe. Throughout Eastern Europe people clung to dog-eared pieces of paper, because without them they were dead.

"Why you to Poland coming?" the official asked.

"Business," Caine replied. Christ, did the schmuck imagine that any tourist would come to Warsaw in the winter for pleasure, he thought.

"What business?"

"I'm a lawyer, here to settle an estate. If I can locate the heirs, some people and your government stand to inherit some money." Caine smiled ingratiatingly.

"What is lawyer?" the official asked suspiciously.

"*Ich bin ein Anwalt,*" switching to German, the lingua franca in this part of the world.

"*Willkommen zu Polska,*" the official responded smartly, and stamped Caine's papers.

The cold wind hit him like a fist as he came out of the airport and stood on line to board the Orbis minibus to the Europejski. As the minibus rumbled over the frozen streets, Caine rubbed a circle on the frosted window and peered out at the gray afternoon. Pedestrians in dark overcoats walked with brisk, ginger steps through the drab frozen streets, like giant awkward penguins. Passing the Plac Zamkowy, he caught a glimpse of the Vistula, frozen in time as if sentenced to eternal winter.

Along the Krakowskie Przedmiescie, signs advertised Western brands of liquor and cigarettes in words full of consonants. Two smartly dressed shopgirls paused at a kiosk advertising the *Zycie Warszawy*. They were stamping their feet in the snow to keep warm, as though performing a Slavic folk dance. The minibus slid gently to a halt at the entrance to the Europejski Hotel like a boat coming in to a berth.

Caine went directly to the Orbis office in the lobby and exchanged traveler's checks into zlotys at six times the official exchange rate. The Poles needed hard currency the way California needs rain in August. He rented a Volga car and then spent a few minutes trying to convince the Orbis man that he didn't need a guide and that he didn't want his hand held. Then he checked in and asked the aging bellboy to bring him a bottle of Dyborowa vodka and a prostitute named Marysia.

The worlds of espionage, crime, and ordinary life intersect in the bedroom. While on a short spell of desk duty at Langley just before he left the Company, he had read a COMINT report on contacts in Eastern Europe. The Warsaw agent-in-place had sent a list of prostitutes who operated out of the major tourist hotels with the tacit approval of the secret police, called the U.B. Marysia was the only name on the list he still remembered.

The hotel suite was furnished in the kind of over-

stuffed baroque fashion that tried to resurrect the
Victorian era. It looked a little like a stage set, Caine
thought. He half-expected the maid to come in and
dramatically announce that King Edward was dead.
He went over to the shuttered French doors that led
to the balcony and looked out at the ochreous clouds
that promised more snow. Along the Krakowskie
Przedmiescie late-afternoon streetlights gave off a
pale sulphurous glow as the light failed, as though
the sun were truly a dying star.

With a hideous leer, like an aging gargoyle come to
life, the bellboy returned with the vodka and the
woman. The leer almost turned to a smile when Caine
gave him a lavish tip. The bellboy bowed and left, as
Caine turned to look at the woman.

She was a stylish blonde, thirtyish and prettier than
he had expected. She was puffing a cigarette through
a gold-plated holder and wore a supercilious expression, or perhaps she just wanted to raise the price. Her
tight dress was red and beginning to fray as it
strained at the seams. She paused for a moment to
study her makeup in a round mirror surrounded by a
bronze frame made up of garish metal cupids, then
glanced around as though she wanted to rearrange the
furniture. Caine watched her as she moved across the
room with an air of studied grace. She was pretty
enough, he thought. The only question was, How hungry was she?

"What's your name?" he asked and when she looked
at him blankly, he repeated the question in German.

"Marysia."

"Come over here."

She approached him, wetting her lips with the tip

of her tongue, then looked at him with surprise as he removed her hand from his thigh.

"How much?" he asked.

"Two thousand, lover," she replied breathlessly and he somehow knew that it was more than she was used to getting.

"I'll do better than that. I'll give you five thousand zlotys for the name of your boyfriend in the U.B."

"*Schwein*," she hissed, her eyes blazing with feigned anger and real fear as she started to back away. He grabbed her arm and threw her on the bed, pinning her down with his weight on top of her. She twisted desperately, then took a deep breath as though she were about to scream and Caine slapped her face hard.

"Who do you know?" he said, his voice soft and cool.

"I don't know what you are talking about," she said, her eyes beginning to brim with tears.

"I'm talking about the man in the Policia Ubespieczenia you pay off, or give it to for free."

"How should I know any of the pigs in the U.B.?"— her voice quavering.

"Shit," he retorted sarcastically. "You know all right. You must be the biggest earner of hard currency in Poland. You're a national asset, so don't give me that shit. If some U.B. officials weren't getting any, you'd be out of business."

She looked at him seriously, as if making up her mind. Her world was full of dangerous men, but he frightened her.

"Let me up, *bitte*," she said. "I need a cigarette." She got up and nervously jammed a cigarette into the holder and lit it. When she turned around, she saw that he had placed five thousand zlotys on the bed. She picked up the money and tucked it into her bodice.

"What do you want to know?"

He poured two large glasses of vodka and for a moment they sat on the edge of the bed, drinking quietly. He felt hollow inside, wondering how he had come to this, acting like a pimp to a Polish whore in a baroque Warsaw hotel room. He felt as if he hadn't drawn a clean breath of air in years. He downed the rest of the vodka in a sudden swallow.

"What's the name of your contact in the U.B.?"

"Grzabowski," she responded, without looking up.

"Is he married?"

"Yes, but—" She looked at him in confusion. So it was the badger game, he decided. Good enough for a quick snatch-and-grab.

"When do you usually see him?"

"It varies," she said and her eyes lit with a bright scorn. "Whenever he feels like it."

"Where do you meet?"

"My place."

"Can you get him there tonight?"

"Why not?" She shrugged.

"Good. Get him there tonight and I'll give you another five thousand."

"What are you going to do?" she asked nervously.

"I just want to talk to him."

"He'll kill me," she blurted out desperately, pressing her fingers against her temples.

"No, he won't. Believe me, he won't."

She looked at his cold green eyes and shivered. Then she bolted down the rest of her vodka, looking for courage in the bottom of the glass.

"I want ten thousand," she said defiantly. Caine smiled and shrugged. "Is there anything else?" she asked.

"Yes," he said, his eyes filling with the dreamy smoke of lust. Anything to fill the sense of emptiness he felt, like an old can emptied of air and about to crumple. She smiled back nervously and with practiced fingers began to unzip his fly.

They had dinner at the Krokodyl in the Old Town marketplace. Marysia was much more animated as she started on her fourth glass of honeyed Soplica, assuming the grand manner of the *belle dame,* to whom dinner at the posh Krokodyl was an everyday affair. The small jazz orchestra was synocopating its heavyhanded way through an old Beatles song. Marysia tried to lead him to the dance floor, telling him that she just loved "moderny" music. Caine bargained with her, as with a child, promising to dance with her after she telephoned Grzabowski to set up the rendezvous. She sulked a bit after the call, but was soon smiling and affectionate as they marched around the dance floor with all the grace of robots who had not quite mastered the art of movement. This was where she belonged, she felt. Or at least that was what she confided to him in a bleary, maudlin voice as he drove the Volga across the Slasko-Dabrowski Bridge to the Praga district on the east side of the river. It was all her first husband's fault, she pronounced with drunken solemnity, swaying against him as he took a corner. When they got to her apartment, Caine took both cameras—the Hasselblad and the Polaroid—out of the trunk and walked up the dark stairs behind her, goosing her to keep her mind off the cameras. She giggled as he grabbed her, twitching her behind as though she were still a seductive young girl.

The one-room apartment was on the second floor, with a double-glazed window that faced a brick wall. The room was shabby and bare, with a sense of desolation revealed in the pitiless glare of the unshaded overhead light bulb. Scattered around the room were little throw rugs and a few knickknacks: desperate feminine touches of color that failed to bring the room to life. There was the sound of a toilet gurgling next door and the apartment stank of cheap toilet water. A small closet, covered by a crepe curtain instead of a door, was set in a corner near the bed. Caine made some room for himself in the closet, loaded the cameras, and slipped the Bauer into his jacket pocket. He opened a bottle of Bulgarian brandy and poured them each a stiff drink. Then they sat on the edge of the rumpled bed and waited.

The hall stairs began to creak under a heavy, slow tread. For a moment Marysia began to pale, and as he headed for the closet, Caine turned and winked at her with a sense of reassurance that he didn't feel. Grzabowski paused at the door, breathing heavily, then loudly knocked. Marysia opened the door with a flourish, handing Grzabowski the half-finished glass Caine had just been drinking. Peering at them through a cigarette-burn hole in the curtain, Caine grinned appreciatively. The girl had a certain style after all.

Grzabowski was an extremely large, heavyset man with wispy blond hair rapidly receding from a jowly red face. He wore a tight-fitting black suit and Caine could smell the musty odor of perspiration from across the room. Grzabowski swallowed the drink and demanded something of Marysia in a harsh, loud voice.

Then without a preamble he reached into Marysia's bodice and grabbed one of her breasts, kneading it in a heavy-handed way, like baker's dough. Although she smiled, Marysia just stood there stolidly, like a cow being milked. As he pushed her toward the bed, Caine began snapping pictures with the Hasselblad. He was glad he had brought the Bauer, he thought. Grzabowski was one of those men who simply bull their way through life, trampling on feelings without even noticing. The only way to make friends with a Grzabowski, Caine mused, would be by pulling a thorn out of his paw. Marysia lay on the bed, her dress pulled up over her hips and her legs spread wide. As Grzabowski prepared to mount her, Caine snapped a Polaroid shot with the flash and stepped out from behind the curtain.

Startled, Grzabowski turned and began to move angrily toward Caine. He stopped when he noticed the Bauer held steady in Caine's hand. For a long moment the two men stared at each other, Grzabowski breathing heavily, rage and confusion mixed in his red face. *"Przepraszam."* Sorry, Caine said. It was one of the few words in Polish he knew. He pulled the positive from the Polaroid and tossed it over to Grzabowski, who studied it briefly and muttered something in Polish. Although Caine didn't understand the words, it sounded like a threat. After all, a U.B. officer had the power to make even high-ranking Party officials tremble. The only power he need ever fear was that of his own superiors. Caine smiled as he approached Grzabowski, whose eyes never wavered from the Bauer. Once you've taken the offensive you must never give them a chance to think, Caine remembered Koenig saying. Caine was still smiling when with a sudden twisting motion, he brought his right leg into a slicing side kick, catching Grzabowski in the groin. The Pole crumpled to the floor with a high-pitched animal scream. Holding himself, he began to retch, as Caine sat down on the edge of the bed. Marysia's eyes were wide with fear, like a cornered animal.

"Now we're ready to talk, Herr Grzabowski," Caine said in German.

"Who are you?" Grzabowski managed to gasp, his hands clasped tightly between his legs.

"Your enemy," Caine replied calmly.

Marysia was staring at him with hypnotic fascination, like a mouse cornered by a snake. She couldn't take her eyes from his, that glowed green as radium with an inner life. Shudders of fear coursed through her body like shocks of alternating current.

"You'd better take a shower," Caine advised her dryly. "This *Schwein* has made you dirty."

Without a word she began to back away from him. In a moment she had gathered her things and was gone. He listened to her footsteps as she tore down the stairs. He heard the front door slam and the sounds of running were lost in the Arctic night.

"She's gone," Grzabowski said. He had struggled to a sitting position on the floor.

"Better for her. Better for us," Caine replied. He lit a cigarette and passed it to Grzabowski, feeling strangely drained.

"What do you want?" Grzabowski snarled, a harsh edge coming back into his German. Caine stuck the muzzle of the Bauer into Grzabowski's ear, as though to remind him of the situation. Then he picked up the Polaroid picture and studied it ironically.

"Not exactly your best side, but still recognizable,"

he remarked conversationally. From somewhere in the building came the sound of someone with a racking cough.

"*Yup tvayu mat*," Grzabowski cursed.

"That won't get us anywhere," Caine sighed. He felt tired and dirty, like a child after a long day's play in the mud.

"Who are you? What do you want?" Grzabowski demanded, a spark of animal cunning in his face. Caine didn't seem to want him dead at the moment.

"I'm a colleague of yours. Interpol," Caine replied, flashing him the bronze badge he had picked up in Las Vegas. Grzabowski looked at his badge as if Caine had gotten it by sending in cereal box tops. "I want some information."

"Why all this?" Grzabowski gestured at the photograph. "Why not just send a Blue?"

"Let's just say that there are too many leaks through our own official channels. German and Austrian leaks, understand?"

Grzabowski nodded knowledgeably. It was commonly known in the intelligence community that the Interpol office in Vienna held secrets the way a sieve holds water.

"If it's not through channels, why should I help you?"

"Because of what will happen to you if you don't," Caine replied ominously. "First of all I'll make the pictures available to everyone from your chief and your wife to the *Zycie Warszawy*," he said, gesturing at the Hasselblad. "Then, I'll implicate you in the worst spy scandal since Maclean hit Istanbul. If anything happens to the girl or to me, I'll lay everything that's gone wrong in Moscow since Prague in '68 right at your doorstep."

"The Russians won't buy it," Grzabowski replied hoarsely.

"You know them better than I do. You tell me if Moscow won't find something they will buy," Caine replied, gambling that a U.B. official taking advantage of hookers was bound to have something he'd want to keep hidden.

"And if I get you the information, what then?" Grzabowski replied, nervously licking his lips like a snake testing the air.

"You get the pictures and the negatives. You never see me again. And all this just for some information that won't compromise your patriotism at all. At the very worst you'll be helping an Interpol agent in an old case that is truly in Poland's best interest. Oh, yes, I'll pay you one thousand cash, in dollars, for your trouble and any inconvenience," Caine added persuasively. It was a standard Company ploy, Caine thought. First the stick, then the carrot, thrown out like a lifeline to a desperate man, sugar-coated with greed. It always worked.

Except that it hadn't bought him anything, Caine mused as he drove from Krakow to Oswięçim. He wanted to think about it, about anything, as a way of taking his mind off the driving. And it wasn't just because being bounced around in a springless Volga while driving across Poland in winter was an interesting way of rearranging his internal organs. The truth was that he didn't know why he was going to Oswięçim.

Large wet flakes of snow splattered the windshield

for an instant before being wiped away by the monotonous slap of the windshield wipers. It had begun
falling as he left Krakow that morning, coating the
green cupolas of the Town Hall Tower with a soft
white topping, like whipped cream on pistachio ice
cream cones. The wind swept the snow across the
endless plain, deadening all sound except for the met-
ronome stropping of the wipers and the soft rumble of
the tire chains. Everywhere there was nothing but the
pale vista of white and gray in an empty world. There
was no sign of any life. Dreamlike, the Volga slithered
down the icy road. He could have been driving across
the Antarctic plateau, an ice planet, forever dead,
where no life had ever crawled out of warm primordial seas.

By rights he should have taken a plane from Okecie
immediately after his r.d.v. with Grzabowski. They
met in the Plac Zamkowy near the statue of King Sig-
ismund. Caine had stood with his back to the rail that
overlooked the open expanse of the Vistula, watching
Grzabowski approach. Grzabowski had tramped awkwardly across the snow, with a weary, reluctant tread,
as though he were a member of the Grande Armée
retreating from Moscow. Caine's eyes rapidly quar-
tered the area toward Jerozolimskie, but there were no
tails. They both carried copies of the *Zycie Warszawy*
to make the switch. A pale cloud of exhaled air
formed around Grzabowski's face as Caine examined
a low-quality photocopy of the Mengele file. The
wind whipped the pages as he quickly leafed through
it. The file contained the Interpol report and the bill
of indictment from Freiburg that he had already seen
in Wasserman's dossier. There was also a bill of indictment from a Moscow court. But as Caine laboriously

picked his way through the Cyrillic script, he realized that it was just a listing of specific murder counts. There were dozens more than in the Freiburg indictment, but no reference to Mengele's whereabouts. It was a dead end.

Without a word Caine placed the file back into the newspaper and handed it back to Grzabowski.

"Why?" Grzabowski wanted to know, his breath rapid and nervous. "Why did you want to see this?"

Caine glanced at Grzabowski's watery blue eyes, wondering if there was anything more than professional curiosity in the question. There was really nothing to say. He shrugged and walked away, the snow creaking under his feet like an old floor.

That should have been it, he thought as he drove. Of course Mengele never headed east; the Communists didn't know anything, or even care. He knew he should have gone directly to the airport before Grzabowski had a chance to think about it. Instead he had checked out of the Europejski and driven to Krakow. And all for no reason at all. Except that he had to. Some instinct, some thought below the conscious level was driving him to Oswięcim and the only rational reason he could give himself was that that was where it all began. That and the knowledge that, as every good agent knew, when you get a hunch like that you follow it. It comes from some part of the brain that thinks more profoundly than the conscious mind. Sometimes it's called "instinct," or "mission feel"; the name really doesn't matter. It doesn't reason, so you have to rationalize what you're doing, Caine thought. It just tells you what you have to do.

The snowstorm had emptied the small village of any sign of life as he drove slowly through Oswięcim.

A single streetlamp cast a pale yellow light that failed
to brighten the drab row of houses along the road. On
an impulse Caine made a U-turn and parked in front
of a *kawiarnia,* its smoky light spilling ineffectually
through the frosted window. He went in and sat down
at the counter. The restaurant was empty except for
the counterman wiping his hands on a dirty, thread-
bare apron and two workmen morosely drinking
vodka at a corner table. The counterman glanced at
Caine without interest. Caine ordered *bigos* and *herbata* tea, then glanced around but no one paid any
attention to him. It surprised him, because the Poles
usually have a lively interest in strangers, especially
foreigners. But in this strange, bleak landscape nothing seemed to matter, as though they were all trapped
in some limbo beyond the grave. Caine ate the *bigos*
slowly, the sauerkraut soggy and wilted. But at least
the *herbata* was hot. He wasn't really hungry, he realized. It was just that he had an uncanny dread of
what he was about to do and had decided to have
lunch as a way of putting it off for a while. At last he
took one more sip of tea and paid the dour counterman, leaving the *bigos* half-finished. When he stepped
outside, he saw that it had stopped snowing.

The midday sky was a solid slab of steel gray. If
anything it seemed even colder and bleaker than before. Except for the soft keening of the wind, the silence was absolute. He got back into the Volga and
started the engine. The sound of the engine kicking
over seemed unnaturally loud. Then he realized that
he was holding the wheel in what was almost a death
grip. He forced himself to relax, and taking a deep
breath, he let in the clutch. There was no need to ask
directions. The main gate of the camp was clearly visi-

ble at the end of the street on the outskirts of the village.

He parked the car by the steel gate, the chilling words written in iron letters arching over the gateposts. *Arbeit Macht Frei*. Work makes freedom. The high barbed-wire fence still stretched out from the gate as far as he could see in either direction. Beyond the fence he could see the vast, snow-covered camp. The naked twisted limbs of a few long-dead trees stood in a line on the other side of the fence, like skeletons thrown up by the frozen earth. In the distance he could see a cluster of boxlike barracks, like a city of cargo crates. Beyond the barracks were the brick chimneys of the crematorium, gray in the bleak afternoon light. The camp lay empty and white under the snow, like bones long since picked clean and crumbling to dust. Just outside the gate was a small wooden guard's hut. On the door of the hut was a small sign with a single word painted in black gothic letters. *Auschwitz*.

He heard the faint sounds of a violin playing a Gypsy melody coming from the hut. He walked over to the hut, the snow crunching under his feet with the sound of someone chewing crackers. The same instinct that had prompted him to come here in the first place was now screaming at him to leave. After a moment he knocked loudly on the door. Abruptly the music stopped. For a long time nothing happened and he was about to go back to the car when the door opened.

A small, wizened old man with a dark complexion peered uncertainly up at him. His dark eyes were almost lost in baggy wrinkles and his wispy gray mustache was stained yellow by tobacco. The old man wore a fraying guard's cap, a moth-eaten Russian Army overcoat over baggy blue serge pants stuffed into high rubber boots, and a sweat-darkened Gypsy scarf around his neck. The skin on his neck was corded and wrinkled like an old turkey that had somehow survived Thanksgiving.

"Excuse me, please . . ." Caine began uncertainly in German.

"Of course." The old man smiled tentatively, his few remaining teeth showing black and solitary, like charred tree stumps in a forest desolated by fire.

"Terrible weather," Caine said, just for something to say. He didn't want to be alone in this place.

"In winter the wind is cold," the old man pronounced, shaking his head. Caine couldn't decide whether he was being sarcastic or merely simple.

"You want to see the *lager, hein?*" the old man said, his German slurred by the syllables of Central Europe. Without waiting for a reply, he shut the door behind him and began walking through the gate. Caine caught up with him in a few strides. They passed under the iron arch and marched toward the barracks, white puffs of breath rising over their heads.

"Are you a Jew?" the old man asked.

"No, why?"

"Not so many people come here. A few Poles and Russians, but mostly Jews."

"What about Germans?"

"Germans?" The old man hawked and spat, the spittle crackling as it hit the icy ground. Then he began to laugh in a strange high-pitched monotone. Somehow the sound of his laugh was eerie, like a human echo of the keening wind. Then he stopped and looked up at Caine.

"*Deutschen, niemals,*" he said. Never. Then he gestured at the wide empty space around them.

"This is where the prisoners were lined up for roll call at dawn. Also for public executions and torture. Once I saw a man torn to pieces by the dogs almost on this very spot. They tied raw meat to his testicles. He was screaming while they ate him. They called it 'special punishment.'"

"What had he done?"

The old man looked at Caine uncomprehendingly. "He was a prisoner. That was his crime."

Caine reached into his coat and took out a cigarette, then offered the pack to the old man, who took one cigarette and pocketed the pack. They lit up and stood for a moment, smoking.

"Everyone was lined up here for roll call, even the dead," the old man continued. "They kept careful records of everyone's number, the Germans. Sometimes it was difficult to tell the living from the dead. There were those who died and still walked around. We called them *Musselmen*. They never lasted long." He shrugged. "Did you know that a man can die and still walk around?" the old man added. "They felt nothing. That's what it is to be dead. To feel nothing."

Caine followed the old man into one of the barracks. They stood in an empty space near the door. Along both walls ran a line of wooden shelves from floor to ceiling, a narrow corridor between them. They began to walk down the corridor. It was intensely cold. Yet even in the bitter chill there was a faint smell coming from the wood itself. It seemed to have traces of urine and carbolic acid and something else. Then as the old man stopped by one of the shelves colored with old dark stains, Caine recognized the scent that brought with it a sudden whiff of Indochina. It was the smell of death. The old man pointed at the shelf above his head.

"That was my bunk," he said.

In spite of the cold Caine began to sweat. He wanted to get outside again, like that feeling of wanting to wake up while in the middle of a nightmare. Instead he quietly followed the old man to the far wall, then back again to the door.

They walked across the parade ground in silence, the only sound the crunch of snow crust breaking under their boots. The old man led him to a long, rectangular brick building. The sign over the door read, BATH HOUSE. Inside, a long line of hooks along both walls led to a set of large tiled rooms. Above each of the doorways was the single word: SHOWER ROOM. The floors sloped towards a drain in the center of the room. On the ceiling directly above the drain was a shower head from which had sprayed Cyklon B instead of water. The walls were in shadows. The only light came from the dim gray corridor.

"When the doors were shut, the screaming always began," the old man said, his voice echoing faintly. "The Jews always sang their death prayer."

"How do you know all this?"

"I was a *Sonderkommando* here. That's how I stayed alive," the old man said simply, flicking his cigarette ash. "While they screamed, we had to search through the clothes, looking for valuables. There were always a few babies hidden by their mothers in the clothes pile. We used to throw the babies in with the next batch. Then we always waited five minutes after the last screams, while the gas was sucked out. When we opened the door, we would find the bodies tangled in a pyramid, sometimes up to the ceiling. They were always covered with blood, as they clawed each other to escape. Also vomit and excrement. That was the hardest job, untangling the bodies. Often we had to break the dead fingers and feet in order to do it."

"Let's get out of here," Caine said, his voice echoing in the gray darkness.

They walked out past the rusting hooks, their footsteps almost muffled and indistinct. Outside the bleak afternoon sky had darkened. The faint clouds of their breath dissolved into the barren air. The old man shuffled his feet awkwardly in the snow that had begun to take on the gray color of the light, as though they were standing in an endless field of ashes.

"Do you want to see the crematorium?" the old man asked with a vaguely disappointed air.

"No."

They stood in the frozen emptiness, like ghosts lost beyond time, the wind ruffling the gray wisps of the old man's mustache. They were like two dying archeologists who had excavated an ancient tomb only to find it empty.

"Tell me about Mengele," Caine said finally.

"*Ach*, that one. Come, I'll show you." The old man beckoned him with a Mediterranean hand gesture that means "go away" to an American and "come here" to a Southern European.

They hiked side by side in silence to a large wooden building, traces of whitewash still visible on the walls. Inside, the old man led him to a large empty room. The only things left in the room were a few decaying pipe fixtures, where a sink had once stood.

"This was Mengele's. *Laboratorium.* He would operate here on his *experimentieren.* Very scientific, *Hauptstürmführer* Mengele." The old man nodded. "Here he would amputate healthy limbs, turn young boys into women, with breasts and everything, even women into men. In this corner"—the old man pointed—"he kept a large glass jar. It was filled with human eyeballs preserved in formaldehyde. They were all blue, the eyes."

Then he stopped, because Caine was smiling. It was a strange, bestial smile, like the death rictus of a wolf. Now at last he understood why he had come, Caine thought. It was going to be so easy to kill Mengele. The old man shuffled uneasily and the moment died. Caine looked around at the room, finding it difficult to imagine the horrors that had happened here. It was just a bleak, ordinary room.

"If you saw Mengele today, would you still recognize him?" he asked.

"He must be an old man by now." The old man shrugged. "Yes, I would recognize him."

"Suppose he had altered his appearance?"

"I would recognize his smile. It was almost like yours just now," the old man added uneasily.

"Anything else? Any other mannerisms? Something he couldn't change?"

The old man took off his cap and scratched his head, as though digging for something. At last he put his cap back on and glanced at Caine. "There is one thing. He used to crack his knuckles before he would operate. Very slowly and carefully. He was proud of his hands," the old man said, jamming his own hands into his overcoat pockets.

Caine followed the old man across the camp to the hut. The frigid wind had strengthened, blowing granules of snow across the lengthening afternoon shadows. When they reached the hut, the man invited him inside. Caine sat patiently on an old army cot while the old man brewed them some *herbata* tea over a little kerosene stove. The wind shrieked through the cracks as they sat quietly drinking their tea. The old man tried the radio, but there was nothing on except for a Polish announcer gloating over the latest inflated production figures.

"It doesn't get good till after six P.M. Then sometimes you can get Radio Warsawy," he apologized.

Then the old man slapped his forehead. He had just been reminded of something and he began rummaging among his things in an old trunk. He pulled out a half-empty bottle of cheap Polish vodka, opened it, and handed it to Caine.

"What's this?"

"For the Silvesterabend. A Happy New Year," the old man explained shyly.

It was New Year's Eve, Caine thought. He had completely forgotten. For a moment he felt a pang of loss. He would have liked to share it with C.J., both of them naked in front of the flickering fireplace and toasting each other with snifters of Courvoisier, instead of here in this desolate place. Happy New Year, he thought grimly, wondering, as everyone does, what the new year would bring. Then he shrugged. For him it was easy. He would either be rich—or dead.

"*Prosit,*" he toasted, sniffing the cheap vodka and

drinking. It smelled like diesel fuel and tasted worse.

"*Prosit,*" the old man's voice bleakly echoing Caine. The old man lifted the bottle to his lips and took a long drink, his Adam's apple bobbing up and down as he swallowed. When he looked back at Caine, his red-rimmed eyes were wet, whether from the icy wind or the vodka, Caine couldn't tell. The wooden cabin creaked in the wind, like a sailboat. The sound made their isolation even more complete. They could have been alone in the middle of the ocean.

"Why do you stay here?" Caine asked.

The old man shrugged.

"My whole family is here. Everyone I ever knew."

"Are you a Jew? Is that it?"

"No, I'm a Gypsy. The last Gypsy."

"I thought that Gypsies wandered."

"They do," the old man cackled, exposing the stumps of his teeth. "I'm a Gypsy who doesn't wander. Where is there to go?"

The old man dug in his pocket and brought out the cigarettes. He took out two, handed one to Caine, and they both lit up. Caine took out his wallet, peeled off a hundred-dollar bill, and handed it to the old man, who stuffed it in his pocket without expression.

"I stay here to remind people that once there were Gypsies," the old man said.

Caine stood up to leave. The old man walked him to the door. Then the old man shrugged.

"I knew about the Jews, but not about the Gypsies," Caine said.

"Everyone knows about the Jews." The old man smiled sadly. "But who remembers the Gypsies?"

CHAPTER 7

In Berlin the pattern changed. It wasn't so much a change in content as in perspective, Caine reflected; like one of those ink-blot optical illusions that looks like a duck's head until it's turned sideways and then appears to be a rabbit.

Caine flew in on the afternoon LOT flight to East Berlin. As the Viscount entered the landing pattern for Schönefeld Airport, he could see the vast flat expanse of the Marx Engels Platz below, like a giant concrete lake that drained the river of concrete that was the Unter den Linden. Dominating the skyline was the Brobdingnagian statue of a Russian soldier in Treptower Park, looking as if with his next giant stride he would be stubbing his toe on the wedding-cake facade of the reconstructed Reichstag. The outsize statue looked big enough to scoop up the Statue of Liberty like a football and run with it. Beyond the statue the monotonous vista of Stalinist gingerbread apartment buildings stretched all the way to the Spreewald. On the western side of the wall he could see the Funkturm Tower in the Messengelände, standing like a modernistic beacon for the glories of capitalism. The Viscount landed in a small series of bounces, like a stone skipped across a lake. After going through Customs, he caught a taxi to the Potsdamer Platz.

As the taxi turned down Friedrichstrasse, Caine took in the furtive air of pedestrians scurrying in the cold wind, like faceless human ants dwarfed by the immense monuments. Hulking over the eastern approach to Potsdamer Platz were the ruins of the *Führerbunker*, where the dying Third Reich had tried to play the last scene of the war as though it were the final reel of *The Phantom of the Opera*. The taxi slowed as it bumped over the tram tracks on Zimmerstrasse and neared the cinder block wall that bisected the city. The apartment blocks near the wall were bricked up and a cleared area twice the length of a football field and filled with tank traps and land mines and barbed wire ran parallel to the wall. At intervals along the barbed wire, skull-and-crossbone signs announced *Achtung, Meinen,* just in case the locals didn't get the idea that wall climbing wasn't an encouraged sport for the *Spartakia.*

The taxi stopped at Checkpoint Charlie, and as soon as Caine paid him, the driver took off with a roar, as though to forestall any objections to having carried an American tourist foolish enough to abandon the glories of democratic socialism. A young Vopo, a Kalatchnikov slung over his shoulder, impassively watched Caine enter the low concrete *Passkontrolle*. A Grepo, resplendent in a blue uniform that made him look like a U.S. Air Force general, mechanically held out his hand for Caine's passport. If it had been a contest of uniforms, the Germans would have won the war, Caine reflected as he handed over the passport.

"What is your name?"

"William Foster."

The official glanced suspiciously up at him. Or perhaps he just looked at everyone that way, Caine thought. He stared at a large wall poster behind the official. On it a sprinter crouched at the starting line, his social realism muscles bulging, as he prepared to run for, "Sport and Health in the G.D.R.," according to the title.

"And your destination?"

"The Berlin Hilton."

The official raised his eyebrows barely perceptibly. Caine was obviously a hopeless capitalist. He stamped the passport as if it were an execution order, then gave Caine one last suspicious glance just to let Caine know that he couldn't be fooled.

"Go through that door to the Customs."

"*Ja, danke,*" Caine said, retrieving his passport.

At the customs tables a Western tour group crowded uncertainly like a nervous herd. Midwestern husbands in checked coats glanced cautionary daggers at their wives, who surveyed the guards with satisfied eyes under lacquered gray hair, as though to silently remind them that they were (whisper it) crossing the Iron Curtain. Near the front of the group a long-haired hippie wearing a brown leather jacket bearing a Canadian flag and on the back a painted fist with the inscription, "Che lives!" paced impatiently, as though he expected to be met by a brass band. A wan blonde in jeans sitting on a suitcase anxiously watched him pace.

Caine waited patiently for his turn. For a moment his eyes met the glance of one of the Vopos and then they both looked away. Maybe neither of them wanted to be there. The busy customs officer barely glanced at the Hasselblad and after he wrinkled all the clothes in Caine's suitcase to conform with the approved border-crossing disorder, Caine was able to walk past the gate and go through the whole procedure again for the American MP's.

From the minute he hailed a Mercedes cab from the taxi stand on Freidrichstrasse, he was dirty. It seemed so improbable that he had the driver circle the Brandenburger Tor twice, just to make sure that the black Opel wasn't simply part of the traffic pattern. For a moment he stared at the triumphal arch surmounted by a warrior's chariot drawn by four bronze horses, while he ran the possibilities through his mind. The last time victorious troops had paraded under the arch was at the end of the Franco-Prussian War. It had remained a symbol of Prussian might until the Red Army had used it for target practice.

Perhaps the Opel simply contained locals with standing orders to tail anyone interesting who crossed the checkpoint. After all, this was Berlin, where you couldn't throw away an empty pack of cigarettes without someone tearing it apart for a drop. Or perhaps someone had made him from his Company days. Or maybe it was Wasserman again. Or maybe—and this was his real worry—it was something else.

The bright neon of the Kurfürstendamm was already lit to dispel the gathering gloom of late afternoon, the sky darkening with gray clouds, as though bundling up for the winter. The electric light flickering over the parade of smart shops and cafés lent an air of forced gaiety to the city. He told the driver to take him to the American consulate on Clay-Allee. As for the tail, he mentally shrugged, let them think he was official.

The consulate was a calculated risk, but he knew he would need some kind of official authorization to gain access to the American Document Center in Zehlendorf. As he had originally noted in the Wasserman dossier, the center contained the only complete set of records on the SS, as well as the best information available on all wanted Nazis.

While he was explaining to the slow-moving Marine sergeant at the front desk that he wasn't feeling well and needed a list of English-speaking doctors, the pattern shifted. As the sergeant reached for a file to hand him a Xeroxed list, Caine caught a glimpse of a trim blond American civilian, a folder in his hand, entering the elevator. For a second their glances met and moved away without recognition, but Caine could feel the prickle of sweat starting down his spine.

"Say, isn't that old Charlie Connors from USC?" Caine asked, gesturing at the closing elevator. The sergeant flicked a heavy-lidded glance to the elevator, then turned back to Caine, his drawl stretching all the way back to Birmingham.

"You mean the blond fella?"

Caine nodded.

"That's Mr. Jennings. He's a trade assistant."

They exchanged a bit of small talk about how Caine must be mistaken and how everyone in the world probably has a double somewhere. Then Caine thanked the sergeant and got back in his taxi, telling the driver to take him to the Hilton. His mind raced as they drove back to the electric brightness of the Kurfürstendamm, because the pattern had shifted and he didn't even know what game he was in. It explained the tail, of course, but not much else because the blond man wasn't Jennings any more than he was the mythical Charlie Connors. He was Bob Harris, who had put Wasserman onto him in the first place.

Once he had checked into his room at the Hilton, Caine locked the door and turned on the television. Then he set to work checking for bugs. The TV program was one of those American action imports that Europeans decry and then snap up like blue jeans. On the screen jiggly girls from the Screen Actors Guild were using choreographed karate chops on overweight villains wearing black shirts and white ties, just in case the audience might forget who the bad guys were. He found the bug fairly quickly in the base of the telephone. With a sigh he lit a cigarette and stretched out on the bed.

Of course, Harris being in Berlin could have just been coincidence. Sure, he told himself. And you could improve your cash flow with the help of the Good Tooth Fairy. He remembered the lecture Koenig had given them at the Farm after they had completed their paramilitary training or, as the trainees called it, the "boom-boom course." Koenig was a short stocky man with a crew cut surmounting an ungainly triangular face that might have been a slice cut from a lumpy pie. Caine had once seen Koenig take apart a burly ex–Green Beret named O'Hearn on the unarmed combat course without getting his shirt wrinkled. Koenig had stood before them in the Quonset hut classroom, lightly tapping a ruler against his palm. He balanced on the balls of his feet, as he paused for effect.

"There are no coincidences in this business," Koenig had said. "None. The moment you spot anything that even smells like a coincidence, you've been blown.

That means you're as wide open as a whore's legs. And once that happens, you've got only three choices: get out, get dead, or get them"—punctuating each *get* with a slap of the ruler against his palm.

For an instant Caine felt a stab of anguish. The bastards wouldn't let him quit. Then he brushed the thought away, because if Harris was running a Company mission, then the sooner he learned the rules of the game, the better his chances of survival would be. He wasn't going to fool himself about how expendable ex-agents were. Right now he knew he was about as welcome as a rent-increase notice.

With a shrug he stabbed out his cigarette and got up. He felt the old familiar tightening sensation just below his solar plexus. It hits everyone differently. With some it's wet palms or shaking hands. Some get shivers down the spine. Some break out in hives. With others it's stomach cramps. In Indochina he had seen men get the shakes, and just before action, he had seen some lose control of their sphincters and piss and shit in their pants. But it hit all of them one way or another. With Caine it was a tightening in his stomach, like a lump of food that had lodged in his esophagus and just wouldn't move or digest. Well, he thought, they can kill you but they can't eat you, using the stock bravado phrase they had used in combat to exorcise the fear. It never really worked, but they used it anyway.

He was going to do the one thing he hadn't wanted to do. He was potentially alerting the Company that he was on a run. Unless—and this was even worse—the Company already knew. He went downstairs to the lobby phone and called the consulate.

"Department one-oh-six, Jennings here," Harris answered.

Normally Caine would have done a number permutation that varied daily. Based on the 106 prompt, he would have responded with the appropriate counter number, like, "Sorry, I was trying to reach the Intershop at Frankfurter Allee ninety-three." Except that he wasn't in the Company anymore and had no idea what the day's sequence was, so he said, "This is an open line and don't tell me you weren't as surprised as I was."

"This is the American consulate. What number do you want?"

"Do you know the Ballhaus Resi?"

"Hasenheide, corner of Gräfestrasse, but I'm afraid I don't know what you're talking about. You must have the wrong number," Harris replied and hung up. Caine was grinning as he hung up the receiver, knowing that the call must have sent Harris up the wall at all the procedures he had broken. Serve the little twerp right, he thought as he went outside and stepped into a taxi. Although the Ritz was nearby, he had the driver double back by way of the Gedächtniskirche, to check for tails. The church's spotlighted spires made it look a little like the Enchanted Castle at Disneyland. He was clean, of course. After all, they knew where he was and where he was going, so they could afford to leave him alone. After a leisurely dinner of roast goose with dumplings, he took a tram outside the Ritz to the Resi.

By the time he got to the Ballhaus Resi, probably the biggest nightclub in town, close to a thousand noisy representatives of the New Germany were crammed around a dance floor no bigger than a throw rug. Thanks to a lavish tip to the headwaiter, Caine was able to share a tiny table from which he could survey the entrance and the stage. On the stage a rock band did a passable imitation of the Rolling Stones. The shirtless lead singer chosen more for his resemblance to Mick Jagger than his voice, screamed that he was sexy while he grabbed the microphone like a steel phallus. Behind the band colored strobe lights flickered across a gushing water display synchronized to the beat, while girls in see-through plastic disco outfits wriggled in ecstasy. The only things missing, he mused, were fireworks and *The 1812 Overture* complete with cannons. But the real attractions of the Resi were the brightly lit numbers and telephones on each table, so that you could dial any member of either sex who caught your fancy, Caine noted, as he sipped his Scotch-flavored ice cubes at ten marks a shot.

He took time to examine his table companion out of the corner of his eye, a chunky dark-haired man in his mid-twenties who kept ostentatiously glancing at his Rolex as if he had something to do tonight besides checking out the girls. He was the new European man, riding the economic boom like a surfer. His watch was Swiss, his jeans French, his disco shirt and jacket Italian, and his slang came from American TV. He nervously jiggled his knees against Caine's and winked at him, conspirators in the eternal quest for the one-night stand. While Caine checked the crowd for Harris, his table partner researched the club for girls.

The telephone rang and before Caine could move,

his partner grabbed the receiver like he was a race-track tout waiting for results of the Kentucky Derby. But it was for Caine. A busty blonde with the heft of a Wagnerian singer at Table 43 waved at him and invited him to dance. At Caine's *"Nein, danke"* she shrugged in an exaggerated manner to show off the low-cut bosom he had turned down and hung up. Caine noted with satisfaction that with the band blaring the telephone was almost completely private, in the midst of the huge crowd.

The second call was also for Caine. This time his partner handed the phone over with a touch of annoyance. It was a pretty dark-haired girl with a sweet gentle smile a few tables away. She had on a tight pink cashmere turtleneck that seemed to glow like neon in the dim light. Caine felt his groin stir as he reluctantly turned down her offer to buy him a drink. He looked at her and thought, another time, another place, another life, and hung up. His table partner looked at him curiously, probably figuring him for a queer, and moved his chair a fraction of an inch away from Caine, not wanting to be guilty by association.

There was a loud series of cheers and catcalls and Caine glanced back at the stage, where the lead singer was working himself into an erotic frenzy. The phone rang again. This time it was Harris. Caine's table partner smiled broadly as he handed over the receiver. The call from a man had confirmed his suspicion. He knew Caine was a queer for sure.

"I'm at table thirty-one. Do you come here often?" Harris said. Except that Caine wasn't playing.

"Only during the mating season," Caine replied, spotting Harris lounging indifferently, his legs crossed, at a table near the door. With his blow-dried blond hair, black pin-striped Cardin suit, and cocktail in hand, Harris looked like he belonged in an expensive whiskey ad.

"I bet you only come here for the classy acts," Harris said, using a code identification. On stage the lead singer was gyrating his hips to the music while the band blasted a hard rock version of Beethoven's Fifth.

"Cut the shit, Bob. I left my Junior Secret Agent kit at home."

"Is that the one with the plastic mask and the water gun that looks like a Luger?"

"Yeah, and fifty snappy sayings to keep the KGB in stitches."

The strobe lights flickered madly and the dancers writhed uncontrollably as the band and the audience went wild.

"What's it all about, Alfie?" Harris asked.

"You tell me. You're the one dealing the cards."

"I think we have a communication problem. I don't know what the hell you're talking about."

"You say that so sincerely, Mr. Jennings. Why don't I believe you?"

Harris shrugged and sipped his drink as the audience exploded into applause and stamped their feet like a giant beast with two thousand legs.

"Then we're even," Harris taunted. "Your passport says William Foster, but I'm not holding it against you."

"That's big of you. Look, let's stop fencing, sweetie. The applause is dying down and my table partner has already got me marked for a queer."

"That's because you look so cute in your three-piece suit. What about lunch tomorrow?"

"I love you too, you sexy thing," he replied. His table partner overheard him and smiled broadly.

"In the Tiergarten, by the elephant cage."

"Just the two of us, lover," Caine said and hung up, suppressing an impulse to plant a cross-bottom fist between his table partner's teeth. He waited till the music started again and the aisles were filled with couples making contact and crowding their way to the dance floor, before getting up and leaving his table partner smirking over the telephone.

It was in the Tiergarten that the teen-aged werewolves and cripples of the Home Guard made a last pathetic stand against the Red Army. The few old trees that managed to survive the Battle of Berlin were cut down for fuel during the frigid postwar winter of '45. During the fifties the ground was reseeded, saplings were planted, and rose gardens once again replaced potato patches. As he walked down the path to the zoo, the only evidences of the war Caine could see were the strange mounds several hundred feet high that dotted the park. The mounds had been constructed of rubble, then covered with soil and seeded with grass. Under the leaden winter sky they looked like tells from a long-lost civilization. Caine wondered what some archeologist from the distant future might make of them. He checked his watch and decided he had enough time for a bite before his r.d.v. with Harris. He stopped at a stand and bought a bockwurst dipped in mustard, which he ate as he walked through the zoo. Harris had used the code phrase "What about lunch . . ." which meant fourteen minutes after twelve.

A plaque on the outside railing of the elephant enclosure identified the elephant as "Shanti." The massive gray animal ambled near the rail, her long trunk searching the concrete lip of the moat for peanuts. Like the rest of her breed, she was a survivor. She had come through the Allied bombings and the Russian onslaught to become something of a local institution. The irony of her name was not lost on Caine, with his linguistic background. It meant "peace" in Sanskrit.

Two small children, their long blond hair tousled by the wind, were throwing peanuts at each other. The little boy chased the girl around the massive bulk of their mother, who watched them with an air of stolid patience. The little girl's shrieks of excitement sounded thin and high-pitched in the air, like the calls of a bird in distress. Caine watched Harris approach and rechecked the large open area. It was secure; Harris was alone. He turned back to the enclosure and watched the elephant until he felt Harris lean against the railing beside him.

"You're looking well, Herr Foster," Harris said, his lopsided grin giving him the boyish charm of a street urchin that women found irresistible. He wore a well-cut camel's hair overcoat that seemed to match his trim blond hair. His blue eyes twinkled with sincerity and as always Caine had the feeling that Harris wanted to sell him something he would be better off without.

"I'll bet you say that to all the girls."

"How's civilian life treating you?"

"I wouldn't know. It looks to me like you bastards are trying to run me without the benefit of a salary."

"Whatever gave you that idea?"

"What are you doing in Berlin, Bob?"

Harris pulled away from him for a moment and looked at him curiously. Perhaps he was remembering some of the things Caine had said when he quit. He reached into his pocket, brought out a handful of peanuts, and tossed them over the moat at the elephant.

"Do you really expect me to answer that? Come on, you know better than that. You were a Company man yourself once, or have you forgotten?"

"No," Caine said. "I haven't forgotten."

For a moment the two men were silent. They watched Shanti's powerful trunk pick up a peanut and put it into her mouth.

"What makes you think we're running you?"

"Not 'we,' you. You're the one who put Wasserman onto me in the first place. Then I run into you here in Berlin, the one place someone interested in Nazis would have to come to eventually. Quite a coincidence, wouldn't you say?"

"Is that what Wasserman wanted you for? Jesus, that's funny."

"Then why aren't I laughing, Bob?"

"For Chrissakes, Johnny," Harris said, smiling his sincere boyish grin for all it was worth. "I thought I was doing you a favor and picking up a little change on the side. I didn't know you were going to go all paranoid on me. Until you walked into the consulate I had no idea you were in Berlin."

"If you were running a mission, would you tell me?"

"Sure." Harris grinned. "Would you believe me?"

"Of course not."

The two men smiled. Harris handed Caine a few peanuts and cracked one open for himself. He spit out a speck of shell and wiped his mouth.

"I was tailed to the consulate," Caine said, his eyes an icy green, like shallow Arctic water.

"Of course you were tailed, marching through Checkpoint Charlie like Napoleon," Harris retorted irritably. "It has nothing to do with you. The Gehlen Bureau has a runner coming across and we want to get our hands on him before they bring him around the corner"—using the German intelligence slang phrase for killing. "As soon as I saw you, I figured those junior G-men had snafu'd and called them off."

Caine lit a cigarette, cupping his hand against the chill breeze. The wind whipped the smoke away as fast as he could exhale it, the pale whiff swirling into the gray air.

"So Berlin is just a coincidence, it that it?"

Harris grabbed Caine's lapel to emphasize his point. Caine let him, knowing how vulnerable that made Harris, since he could snap Harris's elbow by locking the grip and using a base palm blow against the outside upper arm. It was the kind of amateurish mistake that not even a rookie operative would make. But then, Harris was a senior case officer. The kind who moved pins around on a map and never got his hands dirty unless he spilled a drink at an embassy party.

"Look, Johnny. You are out of it. Neither I nor the Company give a shit what kind of a kraut-hunt you and the old pimp have cooked up. You wandered across an open op and I came here to tell you to get off the field because there's a game in progress. That's it."

Caine glanced at Harris's hand for a moment, then back at Harris, who dropped his hand from Caine's lapel as if it had grown suddenly heavy.

"Aren't you even a little curious about what we're up to?"

"C'mon, Johnny, whatever you and Wasserman are up to with the krauts, just tell me it has nothing to do with the Company and I promise to keep it to myself. I won't report it. Scout's honor"—holding up his right hand in the three-fingered Boy Scout sign.

"It's a private beef, Bob."

"Then you have my word."

"Thanks, I'll sleep better at night knowing that," Caine said, the sarcasm heavy in his voice. Harris smiled his patented boyish grin.

"Once and for all, Johnny. The tail was a bureaucratic foul-up and Wasserman paid me an easy five grand for an ex-agent's name. You're off the books. You and I are just two ships that accidentally went bump in the night."

"Then there is no problem, is there? If I see any of your people in my rearview mirror, I'm going to step on them."

Harris shrugged. "Grind them up and feed them to the pigeons for all I care. Christ, you have been out of the game too long. What makes you think the Company gives a shit about the krauts? The only thing that counts these days is oil, kiddo," Harris said, biting his lip as if he had said too much.

Caine wondered about that. He wondered about it for a long time. It was a loose thread and those are the kind that trip you up. Then he shrugged the thought away. The only thing that mattered now was to get at the Mengele records in the official archives. "Then you wouldn't mind doing me a favor," he said.

"Like what?"

"Get me authorization to get into the American Document Center."

Harris looked at him quizzically, as if he were Scrooge being asked to play Santa Claus at the office Christmas party.

"Why should I?"

"Money."

Harris grinned broadly, as though Caine had just handed him a Valentine. He really was the all-American success story, Caine thought, with a shine on his shoes, credit cards in his pocket, and good old-fashioned greed in his eyes.

"That's what makes the world go around," Harris said.

"Funny. Somebody told me it was love."

"You'd be surprised how loveable money can be," Harris replied with a wink.

That was pure Harris, Caine thought. He always had to get in the last cliché, even while picking your pocket.

Harris left after they agreed that he was to call the document center and verbally authorize access for an American named William Foster. In exchange Caine agreed to a drop of twenty-five hundred marks in an envelope addressed to P. Jennings at the American Express office on the Kürfurstendamm. But instead of leaving the Tiergarten after Harris had gone, Caine sat down on a bench and smoked a cigarette, staring vacantly at the bear cage.

If Harris was lying, then he had to get out. Because if he was being run blindly on a Company mission, it could only mean that he was expendable and sooner or later they would bring him around the corner. Even if Harris wasn't lying, the fact that the Company knew what he was up to would queer the pitch for sure, because every intelligence service is playing its own game and security is never that good, no matter how many "Top Secret" and "For Your Eyes Only" stamps are plastered on each page. Intelligence services are more tangled than bodies at a Hollywood Hills orgy, no matter which side they were coming from—which was why an agent could whisper something in a bar girl's ear in Miami and two days later an unidentified body would be found floating facedown in one of the *klongs* in Bangkok.

Of course, everything Harris had said sounded reasonable, and Harris seemed sincere. But then, the world isn't a reasonable place and sincerity was Harris's long suit. It could have been coincidence running into Harris in Berlin. But it was farfetched, because Harris was the thread that tied Wasserman and Mengele and the Company together. If Koenig were here now, he would say that if Caine bought Harris's story, he could let him have the Brooklyn Bridge at an after-Christmas discount price.

Caine looked at the bear enclosure, where Schwips, a big brown male, was idly scratcing his back against a post. He had reached a decision point and he knew it. By rights he should contact Wasserman and tell him that Mengele was bound to be forewarned and the game was called on account of darkness. The permanent kind.

He looked to the south, toward the Steglitz district. He could see the tall rubble mound, dubbed the "Insulaner" by the Berliners, thrusting its way into the skyline. He turned and let his gaze run along the modernistic lines of the Gedächtniskirche, looking like a complicated piece of futuristic computer equipment.

The architects had left one broken steeple from the original structure standing as a grim keepsake of a B-17 raid. Over toward the Strasse des 17 Juni, named to commemorate the day in 1953 that protesting East German workers were gunned down by Russian tanks, stood the blood-red granite spire of the Siegesäule. The column had been built in the last century to celebrate the Prussian victory over France. There was no escaping the war in this city, he thought, because the war hadn't ended in the spring of '45. It had never ended for any of them. It just went on forever in different battlefields. The Middle East, Africa, Southeast Asia. No matter which way you turned, the dead wouldn't stay buried. He thought of the old Gypsy at Auschwitz and that bleak ordinary room where Mengele had conducted his *experimentieren*. And he knew that there was no going back, no matter what the odds were, or what the Company did or didn't have on. The war was still on for him. He wanted Mengele. The job was no longer just business. It had become personal.

The morning was cold, with a clarity that was clean and sharp-edged, as though every object had been carved with a scalpel. A single wisp of cumulus bisected the pale blue sky, like a long strand of white hair. Caine drove a rented VW bug, chosen for its anonymity, through the outskirts of the city to the rural suburb of Zehlendorf. Traffic this way was light and tall, slender trees crowded right up to the road, as though he were driving down a country lane. Clusters of gold autumn leaves still clung to spindly branches, like swarms of brittle butterflies. The undergrowth was green and through gaps in the trees he could see the deep blue of the many lakes that dotted the district. They reminded him of the color of C.J.'s eyes.

He followed Wasserkaferstieg road to its end on the banks of a small quiet lake surrounded by trees. The American Document Center was a long low concrete affair, set like an estate behind a cement-and-iron fence. He gave his name to the guard at the gate and then drove through a tunnel of branches overhanging a private road to the building. Harris had mentioned that the structure was like an iceberg, extending eight floors underground, where the archives were kept in bombproof vaults. Caine handed the Foster passport to the clerk at the reception desk. The clerk checked his name against a typewritten list and handed him a pen and an application form on a clipboard to fill out. Caine filled it out and handed it back to the clerk, then he sat down on a couch to wait. Strewn on the coffee table in front of him were recent issues of *Newsweek* and *Der Spiegel* and an old-well-thumbed copy of *Playboy*. It was like sitting in a dentist's waiting room. The only things missing were the Norman Rockwell prints and copies of articles on the dangers of periodontitis.

After a few minutes the clerk motioned to him and Caine followed him into a large reading room filled with Formica tables and chairs. There was only one other person in the room, a large heavyset German detective in civilian clothes, with the unmistakable air of authority that clings to policemen everywhere, like the indelible scent of aftershave lotion. Caine put him down as a member of Bureau One, the section of the West Berlin police department delegated to investigate war crimes.

He waited for about ten minutes until another wispy clerk handed him a thick four-volume set of three-inch binders, each of which bore the label JOSEF MENGELE, numbers one through four. With a faint sigh he settled himself in the chair and opened the first folder.

For a long while he studied the photographs of the young Mengele attached to the SS records. He realized that after more than forty years they were virtually worthless for identification purposes. Time and age had certainly sculpted that thin-lipped, rather mediocre face into something that no longer had any resemblance to the photo. And although there was no indication of it in the files, Mengele might well have had cosmetic surgery to further obscure his identity. What Caine was after was something more fundamental, some clue to the character of the man that revealed itself to the camera—something that couldn't be changed.

The photographs revealed an intense-looking, thin-faced young SS officer, with dark hair and eyes. He was clean-shaven with a prominent nose and there might have been a touch of vanity in the studied pose he had presented to the camera. He looked more like an Eastern European than a German. Perhaps that had been the source of his boundless hatred of non-Aryans, Caine mused—the fact that he resembled them. For some reason the dark eyes and beaklike nose reminded Caine of a bird of prey. When Mengele operated, that gaze would have revealed no more emotion than a hawk when it killed a rabbit. For the rest, there was nothing there, he decided. It was really a very ordinary face after all.

He skimmed fairly rapidly through the bulk of the first two volumes, which contained records of Mengele's early life, war records, indictments, affidavits concerning a staggering list of war crimes and various warrants for his arrest, requests by different agencies for information, and so on. He began to read carefully when he came to the application for an Argentinian identity card, which had been the last authoritative mention of Mengele in Wasserman's dossier.

On October 27, 1956, the officials of the by-then defunct Perón government, which had been notoriously hospitable to ex-Nazis, issued *cédula* number 3940484 to Mengele under the name Dr. Gregor Schklastro. It was the first of many aliases Mengele had occasion to employ. The files had records of Mengele, a.k.a. Dr. Helmut Gregor-Gregori, Dr. Edler Friedrich von Breitenbach (under which he practiced medicine in Buenos Aires), Franz Fischer, Fausto Rindon, José Aspiazu, Stefan Alvez, Walter Hasek, Heinz Stobert, and even, audaciously, José Mengele. Caine was growing excited and he put down the file for a moment. Mengele was a far more elusive prey than Eichmann had ever been. To hunt him down would be the most extraordinary challenge he had ever faced.

The aliases clarified one point: Mengele was unable to adopt the protective coloration of the South American environment. Whatever identity he assumed, he was unable or unwilling to disguise his German background. Caine smiled. It was the first flaw.

Wherever Mengele was now, he was posing as a German immigrant in his late sixties, probably in a German enclave in Latin America. The target was beginning to narrow.

Given his vast experience in sterilization, it was almost inevitable that Mengele established a successful practice in Buenos Aires, specializing in abortion. He was briefly arrested in 1958 after a woman died on his operating table following a botched abortion. Mengele bribed his way out of jail and entered Paraguay on a tourist visa.

When Mengele fled Argentina, he abandoned his wife Martha and their young son, Karl Heinz, who stayed on in Buenos Aires. They subsequently left Argentina and returned to Europe, settling in Kloten, Switzerland, near the Zurich airport. During the early sixties, while the West German authorities intensified their hunt for Mengele as a result of the Freiburg court indictment, Frau Mengele and her son were located by Feinberg, a Jewish Nazi hunter based in Vienna, who then notified the Zurich police. The last thing the peace-and-order-loving Swiss government wanted was a war crimes trial. In July 1962 the Swiss authorities expelled Martha and Karl Heinz, who then settled in the quiet village of Merano in the Italian Tyrol, where Martha still lived. Martha subsequently divorced Mengele *in absentia* and there had apparently been no further contact between Mengele and his former family. A separate report by Feinberg, referenced in a footnote, indicated that the boy grew up despising his father, as did Frau Mengele.

When his Paraguayan visa expired, Mengele went to the Andean ski resort of San Carlos de Bariloche, where he spent the early part of 1959. There were many cross-references in the files to Bariloche, a luxurious Alpine-like retreat near the Argentinian-Chilean border. First established by a German immigrant named Wiederhold, Bariloche was clearly an enclave for the Nazis, who were drawn to its German atmosphere, that stein-thumping fellowship of beery *gemütlichkeit*, its snow-capped mountain setting so reminiscent of Switzerland and the Tyról, and its proximity to the Chilean border. As the cross-references noted, such Nazi bigwigs as Mengele, Adolph Eichmann, and even Martin Bormann—Hitler's deputy and heir—had often been reported wandering its streets and trails, dressed in *lederhosen* and acting for all the world as if they were still in Berchtesgaden, paying a social call on the *Führer*. In October 1959 Mengele returned to Paraguay, where he was issued a citizenship certificate, number 293348, and established a new medical practice in Asunción.

Even as Mengele calmly and openly went about his business in Asunción, the hunt was intensifying. In Israel, Prime Minister David Ben-Gurion authorized a special commando unit of the Mossad, Israel's general intelligence agency, to initiate two top-secret operations: "Operation Eichmann" and "Operation Angel of Death." According to a CIA report in the folder the objectives of the unit, code-named the "Blue Falcons," were to kidnap Adolph Eichmann and Josef Mengele and bring them to Israel to stand trial.

Meanwhile, on November 13, 1959, the German embassy in Asunción petitioned the Paraguayan Ministry of the Interior for permission to examine Mengele's naturalization papers as a first step toward initiating extradition proceedings. Only five days later Interpol's Paris office approached the Paraguayan authorities with a similar request. A few days later a member of the Blue Falcons was found in Eldorado, Paraguay, his throat slit from ear to ear.

Caine put down the file and looked up at the ceiling, breathing deeply. Then he shook his head wearily. What a balls-up, he thought. They had all crowded around the target, jostling each other in their eagerness to piss into the soup. With a sigh he resumed his reading.

Forewarned by an unidentified Paraguayan leak, Mengele went to ground, next surfacing in Bariloche. Mengele and his bodyguards took over a floor in a chalet at the base of the towering precipice of Cerro Catedral. Using the alias Franz Fischer, he spent much of his enforced vacation hiking the rugged Andean trails.

A frequent companion during those weeks was a pretty blond woman from Frankfurt, named Nora Aldot. They had met at the chalet bar and soon they were inseparable. Mengele had a well-known weakness for beautiful women, and for her part Nora appeared smitten by his old-fashioned Bavarian charm. But Mengele was hot and he knew it. Strangers were showing up in Bariloche and the Argentinian and Paraguayan authorities were being pressured to do something about him. Mengele had his bodyguards and ODESSA *Kameraden* check her out.

The CIA report didn't indicate what, if anything, they found to incriminate the woman. All that was known for certain was that on February 12, 1960, Nora and Mengele and two of his bodyguards went hiking on the Cerro Catedral and that later the three men reported that Nora had fallen in a terrible accident. Nora's battered body was found in a ravine a few days later by the local police.

After a brief and somewhat cursory investigation

an Argentinian police report in the folder recorded the death as accidental and the investigation was closed due to a lack of any further evidence—except that the CIA report on the incident noted that Nora Aldot's real name was Norit Edad, a native of Frankfurt who had immigrated to Tel Aviv after the war. The CIA had concluded that she had in fact been a member of the Blue Falcons. It was the last time the Israelis got close to Mengele, and "Franz Fischer" once again went to ground.

The Blue Falcons were more successful with Eichmann and on May 23, 1960, Ben-Gurion was able to announce Eichmann's capture to the Knesset. But Ben-Gurion's triumph was short lived. The reaction of most Western and South American governments to the Israeli campaign of retribution was almost uniformly negative. The resulting scandals led to the resignation of Isar Harel as head of the Mossad and later to the fall of Ben-Gurion's government. An angry Ben-Gurion stormed off to semiretirement on a kibbutz in the Negev Desert, swearing to never again speak to the new prime minister, his former protégé, Levi Eshkol, who had forced him out of office. Israel was effectively out of the retribution business.

Even worse, the worldwide publicity associated with the Eichmann snatch and trial for war crimes sent fugitive Nazis scurrying for deeper cover. The frightened Nazis were getting harder to get at than ever. Even the complete record in front of Caine contained little information of Mengele's whereabouts between the time of his stay in Bariloche and 1965, except that Caine knew from Ibn Sallah that after the Eichmann snatch the fugitive had tried and failed to relocate to Egypt in 1961.

The record between 1960 and 1965 was a monotonous series of fiascos, as Interpol and Bureau One went through the motions, running down one false lead after another. The Mengele case was becoming a bureaucratic albatross. The situation was muddied still further by the attempts of enthusiastic Jewish amateurs.

In July 1962 the West German government asked the Paraguayans for information on Dr. José Mengele, who was supposedly living in Asunción, according to an Interpol report. A Paraguayan leak let Mengele know about the inquiry even before the Ministry of the Interior officially received the request. Mengele left Asunción and moved to the *finca* of a German immigrant named Krug, near the town of Encarnación on the upper Paraná River, located in a jungle region near the Argentinian and Brazilian borders.

Twelve Jewish survivors of Auschwitz living in Brazil got hold of an Interpol report and formed the "Group of Twelve," dedicated to getting Mengele. In 1965 the group set up shop in Pôrto Mendes, on the Brazilian side of the Paraná. Two members of the group crossed the river to seek out Mengele. Their bodies were hauled out of the river a few days later. The entire group then went into Paraguay, but Mengele had gone to ground once again. After a few abortive raids on places Mengele was thought to frequent, the surviving amateur Nazi hunters had to return to Brazil emptyhanded.

Yet another bizarre attempt to capture Mengele was revealed in a 1968 Argentinian police report. Acting under the authority of an open order issued in Buenos Aires back in 1960 by Judge Dr. Jorge Luque of the Argentinian Federal District Court for the extradition of Mengele to Germany, an undercover police agent in the Brazilian jungle state of Paraná claimed to have killed Mengele. The agent, a flamboyant Austrian immigrant to Brazil named Erico Erdstein, received a tip that Mengele periodically crossed the border into Brazil, where he stayed at the estate of Dr. Alexander Lénárd, a Nazi sympathizer, near the jungle town of Rio do Sul. Erdstein planned to abduct Mengele from Rio do Sul to the frontier town of Puerto Iguassú on Argentinian soil, where Judge Luque's order would be in force. On September 13, 1968, Erdstein arrested Mengele and two companions in Pôrto Mendes and took them on a chartered boat down the Paraná toward Puerto Iguassú.

According to Erdstein's deposition, appended to the report, a Paraguayan patrol boat intercepted them and in the ensuing gun battle Mengele and his companions were killed. Except that a subsequent Bureau One file reported that Mengele was spotted a year later in the Paraguayan province of Amambay. Like the fabled Rasputin, Mengele just wouldn't die. The West German authorities in Frankfurt requested a clarification of Erdstein's claim and, after studying the case, concluded that the three men killed were petty smugglers.

After almost five more years of bureaucratic muddling a special inquiry authorized by the Hesse state court uncovered eyewitness accounts from anonymous sources indicating that Mengele was still living in Amambay. Incredibly, the story was leaked to a staff reporter on the *Frankfurter Allgemeine* and on October 25, 1973, the following story appeared in *The New York Times*:

AUSCHWITZ DOCTOR SAID TO BE IN PARAGUAY

West German justice officials said in Bonn yesterday that Dr. Josef Mengele, the Nazi physician sought for the last twenty-two years for alleged mass murders in the Auschwitz concentration camp during World War II, was believed to have been located in a remote village in Paraguay. Mengele, known as "the Angel of Death," was reported to be in the village of Pedro Juan Caballero, near the Brazilian frontier, in the province of Amambay.

Based on the story, President Goppel, the Minister of Bavaria, contacted the Paraguayan dictator, President Alfredo Stroessner, to request extradition. But Stroessner denied any knowledge of Mengele. In any case it was too late. After all the publicity and an ostentatious search by the Paraguayan police, Mengele had vanished into thin air. Once again the elusive quarry had gone to ground.

Caine closed the last folder and glanced at his watch. It was well past lunch and he had been at it for hours. He lit a cigarette and glanced around the reading room. The detective had gone and the room was empty. His glance fell on the pile of folders in front of him, massive and incomplete, like the ruins of a failed civilization: a bureaucratic monument bearing an inscription as indecipherable as if it had been written in Etruscan. Caine shrugged. As far as he was concerned, all the Mengele hunters combined could have given lessons in incompetence to the planners of the Watergate break-in.

He leaned back and ran a mental tab, plucking the useful nuggets of information like the raisins from a bowl of cereal. Bariloche. The Blue Falcons. Judge Luque. Erico Erdstein. Feinberg in Vienna. The paraguayan authorities, who seemed so solicitous of Mengele's welfare. That could only mean bribes on a fairly large scale. Who had arranged for Mengele's naturalization as a Paraguayan citizen? he wondered. He opened one of the folders and finally found the name he was looking for. Mengele's application for citizenship had been filed by an Asunción lawyer, Cesar Augusto Sanabria. His application had been sponsored by two other German-born Paraguayans: Werner Jung and one Alexander von Eckstein. Cross-references on von Eckstein indicated that he was a leader of the highly visible German community in Asunción.

Caine decided that he could dismiss Mengele's son, Karl Heinz, and former wife, Martha, as potential information sources. That mine had obviously been worked until it was played out. Besides, in addition to their evident bitterness about Mengele, they had been out of the action and too far away from the field for a long time.

But throughout his reading a single question had been running through his mind, repeating itself like a pop melody that you hum once and then keeps coming back, haunting the day. Where had the money come from? Everything Mengele had done—travel, bodyguards, bribes, and so on—had required a great deal of money. He obviously hadn't earned that kind of money with his Paraguayan medical practice, so it had either come from the family business, or the ODESSA treasury.

That ODESSA had vast sums at its disposal was evident. During the war years the SS had systematically looted Europe of its gold, jewelry, and art treasures.

Not to mention all the valuables they had taken from the Jews in the concentration camps. In fact, tons of gold had been extracted from the teeth of Jewish corpses in Auschwitz alone. Yet little of the Nazi loot had ever been recovered. So ODESSA had the means to help Mengele, he mused. Whether they really wanted to was something else.

Mengele must have been a hot potato for the *Kameraden* of ODESSA, he thought. He was very hot and very visible and the practical leaders of ODESSA would probably have funded Mengele only to the extent necessary to keep him away from them. Any large-scale funding would have left a trail back to them as wide as a California freeway.

So the bulk of Mengele's funds must come from the family business. Indeed, as the folders indicated, the Günzburg firm was one of the largest manufacturers of farm and industrial equipment in Germany, with worldwide business dealings. Caine's eyes narrowed. He had hit pay dirt and he knew it. He'd be willing to bet his Mauritian stamp against a political candidate's promise to balance the budget that the Mengele firm had an office in Asunción. If he could just follow the money, it would lead him to Mengele as inevitably as a spawning salmon would lead anyone to his birthplace.

Caine stood up and stretched, his eyes beginning to refocus after all the reading he had done. It was time to begin the search in earnest, where the trail had last disappeared. After returning the folders, he left the center and headed back to the Hilton to check out. He called Lufthansa for a reservation, did some money changing, and made the drop for Harris at the American Express, then headed for Tegel Airport. The last thing he did before leaving Berlin was to stop by the airport telegraph office and send Wasserman a terse, unsigned cable.

He mentally checked everyone boarding the Lufthansa flight to New York, where he would make a connecting flight to South America, but no one seemed interested in him except for one well-dressed woman in her mid-forties. But if she had anything on her mind besides trying him on for size in the plane's lavatory, Caine couldn't spot it. It was just as well, he decided, because the research phase was over. As the jet lifted off the runway, he felt that it was more than just a separation from the earth. The hunt had entered the active phase.

CHAPTER 8

The old-fashioned ceiling fan revolved as slowly as a second hand, a perpetual-motion machine endlessly grinding away eternity. Beyond the drooping palm fronds that formed the thatched ceiling of the open-air *parrillada*, he could see the noon haze hanging over the Paraguay River. It was as if the entropy that will end the universe had already begun. A mosquito whined by his ear and he slapped at it with a gesture that had become automatic over the past four days. On the far side of the earth-colored river the Chaco jungle formed an endless hedge, a dull green wall rippling in the heat waves.

On the broad Avenida McAl Lopez a ragged shoe-shine boy, his bare arms as thin as the straw in Caine's drink, worked on a fat policeman's boots. The boy's movements were slow and desultory in the dense heat that soaked up energy like a sponge. A sand-colored gecko crawled tentatively up one of the wooden posts that supported the thatched roof. With a final flick of his long tail he disappeared into a crack in the wood and it was as though he had never existed.

Even now Caine couldn't get used to the summer heat. He felt suffocated and oddly immobile in the breathless humidity wrapped around him like a rubberized wet suit. With a listless gesture he motioned to the waiter and ordered another iced *caña*, the powerful liquor distilled from sugarcane. The young waiter, his pencil-thin mustache giving him a gigolo's oily charm, served the drink with a flourish, as if he were executing a *verónica* in the Plaza de Toros. Then the waiter walked proudly back to the empty bar, his platform heels clicking like castanets on the flagstone floor.

The rank smell of mud and decay floated up from the riverbank. The shops were shuttered and the streets almost deserted, as the city languidly prepared for the afternoon siesta. A lone army Jeep crawled slowly and deliberately along the riverfront toward Calle El Paraguayo Independiente. For perhaps the twentieth time in as many minutes, Caine glanced at his Omega. His contact was late and the waiter was getting restless. He wanted to close up and go home for his siesta. To give him something to do, Caine called him over and ordered a *carne asada*, although the heat had sapped his appetite.

The indistinct sound of an argument came from the kitchen. Behind his sunglasses Caine's eyes crinkled with a smile as he thought he heard the waiter's voice saying something about *"Turistas locos."* He lit another cigarette, hoping it would help keep the insects away, although so far as he could tell, the smoke didn't seem to bother the insects at all.

He knew when he arrived in Asunción that he couldn't just head on down to Pedro Juan Caballero and ask around the small town for the local Nazi criminal. In effect, that's what a number of the previous Mengele hunters had done. They were the ones found floating face down in the Paraná River. Caine had decided that he would have to locate Mengele long before he could approach the target. When he finally saw Mengele, it would only be when he was closing for the hit.

He spent the first couple of days playing tourist, learning his way around Asunción, and getting acclimatized. The combination of jet lag and the humid one-hundred-plus-degree temperature weakened him more than he had anticipated and he knew that any attempt to initiate the action phase before he was fully operational would be suicidal.

That first morning he had dutifully joined a minibus tour leaving from the curved driveway of the Hotel Itá Enramada, its modernistic white facade and palm trees giving it the appearance of an outpost from Miami Beach. The tour would not only help orient him, but would also help establish local cover as a tourist. A small group of American tourists milled around the spacious palm-lined lobby, checking camera equipment and trying to one-up each other on the bargains they had got on gaudy Guarani handicrafts and silver *maté* cups.

A woman in a flowered print dress and a large straw hat decorated with plastic fruit was reminding her husband for the twentieth time that they had to be sure and get enough samples of *nauditi* lace for the entire family. Her husband, his pink sunburned knees sticking out under Bermuda shorts, pretended he hadn't heard her and fiddled with one of his camera cases. She poked him with her fingers as they boarded the minibus in front of Caine.

"Oh, honey, we mustn't forget Aunt Flo," she said. The man looked unhappily out the window, as if the one thing in the world he wanted to do was to forget Aunt Flo.

Caine settled into a window seat with a silent prayer to whoever had invented air conditioning. A teen-aged blonde in jeans traveling with an elderly woman that he took to be her grandmother, glanced at him out of the corner of her eye to let him know that her glands were working. Give her fifteen years and a couple of failed marriages and she might even become interesting, Caine thought, and turned to the window.

At last the minibus began to move, trailing a cloud of exhaust fumes that hung in the air like brown fog. He watched the corrugated shacks along the river-front slide by, catching glimpses of naked brown children playing soccer in a dusty field. The driver pointed out the ornate Government Palace and minis-try offices on Calle El Paraguayo Independiente, gleaming white in the bright sunlight. The minibus turned away from the river and headed downtown, stopping for a guided tour at the Pantheon of Heroes in the Plaza de los Héroes.

The Pantheon was a white marble structure that looked like the fourth Xerox of the Hôtel des Invalides in Paris. It had been built to commemorate the disas-trous nineteenth-century War of the Triple Alliance, in which the outnumbered Paraguayans had fought the combined forces of Argentina, Brazil, and Uruguay. Barely thirty thousand Paraguayan males, mostly boys, survived the carnage and a sequence of military dictatorships had ensued. As a result of the Chaco border war with Bolivia during the thirties, the mili-tary solidified their power with the establishment of a fascistic regime that still endured, modeled after the

National Socialism that held sway in Germany at that time.

After leading them to a number of tourist shops on Calle Palma, Asunción's bargain-basement version of Fifth Avenue, the driver took them to the Jardín Botánico for more picture taking. Caine snapped photos for his fellow tourists, who squinted into the sun and said "cheese" till it hurt. The man who wanted to forget Aunt Flo took enough snapshots of the orchids to start a florist's catalog.

The grand finale of the tour was a brief boat ride to an island in the river inhabited by a tribe of Macá Indians, selling handicrafts from market stalls. The tourists descended on the stalls like Sennacherib on the fold, waving wads of guaranis and noisily haggling for all they were worth. Some of the chattering Macá women smoked fat cigars while impassive Indian men in loincloths, their dark eyes shuttered like camera lenses, charged two hundred guaranis to pose for pictures. Caine bought a gaudy lightweight *aho poi* shirt to further reinforce his tourist image. By the time the weary tourists staggered off the minibus with armfuls of booty, Caine had decided that a sojourn in a Vietnamese "tiger cage" would beat going on another tour.

Caine found the name of the local office of Mengele & Sons in the Asunción phone book. It was a little anticlimactic, like finding the prize in a box of Cracker Jacks. You always knew it had to be there. He located the office in a modern three-story building on Independencia Nacional near the Braniff office. There was no way to avoid going in, he would have to know the layout.

The cool shade of the hallway soothed his skin like

sunburn lotion, after the blistering morning heat of the streets. The Mengele office shared the third floor with a lawyer's office. Caine entered the Mengele office and stopped at the partition separating him from a petite blond receptionist, who was chewing on a pencil. The walls were hung with blown-up photographs of agricultural equipment, digging into the earth like giant mechanical insects from a grade B science fiction movie. Beyond the partition were a few shirt-sleeved clerks bent over their desks and two doors to private offices. One of the doors bore a brass plate with the inscription, ALOIS MENGELE, PRESIDENT. Mengele's brother.

Caine's eyes narrowed behind his sunglasses as he checked the walls for light switches and alarm wiring. The files he needed would be in Mengele's office, probably in a desk or wall safe. The blonde stopped chewing on her pencil, ruffled a few papers to show she had more important things to do than talk to him, and finally looked up.

"What do you wish, señor?"

"Where is the office of Señor Gomez?" Caine asked, naming the lawyer in the adjoining office. He deliberately emphasized his American accent and mangled the syntax. A gringo who could speak fluent Spanish was bound to be suspect.

"He is in the other office, the next door on the left, señor."

"*Gracias.*"

He left the office and explored the corridor, listening for a moment to the sound of typing coming from behind the lawyer's door. At the end of the corridor a rickety, unlit staircase led him to an alley beside the building. He went back up the stairs to the second floor and came down again, leaving the building by the main entrance. It was then that he saw the procession.

A single drum announced the platoon of soldiers with the inexorable, almost frightening tempo of a heartbeat. Rifles held at port arms with fixed bayonets gleaming in the tropic sun, they marched four abreast down the center of Independencia Nacional. Traffic ground to a halt and pedestrians came to a kind of informal attention as they solemnly lined both sides of the avenue. Caine positioned himself in the second rank of shoppers watching the soldiers approach, their legs kicking high in a measured goose step like a mechanical wave approaching some distant shore.

Behind the soldiers white-robed acolytes carried large ornate icons of the crucified Christ and the Blue Virgin of the Miracles on their shoulders. The icons swayed above the acolytes as though they were riding a raft on a sea of impassive Indian faces. A ripple of movement ran along the lines of onlookers as they knelt and genuflected at the icons' approach. Behind the icons a group of priests and assistants blessed the crowd with the sign of the cross, looking like a flock of crows in their black cassocks. After the priests came another platoon of goose-stepping soldiers, bringing up the rear.

Caine stood transfixed as the procession marched by. He felt an almost superstitious sense of shock and recognition and unconsciously he touched the Bauer, held snug in his waistband at the small of his back, almost as if it were a good-luck charm. Never before had he associated the Church with goose-stepping soldiers and fixed bayonets. As nothing ever had, it brought home to him a glimpse of what life for these people was really all about. No wonder Mengele had been able to go about his business here with complete impunity, he mused.

That evening he attended Sabbath eve services in a tiny synagogue in the Trinidad suburb. The church procession had convinced him that any attempt to directly approach Mengele would only muddy the water and forewarn the target. He needed hard information on local Nazis and it was likely that the Jews of Asunción had some of the answers. If you want to know where the wolves are, you could do worse than to ask the sheep, he thought.

An orange afterlight of the tropic sunset lingered over the streets like a floating veil, bringing little relief from the relentless heat. The street was crowded with gossiping housewives. Ragged copper-skinned children played in a garbage-strewn corner lot. From an open *tienda* a radio blared the rhythms of *música folklórica* as he entered the small wooden-frame house that served as a synagogue.

Inside, about twenty mostly elderly Jews in business suits stood praying in Spanish-flavored Hebrew. Their perspiring bodies swayed ritualistically as they faced a wooden closet covered by a crepe curtain. It bore a crudely painted Lion of Judah standing on a Star of David. Caine awkwardly placed a handkerchief on his head to serve as a yarmulke, wondering what he was supposed to do.

A fat red-faced man in his fifties with bulldog jowls shoved a prayer book at Caine, pointing out the place in the text. Caine shrugged helplessly and the man smiled back with an air of patient resignation. After the service Caine told the man, who introduced himself as Jaime Weizman, that he was an American Jew who was thinking of opening a business in Paraguay and needed advice on local conditions. They arranged to meet for lunch at the *parrillada* and it was Weizman that Caine was waiting for as he checked his watch again.

The only hitch was that he had been tailed by a green Chevy from the synogogue back to his hotel. It was frustrating because there was no reason for it and because he couldn't flush the tail without revealing that he knew he was being followed and thereby blowing his cover. Things were getting hairy too soon, he told himself as he sipped his drink.

The waiter brought over his *carne asada* and went back to the bar, where he settled on a stool and pulled out a tattered paperback. The lurid book cover showed a blonde in a torn blouse being pistol-whipped by a faceless figure in a trench coat. The waiter dived headfirst into the book as into a pool, as Weizman finally arrived in an old Fiat.

Weizman ambled slowly toward Caine, his checked sports jacket refracted in the shimmering heat, as though seen through warped glass. He settled into the chair opposite Caine with a small sigh of relief. With an air of annoyance at the interruption, the waiter put down his book and came over to the table. Weizman ordered a *sopa Paraguaya*, a kind of corn bread quiche, and a cold *cerveza*. The waiter delivered the order to the kitchen and went back to the bar and his paperback.

Caine explained once again that as a fellow Jew he wanted to get to know the Jewish community in Asunción before committing himself to a business venture in Paraguay. As Caine spoke, Weizman's dark eyes regarded him with a disconcerting mixture of friendliness and unhappiness, like a puppy that wants to play and knows it's going to be rebuffed. Weizman patted at his florid, sweating face with a handkerchief, smiling apologetically, as though he were wagging his tail.

"*Perdóneme,* Señor Foster, but you are not Jewish," Weizman said uneasily, his English heavily accented and tentative.

Caine briefly considered lying, then decided against it. He sensed that hidden inside that amiable envelope of flesh was a shy, frightened man.

"How can you tell?"

Weizman shrugged with that gesture of Latin indifference that is mostly indolence. Then he smiled shyly, as though offering Caine a gift.

"After two thousand years, you get a knack for it."

"You're right, I'm not Jewish."

Weizman nodded solemnly. The waiter brought a frosted bottle of beer that Weizman consumed greedily, sucking at the bottle like a starving baby at the nipple. Weizman was like a man who had gone hungry and forever afterward lived with the fear that his food might be taken from him again.

"I'm with Interpol. I'm here to investigate Nazi war criminals," Caine said crisply, flashing the bronze badge he had bought in Las Vegas.

"What war crimes? The camps were all a figment of Zionist propaganda. If you don't believe me, ask any German."

"I did." Caine smiled. "They're all innocent. Hitler fought the war single-handed."

"*Meshuggener.*" Weizman smiled sadly, meaning "crazy" as if it were a compliment. "Do you know the story in the Talmud about the king who visited the prison? Each of the prisoners protested his innocence, except for one man, who admitted he was a robber. 'Throw this thief out of here,' the king said. 'He will corrupt all these innocents.'" Weizman giggled happily at his own story.

"I'm here after some of the guilty ones, even if they are maligned victims of Zionist propaganda," Caine said with a wink.

"Guilt." Weizman looked at him quizzically. "You use such old-fashioned words, Señor Foster. I thought you North Americans were much more up-to-date. Besides, guilt, vengeance, justice, those words passed me by a million years ago. I am a Jew, Señor Foster. What matters to us is survival. That's all, just survival. We're very good at it, we Jews. Survival is the great Jewish"—he waved his hand, searching for the word, as though seeking to pluck it from the air—"talent."

"Do you want to see the Nazis go free?"

"Which of us is truly free, Señor Foster? You, me, the Germans? We are all the prisoners of our past, *verdad*? When the Nazis came to power, the Jews tried to flee Germany. Not one country was willing to take them in, including your United States. There was only one place that was willing to accept them. Do you know where that was, Señor Foster?" Weizman asked, mopping his sweating brow with the soggy handkerchief. "Nazi Germany. Then during the war the world stood idly by, while the Holocaust happened. Europe was flattened, but not one of the death camps was ever bombed. Not one! After the war it was business as usual. The war was over. Who wanted to dig up a past better left buried? After all, the Nazis were only doing their duty, like a good German should."

"If you really believe that shit, why did you agree to see me?"

"To find out what you were after. There are only a few hundred Jews in Paraguay, Señor Foster. We are a small tightly knit community and we survive mostly by staying out of the limelight. So when anyone takes an interest in us, it's dangerous, and we have to know what it's all about."

"Is that why you had me tailed back to my hotel?" Caine asked, with a sudden surge of relief.

"I'm afraid we're not very good at that sort of thing," Weizman apologized.

Jesus, so that's all the Chevy was, Caine thought. Amateurs should never play with professionals. It was like giving children your new Buick and asking them to go play Grand Prix driver on the Santa Monica freeway.

"No, you're not. I'd advise you not to try it again."

"Do you know what it's like to be a Paraguayan Jew, Señor Foster? Our glorious leader, Alfredo Stroessner"—Weizman's lips pursed in a strange kind of unctuous irony as he whispered the name, looking around the empty restaurant to make sure he wasn't overheard—"is descended from Bavarian immigrants. We are under constant surveillance. People who stick their noses into German business just disappear. We have been threatened many times. Even the most casual remark can cause arrest and the whole community is threatened with reprisals. Twice our synagogue was firebombed and when we went to the police, they told us to mind our own business. My Cousin Meyer once identified Eduard Roschmann right here in Asunción. What was left of my cousin's body was found two days later in the jungle by Mennonite missionaries. Don't stir up trouble, Señor Foster. The Germans here still believe in the principle of collective guilt. Whatever you do, we will be the ones to pay for it."

"So just play it safe, is that it?"

"We survive, Señor Foster," Weizman sighed. "It's what we're good at."

"Where's Josef Mengele?"

"I'm begging you, señor." Weizman's bulldog face quivered with emotion. "*Por favor*, let it alone. Let us handle it in our own way."

"That's what the Jews said to Moses when he wanted to challenge the Pharaoh. Fortunately he wasn't paying attention." Caine smiled.

"Such a deal," Weizman giggled. "I was right, you are a *meshuggener*."

"No, I'm just a *goy* with a job to do. Have you ever seen Mengele here in Asunción?"

Weizman hawked and spat into the sand.

"That one. It would give you a chill to see him. He left Asunción years ago and moved to Amambay province in the south. But he used to come back every so often. Sometimes I would see him at the Amstel Restaurant. And once at the Tyrol Hotel in Eldorado."

"When was the last time you saw him?"

"Maybe five—no, six years ago. There was another man from Interpol here then. He also stirred things up. That's when we were firebombed the first time. And for what? Mengele was already gone. We heard that he had left Pedro Juan Caballero and crossed the border to Ponta Porã, on the Brazilian side of the Paraná. The last we heard he had simply disappeared into the Mato Grosso. That was the last anyone ever heard of him and good riddance. He hasn't come back."

"Would you know if he were back in Paraguay?"

For a moment Weizman's eyes searched Caine's face as if it were a map he was trying to read. Then he shook his head with finality.

"He is not in Paraguay. If he were, we would know about it, *comprende?* Besides"—he shrugged—"we have enough Nazis here without him."

"Who leads the Nazis here in Asunción?"

Weizman's eyes turned up and Caine could see the whites as Weizman shifted uneasily in his chair, like a child who has to go to the bathroom.

"Müller," he muttered, actually trembling in terror like a field mouse in front of a snake. "Heinrich Müller. He owns a meat-packing business. Perfect for a butcher, wouldn't you say? But be careful, señor. He has important friends. Political friends."

"Such a deal," Caine said, and stood up. He left a five-hundred-guarani note on the table for the check and extended his hand to Weizman.

"*Gracias,*" he said and shook Weizman's limp, moist hand.

"*Buena suerte.*" Good luck, Weizman said, looking as though he didn't have any to spare. Caine left him sitting there, fervently attacking his *sopa Paraguayo* as though it were his last meal.

Caine was growing impatient. He had been tailing Müller for almost a week without getting a single chance to make the snatch. Of course, snatching Müller might alert Mengele, but since Caine had no intention of letting Müller go, all the Nazis would know for sure was that Müller had disappeared. Then, too, if he could move quickly enough against Mengele, Müller's disappearance wouldn't matter. "Surpries lies at the foundation of all undertakings, without exception," Koenig used to say, quoting Clausewitz. Koenig was fond of quoting Clausewitz. Except that it didn't look like he was going to get the chance to put the theory into practice, Caine mused, because he hadn't found any way to get at Müller.

To make matters worse, inevitably he had been spotted. It was impossible to tail someone in such a small community and go unobserved, so he had taken the opposite tack, blatantly showing up wherever Müller did, making a noisy show as the ugly American tourist with a local hooker on his arm for camouflage. But the ploy only worked short term and time was running out. He had been spotted once too often for coincidence, and now they were undoubtedly wondering who the hell he was and whether or not to terminate him.

Even now Müller was flicking an uneasy glance in his direction across the crowded restaurant. Unless he did it tonight he would have to abort; he was already running too close to the wire. Maybe they were playing Ring-Around-the-Rosie. That very evening before dinner Caine had come back to his room in the Hotel del Lago to find that the hair he had stretched across the doorposts was broken and the keys he had placed in a carefully disarranged pattern in his bureau drawer had been moved. The problem was that the son of a bitch was never alone, Caine mused as he swallowed the last of his beer.

Müller was a big man—nearly six feet—his body still hard and trim under his lightweight sport shirt and slacks. His hair was closely cropped and iron gray, his blue eyes like aquamarines set in a face that looked like it had been hammered out of bronze. Even in his civies he still looked like an SS officer on furlough. He leaned over and whispered something to his body-guard, Steiger, then with a bellow he rejoined his table companions in singing war songs from the good old days. They punctuated their bleary nostalgia by banging their beer bottles on the table in time to the singing, drowning out the plaintive Paraguayan music played by a trio of a harp and two guitars in the far corner.

Steiger was a bullet-headed Neanderthal with a white scar running down his forehead into his cheek. Caine didn't bother to fool himself into thinking Steiger was a pushover. He hadn't gotten that scar from Heidelberg. He had the piggish face of a Brown-shirt bully and Caine was willing to bet that the scar came from the kind of street brawl he probably rel-ished. Steiger made no effort to hide the gun in his waistband, jammed against his beer belly like a truss. It was a naval Luger with a six-inch barrel, the kind that used to be carried by the Wehrmacht paratroop-ers. Also seated at the table were Müller's mistress, an aging blonde who wore a silk scarf around her neck to hide a sagging chin line, and a fat, bald German in a business suit, who crooned the lyrics in a beery off-key monotone.

It had to be now or never, Caine decided, signaling the waiter for the check. He had completed his prepa-rations in Asunción, renting a black Ford and buying everything he needed: flashlight, canteen, binoculars, car flares, fishing tackle with eighty-pound test line, the tin cans of vegetables that he had emptied, the five-gallon can of gasoline. But it was impossible to get at Müller in Asunción. The man's house and office were made of brick and built like fortresses, his pattern of movement constantly varied—and Steiger never left his side.

Then Müller broke the pattern once again. Caine followed Müller's Mercedes to the resort town of San Bernardino on the tropical shore of Lake Ypacaraí. Müller evidently planned to spend a few days with his mistress at his sumptuous lakeside villa. Caine reconnoitered the area till he found the spot he was looking for: a jungle clearing near an abandoned farmhouse, miles from any habitation. Near the clearing was a stagnant marsh pool, oozing with the stench of slime and death. The marsh was bordered with thick mud, black and sticky as pitch.

Using the fishing line and pebbles placed in the empty tin cans, the way they used to around the fortified hamlets, he set trip wires across the overgrown trail from the farmhouse to the clearing. As he worked the smell of his own body heat, the noisy shrieks of the jungle birds, the trip wires, brought it all back. Asia.

He thought he heard the belch of mortars and the rattle of small-arms fire, but when he looked up, there was only the electric whine of insects, like the constant hum of high-power lines and the squawking of a pair of wildly colored parrots. That fucking war just won't end, he thought miserably. He reached for a stick to throw at the birds, then flinched back with horror as it slithered silently into the undergrowth.

But it was no go. Caine had watched the villa through the binoculars from a rowboat well out in the lake. He counted on the glare from the water to cover the glint of sunlight off the lenses. But except for a bit of waterfront fishing with Steiger, Müller hadn't left the villa. All Caine had to show for two days of stakeout were the *surubi* and *armados* fish he had caught, a wealth of mosquito bites, and, in spite of a thick layer of sunscreen, a neon-bright sunburn that made him look like a warning ad for Solarcaine—until tonight, when Müller finally ventured out to La Cordobesa for dinner and the sentimental *Bierhaus* singalong.

Their singing followed Caine out of the restaurant, the lyrics hanging in his mind like an unfinished sentence.

"Wie heist Lilli Marlene, Wie heist Lillie Marlene?"

The question lingered like a Zen koan. It seemed that if he could just find an answer to the riddle of Lilli Marlene's identity, it would somehow contain an answer to the riddle of the universe itself. He shrugged the thought away as he got into the car. Perhaps there was no answer, no real Lilli Marlene. And perhaps the universe didn't mean anything either.

He backed the car into the dark alley beside the restaurant, by the back exit door he had spotted earlier. He opened the locked door with his folding knife and slipped unnoticed into the filthy men's *lavabo* near the door. He latched the cubicle door, folded down the toilet seat, and settled down to wait, trying to breathe through his mouth to minimize the stench.

While he watched the door through the doorjamb crack of the cubicle, he made a slipknot loop from a length of fishing line and put it back into his pocket. Then he took out the Bauer and cocked it. He was counting on the beer and the regularity of Müller's bladder capacity. The last time he had seen Müller out drinking in Asunción, Müller had hit the john approximately every forty-five minutes. It wasn't much, but it was something. More important, Steiger hadn't gone with him.

Caine glanced around the cubicle at the graffiti. The partitions were decorated with the usual badly drawn cocks and cunts and obscene Spanish suggestions that would have required a contortionist to fulfill. That's the part that the Company doesn't talk about when recruiting, he thought wryly. That an agent spends more time in toilets than a janitor does.

Müller's image filled the doorway for an instant and then it was gone. Caine waited until he heard the piddling water sound from the urinal before he quietly unlatched the cubicle door and stepped out. Müller was just zipping up his fly when he heard Caine. He started to turn, his eyes narrowing at the sight of the Bauer aimed at his heart.

"Put your hands up," Caine ordered sharply.

Müller raised his hands slowly, an ironic smile playing across his face.

He didn't looked worried. Probably playing for time till Steiger came looking, Caine thought, his eyes burning bright green as with fever.

"No, against the wall, hotshot," Caine said, gesturing at the wall with the Bauer. He held Müller spread-eagle against the wall and quickly frisked him, keeping the Bauer clear. He knew he had to be quick. Steiger could come in at any second. Now he had come to the danger point. If Müller were to make his move, it would have to be now.

"Put your hands behind you."

Instantaneously with the tensing of the muscles in Müller's shoulders telegraphing the move, Caine slammed the butt of the Bauer with all his strength into Müller's kidneys. Müller's strangled gasp was lost in the hollow thump as Caine rammed his left palm against the base of the skull, cracking Müller's forehead against the wall.

"Put 'em behind you," Caine hissed, and as Müller weakly brought his hands behind him, Caine slipped the fishing-line loop around the crossed wrists and pulled it so tight the line disappeared into the flesh. Müller started to fill his lungs to shout and Caine jammed the Bauer into the same kidney. All that came out of Müller was a hoarse gargle.

"Shut up," Caine hissed, and tightly bound Müller's hands with the remaining length of line. A thin red bracelet of blood formed around Müller's wrists and began to drip on the floor.

"Go," Caine said and shoved Müller ahead of him into the dark corridor and out the alley exit. He kicked Müller facedown onto the Ford's rear-seat floor, fishing in Müller's pockets for the keys to the Mercedes. When he found the keys, he started the Ford, pulled out of the alley, and drove for half a block, stopping alongside the parked Mercedes. Warning Müller not to move, he jumped out of the Ford and quickly opened the Mercedes. He released the hook lock, opened the hood, and yanked out the distributor cap and wiring. Then he slammed down the hood, locked the Mercedes, and was back in the Ford within seconds, heading out of town along the lakefront road. In spite of all that, he knew nothing he did would delay Steiger for long.

He could hear Müller trying to gain leverage

against the rear seat, as he neared the outskirts of San Bernadino. Suddenly he doused his lights and swerved to a stop in a dark private road. Caine heaved the distributor cap and the Mercedes keys in opposite directions far into the trees, then went around to the rear door and tightly bound Müller's feet with another length of fish line. He forced Müller to hop into the front seat, where he could keep an eye on him, and soon they were again speeding out to the deserted farmhouse.

The headlights carved a tunnel of light through the dense jungle darkness as they sped down the unlit asphalt road. The warm, moist wind created by the car's speed flowed through the half-opened window, pressing against his skin in a clammy embrace. Insects splattered like brown raindrops against the windshield until he was forced to use the wipers, smearing the glass with a gummy film.

"Who are you? *Israelien?*" Müller gasped. Since the Eichmann snatch Nazi fugitives had been haunted by the nightmare of Israeli commandos. Now the nightmare was coming true at last.

Müller twisted to look at Caine, his face sweating and taut with pain. But his pale eyes were cold and still in control of it.

"*Bitte,* the line is too tight. My hands are getting numb."

"So what," Caine said.

The asphalt ended and they began bouncing down a dirt road, hedged like a corridor by the dark shadows of trees. Müller gritted his teeth in pain. Every few seconds Caine glanced across at him, then back up at the rearview mirror, which remained pitch-black. He held the speedometer needle poking around fifty, like a compass needle touching north.

"Are you *Israelien*?" Müller asked. When Caine didn't answer, he shrugged and looked away into the darkness.

"It doesn't matter. It had to come. We are both dead men, you and I. Unless you free me, you'll never get out of Paraguay alive. Do you know who I am?"

"I know who you are, Müller," Caine said.

"You know nothing," Müller retorted contemptuously. "I am *Hauptsturmbannführer* Heinrich Müller of the Waffen SS. Did you think I would deny it? I am not like those others, the weaklings, who claimed that they were only following orders. Otherwise they wouldn't have harmed the hair on a Jew's head," he added mockingly. "I did not follow orders, I gave them," he thundered proudly.

"And millions died," Caine said.

"Why not? It was war and they were in the way. We were trying to do what no society had ever done before. To create a New Order for the world and defend our sacred *Vaterland* at the same time. Only a squeamish weakling would let a few Jews stand in the way of what we were trying to accomplish. Besides, what were those lice to me? Or anyone? Shall I tell you something? All anyone ever cares about is himself. It's human nature. If you're honest, you'll admit it.

"I tell you, getting a tiny splinter in your little finger will bother you personally more than the death of thousands of people you don't know. *Ja,* all the rest is liberal posturing"—nodding his head sagely.

"Shut up," Caine said.

"You can't take the truth can you, filthy Jew," Müller muttered, almost to himself.

Caine took the Bauer from his waistband and with a single sweeping movement smashed the butt into Müller's mouth.

"I said, 'Shut up,'" he spat out sharply.

Müller coughed and out came a mouthful of blood and broken teeth. His lips glistened bright red, as if he had smeared on lipstick.

As he drove the remaining few miles in silence, Caine tried to compute how much time he had before Steiger came. Getting a car would take him a few minutes, but that was all. Steiger would know whom to look for and he would only have to ask a few people to find out what kind of car Caine was driving. Then it was only a matter of questioning people until he found someone who had seen the Ford. Only two roads went out of town and he would have to explore a few side ones. Figure half an hour at best.

He glanced over at Müller, who stared impassively into the darkness. His battered face might have been sculpted from stone. Müller knew all he had to do was hold out till Steiger came—Caine was clearly alone. Either he would be rescued or killed—so in any event the pain period would be limited. Müller had no incentive to talk. But Caine had other ideas.

He remembered Smiley Gallagher, his small squinting eyes gleaming with shy pride as he defended his techniques. They were sitting in that noisy bar in Saigon where the MP's never came because Madame Wu had the girls service them with French ticklers if they came in civies, and razors if they came in uniform.

"If all you're after is information, you don't need

lots of time and an elaborate apparatus. All that is required is a basic knowledge of human physiology and the creation of the right psychological conditions. For example," Smiley had said, pausing to delicately pluck a morsel of lemon grass from his plate of *Ga Xa Ot* and chew it with the contented air of a well-fed cow, "suppose you want to interrogate two prisoners from the same outfit. All you have to do is bust them up for a while to see which of them takes it better. Then you question the stronger and when he refuses to answer, you shoot him. Then you cock the gun and put the same question to the weaker one. At that point you couldn't stop him from spilling his guts if you tried.

"The essence of torture is expectation," Smiley said, his soft brown eyes as untroubled as if he were calmly describing the behavior of laboratory animals. "You see, Johnny, the key is that the subject must have the clear notion that the pain will increase indefinitely until he gives you what you want. Oh, yes," he added, like a physics student rewriting an equation, reducing it to its simplest form. "The subject has to feel that you're threatening the thing he loves most, his sight, his manhood, his woman, or his life."

The car bumped slowly across a field to the dark silhouette of the old abandoned farmhouse. After he shut the headlights, the darkness was almost complete. The night was filled with crawling sounds and bird cries and, somewhere, the plaintive shrieks of an animal that he couldn't identify. Caine took the flashlight, fishing hooks and line, and the car flares from a paper bag in the trunk, then put the bag over Müller's head.

Caine dragged Müller from the car and leaned him against the fender. Using the flashlight, he carefully examined the knots around the wrists to make sure they were holding. Müller's clenched hands had turned into dark purplish claws. Soon they would be useless.

"Where are you taking me?"—Müller's voice sounding hollow and muffled from inside the bag. Caine responded with a savage knee to the groin. Today's lesson, class, is to speak only when spoken to, he thought. He waited for Müller to finish retching into the bag, a thread of vomit dripping down onto his chest.

He cut the line binding Müller's legs and prodded him with the Bauer down the trail that was barely discernible in the narrow flashlight beam. Even though he remembered exactly where he had placed the trip wires, he almost missed them in the darkness. He had Müller step carefully over the wires and then shoved the stumbling figure down the trail to the clearing.

Using the fishing hooks and line, he tied Müller to a tree. It was essential that Müller be unable to move and he crisscrossed his chest and arms and legs with so many coils that Müller looked like a fly trussed up by a spider for later consumption. He was careful to leave the head and neck free, so that Müller would be unable to kill himself. When he was finished, he positioned the flashlight in the crook of a nearby tree so he could see what he was doing and checked the Omega. There wasn't much time left.

He removed the bag from Müller's head and lit a cigarette. Müller's bloodshot eyes glowed as red as coals in the pale light. An insect buzzed Caine's face and he slapped at it automatically. They heard a bird shriek not far away and then the shriek was suddenly cut off. Around them the jungle darkness stirred and thrashed like a restless sleeper, spilling the rank smell of the marsh toward them like a pail of dirty water.

"You can scream all you like," Caine said conversationally. "There's no one within miles; that's why I chose this place. And don't think Steiger's going to come to the rescue like the U.S. Cavalry. I've taken care of that. So there's just you and me. Now let me tell you what I'm going to do," he said, unbuckling Müller's belt and pulling down his pants and undershorts. Müller's eyes were almost all pupil, black as a hawk's with fear and rage.

"I'm going to cause you more pain than you can imagine. You won't pass out, you won't be saved, and you won't die. The pain will just get worse and worse until you tell me what I want to know. It's like you said before. All anybody ever thinks about is himself. So I suggest you forget about trying to protect anyone else and just think about yourself.

"I'm going to start on your testicles. After maybe forty seconds or so you might as well cut them off because they'll be absolutely dead and useless. Understand?

"Now then, I'm going to ask you only one time and one time only. Where is Josef Mengele?"

"*Bitte,*" Müller's voice quavered. "I don't know."

"Too bad for you," Caine said calmly and flicked away his cigarette, checking his watch again.

"God in heaven, I'd tell you if I knew. I swear it," Müller shouted desperately, twisting uselessly against the fishing line.

Caine took Müller's soft penis in his hand, pulling it up to expose the testicles. The penis stirred slightly as he flicked open his cigarette lighter and touched the tip of the flame to the testicles.

Müller's body leaped and quivered with electric
shock, as it thrashed mindlessly against the fishing
coils, which began to drip with blood. A piercing
scream seemed to emanate from his very bowels, as
the acrid smell of burnt hair and scorched flesh
reached Caine's nostrils. It was not a human scream.
The body jerked with desperate convulsions and the
stench of charred meat grew very strong as the skin
blistered and began to turn black. The animal-like
screaming went beyond pain or dying and it seemed
to go on forever, like an echoing air-raid siren wailing
desperately for the end of the world. The skin was
gone and Caine could see one of the testicles itself,
blistering and charring as it shriveled to the size of a
pea. Then he became aware that the scream had become a ululation, that it had a pattern, and that
Müller was somehow screaming the word *Peru* as if
it were the name of God.

Caine clicked the lighter shut, grabbed Müller's
head, and banged it against the tree trunk. Müller
continued to wail mindlessly, like a small child. He
slapped Müller's contorted face two or three times.

"Mengele is in Peru?"

Müller tried to look at him with hatred, as if remembering the SS officer he had been, but he was
broken and there was nothing in his eyes except the
dull glaze of pain.

"*Ja, bitte*. No more, *bitte*. No more," he whimpered.

Müller's head fell forward and hung from his neck
like a broken fixture. His rasping breath shattered
into a series of sobs. His face was a death's head, glistening with sweat and tears and blood. Then Caine
heard it. The tinny, rattling sound of the trip-wire
alarm and a sudden crackle of underbrush. Steiger.

Caine moved quickly. He tore Müller's shirt and wadded it for a gag that he stuffed into Müller's mouth. He bound the gag in place with another strip of shirt, his fingers bumping against each other in his haste. Then he grabbed the flashlight and a car flare. Just as he clicked off the flashlight, he heard another jangling rattle and a muffled curse. Steiger had hit the second trip wire. There were only seconds left. He struck the car flare and dropped it near Müller's feet, where it burned cherry-red, like a dying star, as he blundered into the underbrush and rolled behind a tree. For a moment he froze and closed his eyes, so that his vision could adjust to the darkness as quickly as possible.

He knew the Bauer wouldn't stand a chance against the range of the Luger, so he would have to play cat and mouse, hoping to get within range before Steiger spotted him. Even if he could manage it, the .25 caliber shell was too light to risk a body shot. It would have to be a head shot, and he couldn't afford to miss. Steiger wasn't about to hand him the luxury of a second chance.

Caine lay silently, breathing shallowly to minimize the sound of his own breath and straining his ears for any sound of movement. A mosquito's whine by his ear sounded loudly as a plucked guitar string. There was the distant chattering of two birds engaged in a nervous dialogue. And a faint, almost inaudible grinding sound that could have been a beetle chewing on a leaf. Otherwise there was nothing.

Obviously Steiger had also frozen, waiting for him to make a mistake. Caine felt he had a few things going for him. Steiger didn't know where he was or how he was armed, so he would have to be cautious.

Steiger didn't know the terrain or if there were any more trip wires, so he would probably stick to the trail and move slowly. Also the flare light would inevitably draw Steiger like a moth to a flame and at the moment of firing would fractionally reduce his night vision. Finally Caine had the flashlight, which could be used to mislead as well as illuminate.

Even so, Caine knew his chances were no better than fifty-fifty because at this stage he hadn't wanted to risk bringing anything bigger than the Bauer through Paraguayan Customs. When Steiger approached the clearing and first spotted the flare, he would realize his danger and choose to crawl around one side of the clearing or the other, so he could dive into the cover of the underbrush the instant he heard or spotted Caine. If he came on Caine's side, he would be within range of the Bauer, and Caine would have a shot at him. If he went on the far side, it would be a long shot for the Bauer and Caine wouldn't stand a chance. Either way it was an easy shot for the Luger.

His heartbeat sounded loudly as a drum, in the deathly silence. Sweat burned his eyes and the old tightness grabbed at his solar plexus like a fist. It was like being back in Indochina—the jungle sounds, the heat and the death you couldn't see but you knew was out there. It was the terror of a nightmare grown real, and for a moment he felt as if he were drowning in black water. Then he remembered the training at the Farm, Koenig speaking quietly in the tent after night maneuvers on the boom-boom course.

"When you've done everything you can and the fear comes, and believe me, it'll come, ask yourself the question: Is there anything else I can do?" Koenig had said.

There was still one thing he could do, Caine thought. Stealthily, placing his hands slowly one at a time so as not to disturb any animals or leaves or twigs, he began to creep on his hands and toes through the brush toward the trail. When Steiger came, he would expect to find Caine somewhere in front of him and not so close to him by the trail. He crept slowly; each movement seemed to take hours. His eyes caught every shadow and his ears registered barely audible sounds, as instincts millions of years old came alive in him. He had become the most efficient killing machine nature had ever created: the human animal stalking its prey.

As he neared the shadow of a tree at the edge of the clearing, its trunk about half the width of a man, the jungle itself seemed to hold its breath. He crouched behind the tree, steadying the Bauer in his right hand against one side of the trunk and the flashlight in his left hand against the other side. Most people hold a flashlight in front of them near their side. Caine was counting on Steiger knowing that and firing in the vicinity of the light as soon as he saw it. Caine wiped the sweat from his eyes against his shoulder, holding his breath in the dark silence. Come into my parlor said the spider to the fly, he thought.

The sound of a broken twig thrilled through him. It seemed to come from about twenty-five feet away, right around the maximum effective range of the Bauer. It was going to be very close. There was a flicker of shadow in the faint reddish glow from the flare and he thought he heard the faint scuffle of a shoe in the same direction. He no longer had any time to think about it because those primordial instincts had taken over and he clicked the flashlight on. The

beam caught a crouching Steiger, silhouetted for an
instant against the darkness. He was on the far side.
But it didn't matter, because he was already whipping
the Luger into a two-handed stance aimed at the
light. The two guns fired simultaneously. Steiger
missed. Caine didn't.

Steiger crumpled forward and lay still, but Caine
didn't move. He carefully and deliberately placed four
more shots into Steiger. The body jerked spasmodically with the first two shots, as if jolted by electric
shocks. The body received the last two shots without
movement. Caine reloaded the Bauer and listened for
any sounds on the off-chance that Steiger hadn't come
alone. But there was nothing.

He raced over to Steiger, grabbed the Luger, and
fired it almost point-blank into the head. The skull
cracked open like a rotten fruit and bits of brains and
blood sprayed across the ground. Then Caine ran
across the clearing to Müller. But he was too late.

Incredibly, Müller had worked the gag loose by
rubbing the back of his head against the tree. Then he
had committed suicide by swallowing the wadded-up
shirt and choking himself. A piece of shirt strip hung
from the corner of his mouth, like a rat's tail from a
snake's mouth. Caine tried to pull the shirt strip out,
but it tore apart in his hand. Besides it was pointless.
Müller's pupils showed no reaction to the flashlight.

Caine cut the body down and kicked it a few
times in savage frustration. Then he caught himself and
just stood there, listening to the night sounds of the
jungle coming to life once more. He was blown wide
open and there wasn't much time left. His only chance
was to get to the Mengele office before the Nazis had
a chance to react. The only question was whether

Steiger or either of Müller's companions had taken the time to make a phone call.

He carried both bodies to the edge of the marsh and dumped them into the black mud. In a few days they would be unrecognizable; the jungle animals would see to that. Then he drove the car Steiger had used into the ramshackle shell of the farmhouse to hide it from view. Using the flashlight, he carefully examined the Ford, checking the engine, the wiring under the dashboard, and the car's underbody, just in case Steiger had left him a surprise package. He wiped the sweat from his eyes and crawled out from under the car. Everything was clean.

He stripped off his filthy clothes and buried them in the bushes, then washed himself with water from the canteen before changing into a fresh pair of slacks and a sports shirt, congratulating himself on his foresight in bringing them along. Soon he was back in the Ford, speeding along the road to Asunción.

It was nearly two in the morning by the time he parked the car on a dark street off Independencia Nacional. The streets of the business section were deserted at this hour, and the quiet thunk of the closing car door echoed ominously in the stillness, like the sound of a midnight knock at the door. On the corner a single streetlight cast a yellowish glare with the unblinking gaze of a solitary jaundiced eye. Moths and insects swirled and battered themselves against the light, like the souls of the damned desperately seeking entrance to the New Jerusalem. Their tiny corpses littered the glass globe with dark smudges.

Caine opened the trunk and took out another paper bag, containing the five-gallon can of gasoline. He checked his pockets: Luger, detonators, lockpick, flashlight, the Bauer in his waistband, the small lump of *plastique* that he had retrieved from his cache in a safety-deposit box in a New York bank between flight connections. He had saved a small block of surplus *plastique* after the Abu Daud hit in Paris, when they had blown apart *Le Beau Amateur* in the Boulevard St. Michel section as a diversion. If the police stopped him, he could always tell them he was planning to open a retail outlet for urban guerrillas, he thought wryly. Keeping to the shadows, he made his way to the alley exit and up the stairs to the third-floor office.

For a long moment he pressed his ear to the door, but there was no sound. Either he had beaten them to the punch, or they were very good. On his previous visit to the office he hadn't seen any alarm wiring on the office door, but something made him hesitate. Then he realized what it was. The office was the bull's-eye of the red zone. If they were to come at him, this is where it would be. But he had no choice, he decided with a slight shrug. He had already taken two strikes: Weizman and Müller. The office was the only remaining route to Mengele in Paraguay. It was all he had left.

The lock was a standard Yale that wouldn't have slowed the balding, bespectacled "flaps and seals" instructor in Langley long enough to check his watch. But it took Caine almost five minutes with the pick until he heard the faint, satisfying click. In an instant he was inside with the flashlight, checking the drapes and cutting the alarm wire to the inner office. He put the can of gasoline on the desk, checked the window to make sure no light could seep out to the street, then used his folding knife to pry open the desk lock. Using standard burglar procedure, he started with the bottom drawers and worked his way up, so he wouldn't waste time closing the drawers.

The second drawer was full of folders of correspondence in German and Spanish on orders for machinery. Caine scanned the material quickly, looking for references to money being moved from Germany or the Paraguayan office, or anything on Peru. But there was nothing, except for a single cryptic reference in a letter that had slipped behind the drawer and had caught on the slot. The letter was a copy of a memo sent by Alois Mengele to the head office in Günzburg more than a year ago. In it Mengele had mentioned a possible need for funds to deal with "*der Seestern*," or "the Starfish." Apart from that there was nothing, Caine decided, wondering what the hell the Starfish was all about. He would have to blow the safe.

He found the wall safe behind a dusty set of ledgers on a five-tiered wall shelf. He explored carefully for alarm wires, but there didn't seem to be any. The gray *plastique* fitted in a ring around the combination lock like a doughnut on a peg. He was just about to insert the detonator, when the overhead light clicked on.

There were two of them, both of them beefy middle-aged men who looked enough like Steiger to be cousins. They had the same cropped hair, bullying air of competence, and unimaginative eyes. They were the kind of men who reacted to orders with that fanatic Prussian sense of discipline the Germans call *Kadavergehorsam*, which makes a corpse snap to attention. Except that they hadn't come to trade war stories with Caine. One of them carried a 6.35mm Walther PPK, the other a sawed-off twelve-gauge shotgun. The guns bracketed Caine neatly between them like parentheses.

"Put your hands on your head, Herr Foster. Slowly. Very slowly," the taller one with the shotgun said, his English thick with German consonants.

They must have been hiding in the other inner office, Caine thought, cursing himself for not having checked. It was a rookie's mistake. The fatal kind, because in this business there are no second chances. If they had come from outside, he would have heard them.

"You've made quite a mess here," the taller one said, his eyes briefly flicking over the scattered papers, but the gun never wavered.

"Don't worry," Caine said. "I have a cleaning lady coming in tomorrow to straighten up."

"A comedian, Fritz," the taller one said. "Don't you think he's a comedian?"

Fritz smiled. It was not a nice smile. Caine didn't get the idea that Fritz thought he was much of a comedian.

"Place the Luger on the desk. Slowly, with two fingers only on the butt," he ordered.

Caine did as he was told, his mind racing. He was remembering Koenig's famous speech about guns. The one they used to have fun imitating over beers at Clyde's in Georgetown. Harris had been good at it, balancing on the balls of his feet and holding his hands on his hips, just like Koenig, his voice a nasal parody of Koenig's deep frog's croak. Throughout the Company, Koenig's theory was a voice crying in the wilderness, but Caine hoped to hell Koenig was right because it was the only chance he had.

"The man with a gun is as vulnerable as the man he's aiming at," the famous speech had begun. "That's because the very fact that he has a gun makes him think that he won't actually have to use it. That expectation slows his reaction time by as much as half-a-second and if you can get close enough, that's all the time you need. If there are two men with guns, it's even better, because each of them will wait for the other to react first and they have to be careful not to hit each other."

Sure, Caine thought miserably, because it didn't look like these two krauts were disciples of Koenig's theories. Right now he wished that Koenig were here to put it to the test instead of him.

Fritz ordered him to face the wall and lean against it for the frisk. Caine positioned himself so that more of his weight was on his feet than his hands. He noted out of the corner of his eye as he turned to the wall that Fritz shoved the Walther in his belt as he approached, so that he would have both hands free for the frisk. He apparently counted on the taller kraut's shotgun to cover Caine. It was the mistake he had been praying for, Caine thought, and he tried to empty his mind so that the action would be instinctual, which is the way the body works best. If you questioned an Olympic champion on what he was thinking when he set the record, the odds are that he wouldn't be able to tell you, because conscious thought only impedes reflex action.

The frisk, as every police rookie learns, is a vulnerable position for the officer, because he has to come within a range where his reaction time is slower than any movement, making his gun useless. The theory is that the prisoner's weight should be on his hands so they can't be used as weapons without losing balance. At the Farm they were taught the theory's basic fallacy, which was that the wall provided a purchase for a rear kick.

The angle would be critical because he had to guess at the exact instant that Fritz's body would be momentarily between him and the shotgun. With his face to the wall he wouldn't be able to see it. He could only feel it through the aikido concept of *irimi*, in which you sense that an opponent has entered your space and the resulting blow combines the force of his momentum against your own. Caine began the calm, rhythmic breathing that would initiate the instantaneous flow of the *kokyu no henka* movement, remembering the way Koichi would stand there in the gym, oblivious to everything except the harmony of his own breathing.

His mind barely had time to register the hard feel of Fritz's hands starting under his armpits when he moved, lashing backward at the right shin with his heel. He caught it wrong, missing the nerve, but it was all right, because the balance was gone and they both were falling. He felt the hot deafening explosion of the shotgun blast singe his ears as he fell backward on top of Fritz, who reacted immediately even before they hit the floor by wrapping his arms around Caine, pinning Caine's arms to his sides in a crushing grip. His upper arms felt useless, as though caught by a steel band, as they both kicked desperately in an attempt to find something to push against for leverage. Caine managed to twist slightly sideways and brought the edge of his right hand in a slicing motion behind him, past his hip. There was the feel of something soft and then hard as his hand connected with the pelvic bone and the satisfying sound of a grunt from Fritz, as the pain hit his groin and slightly loosened his grip.

He sliced again with his hand, this time connecting solidly with the groin. Fritz's sudden scream was lost in the blinding whoosh of a second explosion, the sudden heat searing Caine's skin. Some of the shotgun pellets had hit the can of gasoline on the desk and it had exploded into a fireball. The room filled with white-hot light that dissolved every shadow in a blinding glare. For an instant Caine's hands were almost free, and as he reached behind him for the Bauer, he caught Fritz's middle finger in his left hand, bending it back with a savage twist that snapped the bone like a dry twig.

Out of the corner of his eye Caine saw the barrel of the shotgun somewhere in the blinding glare of flame and fired the Bauer without aiming, wildly emptying the clip in the direction of the shotgun. He managed to roll to his feet, crouching to avoid the fire searing his lungs like acid. The room was going up in flames like a tinderbox, the taller kraut's wounded body burning as it thrashed feebly on the floor like a half-crushed insect.

Caine braced himself as an enraged Fritz came surging up at him, and almost absentmindedly Caine could hear the distant hee-haw of a police siren. Fritz was swinging a wild right hook and at the last second Caine sidestepped away from it and tried a back-knuckle feint to the temple. As Fritz's arm came up to block the blow, Caine executed a reverse spinning round-kick that missed the solar plexus but caught Fritz in the stomach. Fritz started to double over and Caine locked his fingers and smashed down at the back of Fritz's neck in a two-handed chop that smashed Fritz's head into the corner of the burning desk with a crack like the sound of a well-hit baseball. Fritz crumpled to the floor, his body contorted in an awkward posture of death. Caine slapped at his already smoldering clothes as he leaped for the flaming doorway. There were barely seconds left and with a sudden desperate leap he dived headfirst through the doorway, arms over his head and rolled to his feet in the smoke-filled front office. He bolted through the office door and down the corridor toward the side staircase.

As he ran, he could hear the shouts of police and firemen pounding up the front staircase. Ignoring them, he ducked his head and leaped down the stairs, taking almost an entire flight in a single bound, then tore down the side alley away from Independencia Nacional. He ran down the dark empty street toward the car, the echo of his footsteps lost in the rumble of police and fire engines and the howl of approaching sirens. The breath whistled through his lungs like air through a cracked flute as he ran on. His throat was filled with the bleak taste of defeat, like ashes in his mouth. The game was over. He had blown it.

CHAPTER 9

"*Allah akhbar ashadu an la ilaha Allah wa ashadu anna Mohammed rasul Allah,*" the yearning cry of the *muezzin* came warbling from a loudspeaker in the distant El Aqsa mosque. The setting sun gilded the cluster of stone houses crowded over the hills with a rich patina, as of burnished gold. The metallic Dome of the Rock glowed like a burning ember in the brilliant tangerine dusk. The dome dominated the Temple mount, perhaps the holiest spot on earth. It had been built over the gray rock on which, as the legend has it, Abraham had prepared to sacrifice Isaac. That same rock had been the heart of the Holy of Holies of Solomon's Temple, the resting place of the Ark of Moses. Jesus had called the Temple his "Father's House" when he chased the moneylenders from its courtyard. Later, the prophet Mohammed had ascended to heaven from that very spot, the hoofprints struck by his horse still visible on the surface of the rock, according to the Moslems.

Close by the Zion gate stood the Dormition Abbey where the Virgin Mary passed into eternal sleep. Huddled against the abbey on Mount Zion was David's tomb, which also contained the Coenaculum, the room in which Jesus celebrated the Last Supper. The rosy light painted the city with a glowing silence and Caine fancied he could almost hear the mumble of *maariv* prayers of black-robed Orthodox Jews at the Western Wall. Even the traffic along Rehov David Ha-melekh seemed subdued at the twilight hour, the electric Delek sign at a corner gas station burning white and solitary as an eternal light. Someone had to say it, and finally Temira, Amnon's wife, brought it out, the cherry tip of her cigarette describing an arc in the gathering darkness as she took it from her mouth.

"Jerusalem the Golden," she said.

They were sitting at a table on Amnon and Temira's apartment balcony overlooking the city. Scattered on the table were the remains of the meal, plates of humus and tahini and kabob scraped clean with torn pieces of pita bread. They were sipping Turkish coffee from small demitasse cups, a drink Temira made with as much sugar as coffee.

The faint breath of the evening breeze cooled their skin, after the blistering afternoon heat of the *khamsin*, the hot, scouring wind that blew from the desert of Arabia. The word *khamsin* came from the Arabic word for "fifty," because there were supposed to be fifty such days every year, when instead of the prevailing Mediterranean breeze the wind came hot and dry and full of static electricity from the desert. It was an oppressive and irritating wind and a law, dating from the days of Turkish rule and still on the books in Israel, stated that if a man murdered his wife after three consecutive days of *khamsin*, he was not to be charged, because no one could be expected to put up with nagging after three days of *khamsin*. Now the cool breeze had brought a sense of peace to the spectacular golden sunset, characteristic of the end of *khamsin*.

"The City of Peace," Yoshua said without a trace of irony, putting his cup on the table with a faint clink. Perhaps he really believed it.

"Until the next time the PLO leaves a *plastique* calling card at a crowded bus station," Caine said, stretching his frame restlessly against the chair. He lit a cigarette and watched the exhaled smoke form a cloud, twisted as a challah Sabbath bread, over the honey-colored city.

"We live in dangerous times," Amnon pronounced sententiously.

"Words to live by," Caine responded sarcastically, conscious of the irony that Amnon's clichéd sentence, like all clichés, held a seed of truth.

"And so we do. This land has been a battleground for ten thousand years," Amnon said pedantically, his triple captain's bars gleaming like gold on his epaulets in the fading twilight. He lit a cigarette, his dark face glowing in the match flare like the head of Caesar on an ancient bronze coin. He had the tan skin and curly hair of the Moroccan Jews, with intelligent brown eyes and an intense manner that might have given him the appearnce of an Arab intellectual were it not for the Israeli Army officer's uniform he wore.

"That's the trouble with this country, it's been gorged with soldiers and religious nuts for too long," Temira put in, tossing her long dark hair with a nervous gesture. Amnon looked at her sharply, as though she were resurrecting a long-standing quarrel.

"The trouble with this country is that our very shortsighted God had Moses pick the only damn place in the Middle East where there isn't any oil," Yoshua said, grinning, and they all laughed.

That was what he liked best about the Jews, their finely honed sense of gallows humor, Caine realized, feeling himself relax for the first time in two weeks. They had been among the most frustrating weeks of his life and it felt good to be trying something positive again, even if it blew up in his face. And if the Israelis followed procedure, that's exactly what would happen. But he didn't care anymore. Because unless they could give him a lead, it was all over anyway.

He had escaped from Paraguay following the same route Mengele had used. Abandoning the Ford on a side street of Pôrto Merdes on the Brazilian side of the Paraná, he had taken a river launch to Puerto Iguassú. From there he had hopped a local flight to Buenos Aires to meet with Judge Luque.

The judge was a slender, aristocratic man who proved to be sympathetic, but not very helpful. He could only confirm what Caine already knew. Mengele hadn't been sighted in more than six years. Caine promised to keep in touch if he found anything and caught the morning Aerolineas flight to Bariloche.

It was high summer in Bariloche, the streets and cafés thronged with festive crowds up from Buenos Aires for the Bavarian beer and clear mountain air. German and Spanish were the languages he heard as he brushed by couples in shorts, who spent the time between heavy sauerbraten meals shopping for camera film and sunburn lotion, and every afternoon at three, an oom-pah-pah band gave a concert in the small town square.

But Caine couldn't exactly share the holiday mood, because he was dirty from the minute he had checked

into the Lorelei, an Alpine chalet with a wooden facade carved into more curlicues than an Afro hairdo.
The first time they came at him was on the curving
mountain road on the way to Cerro Catedral, its
snow-capped peak sparkling in the bright sunshine.
Two blond young men in a BMW had tried to force
his rented Mustang over the precipice at the edge of
the road. He had managed to throw the Mustang
across the road in a racing skid that brought him hard
against the cliff face, badly denting the fender. His
hands were still clenched around the wheel as he
watched the BMW disappear around a curve, leaving
a cloud of exhaust fumes hanging over the road like a
memory.

The second time was more serious. It was evening
during the dinner-hour promenade in the plaza, the
couples talking and flirting while the boisterous
sounds of the serious beer drinkers resounded from
the sidewalk cafés. He knew they weren't kidding this
time because it was a front-and-rear tail and when he
tried to reverse, so that he could flush and tail one of
them and find out what it was all about, he discovered that it was a four-man box. They were serious
and professional, the two blond men from the BMW
and the two older types. They took their time because
they knew exactly what they were doing, and he knew
he wasn't going anywhere.

The Foster cover was blown wide open and the
only chance he had was to get out. Somewhere he had
cut one corner too many and the word had gone out,
probably from Paraguay. Like a spider sensing an in-
truder by tremblings in the web, Mengele had become aware of his inquiries and had given orders. The
hunter had become the prey.

What made it all the more frustrating was that there was no clue to Mengele's whereabouts in Bariloche. But that didn't matter anymore because the town had become a death trap for him. His only chance lay in sticking with the crowd. As he threaded his way through the promenade, like a desperate halfback, he latched onto a pretty blond waitress in a dirndl sitting at a café with some friends. They needed a ride to a house party in the hills and the next thing he knew, they all piled into the Mustang. Later he was able to slip out of the party around the time that it got to the jumping-in-the-pool stage. He left the waitress delicately snoring on a pile of clothing in one of the bedrooms, her skirt pulled up over her hips and a naked bleary-eyed young man tugging at her sleeping legs, trying to separate them.

In the morning Caine was able to take the airport bus, hugging the security of the crowd, and safely boarded the first flight back to Buenos Aires. From there he had connected to Madrid, being careful to always keep a crowd between him and the two tails.

The two blond men from the BMW stayed with him all the way to Madrid, where they peeled off. He knew it wasn't because they had lost interest. They wouldn't do that until he had a paper tag tied to his big toe in the deep-freeze box of some local morgue. They were Judas goats, there to identify him to whoever had picked up the contract to terminate him. The fact that they were gone only meant that someone new had picked up the tag. And they weren't playing for baseball cards, because whoever took over had been good and Caine had been unable to spot him until Rome, when he made a break at the taxi stand at Fiumicino Airport. The tail was a tall, well-dressed Mediterranean type with wraparound sunglasses and chiseled features that must have wowed the Scandinavian girls who came to disco on the Costa Brava. He hurriedly grabbed the taxi right behind Caine's.

Caine made the break in the middle of a colossal Roman traffic jam, the Fiats honking and climbing the sidewalks. He handed a wad of lire to the driver, then jumped out of the taxi and weaved his way through the bedlam of horns and noisy Italian comments on his ancestry to a department store, where he picked up a Tyrolean-style hat and raincoat, then added a false mustache to change the image. He left the department store by a side entrance after quickly scanning the crowd for Mr. Sunglasses. Although Caine appeared to have lost him, he knew that he would have to jump back into the frying pan to catch his connecting flight. Fiumicino was the red zone, where they would try to pick him up again. He waited under the big Cinzano sign for the Alitalia flight to Ben-Gurion Airport near Tel Aviv, booked under his own name, until he felt reasonably sure he was clean by the time he boarded.

Things were becoming a little too hairy, he thought. When they forced you to use your own ID to change the image, it was time to start reaching for the rip cord. Then he remembered the stamps and C.J., her long lithe legs opening to him and the little cry of pleasure when he entered her. It was all his if he could pull it off. He remembered the old Gypsy and knew that he no longer had any choice in the matter. He had to go on with it, no matter how many alarm bells he set off, or what kind of nasty little back-alley death they had planned for him.

"Are you done, Signore?" the Alitalia stewardess with the dark eyes that matched her uniform was asking him, gesturing at the pinkish melting ice cubes that was all that was left of his Campari and soda.

"Si, grazie."

"Prego."

He had telephoned Yoshua from Ben-Gurion Airport and it was Yoshua, whom he had worked with on the Abu Daud job in Paris, who had set him up for this evening's meeting with Amnon Sofer, a Mossad staff intelligence officer. So far as Yoshua knew, Caine was still working for the Company. Caine let him believe that and Yoshua didn't press him. One of the advantages of being a spy is not having to do a lot of talking about your work.

"Retribution," said Amnon quietly, picking a speck of tobacco from his lip. Myriad pinpoints of light began to blink on in the gathering darkness, the hills dotted with them like the bivouac fires of an invading army. The air had grown cold and soon they would have to move inside.

"An eye for an eye. The biblical injunction still applies," Yoshua said. Temira began to clear away the dishes and take them inside.

"To be sure, to be sure," Amnon murmured, raising his eyebrow as a signal to Yoshua to leave them alone. Yoshua got up and went inside and Caine could hear the musical babble of Hebrew as Yoshua began talking with Temira. He became aware of the sound of a radio newscast being turned on. The announcer was mentioning the names of politicians and using the word *shalom*, so Caine assumed that he was saying something about peace talks. Amnon pulled a cigarette out of his pack of Dubek's, Caine struck a match, and they both lit up. Smoking was a national epidemic among the excitable Israelis, Caine observed.

"Why is the Company suddenly interested in Mengele? And why does your being here have to be unofficial?" Amnon said.

"I'm an operative, not the DCI. They only tell me what to do, not why." Caine shrugged.

"Retribution," Amnon said again. "We've been trying to get away from that policy for a long time, since the days of Isar Harel."

"That's not what Yoshua thinks. 'An eye for an eye,' he said. And the hate in his eyes was real enough."

"Get any two Jews together and you're bound to get at least three opinions on everything. Anyway, Yoshua doesn't make policy."

"Don't tell me the policymakers don't have to take men like Yoshua into account."

"I remember someone once asked Levi Eshkol—blessings on his memory—how it felt to be prime minister. Eshkol replied, 'You try being prime minister of a country with three million prime ministers,'" Amnon said, chuckling.

"Are you trying to tell me that the Mossad no longer has any interest in the Nazis?"

"Let's just say that we have all the present enemies we can handle. We don't need to go around trying to dig up enemies from the past," Amnon observed mildly. The pale crescent moon hung over the city like an Islamic omen, as if to underscore what Amnon was saying.

"Don't tell me the Jews have decided to forgive and forget the *malachos mavet* of Auschwitz," Caine retorted.

Amnon smiled at Caine's clumsy Hebrew pronunciation. Then he sighed and shook his head, the cigarette tip glowing like a tiny beacon in the shadows of his face. His sad Jewish eyes examined Caine's face carefully.

"*Im eshkahaich Yerushalaim,* If I forget thee, O Jerusalem. No, we haven't forgotten, or forgiven," he said at last.

"Look I don't know what the Company is running or why. My job is to locate Mengele. Period. If there's more, they'll tell me when the time comes. We work strictly on a need-to-know basis, you know that. But I doubt that retribution has anything to do with it. The Company isn't given to subscribing to Jewish philanthropies. Whatever it is, it's strictly top drawer, 'For your eyes only,' because otherwise we'd be running it through channels. Now do you have a lead on the son of a bitch or don't you?" Caine said irritably, standing up. He had played his trump and all he could do was hope that his manufactured anger was convincing.

"All right, you make your point. Sit down, *chaver.* Please," Amnon said placatingly. "I was just feeling you out. We Jews have to argue about everything, didn't you know that?" Amnon said with a wink. Caine couldn't help himself. He let out a snort of laughter and sat down.

He pulled on his jacket. The night had grown cold. "What have you got?" he asked.

"Do you know Feinberg?"

"Only by reputation. Didn't he supply the key lead for the Eichmann snatch?"

"Also Wiese, the Butcher of Bialystok, Ehle, the Mauer brothers, Franz Stangl, the commander of Treblinka, and dozens more. Feinberg operates the Jewish Relief Center in Vienna. No, he *is* the Jewish Relief Center."

"What about him?"

"He came to us about three months ago and told us he might have a lead on Mengele. But he said it would require a large bribe. I believe fifty thousand Deutschmarks was mentioned."

"What happened?"

"Fifty thousand marks is a lot a money, *chaver*. We don't have billions to play with like the CIA," Amnon said with a touch of bitterness. "Anyway, we kicked around the idea and decided not to pursue it. Our resources in money and manpower were already stretched to the breaking point."

"Why didn't you come to us?"

Amnon looked at him scornfully.

"Didn't you say yourself that the Company isn't given to subscribing to Jewish philanthropies. Besides, if the Americans or anybody else had ever really gone after Mengele, he would have been brought around the corner a long time ago. Mengele has survived because of official indifference, that's all. Just indifference."

"Well, we're not indifferent now. And I've got the money. So do me a favor and let Feinberg know I'm coming. And *chaver*," Caine said sharply, "this conversation never happened."

The two men got up and shook hands. Then, almost as if it had been rehearsed, they both looked out at the pale, jumbled lights of Jerusalem, the stars hanging in the night sky, like a heavenly mirror of the city.

"It's a pleasure doing business with you, *Adon*,"— Amnon hesitated briefly, searching his memory for the name Caine was using—"Foster."

* * *

They drove in silence down from the Judean hills toward Tel Aviv, situated on the coastal plain that had been the Via Maris, the pathway of armies since long before recorded history, because it was the only route across the mountains and deserts that separated the ancient empires of Africa and Asia. The car radio was tuned to Israeli pop music broadcast from Kol Yisrael. The music struck Caine as pleasant but a little repetitious. All the songs seemed to sound alike. It was a little like having bad sex, he thought. The sensation isn't unpleasant, but you're not sorry when it's over. Every so often Yoshua glanced away from his driving and over at Caine, as though he wanted to say something but was waiting for Caine to begin.

The headlights picked out the ancient wrecks of World War II vintage armored cars and burnt-out truck chassis that littered the sides of the road. During the 1948 War of Independence the Israelis had tried desperately to run the blockade of this road to reach besieged Jerusalem. After the war they had painted the wrecks with blood-red antirust paint, garlanded them with flowered wreaths, and left them beside the road as memorials. There were times, Caine thought, when it was impossible to escape the notion that the world was nothing but a vast graveyard.

"Do you have any children?" Yoshua asked, and Caine knew that he was thinking about a recent terrorist incident in Metulla where two children had been killed. For a moment the image of Lim, laughing and pregnant in a field of flowering poppies, flashed into his mind. Then he remembered the first time he had seen Lim's daughter, sitting motionless on the porch of the hut and staring out into the rain. He tried to push the image away and forced himself to think of C.J., as she looked in the flickering glow from the fireplace, her long blond hair cascading over them like a shower of golden silk.

"No," he said.

"That's the worst, that's where they really get you. When they get the children," Yoshua said grimly, and Caine suddenly realized that Yoshua was too emotional for this business. Maybe the Israelis knew it too and that was why they had called him back from Paris.

"That's not the worst," Caine said and regretted it as soon as he said it, because he couldn't stop it now. It was like releasing the cork in a bottle of champagne and the images began to spill over, the old tightness closing on his chest like a vise.

"Then what is?"

"The worst are the things we do ourselves," Caine said, wondering how it was that Yoshua didn't know that. Wasn't it Yoshua himself who had said, "In the end we are all murderers"? And then it didn't matter because he was remembering Teu La. He remembered how Dao had looked at him, with that strange mixture of curiosity and indifference, as though Caine had been a spoiled child throwing a temper tantrum, when he had argued furiously against the raid. Even as he had shouted and threatened, he could sense Dao deciding whether it was worth having him killed. Maybe that thought had held him back. Maybe that was why he hadn't tried to kill Dao right then and there.

There was no military reason for it, he remembered shouting. There was no reason at all, because the pull-out had already begun and their only function was to distract Charley to cover the withdrawal. Except that reasons no longer mattered in a world where everything was falling to pieces, while the diplomats at the Paris peace talks had already spent more than a year debating the shape of the table for the parley.

Dao had stood there, swaying and dangerous, his eyes bloodshot from the corn liquor. All of them drunk and miserable in the fetid heat of the bush, the mosquitoes rising around them in clouds thick as mist. They had been savagely mauled for two solid days in the Plain of Jars by the heavy mortars of a full Pathet Lao division, supported by VC artillery. By the third day they were using bodies to make breastworks to crouch under, the bodies bloated black and green with the heat and the unforgettable stench of death that permeated every breath. They burrowed under the damp earth and piles of bodies like insects, the constant explosions blowing the limbs of the living and the dead into an endless rain of bleeding flesh.

When they finally escaped into the bush, it was more of a stampede than a retreat, and when they collected at the fallback site, a muddy clearing thick with snakes and land crabs, they had fallen on the corn liquor with the desperation of desert travelers on oasis water. There were barely two hundred of them left, most of them strangers to him, with the hollow eyes and rabid glare of a pack of starving dogs. Perhaps that was why it had happened. Or perhaps it was because of the wounded they had had to leave behind, like Vang, with his belly ripped open, holding his own intestines in his hands, like strings of sausages. Or Pao, stumbling blindly among the shell holes, talking to himself about getting home for the rice harvest, with one eye ripped completely away and the other eyeball hanging down his cheek from its empty red socket. Or Lynhiavu, who caught a bullet with Caine's name on it, except that he had turned away for a second and when he turned back, Lynhiavu was lying there with a faint Buddha-like smile on his face and his brains dripping out of a hole in his head the size of a baby's fist. Or perhaps . . . well, perhaps it didn't matter why.

"It's murder, Dao," Caine had shouted.

Dao blinked at him like a sleepy owl, then shrugged and took another swig from the jug, stumbling and falling into the mud.

"So it's murder, so what," Dao had muttered thickly. "What do you think war is, you stinking, fucking Yankee? War is murder, not one of your Anglo-Saxon fucking games with rules. There are only murderers and victims," he howled. "Murderers and victims!" grabbing an M-16 and emptying the magazine in Caine's direction, except that he was so drunk that all he did was prune a few trees, their leaves fluttering to the ground like wounded birds.

They were nearing Latrun, the silhouette of the old Arab fort on the hill a dark shadow against the starry night. In '48 Latrun had been held by the Arab Legion to cut off the Jerusalem road. In the end the Haganah had been reduced to attacking the escarpment with green, untrained troops, but all they had managed to do was to soak the wheatfields with blood. Human blood was the one commodity that never seemed in short supply, Caine mused. In the end the Haganah had been forced to build the legendary "Burma road," across the mountains, to outflank the Latrun salient.

"What do you Americans know about the worst, anyway?" Yoshua was saying. "War and terrorism are something you watch over dinner on the seven o'clock news, just before the football highlights."

"I suppose you're right," Caine said indifferently, wishing to God he would shut up. Turning his eyes back to the road, Yoshua flicked his lights and passed an army Jeep on a blind curve. Caine closed his eyes for a moment, with the thought that all Israeli drivers are born fatalists.

Well, what would a fatalist make of Teu La? he wondered. They had attacked the hamlet at dawn, sending a patrol down to the ravine on the opposite side of the village, to cut off any chance of escape. The terrified peasants of Teu La had hidden Pathet Lao arms and guerrillas, and as Lao tribesmen, they had always had a basic sense of superiority to the Hmong, whom they regarded as little better than savages. It had gone beyond war, Caine realized as the Meos moved into the village. It had degenerated into a tribal conflict, a chance to settle old scores.

The sun came up hot and bright into an unblemished blue sky, the dawn evanescent and brief as a single heartbeat. Birds were chirping among the palm fronds and the lazy hum of insects rose from the dried mud fields. Although they were drunk and exhausted, the Hmong moved purposefully into position, just as he had trained them. When Dao gave the signal, they charged headlong, screaming the old war cries, two to a hut. The procedure was always the same. First the grenade tossed into the hut and they hit the ground, flattening themselves against the explosion. Before the smoke cleared, they would leap inside to spray the hut with a carbine, just in case the grenade hadn't got the attention of those inside. Then matches or a lighter were applied to the thatched sides and roof and then they sprinted to the next hut.

In a little while all of the huts were burning, sending an acrid column of smoke up to stain the empty sky. The air was full of screams and war cries and the sounds of firing as Caine jogged toward the ravine, sweat stinging his eyes. There were only a few old men trapped in the ravine, pulling their rags about their bodies as though the cloth could protect them from bullets. All the rest were women and children, wailing incomprehensibly as if they were being punished for doing something wrong. The women pressed the children close to their bodies with trembling arms, their eyes wide and desperate.

Half-a-dozen tribesmen had cornered a pretty Lao girl, her chest heaving and wet with sweat. They were laughing as they ripped her clothes off and pinned her face down over the body of an old woman. Her thin buttocks quivered as they began to take turns mounting her, arguing about whether to start first with her vagina or her anus.

When Caine reached the edge of the ravine, the shooting had already started. Dao was still drinking from the jug and every so often he would stagger to his feet and fire his M-16 into the ravine, the M-16 that Caine had given him. One of the Meo grabbed an infant from its mother, made a funny face to make the baby laugh, then threw the baby into the air and shot it before it hit the ground. A few of them had tied an old man to a tree near the ravine and were shooting their crossbows at him, being careful to avoid a fatal shot. The old man twisted and groaned as one by one, the arrows snicked into his body, until there were so many arrows sticking out of him, he looked like a medieval fresco of the martyrdom of St. Stephen.

They were still firing into the ravine, which was a tangled mass of blood and bodies, limbs still thrashing, like a scene that could only be painted by Goya. A wounded moon-faced woman with a small boy in her arms was trying to scramble out of the ravine, her hand desperately clutching at a tuft of grass. Dao leaned over, as though to help her, placed the muzzle of the M-16 against the child's head, and fired. The head exploded into a thousand fragments and the woman fell back with a scream that went on till Dao fired again.

Caine raised his M-16 and brought Dao into his sights. Dao turned to look at him, his eyes dark and opaque, but he didn't raise his gun. Instead he just shrugged and shouted.

"They're Communists, Tan Caine. That's all. Just Communists. Then we kill them. Then they're nothing. Nothing at all."

Caine tried to squeeze the trigger, but he couldn't because it didn't matter anymore, because nothing did. And because he knew that in some way he had brought them to this. They're ours, he thought bitterly. We're the ones who paid them and taught them how to fight a *civilized* war. That's how it happens. Once the killing starts, there's no place to draw the line. He threw his M-16 into the ravine and turned away. As he walked, a refrain from a song Country Joe had sung at Woodstock kept running through his mind until he thought he would literally go mad with it. Round and round it went with the numbers, like a children's nursery rhyme:

> *And it's one-two-three*
> *What are we fighting for?*
> *Don't ask me, I don't give a damn,*
> *The next stop is Vietnam.*

He saw one of the tribesmen dismount the motion-less body of the raped girl, and apparently dissatis-fied, he pulled an old .45 automatic out of his belt and blew half her head off.

"How did your talk with Amnon go?" Yoshua wanted to know.

"Okay," Caine said wearily. Give it a rest, will you? Just give it a rest, he told himself. He lit a cigarette and rolled the window down a few inches to let the smoke escape out to the rush of cold night air. The images fled back into the night of the soul, like the smoke drawn away by the suction created by the car's speed. Yoshua slowed down as they entered Re-hovot, site of the Weizmann Institute, where much of the work on the Israeli nuclear project went on. The streets were filled with noisy young people in shorts, milling in front of movie houses and sipping ubiqui-tous bottles of *gazoz* soda pop.

"When you left Paris, was Claude still doing busi-ness?" Caine asked. Yoshua pounded irritably on the horn at the driver in front of him, who had the *chutz-pah* to wait for the light to turn green before start-ing to move.

"The Claudes of the world never go out of busi-ness," Yoshua pronounced.

Caine was getting a little tired of Yoshua's brand of saloon philosophy, the kind they print on cocktail nap-kins. The memories were getting to him, he realized, and he was on the verge of telling Yoshua to stuff it.

He held himself back, realizing that that wasn't a good idea; the last thing in the world he wanted was to get the Israelis interested in him any more than they already were. Only Amnon and Yoshua knew him here and he was hoping they would let it go at that.

He thought about Claude, whom he knew only by hearsay as an independent counterfeiter from Marseille who impartially produced documents for the Sûreté Nationale and the Corsican gangs, with a fine lack of distinction for anything except the price. He had first heard of Claude from the suave plainclothesman from the rue des Saussaies who had arranged for his exit from France after the Abu Daud hit. He wanted to get Claude started on a new cover for him even before he saw Feinberg. By now the Foster cover was as effective a bit of camouflage as a red flag waved in front of a bull.

Yoshua dropped him off at the Dan Hotel on the crowded Tel Aviv beachfront. Along Rehov Hayarkon near the hotel entrance, miniskirted girl soldiers walked hand-in-hand with tanned boyfriends, street cafés echoed with boisterous shouts and shabby moneychangers clustered like flies around the tourists, offering to exchange dollars for Israeli pounds at black-market rates that were quoted daily in the *Jerusalem Post*. When he was back in his room, Caine called the international operator and left word for her to call him when she had made the connections to L.A. and Marseille. Then he stripped off his clothes, took a long shower, and went to bed.

He dreamed he was back at the Moonglow with C.J., the surf pounding at the pilings as though they were about to be washed out to sea. He was telling her that he couldn't marry her, because he already had a wife, someone he had left behind in Asia. Her blue eyes were wet and shiny and she was saying something, but he couldn't hear her because the damn telephone was ringing and then he came awake, dripping with sweat, as though surfacing from the sea and fumbled for the phone by his bed. The international operator had finally put his call through, he realized grabbing the receiver. The dull roar of surf came through the earpiece. It was like holding a seashell to his ear.

"This is Wasserman, who is this?" he heard Wasserman's voice say.

"This is an open line, so let's keep it brief," Caine said, hoping that the transatlantic traffic was busy tonight. These days if you want to pass something on the telephone, you might as well take out a full-page ad in the *Times*.

"How's it going?" Good, he thought. Wasserman had picked up his cue. Now let's see if he picked up the tab.

"We've got a solid lead on that lost consignment of angels, but it's going to be expensive to cover the tariff."

"How expensive?"

"Thirty-five K." The extra money might come in handy. Sitting down to play with less than you can afford to bet is the surest way to guarantee losing, Caine thought.

"That's some tariff," Wasserman said, pausing to consider.

"In for a penny, in for a pound. It's part of the deal."

"Nobody likes a *shnorrer*," Wasserman said, and Caine pictured him in the office, glancing at the Monet and lighting a cigar, enjoying his brief moment of power for all it was worth. Where was C.J. now? Caine wondered, feeling a sudden pang of hatred for Wasserman.

"The goods are worth the price," Caine said harshly.

"Is this absolutely necessary?" Wasserman replied equally harshly, and Caine felt that he was hearing the man's true voice for the first time. It was a legitimate question—perhaps the only legitimate question that Wasserman could ever ask him, since Wasserman didn't know how the game was going, or what the scoreboard read.

"Do you think I'd risk a call if it weren't?"

"How do we arrange the transfer of funds?" And Caine felt himself breathing again. He could almost smell his quarry and he badly wanted the game to go on. Perhaps Wasserman had felt it too. In for a penny in for a pound, he thought, a surge of relief coursing through his veins like a shot of alcohol.

"With a certified letter-of-credit bearer bond, sent to me, care of *poste restante* in Vienna."

"Don't be such a *chozzer* next time," Wasserman said with a good-natured tone. He knew Caine must be on to something or he would never have risked a call.

"*Shalom*," Caine said, and hung up. He was smiling as he lit a cigarette and leaned his head on his hands against the headboard of the bed. For no reason, a quote from Shakespeare's *Richard III* had popped into his mind:

"God take King Edward to his mercy,/And leave the world for me to bustle in!"

CHAPTER 10

"So Heinrich Müller is dead. Pity," Feinberg said deliberately, sucking his teeth as though it helped him digest the information.

"Let's not waste too many crocodile tears on him. He wasn't what you would call a choirboy," Caine put in sarcastically.

"That he wasn't," Feinberg agreed. "In a way, he achieved a certain celebrity. You see, Müller was the SS officer responsible for the massacre of tens of thousands of Jews at Babi Yar in the Ukraine. A Russian poet wrote a famous poem about it." The corners of his eyes behind the bifocal lenses crinkled as he ventured an apologetic smile. "I'm afraid I can never remember poetry. Still it's a pity you weren't able to get more out of him. He's been on my list for a long time."

"He wasn't exactly in a talkative mood," Caine observed.

Feinberg smiled appreciatively and began to stuff his pipe with tobacco in a slow, deliberate manner. He carefully tamped the tobacco down, lit it, then dissatisfied with the draw, he tamped it down again, with the precision of an old man who has lived alone for a long time. He would pursue Nazi fugitives in the same careful way, Caine mused, with the strict, plodding attention to detail that was bound to trip them up in the end. Except that Caine was on a deadline, and he knew he could never work that way in any case.

Feinberg was a big man, perhaps six foot, with a large frame that had already begun to shrink with age, giving his untidy navy suit the appearance of being too big for him. His remaining wisps of hair were disheveled and combined with his wire-rimmed bifocals to give him the air of a quiet scholar, far too preoccupied with his work to pay much attention to appearances. Which was probably close to the truth, Caine realized, as he glanced around the cramped two-room apartment on Rudolf Platz, which served as the office for the Jewish Relief Center.

Both rooms of the apartment had every inch of wall space lined with floor-to-ceiling bookshelves bursting with files, creating the claustrophobic atmosphere of a Dickensian counting house—file cabinets that looked as if they had been ransacked, spilled papers onto old desks and a moth-eaten couch, and motes of dust floated like water lilies on the musty air. Scrooge would have felt right at home here, Caine mused. From the front room that served as a cramped reception area came the pecking sound of the petite brunette, Feinberg's granddaughter, at an ancient manual typewriter. The typing was regular and insistent, like the rapping of a methodical woodpecker. Feinberg's desk was piled high with folders, tilted precariously, like paper Towers of Pisa.

"Peru, *ja*, that fits," Feinberg said, pensively tapping his pipe stem against his teeth, unconsciously falling into the rhythm of the typewriter's deliberate tapping. "Quoth the Raven, 'Nevermore,'" Caine thought, following Feinberg's nearsighted gaze to the small grimy window. Through it he could see the jumble of buildings surrounding Saint Stephen's Cathedral and beyond to the heavy afternoon traffic on Franz-Josefs-Kai, along the pea-soup-green Danube Canal.

The traffic moved slowly in the cold rain that had been falling all day. Pedestrians with black umbrellas scurried across the square, looking like moving mushrooms from the third-floor vantage of the window rattling restlessly with the wind. But the gray weather couldn't dampen the spirits of a group of blue-uniformed *gymnasium* students, drinking beer and roughhousing in the small park in the middle of the square. After all, it was *Fasching,* the carnival season when the German-speaking world relentlessly pursues pleasure as if it were a military duty. The season when every night is party night, from posh white-tie affairs like the *Opernball* to all-night student parties in the Brauerei, when beer and *heuriger* wine is downed endlessly from liter-size glasses and adultery is not grounds for divorce. Looking out at the handsome young people larking in the baroque splendors of the city, the streets glistening in the rain, he found it hard to believe that Adolf Hitler had been born in this picture-postcard land.

"Why does Peru fit?" Caine asked.

"About three years ago, I got a letter from a Jew named Samuel Cohen. He owned a small clothing store in Iquitos in the Peruvian Amazon. He claimed to have spotted Mengele in Iquitos."

"That's not much to go on."

"Cohen had been an inmate at Auschwitz and Treblinka, before immigrating to Peru after the war. Naturally I wrote back asking him for details, but he never answered. I wrote again and about six months later I received a note from his wife. She wrote that he had been killed in an auto accident while on a business trip to Lima."

"That isn't why you contacted the Mossad," Caine said disgustedly. He had been hoping for a real lead, instead of a three-year-old maybe. The letter of credit he had cashed that morning and converted into Deutschmarks at the Handelsbank was burning a hole in his pocket. Some instinct had told him that Feinberg was on to something and he was anxious to get on with it. Feinberg's pale-blue eyes were distorted like fish eyes by the bifocal lenses. Once they had saved his life, Feinberg had told him, when an SS guard in a jovial mood had plucked him out of a line of inmates scheduled for the gas chambers, slapped him on the back with a playful gesture, and told him that no one with blue eyes would be sent up the chimney that day. Now those eyes regarded Caine with a steady, serious gaze.

"Why is the CIA suddenly interested in Mengele?"

Caine shrugged elaborately, hoping he wasn't overdoing it.

"That's what I'm supposed to find out. Something's up and Mengele is the key. So our mutual interests happen to dovetail at this point."

"I don't want him killed," Feinberg said sharply, his old man's voice a reedy treble. "I want him brought back to Frankfurt to stand trial. When the crime is so great, no punishment that man can devise will ever fit."

"I thought you wanted revenge. Isn't that what it's all about?"

"*Nein,* not at all. My business is prevention, not retribution. I believe it was one of your American philosophers, Santayana, who said that those who do not remember history will be condemned to repeat it. A major war-crimes trial reminds the public that the Holocaust was not a myth, that it really happened. By reminding people of what happened, we help ensure that it will never happen again"—the old man's eyes glinting with the zeal of the true believer. Perhaps it had been that fire, that consuming sense of a holy mission, that had kept him alive in the death camps, Caine reflected.

"What have you got?"

"You will bring him back to stand trial?"

"If I can," Caine lied, trying Harris's patented smile of sincerity on for size. "What have you got?" Come on, he thought. Come on.

"It will take money, a lot of money," Feinberg said intently.

Caine took a thick wad of Deutschmarks out of his pocket and slapped it onto the crowded desk, as if he were laying down a bet. Feinberg's eyes widened slightly and he allowed himself a nervous smile.

"What have you got?" Caine repeated.

Feinberg relit his pipe, took a few puffs, and then put it down. It was an uncomfortable moment for him. In the jargon of the intelligence trade, he was about to "drop his pants." Come on, sweetie, Caine thought anxiously. Drop your pants and show the boys what you got. The Vaseline is on the table.

"About three months ago I got a curious call from a man who identified himself as Hans Gröbel. He said

he had read about me in the newspapers and he had
some information that he was sure would interest me.
He was in Vienna on business and suggested that we
get together for lunch. I get many such calls." Feinberg smiled apologetically. "Usually they're just a
nuisance, but this time, well, I guess my instincts were
in good working order. Sometimes all the publicity I
get has its uses," he remarked. "At first I was going to
hang up on him, but then he said something about
'ein grosse Fisch,' a big fish, and I knew that it would
always bother me if I didn't see him.

"Anyway," Feinberg shrugged, "we met in a private
dining room in the Griechenbeisl, near the post office.
He was a short, fat man in his fifties, with dark hair
and thick horn-rimmed glasses. He was dressed very
neatly and he seemed very fastidious about his food. I
wasn't surprised when he told me he was *ein Rech-
nungsführer*," searching for the word in English, "*ja*, an
accountant. He seemed very upset because there were
rumors where he worked that on account of the reces-
sion he might be one of those let go. He was very
aggrieved on that point. He felt that after twenty
years with the firm that they were betraying him. In
his bookkeeping he had noticed something funny
going on, and what with his changed attitude about
his employers, he secretly began to make Xerox copies
of certain things. He wouldn't tell me what he had,
but he offered to sell me the lot for fifty thousand
marks in cash." Feinberg's eyes strayed to the money
on the desk.

"I tried to explain to him that, the newspaper stories
notwithstanding, I didn't have that kind of money,
and besides I had no idea what I might be buying.
His papers might be worthless. I tried to bargain with

him, but he was adamant about the price. It was a kind of obsession with him, the sum he had calculated he would need for his retirement. And he kept saying, *ein grosser Fisch,* as if that too were an obsession that he kept doggedly repeating, like a phonograph needle stuck in a groove.

"To tell you the truth, I was beginning to think he was a crank and tried to terminate the meal. Then he told me a little more about himself and I was able to check him out later. What he said turned out to be true and that's when I contacted the Mossad for the money. Unfortunately they didn't come through." He hesitated delicately. "Until now," Feinberg added, leaning forward across the desk.

"It turns out that during the war our Herr Gröbel had worked as an accountant in *Amt* Two of the RSHA. Do you know about the RSHA?"

Caine shook his head, and with a satisfied nod Feinberg went on.

"The Reichssicherheitshauptamt, or Reich Central Security Office, was the centralized bureau set up by the Nazis to handle internal security matters, including the camps. Their office was directly responsible for the death of over fifteen million people. The bureau consisted of six sections, or *Amts,* each of which had a specific function. *Amts* One and Two, where Gröbel worked, handled administrative and financial matters, respectively. *Amt* Three was the SD, the infamous security *Polizei,* which also acted as the controlling department of the entire RSHA. *Amt* Four was the Gestapo, where Eichmann worked. *Amt* Five handled criminal activity, and *Amt* Six was the Abwehr, the Reich's foreign intelligence agency."

"I appreciate the history lesson," Caine said irritably, "but what difference does it make?" Take it easy, he told himself. Don't spook him, because he's got something, and suddenly Caine's senses were completely alive. Something told him he was getting close. Feinberg worked on a shoestring; all you had to do was to look at the office to know that. So he wasn't about to spend fifty thousand marks on hot air and sauerkraut. He had something.

"Don't you see," Feinberg said intently, his eyes sparkling with intelligence, as though with passion, "after all those years with the RSHA, they trusted him. After the war he spent twenty years with the same company, so if there was something funny, something that would indeed lead to *ein grosser Fisch,* he would be sure to spot it."

"But he didn't tell you what it was?"

"No, he didn't. But he did call me about two weeks ago to tell me that he had been laid off and was I still interested. I told him yes and asked him to give me a little more time to get the money. We agreed that as soon as I got it, I would send him a note, care of *poste restante* in Stuttgart. At first I called some people, but since I couldn't be specific, I wasn't getting very far in raising the money. Your timing couldn't have been better, Herr Foster. As soon as I got Amnon's call, I sent the note and Gröbel called me. I'm meeting him, alone, tomorrow night."

"Where?"

"He said *alone,* Herr Foster, and he knows them well enough to mean it. He knows what they would do to him if anyone ever found out that he had been saving those copies for years."

"What makes you think that some funny accounting

is worth over twenty thousand dollars?" Caine asked, playing dumb. He was close and he knew it.

"Because," Feinberg paused to matter-of-factly light his pipe, "for the past twenty years, Hans Gröbel has been an accountant for the firm of Mengele and Sons, in their headquarters office in Günzburg."

Bingo, Caine thought exultantly. Follow the money and it'll lead you right to the son of a bitch's doorstep.

"When do I get to see the goods?" he asked.

"We can go over them together tomorrow night. I'll meet you here in my office at midnight," the old man replied, sucking monotonously at his pipe, like a baby at the breast.

A light, wet snow was falling from an invisible sky, the flakes swirling like moths around the solitary light of a streetlamp. The fat wet flakes decorated the windshield with a fragile lace pattern, forcing him to flick on the windshield wipers every so often. The wet surface of the dark street glistened like black ice as it reflected the electric sign of the tavern. Perhaps if the visibility had been better, or if he hadn't been so tired, he would have seen them sooner.

There were two of them, one on each side of the shiny street. They were both wearing the black leather trench coats that were the hallmark of the Stadtspolizei and made them almost invisible in the dark night. They approached cautiously, ready to dive into a doorway and start firing the second he hit the ignition. He still had time to start the car and make a break for it, but they were almost too close and he knew if he did, he would leave Feinberg exposed and that was what he was there for, to chaperone Feinberg and to see that the exchange went off without a hitch. So he just sat where he was, his hands on the steering wheel and did nothing, a ripple of fear shuddering down the length of his spine. This was the way it would end for him, as it had for so many others. With a silenced soft-nosed bullet in some dark side street, and no one to ever know or care. The morning papers would carry a brief paragraph about a gangland killing, assailants unknown; that was how police departments everywhere handled intelligence casualties. That was how it would happen. It came with the territory.

He let the fear come because it sent a shot of adrenaline through him which he needed desperately, not having slept in two days. After his meeting with Feinberg he had flown to Marseille for an r.d.v. with Claude at that dingy café, two blocks off the crowded Canebière. Claude was a tiny man, almost a midget, with a large skull topped by an oversized beret, which gave him the outlandish appearance of a nineteenth-century bohemian. He affected the air and manners of an *artiste,* as though he were about to join Lautrec for a bout of table sketching and absinthe at the Moulin Rouge.

The café was ripe with the sour smell of garlic and Algerian red wine and Gauloise smoke, and every few seconds Claude glanced up at people he obviously knew, but who never approached their corner table. The café was frequented by serious men, smugglers making the run to Tangiers, ex-Legionnaires and hard-faced rogue cops from the SDECE, who growled softly in the French-Corsican patois of the French underworld and left them alone. They knew how to conduct business, these types, Caine thought.

Claude had already gone through half a bottle of

cognac even before Caine sat down, but if it had any
effect on the little man, Caine couldn't see it. They
agreed on a price of $5,000 for a new American pass-
port and international driver's license, but timing was
a problem. Claude said he would need three days and
he explained something about the watermark problem, as they walked to Claude's studio for the photographs.

After paying him $2,500 as a down payment, Caine
caught a taxi to the airport, but there was some kind
of a labor dispute going on and he had raced back to
the station to catch the express back to Vienna. The
train didn't arrive at the *Bahnhof* in Vienna till late
afternoon and he'd barely made it to the car-rental
agency on the Kärtner Ring, just before closing. All
they could let him have was a VW bug with a sticky
clutch, but time was running out and he took it. He
drove over to the Rudolf Platz and watched the light
in Feinberg's office, until it went out. Then he had
carefully tailed Feinberg to the r.d.v., in a *Heuriger*-
style tavern on Walfischgasse, near the Opera Haus.
Sounds of accordion music and *Fasching* revelry fil-
tered out to the darkening street from the *Heuriger*, as
the snow began to fall. A short time after Feinberg
had gone in, a taxi had dropped off a short man bun-
dled in a dark wool overcoat who answered Feinberg's description of Gröbel. Caine watched Gröbel
pay the driver and nervously glance at the street before entering the *Heuriger*.

However, either his fatigue or the bad visibility had
let him miss the two men in trench coats and now he
could no longer mother-hen the r.d.v. He would have
to be the red herring, mindful of the fact that herrings
usually ended up on someone's plate. As he watched

them approach, he found himself wishing that he'd been able to get the new ID from Claude, instead of being forced to face the Stadtspolizei with the tattered Foster cover.

There was a gentle tapping on the car window. One of the black raincoats was there and he was doing his tapping with the muzzle of a Walther PPK and motioning for Caine to roll down the window.

"Get out of the car," he said, an unlit cigarette dangling from his mouth. It was a bad sign, because it meant he knew how easily a lit cigarette can be spotted at night and that meant he knew what he was doing.

"Do you speak English?" Caine said hopefully, with a wide idiotic tourist grin, spreading from ear to ear.

"Your German is excellent Herr Foster. Outside, please, Police," the man said coldly and he wasn't smiling. Caine got out of the car.

"What are you doing here?"

"Isn't this the way to the American embassy?"

The second policeman had come up and they bracketed him for the frisk, which was handled with quick efficiency. The first policeman hefted the Bauer in his hand for a moment, before slipping it into his coat pocket.

"Interesting little toy. What are you doing with a gun, Herr Foster?" he said calmly, snowflakes clinging to his eyelashes, like tears.

"I'm afraid of the dark."

"He makes jokes, Franz," the first policeman said.

"Funny man," Franz said with a thin-lipped smile as he snapped the handcuffs on Caine's wrists. "We'll have some fun tonight, funny man."

Franz was the one to watch out for, Caine thought,

watching the sensuous way he smiled and almost subconsciously caressed the Walther with his fingertips.
When he squeezed the trigger, it would be with an
expression of pure enjoyment. In a way Franz reminded him of Van Dagen, the Belgian ex-
Legionnaire and mercenary he had met in Paris just
after the collapse of Biafra. Violence was a narcotic
for these men, the confrontation with death the ultimate trip. *"L'heure douce,"* the sweet hour, was the
way Van Dagen had referred to combat. The sweet
hour.

The two men marched him over to a black
Mercedes parked across the street. The first police-
man opened the rear door and gestured with the
Walther.

"Get into the car."

"I think I'd rather walk. It's such a lovely eve—"
Caine couldn't finish the sentence because Franz had
savagely jammed the muzzle of his gun into Caine's
solar plexus, doubling him over against the rear
fender.

"Get into the car."

"On second thought, I think I'll get into the car,"
Caine managed to gasp, and climbed in with Franz
right behind him. The first policeman got into the
driver's seat and pulled out, the wheels slipping
slightly on the slushy surface. Caine glanced over at
Franz, who smiled back with his sniggering look, except that his eyes were as blank and empty as those on
a monument. Caine was worried because it was all
wrong. And then he had it. They had called him by
name! They knew who he was and he had made a
fatal error. He wasn't the red herring, he was the tar-

get! They hadn't been after Feinberg or Gröbel, they had come for him.

It was all wrong, because it meant that they had been put on him by either the Nazis, or else—and it was just as bad—Harris had lied and the Company was running him on a blind mission. Either way, the pickup meant that they weren't really interested in interrogating him, because all he knew was that Mengele might be somewhere in Peru. What it meant was they they were going to terminate him and there wasn't a damn thing he could do about it, because Franz was holding the Walther very steadily and he didn't look like he was going to make any mistakes. He hadn't realized that Mengele's reach could extend all the way to the Vienna Stadtspolizei, unless it was Company business. Their reach could extend to Tierra del Fuego, if they wanted to.

The Mercedes slithered down the heavily trafficked streets, the snow falling through the beams of the headlights as though it would never stop, as though a new Ice Age were beginning. Franz fished into his pocket for a stick of gum and began chewing it, but the gun never moved from the vicinity of Caine's ribs. He would know for certain what they were going to do when they reached Schotten Ring. If they turned into the Ring toward the Danube, it meant that they were taking him to the central police station for questioning and there might be a way out. If they headed out on Währingerstrasse toward Kahlenberg, then it was a one-way trip and they just wanted to do it without fuss in a quiet place. Caine didn't think they would take him to the Vienna Woods to listen to an open-air concert in three-quarter time.

The first policeman concentrated on his driving, as

he slowed to approach the intersection, occasionally flicking his eyes to the rearview mirror to check on Caine. Their motion was smooth and almost dream-like, the only sound the slapping of the windshield wipers and the low rumble of the snow tires on the wet pavement. They bumped carefully over the slick tram tracks and then there was the tick-tick of the di-rectional signal. A pretty blonde with a bottle in her hand in a crowded BMW in the adjoining lane glanced over at him and then waved the bottle play-fully at him. She drunkenly mouthed a one-word invi-tation: *Fasching*. She ran her tongue lasciviously over her lips and smiled, her eyes bright with seduction. She reminded him a little of C.J. He wondered if he would ever see her again. He tried to smile back, but it was impossible because the Mercedes was making the turn across the intersection. It was Währinger-strasse.

"Don't worry," Franz said, stopping chewing long enough to give Caine a comforting smile. "We just want to take you to someplace quiet and ask you some questions."

Of course, Caine thought. They didn't want him to panic into giving them any trouble, because he couldn't stop the sweat from breaking out over his face and Franz had picked up on it at once. They were very good and only wanted to keep it clean. This way to the showers, they had told them at Auschwitz. A surge of anger coursed through him and he let it happen because he needed the adrenaline. He wasn't about to die like a steer being led to the slaughter. In the darkened car his eyes glowed as green as the dash-board dials as they began to go through the suburbs.

"Questions about what?" he asked.

Franz's thin lips parted in a smile as the gum flicked between his teeth like a snake's tongue.

"You can tell us all about *der Seestern*. In fact, I'm sure you'll want to cooperate, won't you, funny man."

"Shut up, Franz," the driver said sharply.

"He knows all about it," Franz said airily. "Don't you, funny man?"—jamming the Walther hard into Caine's ribs.

"You got a big mouth, Franz," the driver said angrily.

Der Seestern, the Starfish again, Caine thought rapidly. What the hell was going on? Who or what was it? Except it looked like he would never find out because Franz wouldn't have ever mentioned it if they had the slightest intention of letting him live. The question was rapidly becoming academic, he realized. The only thing that mattered now was sheer survival.

It would have to be in the car, he knew, his eyes flicking around the interior of the Mercedes without moving his head, measuring distances. Once he started moving, he would be irrevocably committed and there would be no time to see and no chance to correct. It had to be inside, because outside the car they could create any distance they wanted and Franz would be smiling and chewing his gum as he fired into Caine's body, making his last futile run. That was the one thing he must never do: give up. He had seen many men collapse and die in Asia because the organism just gave out, and it was always the same. The collapse of the will to go on suffering, to live, invariably preceded any physical collapse. No, it would have to be inside the car, with the driver too preoccupied to do anything for the first four or five seconds. That left only Franz to deal with. He began to move his body slightly, to get Franz conditioned to his movements. The door on his side could be used as a fulcrum, but he needed a natural movement for the reaction to occur, like the slight lean on a curve.

Time was running out; they were already nearing the *autobahn* beside the woods. The tall, dark shadows of trees, gleaming and heavy with snow, began to crowd down to the road. He began the rhythmic *kokyu* breathing, because it had to come now and he wanted to clear his mind and to look a little sick, with sweat induced by slight hyperventilation, to fractionally decrease the distance between him and Franz. Given the way he felt, he didn't think looking sick was going to be anything of a problem. Franz looked over at him, annoyed. He wanted it clean. *Alles in ordnung*, everything in order, Caine thought.

"Don't try it," Franz said, the gun held steady, as if a statue were holding it. Franz was good. He had noted Caine's movements and he was ready. It wasn't going to work. Caine sighed with defeat and slumped back a tiny bit closer to the door. Franz smiled happily as he chewed, his teeth a pale phosphorescent blue in the dark car, almost like the color of the snow at night. Caine had been right about him. He was truly going to enjoy the killing.

The Mercedes skidded slightly as the first policeman took a wide curve into the woods and began to reduce speed. Caine let the hate and anger come from the dark and ancient corners of his subconscious in a blinding surge, drowning any conscious thought. Those ancient instincts that could transform a man into a berserk animal, would make him fight without quarter for his very existence, as the centrifugal force allowed him to complete the lean against the car door.

The instant his shoulder hit the side, he twisted slightly and kicked savagely with a recoil movement of both legs at Franz's gun hand. The explosion of the gun going off echoed deafeningly within the confined space of the car, succeeded by a roar of cold air as the window beside his head shattered and exploded out to the darkness. His right foot had Franz's forearm pinned against the opposite door, as a savage pain flooded up from his groin from a blow by Franz's left hand and Caine kicked again with his left foot, feeling it connect with bone. The car slewed sideways as the driver tried to brake on the icy road, but Caine couldn't worry about that as he slapped his palms together and whipped the twin hand edges at Franz's temple with everything he had in him. Franz tried to duck the blow, howling at the driver, as the blow caught the side of his neck, stunning him for a second. That was all Caine needed. With a sudden heave he sprang for Franz's throat, his bound hands like steel claws that bit mercilessly into the flesh, and with a surge that seemed to emanate all the way from his groin, he smashed Franz's head through the opposite window, exploding the glass and covering them both with screaming wind and blood.

He scarcely had time to register the fact that Franz's badly gashed skull and neck had gone slack, when he sprang for the driver, who was fumbling at his shoulder holster while he frantically tried to control the erratically skidding car with one hand. Caine brought his hands over the driver's head and yanked back and down with all his might, using his weight and legs against the front seat, as the handcuff's chain bit deep into the driver's neck. He pulled the head down backward across the headrest, trying to snap the straining neck, but the man was incredibly strong and he was still holding the wheel as the car skidded wildly out of control. The driver had managed to free his Walther and twisted his arm backward to point it at Caine. But Caine's hands were locked fruitlessly around the driver's throat and there was nothing he could do except haul at the neck. His body tensed involuntarily as he waited for the split second of sound that would be death, the muzzle pointed into him. Then there was an explosion and sudden savage G-forces were tearing at him as the car smashed into the trees and the driver's body tried to leap through the windshield, despite the handcuffs around his neck. Caine felt his arms being wrenched out of their sockets with the force and then there was only tangled darkness as the car began to roll over. He felt a dull blow somewhere in his body, but he didn't know where, because it wasn't his body anymore and then there were only flickering images and somebody screaming with a voice like his own. Then there was nothing.

Death is cold. He hadn't known that it would be so cold. And dark and wet. He tried to move, but he couldn't, so he simply rested and tried to see. He was looking at a strange rounded shape that formed out of the darkness, and it took him a long while before he realized that he was staring at his own shoe as it rested against the roof of the Mercedes. He was pinned under the heavy body of the driver, his hand-cuffed hands still locked around the man's throat. Like an electrician testing circuits, he tried systematically to feel the damage to the different parts of his body, but he could feel only two sensations, numbness and pain. But at least nothing seemed to broken. Something had hit him near his eye. It felt sticky but he could still see.

The driver's body was heavy on him and he tried to free himself, but the body was immovable. A feeling of lassitude and warmth stole over him and he felt himself smile. It felt good to rest and he decided not to move. But somewhere in the darkness an alarm was going off and it took his groggy mind a while to realize that some part of him was screaming at him that the warmth was an illusion, that if he didn't move, he would die. But I can't move, he reasoned with the voice that was him. I tried and besides I don't feel like it. Don't give up, the voice cautioned, and then it handed him a memory from the brain's data bank.

It was Hudson's voice giving them their final instructions before the drop. Hudson was a grizzled Green Beret master sergeant who taught survival training for pilots, Special Forces, and Company types heading for Vietnam. He was shouting over the roar of the engines as they prepared for a parachute jump into the Chiriquí forest of Panama, for one week on their own in the jungle. Hudson cupped his hands and shouted,

"When you can't go on anymore, when all you want to do is just lay there and die, when you've given up completely, remember my voice. Remember just one thing. TAKE ONE MORE STEP! Just one. If you do, it will save your life. Because once you take one step, you're bound to take another."

All right, Hudson, all right, he thought irritably. Just one, you bastard. And summoning up all his strength, he managed to pull his hands from around the driver's head. The head lolled loosely against his chest, the neck broken. With sudden disgust at the thought of lying there under a corpse, he heaved sideways and managed to partially free himself. From a dozen parts of his body came shooting signals of pain. With another heave he managed to roll the body off him, then he had to rest. He panted heavily, his eyes glazed with fatigue and pain, like a winded animal. He began to paw at the already stiffening body of the driver with his own stiff and frozen hands, searching for the Bauer. He found it still stuck in the driver's belt and dropped it into his jacket pocket. He shook his head, trying to remember something.

The keys, he thought dully. He had to find the keys to the handcuffs. Who had put them on him? Franz, he remembered. Where was Franz? He looked around. Franz wasn't in the smashed, overturned car. Slowly, and with frequent pauses to rest, he managed to crawl inch by inch through the shattered upside-down window and into the snow. When he finally looked up, he could see the dark blot of Franz's body lying in a snowdrift about ten yards away, where he had been thrown clear. Caine managed to crawl over on all fours, like a wounded animal, leaving dark prints of blood crystallizing on the snow.

Franz was still breathing, Caine realized as he began searching him for the keys. He found them in the pants pocket and it took him many tries before he was able to insert the key into the lock. Finally he held the key between his teeth and managed to turn it that way, releasing the fastening. Then like a toddler trying his first steps, he painfully managed to pull himself erect with the help of a tree trunk.

He took out the Bauer and briefly debated shooting Franz. Then he decided against it. The first Stadtspolizei on the scene might take the whole thing for an accident and he would need as much of a head start as possible to get clear of Austria and pick up his new cover in Marseille. He glanced at his watch and then down again at Franz. He still had forty-five minutes to make his r.d.v. with Feinberg. As for Franz, he would probably freeze to death in a little while anyway. He put the Bauer away and began to stagger toward the road.

"Mein Gott, what happened to you?" Feinberg said, his eyes wide behind his glasses at the sight of Caine swaying drunkenly in the doorway. Caine's suit was torn and filthy and soggy with melted snow and blood. His hair was matted and his face was red and blue with bruises, like patches of raw hamburger. One of his eyes was swollen shut, the puffed skin showing all hues of a rainbow.

"I cut myself shaving," Caine muttered thickly.

"Let me call a doctor," Feinberg said anxiously and helped Caine over to the old sofa.

"There isn't time. But I could use a drink," Caine said through swollen purplish lips. He sat gingerly on the sofa, while Feinberg bustled through a metal file cabinet, finally coming up with a bottle of schnapps that he uncorked and handed to Caine.

"Prosit," Caine toasted and drank deeply. The warmth of the harsh liquor flooded his veins like a benediction. He took another drink and passed the bottle back to Feinberg, who tilted it in a toast.

"L'chayim, to life," Feinberg said and took a swig. To life, Caine thought, and smiled, remembering the icy feel of death in the overturned Mercedes. Amen, he thought. Good or bad, here's to it.

"What happened?" Feinberg asked, a genuine concern written over his sad Jewish face.

Caine shrugged. "I'm not sure, but a couple of boys from the Stadtspolizei tried to take me for a one-way ride to the Vienna Woods."

"What happened to them?"

"Let's say that I made a lasting impression on them," Caine replied, and smiled grimly. Feinberg shuddered. It wasn't a pretty smile.

"Can what happened be traced back to this office?"

Good, Caine thought. Feinberg was thinking like a professional.

"No. You're clear. Have you got the goods?"

Feinberg nodded excitedly, his eyes gleaming with enthusiasm. He went over to the desk and brought back a sheaf of Xerox copies.

"I was just going over it when you arrived. Look for yourself. I've marked the significant entries with blue ink."

Caine quickly scanned the pages, the certainty sprouting up within him like a mushroom after a rainstorm. Over a period of almost six years the firm of Mengele and Sons had made quarterly contributions averaging around seventy-five thousand marks to a medical hospital in the Peruvian Amazon, near the town of Pucallpa, called the Mendoza Institute. The drafts had been countersigned by the head of the institute, a Dr. Felix Mendoza. Audaciously, the company had taken the contributions off their corporate income taxes as a charitable deduction.

"Who is this Dr. Felix Mendoza?" Caine asked.

"I was waiting for you to ask," Feinberg said, the excitement sparkling in his voice like the bubbles in a glass of soda pop. He went back to the desk and brought over an opened copy of the *International Who's Who*. He handed it to Caine, who devoured the entry on Dr. Felix Mendoza.

The brief paragraph indicated that Dr. Felix Mendoza had been born in Lima and had studied medicine at the University of Munich. In 1973 he established the Mendoza Institute as the first medical facility for the natives of the Peruvian Amazon. The institute had been patterned after the Albert Schweitzer Hospital in Ghana and had the enthusiastic support of the Peruvian government, which had publicly hailed Mendoza as "the Schweitzer of South America." As a result of his charitable efforts for the Indians, Mendoza had been twice nominated for the Nobel peace prize.

"Have you got an atlas?" Caine asked, and Feinberg ran to the shelves and found it almost immediately. They jostled each other in their excitement, until they found the map of Peru. With a cry of triumph Feinberg stabbed at the map with his finger.

"There it is!"

His finger pointed at the dot marked PUCALLPA. It lay several hundred miles south of Iquitos, along the Amazon tributary called the Ucayali. Iquitos itself was situated near the juncture of the Ucayali and the Amazon rivers. For a long moment the two men looked at each other, their eyes bright with discovery.

Got you, you bastard! Caine thought exultantly. All the pieces fitted perfectly. Müller's anguished cry of "Peru." Cohen's sighting of Mengele in Iquitos and subsequent death in Lima. The payments of Mengele and Sons to support the jungle hospital. The almost complete safety and isolation provided by the jungle hospital, founded in 1973, the year Mengele had gone to ground in nearby Paraguay. Mendoza's education at the University of Munich, Mengele's alma mater. Even the brazen similarity in the names: Mengele—Mendoza. He was dead certain. The hunt was over. He had found Josef Mengele.

Caine smiled broadly and then the two men were hugging each other, Caine wincing at Feinberg's embrace. Feinberg grabbed the bottle and raised it in a toast. Suddenly his eyes were brimming with tears as he pronounced the ancient Hebrew prayer of thanksgiving, with a bittersweet quaver in his voice: "Blessed art Thou, O Lord our God, King of the Universe, who has preserved us and sustained us and brought us through to this time," and he drank a long swallow of schnapps.

Caine raised the bottle to his lips. "Amen," he said, his one good eye glinting green in his swollen face, like an emerald in a statue of Buddha.

For the moment it didn't seem to matter that he had stumbled across something called "the Starfish" and that it wasn't very friendly. It didn't matter that he didn't know what the game was, or who the players were. Or even that he was hotter than August in Death Valley. All that really mattered was that he had pulled it off. He had managed to do in seven weeks what five governments were unable to accomplish in thirty years. Of course, he had to admit, they hadn't been trying very hard. In his mind's eye he was already composing the cable he would send to Wasserman from Marseille: "Have located the missing parcel. Stop. Initiating Phase two."

PART II

"Hasn't it occurred to you that if Cain had not killed Abel, it would have been Abel who would have ended by killing Cain?"

—*Miguel de Unamuno*

"The Gods are mighty; but mightier still is the jungle."

—*Amazonian proverb*

CHAPTER 11

Sudden clouds extinguished the sun and, just like that, it was raining. The rain fell with an oily hiss into the earth-colored river. Large heavy drops shattered the placid surface into ripples. Where a moment before he could see the endless vista of jungle crowding the river-banks, now there was only a gray wall of water.

The engine of the riverboat droned monotonously as the boat glided upriver against a current so slow it was impossible to determine its direction merely by looking through the open windows of the salon. The salon attendant, his dark Indian eyes impassive as always, lit a kerosene lamp to brighten the salon and brought them a fresh round of Cristal beer, the brown bottles sweating in the humid jungle heat.

"Well, at least the rain might keep the *moscas* away for a while," Caine said, idly scratching a mosquito bite on his neck.

"Don't scratch. The slightest break in the skin turns septic in this climate," Father José rebuked him gently and took a long pull at the warm beer. His large work-gnarled hand wrapped around the bottle was covered with millions of black spots, the vestige of countless *borrachudo* bites. *Borrachudos* were tiny poisonous flies that filled the air like clouds, and their stings were known to have driven men mad. Caine took another swig of the beer and placed his bottle on the table, where it stood trembling with the engine vibration.

"This climate would try a saint's patience," he said irritably, wiping his brow with a forearm already swollen by mosquito bites.

"You're right about that," Father José agreed, his consonants in English still retaining a faint echo of his native Dutch. "It's no accident that the Indians call the Ucayali, *Río de los Mosquitos.*"

"And yet you stay on here."

The priest shrugged and drained his beer, signaling to the attendant for another.

"It's what God wants me to do," he said simply. He was a big man with brooding brown eyes and a luxuriant black beard that cascaded down the front of his dirty gray surplice, which had once been white. "It's been almost fifteen years now," he added, shaking his head with wonder. "When I first came to the Amazona, I thought it would only be for a two-year mission, but there was so much to do that I couldn't leave. Now I don't suppose I ever will," he said sadly, for the moment his dreamy eyes filled with the memory of the lost windmills of Haarlem.

"Then why did you become a missionary?"

"Oh, that all goes back to when I was a small boy growing up in a village near Haarlem. When I knew that I wanted to be a priest, I began to read the Bible with an incredible intensity, poring over every word. And a single sentence of Christ seemed to burn itself into my soul: 'Whatsoever you do to the least of my brothers, you do also to me.'

"It was as if the words had been branded on me. I

couldn't get rid of it. Finally I understood what God required of me. To help the least of men. Mind you," he said, pausing to drain another bottle of Cristal, "had I known what I was letting myself in for, I'd have spent more time arguing with God about choosing someone else for the job.

"When I first came out here, it was to replace Father Antonio at the Franciscan mission near Requena. He had been killed trying to make contact with the Achual Indians, who are kissing cousins to the Jivaro. Not long after, an Achual tried to sell me Father Antonio's head. It had been shrunken to the size of an egg."

"I thought head-hunting had been outlawed."

"I'm afraid you don't understand," Father José said gently, his voice almost lost in a deafening explosion of thunder. A sudden flash of lightning brightened the salon with harsh white light and a long rumble of thunder underscored his words like a drumroll.

"*Urumuha,* that's what the Indians call this kind of a thunderstorm," the priest said pensively, almost to himself. The light of the kerosene lamp glowed like embers in his eyes. "You see, there is no law here," he went on.

"The Indians are not like us. You and I are savages with a veneer of civilization, but the Indians lack even the veneer. They are simply savages. Even after fifteen years of living with them, I still have absolutely no idea how they think, or if they even think at all, as we know it. I never know on any given day whether they'll welcome me or kill me for no reason at all."

"This river"—gesturing at the salon window—"covers more than distance. We are going upriver as much in time as in space. The Amazona is the last unexplored place on earth and with good reason. If you want to know how old the world really is, the Amazona will teach you. Make no mistake, señor, the jungle is more ancient than you can imagine and *civilization* is merely a word."

"That sounds like a warning, Father."

"It is, Señor McClure. To enter the darkness of the Amazona is to enter the darkness of your own heart," the priest said, his dark eyes brooding, and Caine knew that he was really speaking about himself.

"Call me Mack," Caine said. He liked that touch. It gave his cover a sense of reality. He looked out the salon window. The storm had ended as abruptly as it had begun. The hot, heavy sun was shining brightly on the brown water, the jungle steam rising over the trees forming a glistening curtain of rainbows. Once again they could hear the raucous chatter of the parrots, invisible in the greenery along the river.

"*Salud,* Mack," Father José said, starting another bottle of beer, pouring the amber fluid down his throat as though he were filling a bottomless tank. Caine shrugged and followed suit. It didn't matter how much they drank; they sweated it out as quickly as they poured it in.

"Well, I don't know how much success you'd have with us civilized types either. I'm not exactly a Lenten Special, Father," Caine said, slapping at a *mutaca,* a stinging insect almost twice the size of a horsefly. He felt the soft squashy body crack under his fingers and disgustedly flicked it away.

"Few of us are," the priest said, a shy smile revealing itself amidst the dark foliage of his beard.

"I'll tell you the truth, Father. When I go into a cathedral and see starving Indians spending their last centavo to buy some silver medal to hang on an icon, it makes me want to puke. The Church has done terrible things all throughout history."

"Terrible things," the priest agreed amiably.

"You know, Padre," Caine said, a broad smile breaking across his face, "I get the feeling you've had this conversation before. More than once, maybe."

"More than once," Father José answered with a grin of his own. "You'd be surprised how often people say the same things to priests. You know, to the Indios I'm a kind of white man *brujo,* a witch doctor of sorts. I sometimes wonder if white people don't think of priests in a similar way."

"*Salud,* Father. Here's to witch doctors everywhere," Caine toasted, the beer foaming over his mouth, giving him the momentary appearance of a slavering animal.

"*Salud,* Mack."

Caine glanced out of the salon window at the unchanging landscape of river and trees. An Yagua fisherman stood in a dugout pirogue on the placid surface of the Ucayali, his bow poised and motionless. He released the reed arrow that was as long as he was, the line uncoiling behind it. As the riverboat drew abreast of the dugout, the Indian was already reeling in the fish, a great brown *paiche,* impaled and wriggling on the barbed arrow. The jungle steamed wetly in the sun, like a damp fire, and the green of the forest faded in the strong white light.

"Tell me about your plans," the priest said. Conversation was as much a staple of life for white men in the jungle as *mandioca* root was for the Indians. Caine lit a cigarette and offered the pack to the priest, who shook his head and began fussing with an old briar pipe, the stem bitten and broken as though it had been gnawed by some animal.

"I'm a kind of advance man for Petrotex, a major oil company headquartered in Houston. We're interested in obtaining a drilling concession from the Peruvian government. As I explained to the Minister for Jungle Development, my job is to explore the site with an eye toward logistics, local conditions, labor supply, medical facilities, and what not before we actually make a bid for the concession. I have the minister's authorization right here," Caine said, tapping the sweat-stained pocket of his khaki shirt. He hoped that he had sounded casual enough about his interest in "medical facilities." He wanted the priest to be the first to mention the Mendoza Institute.

"Another rape of the Amazona," Father José said pensively. "It's been going on since the days of Orellana and the conquistadors. Did you know that the Amazona contains more than a fifth of all the fresh water in the world and that it supplies about a quarter of all the oxygen on this planet?"

Caine nodded and the priest sat back in his chair with a satisfied air.

"It'll mean a lot of money for the people here," Caine said defensively.

"It will also mean the rape of the environment and the destruction of the Indian cultures. All the Indios will be reduced to the status of *caboclos,* half-breeds, who have no place of their own, belonging neither to the Indian or the white worlds. Still," the priest sighed, exhaling a thick stream of pipe smoke, "it doesn't matter. The jungle will win out in the end. It always does."

"What can you tell me about medical facilities?

Minister Ribiero mentioned something about a jungle hospital near Pucallpa," Caine prompted. He had to get the garrulous priest talking about the Mendoza Institute, so that he could get a feel of what he was up against.

"You mean the Mendoza Institute?"

"I think that was it. Yes, that sounds right."

"An extraordinary man, Dr. Mendoza," Father José remarked. He put down the pipe for a moment and spit into his hand. Then he rubbed the tobacco-stained spittle over his hands and face. "Keeps away the mosquitoes and *borrachudos*," he explained apologetically, his ascetic face gleaming with sweat and spittle. Caine glanced out of the window at the river, hoping he wasn't overplaying his interest. The gray back of a freshwater dolphin momentarily broke the flat brown surface of the river alongside the boat, its dorsal fin reminding Caine of a shark. Father José struck a match and relit his pipe.

"Do you know him?" Caine asked.

"Oh, yes. I've been to the institute several times. In just the five or six years he's been here, he has accomplished miracles. The Indios around Yarinacocha think he's a god. His word is law from the Santiago to the Ucayali."

"Which tribes are around there?"

"Mostly Chamas, Yaguas, and Shipibos. Simple folk and relatively peaceful. Not like the Achuals. But Dr. Mendoza is an extremely private man. He doesn't like outsiders and rarely allows visitors. The only access to the institute is by river and the Peruvian Army has a gunboat on the Yarinacocha to discourage intruders. I sometimes think that he's trying to expiate some past sin by burying himself in the jungle. Perhaps that's just a priest talking," he mused, thinking out loud, as do many solitary men.

"Tell me, hasn't anyone ever wondered about what Mendoza did before he came here?"

Father José frowned and he looked sadly at Caine.

"In the Amazona one learns not to ask a man about his past. Dr. Mendoza himself never speaks about the outside world. When he found out that the government had nominated him for the Nobel prize, he was furious. They say he wrote the authorities an angry letter, demanding that they withdraw the nomination. A very private man, Dr. Mendoza," the priest said. "Still, thanks to his efforts, malaria and tuberculosis and death by snakebite have almost been eliminated among the Indios."

"Why this mania for privacy?"

"Dr. Mendoza is a brilliant man. In addition to practicing medicine, he researches tropical diseases and collects botanical specimens." For a moment Caine was reminded of Mengele's *Experimentieren* and his eyes glittered like green fire. "He's also a linguist and something of an ethnologist," the priest went on.

"He says that he doesn't want outsiders to contaminate the Indios with the white man's culture. I daresay he has a point. Most of the white men who come to the Urubamba are fortune hunters, fairly disreputable types seeking out gold, or carrying some dubious map to Vilcabamba, the fabled lost city of the Incas. I can understand why Mendoza doesn't want them around. All the white man has ever brought the Indios are trinkets, misery, and diseases against which they have no natural immunity."

Father José paused and signaled to the salon attendant for another round of beers. His thin bronzed face glistened with sweat.

"And the Word of God," he murmured, almost to himself, "although I fancy the Indios think of Jesus as the white man's god. I suspect they've mentally placed Him in some niche in the Pantheon of Gods, somewhere between the river god and the sun god."

Caine stood up and stretched; he had to think. With the institute so isolated and protected by Indians and the Peruvian Army, he would have to reevaluate his escape route. Father José looked up at him.

"I'm going downstairs, perhaps it's cooler there," Caine said and stepped out of the salon, the half-finished bottle of Cristal in his hand. He went down the stairs and passed through the feral smell of a family of Campa Indians camped around the cargo cases of plantains, and the sharp, putrid stench of stacked alligator hides, toward the flat prow of the riverboat. He stood gazing at the placid, almost solid surface of the river slowly passing underneath. There was no break in the brown water or in the edge of the jungle, brooding like a dense green fog on the riverbank. He took another long sip of beer, finishing the bottle, then tossed it over the side. It bobbed on the surface like a sleek fish, in the wake of the boat. He watched it till it was too far away to see.

After leaving Vienna, Caine had gone to Marseille to pick up an American passport in the name of Ross Payne from Claude. He used a doctor recommended by Claude to treat his bruises from Vienna. The doctor told Caine that he had been lucky; the doctor himself refused to drive because of all the crazy drivers. He put a fresh bandage on Caine's eye and told him it would probably heal in a week or so. Caine threw the bandage away as soon as he left the doctor's office.

Using the Payne passport, which he planned to keep as a backup cover, he had flown to New York and then on to Houston, where he had a secretarial service type up a résumé and a letter applying for a job as a geologist with Petrotex. He managed to get an appointment with the chief geologist, named James McClure. He arranged for the secretarial service to call McClure with an important private call during the interview, and while McClure stepped out of the office to answer the call, Caine stole a sheaf of Petrotex stationery.

Using the stolen stationery, he had written to the Minister for Jungle Development in Lima, describing the purpose of his forthcoming trip and hinting delicately of potentially huge bribes for possible oil-drilling concessions in the Peruvian Amazon. Then he went to the city hall and got a Xerox copy of McClure's birth certificate, which he used to apply for a passport. He also had business cards with the Petrotex logo made up in the name James McClure. In a world of computers and bureaucracy it is easier to steal a man's identity than his small change, Caine thought sardonically. Armed with the McClure passport and a self-typed letter of introduction on Petrotex stationery, he flew to Las Vegas, where he dug up the suitcase with the guns. He took a Greyhound bus from Las Vegas to Los Angeles to avoid airport security. In L.A. he contacted a Marina travel agency to arrange an Amazon hunting safari, to facilitate transporting the guns. But he didn't pack all the guns. Acting on a hunch, he deposited the S&W .44 Magnum revolver and shells and $2,000 in cash in a safety-deposit box in a Hollywood branch of the Bank of America. Then he called Wasserman.

Wasserman took the call in his Mercedes, somewhere on the Pacific Coast Highway. Caine briefly brought Wasserman up to date and they arranged for Wasserman to acquire an additional cover passport for Caine, in case it became necessary as a backup. Caine would contact Wasserman through a classified ad addressed to C.J. in the Personals section of the L.A. *Times*, in case of an emergency or once the job was done, if he needed help in getting out of Peru. Wasserman seemed surprised when Caine asked him if he'd had any further contact with Harris and there was a note of irony in his voice when he told Caine that C.J. was at the beach house.

They made love on the living room carpet, tearing off their clothes from the minute she opened the door to him. She climaxed in a wild series of shudders, arching her back and moaning his name over and over, her long fingernails digging into his buttocks. Later they relaxed over sandwiches and chilled Chablis on the balcony overlooking the beach. The ocean breeze rustled the fringes of her long hair as they ate, her serious blue eyes never leaving his face. Once she reached over and touched his cheek and even now, here in the jungle, he could still feel that soft, almost imperceptible touch, as though it had left a permanent scar.

"I thought I would never see you again," she said.

"I'm like the bad penny that always turns up," he shrugged.

"Are you a bad penny?" she asked, her eyes serious and intent, as though she were asking him to tell her fortune.

"Not for you," he said and they both looked away for a moment, knowing that it was a commitment.

"Why me?" she asked thoughtfully.

"Because you're the only woman in L.A. who hasn't asked me what my astrological sign is," and they were laughing easily and lightly for the first time. She wrinkled her nose and made a face at him, like a little girl.

"What is your sign, anyway?"

"Slippery When Wet," he grinned, and she answered with a smile full of sexual complicity.

That was how he remembered her now, the faint scent of lovemaking still on her, her eyes blue and squinting slightly in the bright sun, her smile as breezy as her long blond hair, the sounds of children playing on the beach drifting up to the balcony, like smoke in the wind.

But the same hunch that had made him leave the revolver in the safety-deposit box still troubled him. There was more to the job than just the hit, but he couldn't put his finger on it. It bothered him all the way to Lima, where he had met with the minister and made even stronger hints about bribes and the joys that American technology and Coca-Cola could bring to the jungle. When Caine left the office, Ministro Ribiero gave him a letter of authorization to the local officials and a warm *abrazo*, the Latin American hug of friendship.

But it was still bothering him as he reviewed everything that had happened since he had met Wasserman, on the long flight over the Andes from Lima to the jungle port of Iquitos, where he had boarded the riverboat to Pucallpa. It was, Caine thought, a little like having a tooth pulled. Time and again, your tongue explores the gap. Something was missing and he couldn't let it alone. There were too many loose ends: Harris in Berlin and his remark about oil, which might have subconsciously prompted Caine to use the Petrotex cover; the Company—and most of all the two references to "the Starfish," whatever that was. The first, the memo he had seen in the Mengele office in Asunción; and then the two goons who had wanted to ask him about it in Vienna. He shook his head, as though to clear it, and wiped his sweating forehead on his sleeve. He had enough to do as it was. Mengele's jungle isolation made the hit extremely chancy and he might have to tackle the jungle itself as an escape route if the army and the Indians closed the Yarinacocha to him.

He went up to his cabin and prepared a small jungle-survival kit, which he packed in a waterproof plastic suitcase. As he packed, he felt a disquieting sense of dread. It was like Paraguay all over again. In addition to the Colt AR-15 rifle and a machete, he packed a small knapsack containing a mosquito net, insect repellent, iodine, a compass, a small aluminum pot, salt tablets, Halezone tablets, fishing hooks and line, a flashlight, a plastic canteen, a wad of coca leaves, four chocolate bars, matches in a waterproof case, the Payne passport and a thousand dollars in dollars and Peruvian soles, the clips of 5.56mm ammunition, and three packs of cigarettes.

He lit a cigarette and went up to the pilot's cabin, still troubled by "the Starfish." In the back of his head he could hear Koenig's voice, like a conscience that he couldn't shrug away. "In this business, it's what you don't know that'll kill you," Koenig used to say.

He watched the pilot steer the riverboat for a long

time. The landscape hardly changed. Always there was the flat, muddy surface of the river hedged by the dense tropical foliage, the monotony occasionally relieved by the wedge-shaped ripple of a water snake, or the screech of a spider monkey from a nearby tree. With an easy movement the Shipibo pilot turned the boat to port toward the far bank.

"Why did you do that?" Caine asked.

"To avoid sandbars, señor. It's best for the *barco* to follow the deep channel."

"Doesn't the channel ever shift?"

"*Sí, señor*," the pilot grinned widely, his teeth bright in his dark, tattooed face. "The channel is always shifting. It is never the same twice in this *madre* of a river. This river will trick you every chance it gets."

"But how did you know that the channel ran to the port side? There was nothing in the surface of the river, no landmark to show you where it was."

"The river did show me, señor," the pilot laughed. "I saw where the floating leaves and bits of wood were. They follow the current to the sea. Where they go, the current is fast and the water is deep. The river is a woman, señor. She is beautiful, but sometimes unfaithful. You must learn to follow her moods, otherwise she will swallow you up."

Caine took out his cigarettes, offered one to the pilot, and they both lit up. Koenig had been right, Caine thought. He'd have liked the Indian pilot, because they both believed in searching for the overlooked bit of information, and they both knew that it's what you don't know that'll kill you.

"When will we reach Pucallpa?" Caine asked.

"Two, maybe two hours and a half, señor."

* * *

They docked in Pucallpa in the sweltering noon heat, even more oppressive now that there was no longer the faint river breeze of the boat's passage to cool them. The port was like a junkyard, a tangle of scrap metal huts and warehouses scattered along the mud flats, with haphazardly angled corrugated roofs stained red with rust and crowded with small power-boats, *lanchas,* and Indian rafts. The mud flats were streaked yellow and red with sawdust that flowed down to the river from the sawmill on the bank.

The boat docked by an old wooden pier, its pilings black with sewage and oil slicks floating on the scummy surface of the water. The ripe stench of mud and decaying matter rose with the heat waves to Caine's nostrils. On the other side of the pier, sweating *campesinos,* naked except for ragged loincloths, loaded a barge with stacks of freshly cut lumber, stained red as thought the sap were blood. Next to the riverboat floated a dugout pirogue full of chattering Shipibo women weaving a reed mat. The women were as bright and pretty as jungle birds in their colorful skirts woven in intricate geometric designs, and long, straight black hair. The Shipibo women are among the most beautiful in the world, Caine thought. With their lightly tanned skins and pretty, vaguely oriental features they reminded him of a Gauguin painting. They seemed out of place here, floating like water lilies on this dung-heap outpost of civilization.

Planks had been stretched from the boat's flat lower deck to the wharf, and a large group of *caboclo* laborers were attempting to manhandle an old Chevy from the deck to the pier. After a great deal of shouting and violent gesturing they managed to lift the car and carry it onto the dock. It had never occurred to any of them to simply drive the car over the planks to the dock. Father José was right, Caine mused. We bring them the dubious gifts of civilization that they truly don't know what to do with. Almost as if Caine's thought had summoned him, the priest appeared beside him at the rail of the upper deck. He had come to say good-bye.

Father José embraced Caine with a rather formal *abrazo*, his expression a disconcerting mixture of warmth and anxiety. He was oddly nervous, as though he had something to say that he really didn't want to put into words. He tugged anxiously at his beard, as if it were a bell rope, then he looked searchingly into Caine's eyes and brought it out.

"I have seen eyes like yours before, Señor Mack. Yours are green and those of the jaguar are black, but you have the eyes of a jaguar. I have seen them over the sights of my rifle. They are the eyes of a hunter, señor." The priest paused. "I think perhaps we shall meet again."

"Who knows?" Caine said, warmly returning the priest's *abrazo*. "So long, Padre."

"*Vaya con Dios.*" Go with God, the priest replied and looked away.

Caine spent the next few hours dealing with local authorities, who sent him from one fly-specked and sweltering office to another. The offices were crowded with *campesinos*, timidly waiting their turn with the quiet, stolid patience of animals. The sullen heat and bureaucratic confusion gave him the feeling that he was in the outer offices of hell, unable to find anyone who knew what was going on. Finally a small, short-tempered army officer stamped and countersigned his letter of authorization from the minister, approving his visit to the Mendoza Institute. Caine searched the docks until he found a Chama Indian with a *lancha,* a large dugout canoe powered by an outboard engine, who agreed to take him to the institute.

It was late afternoon by the time they headed up the Yarinacocha. The lake was placid, its deep-green surface reflecting the intricate herringbone pattern of clouds, the shores shrouded with foliage. The bright scarlet of a macaw flashed among the palms and a small band of howler monkeys shrieked at them from the refuge of a *kapok* tree. Caine smeared on more insect repellent as the *borrachudo* began to attack in droves. His guide, Pepé, a short, stubby man wearing only the sacklike brown *cushma* of the Chamas, smiled at his discomfort and offered him a coca leaf to chew. Caine shook his head and Pepé shrugged. The insects didn't seem to bother him at all.

A sun ray of pure white light streamed from a cloud edge to the sparkling surface of the lake and for a moment the Yarinacocha achieved an almost artificial prettiness, like one of those three-dimensional electric beer signs that brighten dark bars with the illusion of a mountain stream. The sound of a diesel engine drew Caine's attention and he saw the small Peruvian Army boat, with an old .30 caliber machine gun mounted on the bow, approach the *lancha.* The gunboat drew alongside and Caine boarded and showed the officer his authorization. The officer offered Caine a gourd of *masato,* a strong Indian liquor, and they toasted Ministro Ribiero and the President of the United States. Caine gave the officer a pack of cigarettes and the officer warned him about a nest of *caimán* alligators on the western bank of the lake. They parted with an *abrazo* and as Pepé pulled away, Caine pulled out the Winchester and sat under the thatched sunshade of the *lancha*, the rifle across his knees, scanning the surface for *caimáns*.

It was nearing dusk as they approached the western bank of the lake, the surface a flat yellow reflection of the sky. Suddenly Pepé was swinging the *lancha* around and pointing at the bank. Caine eased into a crouch, reminding himself to squeeze slowly and steadily in the uncertain light, only the nostrils of the *caimán* protruding above the surface.

"*Espera,*" wait, Pepé said, moving the boat closer in a wide arc, but Caine had the alligator's head in his sights. The crack of the rifle echoed across the water and for a second, he thought he had missed, the *caimán* floating motionless as a log. Then the water seemed to explode with wild thrashing, the powerful tail slapping the water as if the animal were trying to beat it to death. The water near the bank turned a frothy pink, and Pepé was pointing at the thrashing animal in excitement. Then Caine realized that he was pointing at the snouts of other *caimáns*, moving silently toward the wounded alligator, the water commotion calling them like a dinner bell. He had to be quick, he realized, and put another shot into the alligator's arched back. It took two more shots before the *caimán* lay still. Pepé tied the animal to the boat with a liana line and it took the both of them to drag the six-foot beast to shore. As they dragged it up on the mud, the tail began to thrash again and Caine dropped the rope and, aiming carefully, placed another shot between the dead, bleeding eyes.

They made camp near the bank, Pepé assuring him

that it was impossible to attempt a jungle trail at night. Soon they had a fire going, a pot of *farinha* bubbling on the fire, and thick steaks cut from the *caimán*'s tail broiling with a soft sizzling sound. While Pepé busied himself skinning the *caimán* and hacking off fillets of meat, Caine walked into the jungle to relieve himself. He waited till Pepé turned away, so he wouldn't see Caine carrying the suitcase with the survival kit. He moved cautiously up the trail, finding his way by the pallid beam of a flashlight and cutting blaze marks on the trees so that he could find the location again.

He stopped at a tall stand of *cedro* trees, the center tree dead, its core hollowed and eaten away by a swarming colony of termites. He anointed the termites with his urine, the frightened insects milling blindly in the sudden wash of water. Then he wedged the suitcase into the hollowed-out trunk and covered it with handfuls of dead leaves and damp earth. He carefully marked the tree with three parallel blazes and inspected the trunk with his flashlight, making sure that no traces of the suitcase could be seen. With any luck it would never be used. He hadn't needed the warnings of the priest. That week of survival training in Panama had convinced him that he had a better chance of surviving Russian roulette with all the chambers loaded than in tackling the jungle on his own.

He walked back to the camp, guided by the flickering light of the campfire. Pepé was crouched over the fire, stirring the thick, soapy *farinha* with a twig. There was something very ancient in the way he tended the fire, like a Stone Age man, more animal than human. He looked up at Caine and smiled, gesturing at the charred alligator meat. If he had noticed the missing suitcase, he gave no sign of it. Caine squatted near the fire, not because it was cold—far from it, the darkness bringing little relief from the relentless heat—but because the smoke seemed to keep the insects away. The *caimán* steak was surprisingly good. It tasted a little like rubbery chicken. But Caine could only stomach a few mouthfuls of the thick, bland *farinha* paste. Undaunted, Pepé shoveled the stuff in at an amazing rate.

Caine lit a cigarette and exhaled slowly. The dense canopy of branches above the camp shielded them from the black sky, sprinkled with stars. He got up and walked down to the lake, its flat surface sparkling with starlight. The darkness vibrated with the whisper of black wings and a primordial ripple of fear shivered down his spine. The vampire bats were coming out to hunt. One way or another it would all be over tomorrow, he thought. He wondered if he would ever see the stars again.

On an impulse he squatted down and cupped the water in his hand to drink. A single star glittered from the center of his palm, like a diamond, and he drank it. The lake water tasted like rain. Near the bank a snow-white heron awkwardly poked at the mud, digging for insects. Then it flapped its great wings and swooped over the lake, the reflection of its white body bright as the moon on the still water. The silence was broken only by the faint splash of an electric eel as it momentarily rippled the surface.

As he walked back to the campfire, the darkness began to come alive with jungle sounds. A spiderweb tickled his face and he brushed it away. From the branches above came the shrill cry of a toucan, as though it were sounding an alarm. The lakeshore echoed with the hum of cicadas and the restless croaking of frogs. Pepé had stretched a hammock for Caine between two palms and curled himself like a great monkey on a bed of reeds. A mosquito sang in Caine's ear and he slapped at it with a perfunctory gesture. He rummaged in his backpack for the mosquito net and draped it over his head. The white netting gave him the appearance of a ghost in the flickering firelight. He settled himself precariously on the hammock, which swayed gently, as he eased the Bauer from the small of his back.

The morning was already hot and humid, the sun sparkling on the lake, as they broke camp and headed up the trail. Caine carried a backpack and the Winchester in his hands. Pepé had tied Caine's two suitcases together with liana rope and carried them, like a bulky pack, on his back. The little Indian seemed bent double under the load, but it was all Caine could do to keep up with him. As he hiked, his eyes searched the trail looking for landmarks. But there was no horizon to guide him, only the jungle that crowded around them like a massive green wall. It took them three hours of hard march to reach the institute. By the time they arrived, Caine's khaki shirt and slacks were black with sweat.

The institute was set in a large clearing, bisected by a small, clear stream. It was quite a settlement, with about twenty whitewashed bungalows and huts laid out in neat, rectangular order. The dirt paths were lined with stones and someone had planted a colorful flower garden near the largest bungalow, which he assumed was the infirmary. An Yagua woman in one of the huts was making a clay pot by the oldest method known to man: rolling worms of clay between her palms and layering them, one on top of the other. A wizened Shipibo, naked except for a palm skirt, was slowly sweeping the porch of the large bungalow with a palm frond broom. Caine could hear the high-pitched shouts of Indian children playing on the banks of the stream, where a number of Indian women were doing their washing. As Caine approached the main bungalow, a spider monkey ran up the porch and climbed a trellis, twined with flowers, turning to screech at him from the top. Caine put down his pack and gun and stepped up on the porch.

He wasn't prepared for his first sight of Inger. She stepped out to greet him, her sleek blond hair cut short and close to her head, gleaming like a golden helmet in the sun. She was thin and wore a white shirt and blue jeans. Her eyes were almost violet and fierce as a bird's and they made him feel as if he ought to apologize for something, but for what he couldn't say. She was very beautiful and she looked as if she would be more at home on the cover of *Vogue* than in this bizarre setting. Her intense gaze examined him with a kind of clinical curiosity, as though she were a man looking over the girls at a singles bar.

"*Buenos días, señorita. Yo soy* James McClure, *de la compañia* Petrotex. I'm looking for Dr. Mendoza."

"We've been expecting you, Señor McClure. The colonel radioed us from Pucallpa that you were coming," she said, her English faintly flavored with a Spanish accent. She extended her hand and shook his smartly. "My name is Inger. I'm Dr. Mendoza's daughter. If you'll follow me . . ."

He followed her hard little behind, clearly outlined

by the tight jeans, toward the main bungalow. His groin began to tingle as he imagined how she'd be with her rump stuck out and open to him. Christ, what a time to think about sex, he told himself. She opened a screen door and they entered a large ward-like room, filled with hospital beds and the faintly acrid smell of disinfectant. About a half dozen of the beds were filled with wheezing Indians, their faces tattooed black and red. Their eyes regarded him with a silent curiosity, as they made their way down the aisle.

"These are mostly tuberculosis cases," she remarked matter-of-factly as they approached an old man wearing a lightweight white shirt and slacks, seated on the edge of a bed and carefully peering into a young Indian boy's throat with a pocket flashlight.

The old man patted the boy on the head and stood up to face Caine. The doctor was of medium height and his body was still trim and tan. He appeared to be in his mid-sixties and his hair was white and neatly cut to a medium length. He wore a trim white mustache and his eyes were black, like lumps of coal set in his face. His expression was friendly and if there was any resemblance to the photographs of Mengele, Caine couldn't see it. The old man smiled and nodded his head in a kind of formal European bow.

"I am Dr. Felix Mendoza," he said.

CHAPTER 12

If they were selling the milk of human kindness by the quart, Dr. Mendoza could have opened a dairy, Caine decided irritably. It was annoying, because Mendoza didn't fit his expectations. Certainly no one who observed him working on the little Chama boy would have ever mistaken him for the infamous Mengele. The boy, his skin flushed and sweating, was about six years old. He had been carried into the examining room by the anxious father, a short, squat Indian, his face tattooed with red and black stripes, who still carried a blowgun. The Indian stood silently next to Caine, mechanically chewing a chaw of coca leaves as he watched the doctor prod the child. The heat was intense in spite of the electric fan that rotated its face back and forth across the room, like a robot programmed to answer "no."

Inger removed the thermometer from the boy's rectum and examined it critically. Mendoza poked the boy under the left rib cage and the boy squirmed like a wounded animal and began to cry.

"Thirty-nine point five Celsius," Inger said, her violet eyes burning with something that could have been anger, or hatred.

"It's going to be close," Mendoza muttered irritably.

"This fool has almost left it too late"—gesturing at the father. The Indian blinked stupidly, his blank eyes bulging out of his head, like frog's eyes, and began to tremble. The white god was angry.

"The Chamas believe that disease comes from invisible poison darts directed at the victim by some enemy. So he probably took the boy to a *brujo*, a witch doctor, to exorcise the bad magic. By the time this fool brought him to us, it was touch and go," Mendoza remarked to Caine, a faint trace of German evident in his English.

"Now the symptoms are not so clear; complications may have set in. In these parts fever can be caused by a thousand things. So we consider the symptoms," he said, holding up his hand and counting them off on his fingers, one by one. "High, intermittent fever; blood pressure is quite low, ninety over fifty; respiration rate high and somewhat irregular, with signs of some bronchopneumonia, or pulmonary edema."

"The urine shows signs of albumin," Inger said.

"I don't think we have time for a blood test," Mendoza said and turned irritably to the Indian.

"*Iai?* He is eating?" he demanded in pidgin Chama, pointing at the child. The Indian anxiously shook his head and trembled.

"How many days?"

The Indian held up four fingers and acted out vomiting and diarrhea, with sign language.

"The key factor is the enlarged spleen. It's quite tender. Here you can feel it," Mendoza said, and placed Caine's fingers on the boy's abdomen. Caine could feel something swollen move under his touch and the child squirmed and screamed with pain.

"Forget the blood test. It's falciparum malaria.

We're lucky he was brought here today. By tomorrow, if he had lived, it would have degenerated into black-water fever," Mendoza said, staring at the Indian, who squirmed uncomfortably under his gaze, like a child, his face smeared with chocolate, who says he doesn't know what happened to the cake.

"We'll start him with two hundred milligrams of chloroquine," Mendoza said to Inger, who prepared the syringe. Mendoza patted the child's head paternally and turned him over. He popped the hypodermic into the boy's buttock and told the father to take the boy and follow Inger to the infirmary ward, but the Indian stood there with his head bowed, waiting for the white god to punish him. The Indian's hair was alive with lice and Caine felt his skin crawl and moved away from him. Mendoza reached into his shirt pocket and brought out a piece of sucking candy, which he offered to the Indian.

"*Iai*, eat," Mendoza said in *lingua geral*, used between the Amazona tribes much as Swahili is used between the differing tribes of east Africa. The Indian looked at him blankly.

"*Oarishama*, good," Mendoza tried, and smiled. The Indian put the candy into his mouth and smiled broadly. He had been reprieved. He picked up the boy and the blowpipe and followed Inger into the infirmary. As he left, Mendoza called out to Inger, his eyes twinkling with self-satisfaction, "And have Maria shampoo his head. It's crawling."

Now was the time to do it, Caine thought. While they were alone, before the next patient came in. But suppose he was wrong. Suppose Mendoza wasn't Mengele. In spite of all the clues it was impossible to imagine this dedicated man, who treated the Indians with such kindness, as Mengele, the ruthless exterminator of what he regarded as inferior races. Jesus, what did you expect? To find the place festooned with swastikas and barbed wire? he asked himself sardonically. But still, what if he was making a mistake? He would have to wait till he was sure, he thought, accepting a cold glass of papaya juice from Mendoza, who sat on the edge of the examining table.

It began to rain slowly and steadily, the drops clattering like pebbles on the corrugated metal roof of the bungalow. The rain was as warm as bathwater and had that same feel of dirtiness, of having been already used. A black and tan moth, as large as a hand, blundered against the window screen, its wings beating feebly against the wire mesh. The patter of the raindrops was swallowed by the cough of the diesel generator that supplied electricity to the institute, as it started up. For a moment the electric fan paused in its endless oscillation, the blades becoming visible, and then resumed its mechanical survey of the room, barely stirring the dead, humid air.

Was it possible? Caine wondered. It seemed incredible that he could be sitting here calmly sipping papaya juice with the man he had hunted over half the world— the man he was being paid half a million dollars to kill.

"You're not a journalist, are you?" Mendoza asked him good-naturedly, but his dark eyes were masked with a trace of suspicion. Caine shook his head and lit a cigarette, the smoke tasting of disinfectant and vegetation and the earthy smell of the tobacco-colored rain.

"Because I don't want the world to discover me the way they discovered Albert Schweitzer. They turned him into a celebrity, a commodity for public con-

sumption, like some overdeveloped Hollywood star-
let," Mendoza said with disdain. "After a while the
publicity-seekers and professional do-gooders outnumbered the lepers. Any publicity would only interfere
with my work and contaminate the Indians. You've
seen for yourself how hard it is to get them to give up
on their *brujos* and bring the sick here. Had I seen
that little boy twelve hours later, I wouldn't have
been able to save him. Fill this place up with white
men and we'll never be able to get them out of the
jungle to where we can help them."

"I'm just an oilman, Doctor. I'm here to establish
medical facilities for our drilling crews. It can mean a
lot of money for you. Money for equipment, drugs,
even research, if you like."

He dropped the word *research* like bait, hoping
Mendoza would pick it up.

"What research?" Mendoza looked sharply at him.

"I was told by Father José that you were interested
in studying tropical diseases."

"Oh, that," Mendoza said, his eyes troubled. "No, I
don't do research anymore, Señor McClure. And I
don't want your oil crews here either. Your people can
only interfere with my work here."

"That's all I'm trying to do, too. Just my job, Doctor."

A little Shipibo girl who barely came up to Caine's
knee wandered into the room. Completely naked, she
gravely reached out a hand to Mendoza, who placed a
piece of sucking candy in it. Her other arm had been
amputated above the elbow. She put the candy into
her mouth and padded out the door.

"Snakebite," Mendoza explained. "Probably a *fer-
de-lance*. The Indians tried to treat it with river mud,

parrot feathers, and *brujo* chants. By the time we caught it, we had to amputate." There was no emotion in his face and Caine was reminded of Mengele's bleak *Laboratorium,* where healthy limbs were amputated as a matter of course. He would do it tonight, he decided, using the cover of darkness to get back to the camp by the lake, where he had instructed Pepé to wait for him with the *lancha.*

"Why don't we discuss it tonight over dinner," Caine said. "At the very least you might consider letting Petrotex make a financial contribution to your work."

"As you wish, Señor McClure. But I'm quite firm about my policy of noninterference. I only saw you as a courtesy to Ministro Ribiero."

"We'll talk at dinner," Caine insisted, trying Harris's sincere smile again. He was beginning to get it right, he thought. Soon he would be like Harris and he wondered if Harris himself knew when he was being sincere.

"People come and go in the Amazona, like bits of debris in the river," Mendoza said, and shrugged. It was almost a threat, Caine thought, and he was about to confront Mendoza right there and then, but didn't because Inger appeared in the doorway, and he was certain now that the flame in her eyes was hatred.

They walked across the compound in the rain, Inger pointing out everything of interest, in a kind of breezy, nonstop chatter, as though she were the local Welcome Wagon lady. The rain flattened her short, boyish yellow hair and plastered her clothes to her skin, giving her the compelling appearance of a Rhine maiden washed ashore by the river—one of those legendary Loreleis who lure sailors to their destruction.

Caine followed her slim, young figure to the lab, where a heavyset middle-aged German technician named Guenther sat peering through a microscope at blood slides. Guenther nodded gravely to Caine and solemnly explained his work, spoken in a monotonous tone, as though he were reading a legal contract out loud. He declined Caine's offer of a cigarette, and when pressed, he indicated that the only thing he felt the lack of was a new centrifuge.

Inger introduced him to Helga, Guenther's wife, in one of the bungalows set aside for special cases. Helga was a short, stout woman in a white nurse's uniform who spoke only German. She had hard, piggy eyes, blotchy cheeks that reminded him of a figure in a Hals painting, a mouth that opened and closed like a trap, and Caine had little difficulty in picturing her as a matron in a concentration camp. Helga acknowledged Caine with a grim smile and he felt a prickle at the back of his neck. His certainty about Mendoza's identity was beginning to grow.

Helga was adjusting a bottle of an aromatic amide solution of 2-hydroxstilbamidine set up for intravenous feeding into the arm of a teen-aged Yagua boy, the left side of his face, ear, neck, and chest covered with horrible sores from blastomycosis. The air in the hut was thick with the sickly stench of rotting skin. The boy barely glanced at them, never taking his frightened eyes off Helga, who busied herself with the butterfly clamp that controlled the intravenal flow as though she were rigging up some kind of white man's torture device.

It was only after Inger had shown him everything—the bungalows and huts where the families of the patients stayed; the operating room; the storage rooms full of food supplies, drugs, and medical equipment; the generator shed; the kitchen and dining room; the vegetable patch and barnyard pens for chickens, pigs, and goats—that she took him to her bungalow.

"What's in here?" Caine asked, his face shiny from the rain.

"This is my room," she said, her violet eyes hooded like those of a cobra, and she began to unbutton her shirt. Caine started to back away from her, his senses bristling with the prickle of danger. To go to bed with her would be like mating with a barracuda, he thought. She had the same air of streamlined beauty and deadly efficiency, as if she were made of very fine, very cold steel. She took off her shirt and faced him, her small pointed breasts not much bigger than a young girl's, the nipples erect like tiny daggers. She pressed herself against his wet shirt and kissed him, her sharp teeth gnawing at his lip as though she wanted to draw blood.

"Well, what are you waiting for? Take off your clothes!" she ordered harshly, her eyes almost phosphorescent in the humid midday gloom.

"I don't think this is a very good idea," Caine said, gently pushing her hands away, but he never got a chance to say why, because she slapped his face savagely, her eyes blazing with a hate-filled passion, her teeth bared in an animal growl. Without thinking, Caine slapped her back as hard as he would a man, knocking her backward and splitting her lip. With a cry she sprang at him, spitting like a cat and clawing at him with her fingernails. He grabbed her arm and using a hip-roll, threw her to the floor. She licked at the blood on her lip with a long, pointed tongue and her eyes glittered like sapphires.

"Yes, oh yes, oh yes," she sobbed, and he was startled by the sudden knowledge that this was what she wanted. She liked it! She crawled over to him and began to lick his muddy shoes, her mouth a smear of mud and blood, then she tore off her wet jeans and panties and began fumbling with his belt buckle. He felt her biting his shoulder, as she pulled him down on top of her, her legs spread wide and her pelvis humping madly against his. He entered her moist, tight vagina that burned hot enough to scorch him, her rhythmic thrusting moving even faster against him, like a mindless machine running out of control. He pinned her arms to the ground, his body pounding into her as though he wanted to split her open.

"Hurt me, hurt me," she gasped, sucking the rain and sweat from his neck like a vampire. He thrust deep into her, impaling her on his cock, realizing that this was as close to rape as he had ever come, their mating the ultimate savage battle of the sexual war.

"Fuck me, you animal, fuck me hard! You animal, you animal!" she screamed in time to his thrusts and she climaxed with a piercing cry. He pounded even harder at her slackening body, his cock stabbing into her, as though he were trying to kill her with it and when he came, it was with a desperate grunt that brought little sense of relief, drops of semen spilling out of her onto the floor between her legs.

They lay there for a long time, motionless as bodies on a battlefield, the only sounds their labored breathing and the clattering of the rain on the corrugated metal roof. Gradually he became aware of the weight of his body on hers, his nose buried in the golden thatch of her hair, which smelled like wet straw. He eased himself off her gingerly, his back still sore from the crash in Vienna.

There was a moment when the lulling sound of the rain, the whisper of the wind as it rustled the palm fronds, the sweet and sour smell of sex, and the sticky, jungle heat made him think of Lim and the sickly, cloying scent of Asia, of the soft times of loving when the war was only a shadow in the corner and all that mattered was the two of them sheltering from the storm, safe within each other's arms. But when he looked into Inger's cold, sparkling eyes, he knew that what they had experienced was not lovemaking, but something far more ancient in its mindless savagery. The priest had been right, he mused. To enter the jungle is to enter the primordial darkness of the heart.

Almost as if he had summoned it with his mind, a giant black beetle, the size of his palm, crawled out of a dark corner and across the wall, its shiny pincers open and threatening, its very existence a declaration that the Jurassic Age hadn't ended, that hideous monsters still stalked the earth. With a sigh he reached for his discarded shirt, pulled a crumpled cigarette from the pocket, and lit it.

"Don't think this means anything, because it doesn't," Inger said bitterly, getting up from the reed mat and lying down on her narrow bed. He sat beside her, exhaling the smoke as if it were a sense of regret and flicked his ashes on the floor.

"I'll bet you say that to all the boys," he said.

"You bastard!" she snapped, her eyes flashing. She tried to slap him again, but he easily caught her wrist in his hand.

"Don't," he warned, "or I'll break it. This time it

won't be for fun." And his eyes glittered as coldly as hers.

"You think you're really something, don't you?"

"Tell me, is it just me, or are you out to get the entire male sex?" He felt her wrist relax and he released it as if it were something dirty.

"You're so damn smart, you figure it out," she sneered.

"Let's not pretend you didn't want this. You brought me here."

"Of course I used you. Who am I supposed to fuck around here? The Indians? I'd sooner do it with one of the goats out back," she retorted, her face contorted with disgust. Perhaps some of that disgust was for herself, he mused. The sound of the rain was lighter now. Soon it would stop.

"No, it's more than that," he said finally. "You hated me from the minute you saw me. But why? Who am I to you?"

"My father is a brilliant man," she said.

"Yeah, I'll bet he's a wow doing his Great White Father act for the Indians," he said, egging her on, his senses alert and probing. Danger, as real and palpable as the black beetle, had entered the room. She had something to tell him if he could just needle it out of her.

"He's more of a man than you are, old as he is. Someday the world will recognize his genius," she said defiantly. "Take that magnificent diagnosis he did on that little Chama boy. It was my father who discovered that blackwater fever is a complication of falciparum malaria. He wrote a paper for *Lancet*, proving that blackwater fever is an antibody-antigen reaction resulting in intravascular haemolysis, but the fools refused to publish it. They said that his research methods weren't rigorous enough, that his results weren't conclusive! They wanted control groups. Control groups!" she said, her eyes blazing.

The rain had stopped and the outside air was thick with sunshine. A rainbow had formed in the sky over the compound, the colors rich and sparkling, like some giant snake curved over the jungle. The air steamed in the relentless heat and clouds of mosquitoes rose like columns of smoke in the strong light. Pockets of mist lay over the mud puddles, white and gleaming, as though it had snowed during the storm.

"What's wrong with control groups?"

"What do you know, anyway?" she retorted.

"Not much, I guess."

"My father established the institute to help the Indians, not to experiment on them. He's too kind a man for that. That's why they worship the ground he walks on; that's why we all do. He's the finest man I've ever known. Hell, he's the only real man I've ever known."

"He seems to treat the Indians very well," Caine said carefully.

"It's not just the Indios, it's everyone. He's an incredible philosopher and medical researcher. He's a linguist and an anthropologist. Someday his theories on the origin of the Indian races will revolutionize our knowledge of the development of man. He's even an architect. He designed and built everything you see here. When he came to the Urubamba, all this was nothing but malaria-infested jungle. He did it all by himself. And that's not all. He's a zoologist who has classified dozens of new insect and bacterial species. Even in this place he's brought us the culture of the world. He's a brilliant violinist. You should hear him

play Mozart and Schumann. It's glorious," she rhapsodized.

"What about your mother?"

"She died when I was a little girl. She was his mistress in—" she hesitated, "—in another place. But she
wasn't worthy of him, that's why he never married
her. That's right," she declared defiantly, thrusting
her chin out as if it were a weapon. "I'm a bastard!
My father didn't have to take me in, especially with
all he had to do, a busy, important man like him, but
he did. He's the most wonderful man in the world!"

"The way you talk about him, he sounds more like
your lover than your father."

"He was," she said simply. Her words hung in the
air between them like a curtain. He turned to look at
her, the side of her face lit with a bright bar of sunlight, her hair a splash of gold in the drab room. She
was lying on her side, her head supported on her arm,
her expression as motionless and veiled as the Sphinx.
She ignored the fly sipping at a bead of sweat in the
hollow where her neck joined her breastbone. With
her golden helmet of hair, her virginal, almost boyish
face and flat chest, she might have reminded him of a
young knight, an adolescent Parsifal, were it not for the
damp triangle of curly, light brown pubic hair. For
the first time he looked around the whitewashed
room.

The room was as bare as a nun's cell, with none of
the usual feminine dust collectors. The furniture consisted of the narrow bed, a nightstand, chest of drawers made of cedar, and an old mahogany standing
closet. The furniture had the heavy look that was
fashionable in Europe during the thirties. A crude
dressing table, mirror, and a chair completed the

room. The bed and the closet stood on legs set into coffee cans filled with liquid disinfectant, the acrid aroma permeating the room. The whitewashed walls were bare except for a colorful glass display case of butterflies and a large framed black-and-white portrait of Mendoza hung over her bed. A gauzelike mosquito net was draped over one of the bedposts, like a shroud, and a single screened window looked out over the vegetable patch.

"Where was all this?" he asked.

"We were living in—" She hesitated, and he could have sworn she was about to say Paraguay. Then she shrugged, her thin shoulders looking frail and white in the bright afternoon light.

"We moved around a lot. After my mother—" She stopped and began again. "Anyway, there was nothing permanent in my life. There were no other children to play with. We were very isolated. All I had was my father."

He could picture her as a small, solemn little girl, isolated on the *finca* in Pedro Juan Caballero, her only companion, a doll. How lonely it must have been for her in that gloomy house, populated only by that maniacal man and the brooding ghosts of old crimes, he thought, feeling the first stirrings of a kind of sympathy for her. But pity was expensive baggage. Dao had taught him that, he remembered. He wasn't there to pity her. He was there to kill her only real lover, her messiah, he thought disgustedly.

"It was a hard time for my father. He must have been very lonely. Even as a child I knew that my father was a great man, but one whose genius had been rejected by the world, by blind fools who couldn't hold a candle to him," she said with a voice that seemed to come not from her, but from the shadows of the room. It might have been the black beetle that was talking. He could hear the croaking of the frogs. A macaw was squawking nearby with a voice that was almost human.

"One day, I must have been about twelve years old, I got into one of my father's medical books with my coloring crayons. I ruined it," she said happily, a faint Mona Lisa smile bringing a dimple to her cheek.

"I must have colored every page. My father was furious. I remember him shouting at me and I ran to the bathroom to hide. I suppose I wanted his attention. Even then I wanted him all to myself. It felt good somehow, with him pounding in fury at the bathroom door, screaming at me to come out. It was scary, but it was exciting, too. I could feel myself tingling and getting wet between my legs, but I didn't even know what it was. I had no one to tell me what those feelings were all about.

"Finally he smashed in the bathroom door and stood there, panting. I was cowering on the floor, looking up at his red, angry face glaring down at me. It was terrifying and yet there was also that tingling sense of excitement. Then he grabbed me by the arm and he sat down on the folded-down toilet seat. He took off his belt and dragged me across his lap, pulling up my skirt. He tore off my panties and I was completely exposed and helpless. He beat me with his belt while I squirmed and screamed, but he wouldn't stop. The pain was terrible, but it felt good too, somehow. I knew he was right to punish me and I loved him for it. Then I felt his hand fumbling between my legs and it felt wet and good. He slapped my thighs apart and I didn't fight. I only wanted to please him.

Then he took me, right there on the bathroom floor. And I loved it, do you hear? I loved it! I was proud that I could give pleasure to this great man, my father."

"A great man," Caine echoed, his voice a bleak murmur that she either didn't hear, or ignored.

"That was how it all began," she said with an air of quiet dignity, like that artificial solemnity that people tend to wear in church. "We were lovers until he sent me away to school in Switzerland. And even if he was my father, he was more of a man and a better lover than any of those fumbling, posturing Swiss boys we used to sneak out at night to see. Because I loved him! And he loved me!" she declared defiantly.

"Love," Caine snorted. "Is that what you call it?"

"Yes, love!"

"Yeah, well, in my country we call it incest and statutory rape."

"I knew you wouldn't understand," she hissed through clenched teeth.

"You're right." He shrugged. "I'm far too crude to ever understand the finer points of child molestation. But there's just one thing I don't understand: Why are you telling me all this?"

"Because I wanted you to know what a wonderful man you've come to destroy."

He grabbed her arms so tightly that she winced, and he stared intensely at her cold, perfect features. His eyes were like tiny green lights and at that instant he was ready to kill her. His body was desperate for movement, but he had to find out more.

"Where did you get that idea?"

She shrugged listlessly, as if the answer was self-evident.

"You're from *der Seestern,* aren't you?"

Her answer rocked his head back like a slap and his hands slid lifelessly away from her arms. The Starfish again! And all he could think of was how right Koenig had been about how it's what you don't know that'll kill you. Because her words were his death sentence. That's one for the books, he thought with savage irony: hearing your own death sentence pronounced conversationally by a naked woman.

It was proof positive that Mendoza really was Mengele, he thought. It tied Mendoza to Vienna and the Mengele office in Asunción, where he had found the memo. Not that it mattered anymore. Because it was a setup and he knew he'd never leave the institute alive. Whoever or whatever *der Seestern* was, they had been running him on a one-way mission. Because there was no way out. They had been expecting him! He had flown into the institute like an insect into a Venus flytrap. No, he amended the thought bitterly, looking with a sense of revulsion at her cold beauty, she was the Venus flytrap. He tried to joke his way out of it. He needed time, desperately.

"Actually, I'm from a company called Petrotex. We're into oil, not fish."

"We've been expecting someone, Señor McClure or whatever your name is. We knew it would have to be an outsider, a professional. As soon as we heard you were coming from Pucallpa, we knew it was you. From the second I saw you I was certain of it. That's why I brought you here," she said, her eyes sparkling with satisfaction.

"Will you kindly tell me what the hell *der Seestern* is all about?" he demanded irritably and made his move. He shoved her aside and started toward his pants, where the Bauer was, discarded on the floor near the door. But he was too late.

"That is something you and I will have to discuss, Señor McClure, or is it Foster now?" Mendoza said amiably from the doorway.

Mendoza wasn't alone. Helga stood against the far wall, pointing the Bauer at Caine and smiling grimly, her mouth opening and closing like that of a fish. Caine slumped back on the bed in utter defeat. He was disgusted with himself for having been caught by lust, the oldest trap in the business. And this time there was no way out.

He couldn't even try a bluff about his identity to hang on to the McClure cover, because of the tall, blond young man in jungle whites standing next to Mendoza. He looked familiar to Caine; he was one of the men in the BMW who had tried to run him off the road near Bariloche. That he recognized Caine was apparent by the calm certitude with which he pointed the barrel of Caine's own Winchester at Caine's chest, the muzzle opening looking as large as the mouth of the Lincoln Tunnel.

CHAPTER 13

"Did you enjoy having sex with my daughter?" Mendoza asked.

"You ought to know," Caine retorted, and Rolf, the blond man from the BMW, savagely slapped his face. Caine spat out a mouthful of blood and grinned. He had expected something more sophisticated from the Angel of Death of Auschwitz.

"What is your name, anyway? McClure, Foster, or Caine?" Mendoza asked conversationally. They had been through his knapsack and found the other passports, he realized. He shrugged his shoulders as best he could, with his hands and feet tied to a steel chair in Mendoza's laboratory.

"Foster's good enough," Caine lied. He was a professional spy; he'd be telling lies on his deathbed.

"As you wish," Mendoza muttered through his thin lips. And then he was staring at Caine's icy green eyes and the cruel smile that came to Caine's mouth, blurred with blood, like a smeared painting.

"Dr. Mengele, I presume," Caine said.

"Of course," the old man snapped and gave Caine a perfunctory Prussian nod that oddly managed to be both contemptuous and respectful. He was leaning against the lab counter, his hands on his hips and his legs crossed at the ankles. Helga stood nearby, a glint of satisfaction in her piggy eyes, the Bauer still in her hand. Rolf stood near Caine, his hands balled into fists, anxious to start beating Caine, like a dog straining to slip the leash. Inger had gone. Caine sighed and shook his head.

"I walked right into it, didn't I?" Caine said.

"You are to be congratulated for having gotten this far, Herr Foster. You are the first man to find me in more than six years. How did you find me? Müller?"

"Sure, Müller," Caine said. Maybe the bastard would think he was safe now and it might be easier for whoever came after him to get Mengele, he thought.

"I thought as much," Mengele muttered. "You're a dangerous man, Herr Foster. Five of my *Kameraden* are dead thanks to you: Müller, Steiger, Hans and Fritz in Paraguay, Klaus in Vienna and Franz is crippled for life. Very impressive," he admitted. "You must have Aryan blood in you. I would be curious to know your racial heritage. What were your parents?"

"Well," Caine smiled, "my father was Little Black Sambo and my mother was Golda Meir."

"*Schweinhund!*" Rolf shouted, and Caine saw the slap coming. At the last second he turned his face into it and caught the bottom of Rolf's little finger between his teeth. He bit savagely as Rolf screamed in pain and didn't let go until Helga kicked the inside of his knee, the pain flooding through his body. Caine spat out a thick stream of blood, together with a tooth and a piece of Rolf's finger.

"Fucking American!" Rolf cursed, nursing his hand and glaring balefully at Caine; but didn't try to slap him again.

"And don't you forget it," Caine said coldly, rage coursing through him. His eyes were slits and he swore to himself he'd stay alive. He had only one thought now: to kill Mengele and Rolf, no matter what. He let the rage come because it would keep him going. He was still the hunter, he told himself.

"If you were about to be tortured yourself, what would you do?" he had asked Smiley Gallagher that time at Madame Wu's.

"There's only one sure way to survive torture," Smiley had said, his breath wafting the sharp smell of fish sauce at Caine, that odor of fish that was as much a part of his memory of Vietnam as the stench of death itself.

"And that is?"

"You must never, under any circumstance, allow yourself to get caught," Smiley had giggled.

"I was right, Herr Foster. You are a dangerous man. It's a pity I'm going to have to kill you. In some ways we are very much alike," Mengele said calmly, his eyes as dark and empty as outer space.

"I'm nothing like you, you motherfucker," Caine growled.

"Oh, but you are," Mengele said with a mocking smile. Caine recognized the smile. It was exactly as the old Gypsy had described it. Wasserman had been right, he realized. Mengele was no ordinary sadist.

"In a way it is fitting that we should meet in the jungle like this, you and I. We are both strong men who know that the world is a jungle, where only the strong survive," Mengele went on. "We are both killers, outcasts, who make our own rules. Neither of us is bound by the conventional morality of the bourgeoisie. And spare me your protestations of innocence. If I'm a murderer, so are you. After all you came here to murder me, didn't you? So you see, we have something in common after all."

"I'm not even in your league," Caine said angrily, a fine spray of blood spattering his shirt. "I never sent millions of human beings to the gas chambers. I never shot innocent women and babies. I never cut out eyes or healthy limbs. I never buried people alive or used them like laboratory animals. I never fumigated lice with mustard gas. You have that distinction all to yourself, you disgusting pervert!"

Mengele's black eyes bored into Caine, the dark irises like openings to a vortex of emptiness. They were the eyes of a machine. Mengele shook his head, as though he was troubled.

"I don't suppose you'll believe me when I tell you that I sincerely regret what happened in those days. That whole period is like a bad dream that I can hardly remember. It was all so long ago," Mengele said, his mouth twitching with an old man's tremble.

"It's true," he whispered, his eyes wide and fearful, as though he was seeing ghosts. "I did terrible things. We all did. It was as though we were possessed by demons. Men are capable of anything. Anything! Did you know that? Once you let the demons slip their leash, the most horrible things can happen. We gorged like leeches on the blood of our victims. We were drunk with it. I, worst of all. There was no stopping it.

"It was like a long sickness. When I think of it, it's as though I had no part in it. It's as if I were recalling a stranger. It's true, I was insane then, but so was the whole world. Everyone contributed to the crime. Everyone!" he thundered. "There are no innocents! We live in a jungle where every living thing survives by murdering other living things. We are all assassins, so who are you to judge me? How can you, a murderer, judge me for murder?"

"Who's better qualified?" Caine asked simply.

Mengele turned away, his hands gripping the counter for support. With shaky hands he poured himself a glass of papaya juice from a pitcher and sipped at it. He offered the half-filled glass to Caine, who shook his head. Mengele took a deep breath, and when he began again, there was a whine of self-justification in his voice.

"I am not the man I was. You must believe me. Look at me! I've changed over the past thirty-five years. You've changed! The world has changed, so why not Mengele? Look at this place," he said, gesturing at the laboratory. "This is my penance. I've dedicated my life to helping men, not killing them. Can't you see that? What more must I do? I only want to preserve life."

"Why don't you go back to Germany to stand trial. They'll give you a chance to testify, I'm sure. You can tell them all how wonderful you are."

"What good will that do? Will my testimony and death bring back even one of all those millions? Will it? At least here I can be of some use. There are hundreds, thousands, of Indians who are alive today because of me. By staying here, I do the greatest good for the greatest number. Isn't that truly what morality is all about? I shall finish my life here in the jungle," he said definitively, nodding his head.

"You're so full of shit, it's coming out of your ears," Caine retorted. "What about all the people you had killed who tried to bring you to justice? What about Nora Aldot? Shit, you haven't changed!"

"Surely every human being has a right to survive. How can you condemn me for simply trying to stay alive? I didn't go after them, they came after me. How can a dead man do penance?" Mengele argued persuasively, his hands outstretched as though he were addressing a jury.

"You fucking malignancy!" Caine said coldly, his eyes fixed on Mengele, like a cat on a mouse. "Do you think there's anything you can say or do that'll wipe out what you've done? Do you?"

Mengele's eyes, caught in Caine's glance, were as hollow and empty as the sockets of a skull. His hands clutched at the counter behind him as though to a life preserver.

"Is there no redemption, then?" Mengele asked in a tremulous whisper. Caine shook his head solemnly from side to side, though somewhere he knew that the question would always haunt him. When he opened his mouth, blood dribbled over his lower lip and down his chin, giving him a reddish goatee.

"Not for you," he said finally.

"Damn Jew!" Mengele screamed wildly and lurched against the counter, smashing the pitcher and glass to the floor, slivers of glass exploding like tiny pieces of shrapnel. "Jewish scum!" Mengele howled, his face suddenly and totally red, like the eye of a mud hen.

Helga cocked the Bauer and shoved the muzzle against the bridge of Caine's nose, her fat face gloating with satisfaction.

"Now, Herr Doktor?" she asked hopefully. "Can I kill him now, this *Schweinhund*?"

"*Nein*," Mengele snapped authoritatively. "We still have questions to put to Herr Foster."

Mengele stood there arrogantly, once more in complete control. His pupils were cold pinpoints, like those of a hawk. Out of the corner of his eye Caine watched Helga waddle away, her bloated body jiggling with disappointment. Then with a shattering sense of déjà vu Caine watched fascinated as Mengele carefully cracked his knuckles, one by one, precisely as the old Gypsy had described it, and when Mengele coldly examined Caine again, Caine couldn't repress a shiver, because he was finally seeing what only the dead had seen. Dr. Josef Mengele was about to operate.

"I have wasted enough time with you on idle discussion. I want to know everything you know about the Starfish Conspiracy," Mengele announced.

That was it, Caine thought. The Starfish Conspiracy. It was the unknown factor that from the beginning had dogged his footsteps like a shadow, till it tripped him up in the end. He didn't need to look at Mengele's impassive face to know that unless he gave Mengele something to chew on, they would make his death extremely unpleasant. Not that it mattered now. Not that anything did.

"How long have you known about it?" Caine admitted.

"Over a year. It's taken you a long time to track me down."

"Who told you about it? Müller? I knew that was a mistake," Caine said, guessing.

"Excellent," Mengele said, raising his eyebrows. He was clearly enjoying himself. "Yes, Heinrich was one of the few *Kameraden* who refused to betray me. Now its your turn to answer my questions. Tell me, Herr Foster, who sent you?"

"I'm a field agent for the CIA. Did you know that we were involved?"

"I see," Mengele muttered disgustedly. "So that was the fifth arm of *der Seestern.*"

So that was it, Caine thought excitedly. The Starfish was named for a five-armed conspiracy with a single objective. ODESSA, Mengele's former *Kameraden*, was one arm and the CIA might be another, if Harris had lied to him in Berlin. But why did they want Mengele out of the way?

"Why did they want you out of the way?" he asked.

"I don't know," Mengele admitted. "Unless it was—"

And then Caine had it. There could be only one reason that Mengele was a danger to them, even in his jungle hideout. Because it might come out.

"Unless it would be bad publicity for them," Caine finished for Mengele. He shook his head, because the whole thing was insane. It meant that all of them—Wasserman, Harris, Gröbel, and God knows who else—had all been in on it.

There is a moment in every agent's life when he wonders if he has become truly paranoid, because he begins to suspect everyone of conspiracy. Caine wondered if he had reached that point. The whole thing was getting all mixed up, he thought, and he had to consider dismissing the whole idea as impossible. Then he shrugged mentally, because it didn't look like he was ever going to find out.

"I walked right into it, didn't I, like a fly blundering into a spiderweb?" Caine said disgustedly. "Müller alerted you about the Starfish Conspiracy, so you knew they would send someone. I set off alarm bells in Paraguay, Bariloche, and Vienna to let you know I was on the way. The colonel in Pucallpa let you know

I was coming by radio and you had Rolf here to identify me, just to make sure. Inger was the decoy, in case I had any tricks up my sleeve. All you had to do was sit back and wait, like a spider in the middle of his web."

"Just so," Mengele said. "So there's only one thing left before we finish with you, before I step on you like an insect. Where is von Schiffen?"

"Von Who?" Caine asked. He was genuinely astonished.

"How tiresome," Mengele remarked. "And our discussion was going so well," he sighed. "Still, I'll give you one more chance. Perhaps your position isn't entirely clear. You are going to die. It's up to you whether we do it quickly, or whether you die a few days from now, screaming in agony, begging for me to kill you. So I'll ask you once again, where is von Schiffen?"

"Why do you want to know?"

Mengele shrugged. This agent was a dead man in any case. It didn't matter what he told him. Besides, the man clearly had Aryan blood in him. Perhaps he could be reasoned with.

"Von Schiffen is the Starfish, didn't you know? Once he learns that you failed, he will send others. I have to eliminate him before he gets me. Have you forgotten what I said before? I want to live. Surely every human being has a right to fight for his survival. Now, where is von Schiffen?"

Caine took a deep breath, returning Mengele's cold gaze with his own ruthless stare. It was time to show and tell—only he didn't have the foggiest idea who von Schiffen was, and even if he did, it wouldn't matter. The only consolation he would have as he died was that Mengele would still be worrying about this von Schiffen character. It wasn't much, he reflected. But still, men have died for less.

"Whatever gave you the idea that you're a human being?" Caine said carefully.

Mengele smiled and Caine knew he had been right. It was not a human smile. He had to hang on to one thought now, only one. If he ever got free again, even for a second, he would kill Mengele as mercilessly as he would a plague-carrying rat.

"That was a very foolish thing to say. You see, here in the jungle one has no need of elaborate torture apparatus. The jungle itself provides all the discomfort necessary to persuade you to do anything I say. Take him to the Anthill," Mengele ordered.

Rolf placed the muzzle of the Winchester against Caine's back as Helga began to carefully untie his feet, squatting between his legs like a giant toad. It was useless to hope, Caine realized. He could barely move.

"I don't think I'm going to like the Anthill," Caine said. He really didn't think he was going to like it at all.

"*Nein*, I'm sure you won't," Mengele said, and patted Caine's hair paternally with the same comforting air of a doctor prescribing foul-tasting medicine for the patient's own good that he used as a bedside manner with the Indians.

"We built a tin shed over an anthill," Mengele said conversationally. "Of course, the shed is incredibly hot and uncomfortable, like an oven in the sun. But that is nothing. You see, my friend, this is the Amazona and these are fire ants. Any one of them is from two to five centimeters long and can give you a bite far more painful than any beesting. You will be bitten thousands and thousands of times. They never stop.

"You can scream all you like. There's no one to hear you except the ants and the Indians. And they won't mind or help you, I assure you. Usually after two or three hours on the Anthill, even a strong man goes completely and permanently insane. I may decide to keep you there for days. It's up to you." Mengele smiled and affectionately pinched Caine's cheek. "Now get him out of here. He has taken up too much of my time already," Mengele snapped to Rolf and Helga.

They forced Caine into a squatting duck walk, his hands and torso still tied to the chair. Rolf prodded him with the Winchester toward the door, Helga never taking her eyes off him. Now he knew how a cripple felt, he thought as he paused near the door, throwing a last glance back at Mengele, who smiled.

"*Auf Wiedersehen*, Herr Foster," Mengele said.

"*Heil* Hitler, you creep," Caine retorted with a bravado he was far from feeling, as Rolf kicked him and he fell heavily to the ground. Rolf kicked Caine to his feet and prodded him across the compound in his awkward squat, while the Indians watched his progress with silent, open stares.

A shadow crossed his face for a second and he glanced up at the blinding bluish-white glare of the tropic sun until he could make out the black speck of a large bird in the blue immensity of the sky. For a moment he wondered where Inger was. Then Rolf prodded him again with the gun and they resumed their slow pilgrimage across the compound to the small corrugated metal hut that stood at the outskirts of the institute on the leafy fringe of the jungle. All the way across, Caine had only a single thought in his mind: kill Mengele.

Helga unlocked the door to the shed and the heat from the dark interior almost knocked them down. It was as blistering as a sauna. As his eyes adjusted to the gloom, Caine could make out the anthill, a low sand-colored mound swarming with scurrying dark rust-brown insects about half the size of his little finger. A few Yagua Indians had come up to the door of the shed to watch what was going on. As the light from the doorway invaded the hut, the ants ran about in turmoil and Caine felt his flesh crawl. He had that same feeling of unreality as in a nightmare—that feeling of helplessness as the worst you can imagine is happening and you can't do a thing to stop it.

"Oh, shit," he muttered. With a curse Rolf shoved him into the shed and kicked his legs from under him. Caine fell heavily onto the anthill, landing on his side. The mound seemed to boil with a frenzy as the excited insects milled and ran about in confusion.

Rolf and Helga quickly tied the chair arms with hemp line to rusty hooks on opposite sides of the shed, slapping at the insects on their clothes as they worked. Then they hastily retreated to the door to watch. Helga took a spray can from her dress pocket and she and Rolf sprayed each other, while the Indians began to giggle at the strange antics of the white people.

Caine felt the first bite almost immediately on his calf and he screamed desperately. It was like being stabbed by a white-hot knife. His body began to twitch uncontrollably as tears rolled out of his eyes. There was another bite on his arm and another on his cheek and he screamed again. With horror he realized that he had never really known pain before. Not like this. His body thrashed spasmodically and he screamed again and again as thousands of insects swarmed over him, running and biting. It was like touching fire, like being burnt alive, each bite raising a bright red welt on his skin.

His screams echoed in the dark, stifling shed. His skin was crawling with maddened ants, and they were biting his thighs, back, and stomach. He felt his mind shrivel like burning paper as his body seemed to explode with agony. "Help me," he begged. "Help me!"

For one horrible moment he opened his eyes and saw the Indians in the doorway. They were laughing and slapping each other on the back, almost falling down with laughter, as though they were watching a hilarious slapstick comedy. Rolf and Helga smiled grimly at each other as they regarded Caine, his body almost black with a moving surface of insects. He screamed desperately as an ant bit his eyelid. Then the doorway went dark as Helga slammed the door shut and locked it. Caine was alone in the crawling darkness.

The pain seemed to get worse and worse, his body quivering with hundreds of burning, stabbing wounds. In desperation he tried a Zen mind discipline, attempting to concentrate on each bite, to experience it into disappearing—but it was impossible. His screaming nerves were feeding in too much pain from too many points and the agony was unbearable.

He could feel his skin crackling and sizzling like meat on a grill, as the pain grew and grew and there was nothing left of him, no part of him that wasn't pain. The frenzied ants crawled under his clothes and stampeded into every crevice of his body. They swarmed through his hair, into his ears and nostrils, across his screwed-tight eyelids, and into his mouth. His skin and clothes were black with the rustling, scorching mass of them, piercing him again and again with sharp, stinging jaws. He felt his mind going as the top of his head seemed to explode. Please stop, someone was whimpering over and over and he didn't even know it was him. And some part of him broke and he lay there quivering like jelly, his tears and sweat soaking into the ground and everything was darkness and pain and crawling terror.

He was in hell, a noisy, burning hell filled with laughing, tormenting demons who devoured his living, screaming flesh with the mindless savagery of machines. He was in a black, fiery tunnel, the darkness growing to engulf him, and even as he welcomed it, the bliss of nothingness, of death, he knew that the world was a horror, a place of madness. And he became one with the insects devouring him and as the horror carried him to the crawling, cruel insect that he finally knew himself to be, a single thought filled his tiny insect brain, black with hate: kill Mengele. Kill Mengele. Kill Mengele.

CHAPTER 14

The water was dark and steaming, boiling with the heat and grotesque alien shapes. A school of piranha were tearing at his flesh in a feeding frenzy. The salt taste of the water was the taste of blood, and like the fish, he was feeding on his own bleeding flesh. The dark shape of a shark, blacker than the darkness, ripped away his groin and he could almost see the bloody remnants of his manhood dangling from the gaping maw of the shark's saw-toothed jaws.

"Is there no redemption, then?" the shark asked him as it gulped and swallowed his flesh.

"No, there is no redemption," he heard his dead, grinning skull say. His bones, picked clean by the piranha, began to rise in the current.

His skeleton rose slowly as the bubbles, like the time he had gone for his scuba certification dive near Anaconda Island, his instructor holding his chin up as they ascended. He had removed all his gear and left it on the ocean floor and they swam up together, forty feet toward the surface, exhaling all the way until he couldn't exhale anymore and his chest began to burn for air. And still they rose, the water growing lighter and lighter as they neared the brightness that was the surface. Then it was brighter, and then it was dark again.

He opened his burning eyes, shimmering with fever. It was dusk. A giant red sun filled the jungle with fiery light, the edges of the leaves glowing as though they were burning. He could hear the chirping of the cicadas and the monotonous croaking of the frogs. From somewhere came the sweet, acrid scent of insect spray and he could feel the fish still nibbling at his groin.

His body radiated heat like a star and simply to breathe was agony. Descartes was wrong, he thought. I feel pain, therefore I am. And then he glanced down and saw his arms, still securely bound to the arms of the chair. His skin was mottled with red welts that seemed to cover his body. He saw the top of Inger's head between his knees, her metal-bright hair glowing like an ember in the dying red light. She was sucking his cock. Madness, he thought. The universe is a mad dream.

He sat lifelessly bound to the upright chair, like the corpse of an African tribal chief. Inger had obviously dragged him to the doorway of the shed, where she had sprayed him and the area around the door with insect spray. He watched her with indifference as she moved her head, sliding his penis in and out of her mouth. He felt nothing but the pain and a mild sense of amazement that his penis could even get hard, because his body no longer seemed to belong to him. He stared at his bound hands, at the somehow reptilian network of crevices that covered his knuckles, spotted with welts from the ants, and saw for the first time what a prehensile claw his hand truly was. He willed his finger to move and was surprised when it did. It seemed to be the dead claw of some extinct animal, with a life of its own. Almost as an afterthought, he realized, with a surge of pain, that he was still alive.

Inger stopped sucking for a moment to look up at him, her mouth drooling like a beast, her eyes glowing like rubies in the fiery sunset and he knew that the fire in her eyes was madness.

"I wanted to have this one more time before they killed you," she said, baring her teeth savagely.

As she bowed her head again to his groin, his leg lashed out, his shin catching her under the chin. He heard her teeth click as she tumbled to the ground. He rocked forward in the chair and fell on her stomach with his knees, knocking the breath from her. It had all happened without any thought; his actions had become totally instinctual. Every movement was agony for him, but that didn't matter because he had only a single raging thought: kill Mengele.

He somehow managed to stagger to his feet as she lay there groaning and trying to get up. He planted his foot across her neck, pinning her to the ground and choking her. She struggled feebly against his weight, but Caine was implacable.

"Untie my hands or I'll kill you," he threatened, his eyes burning like the flames of hell itself.

"No," she gasped and struggled desperately, but he leaned even harder, as though he wanted to stamp her out of existence.

"Untie my hands, you fucking animal," he rasped.

"Yes, master. Oh, yes, master," she managed to gasp and her hands fumbled at the knots around his wrist.

Caine squatted down, his knees on her chest, while she feverishly tore at the knots with her nails. The moment he felt the rope loosen, he freed his hand and grabbed her throat. He ordered her to untie the other hand and the seconds passed like hours till the moment he felt the knot give and he was free.

With a wide cruel sweep he slapped her face with every particle of strength in him, breaking her jaw. Then he grabbed her hair and hauled her into the chair. He gripped her hair tightly, as though he wanted to tear it out by the roots. Her eyes were wide with pain and horror as she stared up at him. And there was something else in them. It was beyond submission. It was, almost, gratitude. Because Mengele wasn't her true love. Or the whip smacking against the leather boot. It was death she loved. He saw that now. Death and his handmaiden, pain. That was why she wanted and obeyed Caine, even as she trembled at the sight of him. With his hellish eyes and bloody, mottled skin he looked like nothing human.

"Where's Mengele?" he rasped.

She tried to speak, but only unintelligible grunts came out of her broken jaw. He gripped her hair even tighter and twisted her head.

"If you can't talk, point, you cunt," he growled in her ear.

Her trembling hand pointed at the laboratory, where a single light was burning in Mengele's office. She clutched at his grimy shirt as he began to pull away and shook her head desperately, her shiny eyes imploring him to stay. He shook her off and grimly tied her to the chair, gagging her mouth with a strip of her shirt.

He dragged her bound and moaning body back into the metal shed and closed the door. Then he began running toward the laboratory, his black figure almost invisible in the shadows of evening. Every step was agony, his brain burning with the high fever from the ant bites, but Caine was beyond mere pain. He was the hunter, closing on his prey.

As he approached the laboratory, he could hear the lilting sound of a violin playing the "Blue Danube" waltz. A mosquito bit his neck and he could have laughed because he scarcely felt it. He stopped to catch his breath in the shadow of the laboratory, then cautiously tiptoed to the lighted window and carefully peered inside through the screen. Mengele was standing near the desk, his eyes closed, playing his violin for Guenther and Helga, who were seated side by side on folding chairs, their faces rapt with the sentimentality of the music. Caine began to tiptoe around the building toward the front door. He had no plan, only the single consuming thought: kill Mengele.

He crept as silently as a shadow up on the porch and opened the screen door. The sound of the music was stronger now and it reminded him of Wasserman's story, about how Mengele had ordered the inmate orchestra to play Strauss waltzes as the Jews were led to the gas chambers. His mind barely had time to register the fact that the sound of his footsteps was covered by the music before he was moving quickly through the doorway into the office.

Mengele saw him first and froze, his face a mask of shock and horror. Caine's blood-splotched face, glittering green eyes, and savage, implacable movement gave him the appearance of a specter from hell. He moved irresistibly toward Mengele, who began to back away in terror against the desk. Caine's first move was a spinning round kick that caught Guenther in the back, knocking him to the floor.

Helga sprang for a table against the wall and grabbed a scalpel, whirling to face Caine. As he moved toward her, she slashed at his face with the blade. Automatically Caine went into one of the sequences Koenig had rehearsed them in, over and over, till they could do it in their sleep. He blocked the slash with his left forearm and kicked savagely at Helga's midsection, staggering her against the table. She tried to block the right hand chop he aimed at her temple, leaving her left side open, and he finished her with a lightning left uppercut to the ribs. He felt the rib crack under the rubbery layer of fat and whirled to face Mengele as she sank to the floor, but by that time Guenther had a massive forearm locked around Cain's neck in a choke hold from behind. Caine immediately unlocked his knees and sank down, grabbing Guenther's forearm with both his hands. Then he bent forward at the waist with a sudden jerk, sending Guenther flying over his head and toward the wall. Guenther's head cracked against the edge of the table and he collapsed in a heap on the floor, like a puppet whose strings have been cut. His neck was broken.

Mengele was fumbling at a desk drawer, probably for a gun, but before he could grab it, Caine had lunged across the desk, his fist smashing against Mengele's shoulder and knocking him against the wall. Mengele cowered against the wall as Caine stalked him, their eyes locked on one another.

"*Nein, bitte,*" Mengele whimpered. "I can make you a rich man, a million—" and threw a clumsy right hook at Caine's head.

Caine sidestepped the punch, blocking it with his forearm, and put all his rage into a savage right hook to the ribs that came from his toes. Mengele's ribs snapped like dry twigs and he sprawled across the desk, howling in pain and kicking desperately out at Caine. A wild lucky kick hit Caine's midsection, knocking him back, and Mengele scrambled to his feet, his hand holding his ribs. Caine could hear the sounds of movement and voices from outside. He was running out of time. Rolf and the Indians would be on him at any moment. He remembered what Koenig had taught him, that you only use your body as a last resort. "No matter where you are, there is always a weapon at hand. A rock, sand, a bottle, anything will do," Koenig had said.

As Mengele rushed for the door, Caine grabbed a ballpoint pen from the desk and raced after Mengele, cornering him in the lab. Mengele stood there panting, his tongue lolling like a heat-stricken dog, his eyes darting around frantically. He threw a flask at Caine and Caine barely managed to duck out of the way. Before he heard the flask smash behind him, he had already begun to move.

He aimed a stab at Mengele's eye with the pen, but the stab was a feint and as Mengele's arm came up to block the blow, Caine side-kicked Mengele's groin. The back of Mengele's head was exposed as he doubled over with a high-pitched scream. Caine stabbed at the back of Mengele's neck, ramming the pen into the small indentation between the neck and the base of the skull. Caine felt a sudden tremor as Mengele's body collapsed. He had hit the foramen magnum, perhaps the most vulnerable spot in the human body. Mengele was dead before his body hit the floor.

A savage exultation flooded Caine. It was like nothing he had ever felt before. A sense of pure joy and freedom beyond orgasm that only the gods can know.

He let out an insane animal yell that was both terrible
and awesome—the triumphant howl of primordial
man, the killer ape. The hunter had made his kill and
for an instant the jungle itself stood still.

A wide-eyed Indian face peered at him from the
front doorway. Caine grabbed a flask and heaved it at
the Indian, and the head disappeared. The flask shattered harmlessly on the doorpost. He suddenly became conscious of the babble of voices outside and
the sounds of running. His body still tingled with the
thrill of what he had done, but he knew he had almost
run out of time.

He picked up a small corked vial that contained
some tissue specimen floating in formaldehyde and
slipped it into his pocket as he ran back to Mengele's
office. Helga had managed to get up on all fours and
was slowly crawling, like a massive sloth, toward the
scalpel on the floor. Caine kicked her in the side, connecting with the spot under the ribs that boxers aim
at, and she dropped as though she had been poleaxed.
He grabbed the scalpel and ran back to Mengele's
body.

Mengele's hand was curled and grasping as Caine
turned it over. It looked like a bird's claw. He slashed
quickly at the first joint of the thumb, the blood spilling over his hands and onto the floor. He felt no re-
pugnance as he sawed away at the ligaments of the
joint. It felt good to have Mengele's still warm blood
bathing his hands, almost as though he were enacting
some ancient, savage ritual, washing his hands in the
blood of his enemy. The scalpel grew slippery in his
hand and he had to wipe his hands on Mengele's shirt.

He glanced up to see three or four Indian faces staring at him from the doorway, their eyes wide with

horror at the hellish spectacle of the white man kneeling over the body, dismembering the white god, Mengele. They were too frightened to attack or even move. None of them had ever seen anything like it. The white man with the bleeding face was a jungle demon incarnate.

"Justice," Caine shouted at them, his body swaying drunkenly as he straightened up, his eyes burning with flames that were not of this world.

"For the Jews," he cried, and then he remembered the old Gypsy at Auschwitz. "And the Gypsies. And for all the poor bastards from whom God hid His face when they cried out to Him!" he spat out. "And for me," he said with quiet intensity. "Caine, the killer."

And he lifted Mengele's dead hand to his lips and savagely bit off the thumb at the nearly severed joint. He spat the bloody joint into his hand. A sense of release came over him, like a baptism, and he flung the hand away from him and stood up. His lips were red and glistening with Mengele's blood.

He glared at the Indians and began to walk toward them, as they started to back respectfully away from him. Like all primitives, they knew that madness is inspired by the gods. Then he stopped. He heard Rolf angrily cursing in German and Spanish, outside. He was screaming at the Indians to get out of his way. Caine had only a few seconds left.

Instantly he whirled, leaped over the body, and ran for Mengele's office, clutching the bleeding finger in his fist. The doorpost cracked with a loud snap from the .300 caliber slug as he ran past it. He charged across the room and dived headfirst through the window, tearing the screen away and taking it with him as he rolled on the dark ground. He ran across the dark compound with sudden zigzags, like a fleeing rabbit, as the shots of the Winchester echoed through the night.

He stumbled and seemed to hear the hum of a bullet as it whizzed through the space where his head had been. He was tumbling in the mud and suddenly found himself waist-deep in the stream. He dived under the surface, letting the current carry him toward the black wall of the jungle's edge.

The water was cool and soothing as he floated with the current. It felt like balm to his burning skin and the tension began to drain away. He wanted to float forever down the stream, like a log, drifting into a peace he had never known. The coolness touched him with a sense of absolution and he was almost asleep when he came to with a sudden jerk, thrashing and sputtering in the stream. A part of his mind was sounding a desperate alarm—unless he got moving, they would kill him.

He waded to the mudbank and staggered up the slope, somewhere near the edge of the clearing. He had to find the trail back to the Yarinacocha before Rolf and the Indians tracked him down. The darkness was almost complete and it was impossible to orient himself. Even if he found the trail, to attempt the jungle by night was madness. He was sure to lose his way in minutes. But to stay was certain death. Hell, it was death either way, he reasoned. Reason, that was pretty good, he thought. For the first time since they had marched him to the Anthill, his mind was reasoning again. He began searching for the mouth of the trail among the dark trees.

One by one the lights of the institute clicked on, casting dim pools of light over the compound. Soon the Indians would be after him, he knew. They would try to get him before he faded into the dark bush. But the light was a godsend. It would help him to find the trail and he ran faster. He thought he spotted the opening where he and Pepé had emerged from the trees and headed toward it at full speed, when he collided with an Indian, suddenly emerging out of the artificial twilight.

Caine lay dazed on the ground for a moment, then leaped to his feet as the Indian sprang at him, his tattooed face like a ferocious demon mask. Caine pivoted, his feet slipping in the dirt, moving into a clumsy spinning back-kick that luckily caught the Indian high in the chest, knocking him down. Caine didn't hang around to finish the Indian off. He had to get to the safety of the trail. He didn't think they would try to track him in the darkness; that would make them crazier than he was. Suddenly an opening in the trees was before him and he dived into it. Darkness swallowed him as he staggered down the trail, his chest heaving desperately for air.

Somehow he stumbled on through the darkness, branches whipping at his face, until his legs finally collapsed under him. The pain washed over him in waves, his body shivering with the violence of it. There was no end to it, he thought dully. The blackness of the jungle was ominous and eternal, like that of the grave, and his imagination populated it with snakes and scorpions and ugly, crawling shapes. So this is what it's like to be blind, he thought with a shudder, and a feeling of helplessness and horror engulfed him. Stop it! he warned himself. That way madness lies. Who wrote that line, anyway? he wondered. Somebody. Shakespeare, probably. You're alive, damn it. Alive! You did it, you son of a bitch. You pulled it off!

His breathing had grown more regular and the shivering began to ease off. Where was the thumb? he wondered, and it took him a full minute before he realized that it was still clenched in his fist. With fumbling fingers, he took the vial from his pocket and plucked out the tissue specimen. He put the thumb into the vial, recorked it tightly, and replaced it in his shirt pocket, buttoning it securely, the sharp smell of the formaldehyde filling his nostrils. He'd swap the thumb for a cigarette in a minute, he decided. If there was a part of his body that didn't hurt, he couldn't feel it.

They were sure to close his escape route, he knew. By morning Rolf would have radioed Pucallpa and the gunboat would be alerted, so the Yarinacocha was out. And even if he could somehow make it back to Pucallpa, the town was too small and isolated for him to evade the authorities and the Indians. Pucallpa would be a death trap, he realized.

Jesus! He had them all after him now: the Peruvian Army and *policia*, the locals, the Nazis, the Chamas, Yaguas, and Shipibos. And he was on their ground, not his. For him there was only the jungle, where no man can survive alone for long. They had him boxed, all right. And in the morning Rolf and an army of Indians would be on his trail, and they could move twice as fast as he could. It was hopeless.

If he could just get back to the survival pack he had hidden, he thought. It was his only chance. He thought about the AR-15 carbine hidden in the tree, and felt better. If he could just get back to it, he could take a few of the bastards with him, he reflected grimly. Christ, he wanted a cigarette badly. There were cigarettes in the survival pack, he reminded himself. He had to get back to it.

What time was it, anyway? He brought his wrist up to his eyes, the radium watch dial glowing in the darkness, like a constellation of stars. His eyes fastened greedily on the tiny specks of light. A quarter after nine. It was still early, in spite of everything that had happened. The night seemed endless.

Where was C.J. now? he wondered. Probably having dinner in some fancy restaurant, her face glowing from an afternoon on the beach, surrounded by the murmur of conversation and the tinkle of cocktails. Did she think of him, or was she really taken by all the superficial charm of the people around her? He felt a kind of contempt for their world of surfaces, filled with those who do not know that the ocean is not the surface you can see, but the depths that cannot be seen. Suddenly he began to laugh, because as desperate and painful as his situation was, he was luckier than they were. He was alive! He could feel life pulsing through his veins. He wondered if C.J. could ever see things that way.

He felt something move across his foot and he froze, the sweat rolling down his face as though it would never stop. Something long and slow and he knew it was a snake. And then the movement stopped and he was sure that within inches from him, somewhere in the darkness, the long, forked tongue was flicking out, sensing the air for the heat of his body, waiting to strike. He held his breath in terror. The slightest sound or movement would give him away. His instincts, harking back to tree-dwelling days, were screaming at him to run, but he couldn't move. What was it? he wondered desperately. It was too light for a boa constrictor and that meant it could well be poisonous. There was no sound of rattling, so it probably wasn't a bushmaster. It could be anything, a *fer-de-lance*, a palm viper, or a deadly coral snake. Whatever it was, it wasn't his idea of a house pet. A bead of sweat hung on the tip of his nose, itching maddeningly. Go away, his mind screamed and it was almost worth getting killed just to scratch his nose. If he could just see its head—but it might be anywhere.

The screech of a howler monkey sounded from the darkness far above him. The cry was taken up by a trio of macaws and the jungle came alive with chattering cries. And then a slender, pale shaft of light touched his foot. It was the moon! he thought exultantly. If the snake would just move, he had a chance to get away. He could just make out the trail in the dim, ghostly light. He had to get out of there! Move, you bastard! Move!

At last, after what seemed like an hour, he felt the snake slither on and on across his foot and disappear, with a faint rustle of leaves, into the darkness. It must have been a good eight feet long! He forced himself to wait for at least twenty seconds more, counting them as if they would never end. He moved his stiff legs and broke into a run down the trail, feeling his way as much as seeing. It was time to perform the classic, military maneuver known as "Getting the fuck out of there." He had to put as much distance between the institute and himself as possible before daylight. The distance he covered this night was all the head start he was going to get. If only he had a flashlight! Or a cigarette, damn it, he thought, rubbing his nose gratefully as he ran.

The night passed in a kind of twilight daze, like that odd moment between sleep and waking when one is not sure which is the reality and which the dream. His brain was dizzy and increasingly confused. He couldn't tell whether it was fatigue, or the darkness, or the pain, or the rising fever from the ant bites. Time and again he lurched into trees and bushes, bouncing against them, like a beaten fighter against the ropes. Each time they knocked him down, he would scramble up again and stagger on. He blundered into invisible spiderwebs that tickled his face with long, sticky fingers. With a shudder he tore through them with flailing arms and stumbled ahead, his skin crawling with the feel of hairy legs and no way of telling whether they were imaginary or real. He was completely exhausted, yet he went on and on, hardly knowing what he was doing. His arms hung like dead weights from his shoulders and his head swayed drunkenly, lolling on his panting chest.

It was nearly midnight when he finally collapsed. He tried to crawl to his feet, but he couldn't make it and fell face-first into the decaying earth. Got to rest, he thought stupidly. You can't rest, another part of him said. If the Indians don't get you, the bugs and snakes will. You can't lie down on the ground in the jungle. It was as though he had three selves: one that obstinately refused to move; a second that insisted on it; and a third that observed the debate as though it were a tennis match.

Your only chance is to rest, he told himself. No, your only chance is to move; there's time enough for rest in the grave, he countered. Somehow he got to his feet again, stumbled ahead, and then he was down again. Can't stay here, got to move, he thought dully, licking his dry lips with a tongue that felt raspy as a file. Take one more step, Hudson's voice was screaming at him from the darkness and he was up again, lurching farther down the trail and then he was down again, sprawling in the rank, moist dirt.

The darkness was complete and he couldn't tell whether it was the night, or whether he had blacked out. Got to get off the trail. Can't let them find me here, his thoughts clinking dully against each other like coins in a nearly empty purse. He crawled heavily into the bush and blindly pulled at palm fronds to make a rough bed. The frond edges cut his fingers, but he was already in so much pain that he hardly felt it. He collapsed with a dry rustle on the small heap of fronds and then there was only the darkness.

Caine woke with a start at the cracking sound of a broken twig. The jungle was bright with the milky light of morning and the merry chirp of birds. The air buzzed with the sound of insects and it took him a few seconds before he remembered where he was. Through the dense foliage he could see the naked, brown figure of an Yagua on all fours, sniffing the ground like a dog. They were tracking him!

The Yagua stood up and carefully inspected the bushes along the trail. He was carrying a blowgun, a bamboo quiver of darts dangling from it. Caine knew that the darts were tipped with curare. Just to prick your finger with one of the darts would cause death within fifteen seconds, and he remembered Father José telling him that the Yaguas could hit a parrot at a hundred yards with their blowguns.

He needed a weapon desperately, he thought, his skin shiny with sweat. The Indian's gaze passed right across the sun-dappled foliage in front of Caine, and Caine's muscles tensed into knots. A shout sounded farther down the trail and the Yagua turned and trotted away. As he disappeared from sight, Caine began to breathe again. He glanced down at his sweat-slick arms, the skin swollen and welted as boiled sausage and he began to panic. The heat was intense and he couldn't tell whether it was fever from the ant bites, or just the sun.

"Are you okay?" Hudson's voice sounded in his ear, just as it had when he had sprained his ankle on their first twenty-mile cross-country march in Panama. Hudson had shown him how to tightly bind the ankle, but Caine didn't think he could walk on it. Hudson just stood there glowering at him.

"When I say 'Are you okay?' I mean, are *you* okay? I don't mean your ankle. That's just pain and pain is just pain. It's no excuse for not doing anything. What I want to know is, are *you* okay?"

"I'm okay, Hudson, I'm okay," Caine muttered, just as he had that time in Panama. He scrambled painfully to his feet and began to check his pockets, but there was nothing he could use for a weapon. He began to move slowly through the bush and cautiously started hiking down the trail, keeping his eyes peeled to the ground till he found what he was looking for: a dead branch of hardwood, about an inch in diameter. With difficulty he broke the branch into two roughly equal pieces, each about eight inches in length. He tied the two sticks at the ends with a length of tough, slender vine, which he cut by chewing with his teeth so that the sticks were connected by a two-inch-long stretch of flexible vine. He got a sense of power by

just holding the crude *nunchaka* he had just constructed. It wasn't the greatest weapon in the world,
but he felt better just having it. You used it by holding one stick and whipping the other at your opponent, and it was efficient enough to have been outlawed as a deadly weapon by the state of California.
He grimly looped the *nunchaka* through his belt and
started down the trail toward the Yarinacocha.

Caine could hear the sounds of the Indians crashing
through the bush long before he could see the shimmering light of the sun reflecting off the water. He
quickly abandoned the trail and angled into the undergrowth, toward where he estimated he had cached
the survival pack. If he could just get to the pack before the Indians spotted him, he might have a chance,
he thought anxiously. Then he heard something and
froze.

The Indians were all around him. He could hear the
faint rustlings of movement as they picked their way
through the jungle. Down toward the water a voice
that sounded like Rolf's was snapping orders in a muffled tone. There was a shout and then an ear-piercing
scream that was cut off as suddenly as it had begun.
The sweat poured into Caine's eyes, stinging them
sharply, and he blinked to clear them. He wearily
leaned his forehead against a tree, the rough bark
scratching his skin. Why didn't they find him and just
get it over with? he wondered.

When he finally opened his eyes and focused them,
he realized that he was staring at a strange marking
on the trunk. His heart skipped a beat when he recognized it. It was the blaze he had cut the night before
last, to mark the way to the survival pack. He started

into the clearing toward the three *cedro* trees and then froze. A wide-eyed Yagua was staring right at him, the blowgun already being raised to his lips.

Caine dived sideways into the brush as the poison dart thunked into a tree trunk, vibrating inches from his head. He rolled and, in complete desperation, charged at the Indian, who was raising the blowgun into position for another shot. He wasn't going to make it, because the gun was pointed right at him and there was no way to miss at this range. Caine tucked his head and went into a forward roll, the dart ruffling his hair as it passed. With a loud war cry, the Indian dropped the blowgun and whipped out a knife.

Caine scrambled wildly to his feet and pulled the *nunchaka* from his belt. Warily the two men crouched and began to circle each other. The Indian slashed at Caine and he pulled back just in time, the glittering blade just missing the tip of Caine's nose. The Indian shouted again for help and Caine knew he had to end it right away. He stumbled and the Indian thrust forward at Caine's belly, but the stumble was a feint and Caine completed the move with a slicing crescent kick that knocked the knife hand sideways. Caine whipped the Indian's arm with the *nunchaka* and the Indian screamed and dropped the knife. Caine whipped the *nunchaka* back horizontally with a wrist flick. The stick crashed into the side of the Indian's head with a loud crack, knocking him to the ground. The Yagua lay unmoving, a thin trickle of blood seeping from his ear.

Caine didn't take the time to check whether he was unconscious or dead; he raced for the center tree and tore wildly at its hollow core for the survival pack.

He wrestled the suitcase out of the trunk and scrambled into the foliage only seconds before the clearing filled with chattering Yaguas and Chamas. Caine rolled behind a dead tree trunk which was swarming with termites and cautiously zipped open the suitcase.

The AR-15 came to his hand like an old friend and when he slammed the first clip home, he no longer cared whether they heard him or not. His eyes had gone flat and cold. He was the hunter once more. He carefully peered over the trunk at the clearing.

There were half a dozen Indians running toward him, three of them wildly waving their machetes. Caine swung the gun into firing position over the log and began rapid-fire, aiming at the farthest one first and working back toward the lead Indians. They went down like figures in a shooting gallery and the two lead Indians didn't realize what was happening at first. Then they turned to flee and he got them in the back, just like that.

Silence filled the clearing, palpable as the humidity, as Caine grabbed the knapsack and headed back toward the trail. He had to get across to the other side before Rolf got there. Caine hesitated at the edge of the trail, crouching in the age-old stance of the jungle predator, his senses alive to any movement. A sudden stab of pain drilled his cheek and he almost cried out. He winced and an insect the size of a dragonfly buzzed his ear and was lost in the trees. He had been bitten by a *mutaca* and almost immediately he could feel the skin on his cheek tighten as it began to swell.

The trail was clear; all he had to do was cross it. Sure, he told himself, but he couldn't make his feet move. How many times had they tried to cross empty trails in Laos, only to get cut down by the unseen enemy? Go on, you bastard, do it, he urged, but his feet were frozen in place. He wiped the sweat from his eyes with his sleeve. The dense greenery across the trail beckoned him like a distant view of Shangri-La. Why does a killer cross the road? he asked himself stupidly. To get to the other side, you gutless son of a bitch, he answered, jeering. Do it! You're a dead man anyway, so just get it over with. That's not why you cross the road, he amended. You cross it because you can't stay here. And he stumbled awkwardly across the trail and crashed into the trees.

Rolf and the Indians would be along at any second, he realized, and feverishly dug in the knapsack for a length of fishing line. Rolf had the Winchester, with its greater range, but he had the AR-15 for firepower. Rolf was the key. If he could get Rolf, the Indians were odds-on to run for it. Then he saw two Chamas far down the trail and fired at them. They dived into the foliage for cover. He had to move quickly.

He tied one end of the fishing line to the bush and crawled through the scratching, tearing undergrowth to a tree about twenty yards away, trailing the line behind him. He propped the knapsack beside the tree as a shooting rest and took up the slack in the line. Now all he had to do was wait.

Sweat blinded him and he had to keep wiping his eyes with his sleeve. It was Laos all over again, he thought. It was like a wound that wouldn't heal, a dull ache that never went away. "You never came back," C.J. had said. It was exactly the way it had been for them. The fetid heat and sounds and stench of the jungle and always the enemy, invisible and yet you knew they were there. It had come back, that awful sense of frustration, because you never saw them, not even when they got you. You would lie there, your life draining away, while the medic told you it wasn't bad, you would make it. You were one of the lucky ones, boy. You were going home. And you could look up and see the lie in the medic's eyes, because he wouldn't look at you and you knew it was bad, because you couldn't feel it and those were the ones everybody said were the bad ones. And they would check your dog tags, for the blood-type, the medic said, but you knew that it was for the records before they shoved you into a body-bag. And there was nothing you could do, so you just lay there, feeling your life drain away and thought that you had come so close; you had almost made it. But it didn't matter anymore, because C.J. had been right all along. He had never come back.

He whirled at a sudden rustling sound behind him, his heart fluttering like a trapped bird, but it was just a large turtle plodding through the undergrowth. Rolf would send the Indians around to outflank and flush him, he reasoned. He had a fairly decent field of fire, he thought, peeking carefully around the tree, but there was nothing to see but the dappled greenery along the trail. Where was Rolf? He had to draw his fire. If he waited much longer, the silent Indians would have him boxed. His nerves were screaming, like a fine wire being drawn tighter and tighter, until he couldn't stand it anymore.

He jerked cautiously at the fishing line and the bush rustled harshly. Almost immediately the thwang of arrows flew at the bush, followed by the crash of the Winchester. Damn! He hadn't spotted it. He desperately jerked the line again and the Winchester fired again, followed by a sudden, arching rain of arrows and darts at the bush. Caine jerked the line feebly once more and waited breathlessly.

An Yagua cautiously emerged from the undergrowth, his eyes rapidly darting about. Something must have frightened him, because he pressed back against the foliage. Come on, you kraut bastard, Caine pleaded silently. Then there was a movement, as a hand or something shoved the Indian forward from behind and Caine fired rapidly, emptying the clip at the bush behind the Indian.

As the Yagua tumbled dead to the ground, Caine slammed home another clip and continued firing at the bush until the clip was empty. Suddenly there was a murmur of voices and he could hear the Indians running, the sounds receding in the sullen heat. Caine loaded another clip and sprinted back across the trail, diving into the brush for cover, but nothing happened. He crept in a wide circle until he neared the bush he had been firing at. He went down on his belly and crawled slowly, one step at a time, until he was within close range. Then he snapped into a kneeling firing position and put half the clip into the area around the bush.

The jungle was silent except for the endless insect whine that was as much a part of the jungle air as the heat and the humidity. Caine crawled on his belly until he saw the bodies. Rolf was lying facedown, his back stained a dull red with blood. Next to him, a dead Yagua lay curled in a fetal position, part of his face scooped out, leaving a bleeding red mass. Someone must have run off with Rolf's Winchester, because it was gone, he noted. Caine kicked Rolf's body over, but there was no need for a coup de grâce. He could see that at a glance. Caine stared down at Rolf's dead eyes.

"I forgot to tell you. I cheat," he said to the dead, staring eyes. A cluster of insects had already formed near the body, feeding on the blood that seeped from Rolf's chest.

Caine ran back to the trail and retrieved the knapsack and fishing line. He trotted down the trail till he reached the edge of the water, the placid surface sparkling in the sun. There was no sign of the *lancha*. They must have sunk it, he mused. In the far distance, he could just make out the gunboat as it patrolled near the shore, the sound of the diesel engine like a distant insect buzz. Rolf must have radioed ahead, he thought with chagrin. The Yarinacocha and Pucallpa were closed to him for good. The trap had snapped shut.

He found Pepé's body on the mud flats, near the water. The *caimáns* hadn't gotten to him yet. His stomach had been pierced by a long Yagua arrow, the barbed point extending almost a foot out of his back. A deep rust-colored gash showed across the nearly severed throat, where a machete had mercifully put Pepé out of his agony. Caine sank to his knees in the rank mud beside the body. For the first time since he had found Lim's body that day in Laos, and for no reason he could fathom, he began to cry.

CHAPTER 15

"Plucking a parrot is not one of the more entertaining ways of spending your time," Caine said, and was suddenly aware of the sound of his own voice. How long had he been talking out loud to himself? he wondered. Ever since the stream, yesterday. It was the loneliness, the complete isolation, he surmised. The dense, endless green of the rain forest had cut him off from the rest of humanity as completely as if he were an astronaut, marooned on an uninhabited planet.

"A fugitive and a vagabond shalt thou be in the earth," he recited loudly to the big, brownish spider, near the center of the giant web, just a few feet away. The web was as large as a bedsheet. It glistened with a poisonous, iridescent shimmer in the relentless heat, but it screened out the insects on that side. That was one of the reasons he had chosen this spot as a campsite.

Where was that line about being a fugitive from anyway? he wondered. Probably the Bible. It sounded like the Bible, he reflected. He shook his head and resumed plucking the bright green feathers, one by one. It would be good to taste meat again, he thought. It had been a lucky shot. The parrot had been just sitting on a branch, barely ten feet over his head and he had fired the carbine at once, without even taking the time to aim.

This was the fourth day, he remembered. The second since the impassable mangrove swamp had forced him to abandon the bank of the Yarinacocha. He still wasn't sure whether he had made the right choice.

"We are all constantly confronted with choices. What makes a survival situation different is that there are no second chances. In the jungle the punishment for a mistake is death," he remembered Hudson saying just before they jumped from the plane.

Well, he would know in a day or two, he shrugged. Of course, standing on the mud flats looking down at Pepé's body, there really hadn't seemed to be much of a choice.

For the Chamas and Yaguas who lived south of the Yarinacocha, between the institute and Pucallpa, he was an outcast, a murderer. Even if they feared him as a demon, he knew they wouldn't hesitate to turn him over to the Peruvian Army authorities, who probably wouldn't bother with the niceties of a trial. Even if they did, he could think of better ways to spend the rest of his life than in some hellhole of a Peruvian prison.

That left only the jungle as a way out. It was a long shot, but it was the only shot he had. The jungle north of the Yarinacocha was largely unexplored. That area was Achual country, the most savage tribe of the southern Amazon, where no Chama or Yagua would dare venture. Father José had told him that the Peruvian Army had twice sent military expeditions into Achual country. No trace of either of the expeditions was ever found. The jungle had simply swallowed them up. So Caine would be safe from the Chamas,

Yaguas, the Nazis, and the authorities; they would simply assume he had died in the jungle. God knows, that was a reasonable assumption, he reflected. Because the jungle was doing its best to kill him.

Starting out, the plan had not seemed that crazy. It was only thirty to forty miles from where he stood on the mud flats to the banks of the Ucayali. There were no mountains, ravines, or major topographical obstacles between him and the river that anyone knew of, and no matter which way he went, so long as he headed roughly east, he was bound to strike the Ucayali.

Once there he could raft, or get a boat to take him downstream to Iquitos, where he could catch a flight to Lima. He doubted that the news about Mendoza would reach that far, and even if it had, they would be looking for McClure, not someone named Payne. Thirty miles wasn't so much. A good marathon runner could do it in under three hours easy. He ought to be able to do it in a day or two, he had reasoned. He had the survival kit and the carbine and the training to do it. All in all, the idea seemed plausible.

Except that he hadn't really taken the Amazon into account. He was alone and unaided and the jungle was trackless. The total distance for him wasn't thirty miles, but perhaps two or three times that, because he could hardly travel in a straight line. And whether or not he had realized it when he began his march, he was in a desperate race against time.

Because the real dangers of the jungle are not the spectacular one that people imagine. Certanly no one in his right mind would want to cozy up to a *caimán* alligator or a poisonous snake, Caine reflected. But by and large, these creatures are timid of men and are rarely encountered. The true dangers of the jungle were the mind-sapping heat, insects, and bacteria, which were inescapable. The jungle destroyed a man slowly with thirst, pain, and disease, like an insidious poison. Caine knew that he had to get to the river before gangrene from a tiny, unnoticed scratch, fever, and malaria would inevitably bring him down.

He had started his march along the bank of the Yarinacocha, weaving his way through the endless thicket of brooding trees strung with liana vines that grew as thick as a man's thigh, and dense saw-toothed grasses. The air was heavy with a rank smell of vegetation and black mud that sucked loudly at his already rotting jungle boots. Caine carried the knapsack on his back, the canteen and machete at his hip, and the carbine slung over his shoulder. He wore the mosquito net loosely over his head, like a ghostly bag. Every so often the foliage was too thick and he would have to hack his way through with the machete.

His head pounded from the hammer strokes of the blinding tropic sun. The attack of countless, stinging mosquitoes and *borrachudos* was relentless. His body ached with every step, the mud clinging to his feet like lead weights, and he had to stop every hundred paces or so to sip water from the canteen.

Paradoxically, in the rain forest where it rains at least once a day, even during the so-called dry season, it is thirst that is the greatest problem, he reflected as he waited for the mud to settle in a hole he had dug about four feet from the bank. The hole filled with muddy ground water and once the mud settled, he could fill the canteen, add a Halezone tablet, and drink the brackish liquid. The problem wasn't a lack of water, but that it was virulent with bacteria and animal and vegetable poisons. Clean, fresh water was simply unavailable, yet he needed a lot of it—the fever, heat, and his exertions vastly increasing the natural rate of dehydration.

Judging by the bits of floating leaves and bark, the current near the bank might just be a little too swift for the piranha and he decided to chance it while waiting for the mud to settle in the hole. He quickly stripped naked and eased himself into the tepid, brown water, moving as little as possible. The feel of the water was delicious as it soothed his skin, burning with the fever from all the ant and other insect bites. He couldn't relax for a second, though, and cautiously kept his eyes peeled for piranha, electric eels, *caimáns,* and water snakes. A sudden ripple near his toes had him scrambling frantically out of the water and onto the bank, like a slapstick character in a silent movie. He hurriedly smeared handfuls of mud all over his body, to soothe his skin and protect it from the insects. He was brown as a Negro with the mud, as he quickly climbed back into his filthy clothing. He filled his canteen with the tobacco-colored water, took a long swallow, and resumed his march.

All in all, he made pretty good progress that first day. The mud had proved fairly effective against the insects, and as a bonus, it seemed to cool his fever and help heal the ant bites. But as the drying mud began to crack and flake off in the intense heat, his skin began to itch maddeningly. He had to clench his fingers desperately to prevent himself from scratching as tears of frustration stung his eyes. The tiniest break in the skin could turn gangrenous.

He made camp about fifty yards from the lake to

avoid the dense fog of mosquitoes that gathered at the water's edge. He still had a good two hours of daylight, but there was a great deal to do. He hacked a tiny clearing with the machete and constructed a rude bamboo-and-vine bedframe. It was essential not to sleep on the ground. He laid a bed of palm fronds on the frame and dug a mudhole in the bank for water. A late afternoon shower had soaked the deadwood, but he managed to collect a good supply of kindling from the hollow, inner lining of a dead cedar trunk. He also collected a dozen handfuls of dry fibers, found at the bases of palm leaves, for tinder. It was time to forage for dinner.

He found a large, fungus-like colony of purslane growing near the mudhole. The nondescript yellowish flowers hardly looked inviting, the reddish stems fleshy as giant worms, but it would make a tolerable salad—except for the roots, which were poisonous. He collected an armful of stems, leaves, and flowers, enough for dinner and breakfast as well.

He killed a saucer-sized pimpled frog and cut it into bleeding pieces with the machete. He threw about half the bleeding pieces into the water for chum, then used the rest for bait, his fishing hook and line attached to a long, bamboo pole. After about half an hour, he had caught three razor-toothed piranha, which he hauled out, wriggling and snapping at the hook with angry jaws. He killed them by slapping them repeatedly with the flat of the machete. They were about four to five inches long and most of that was mouth. The trickiest part was cutting the hooks out, because the dead jaws would still snap shut spasmodically. After he retrieved the hook from the last fish, the steel slashed with bright tooth scars, he gutted the fish with the machete and soon had them broiling on sticks over the fire.

The last thing he did before settling down to dinner, the trees glowing red from the sun, as though reflecting a distant battle, was to strip. Dozens of leeches clung to his legs, their black, slimy bodies fat with his blood. The only way to get rid of them was to touch them with the tip of a lighted cigarette, one at a time. The leeches would shrivel and dance with a foul, crackling smell before they would drop off. As each one fell, he daubed the tiny, puckered wound with iodine. Soon his legs and feet were splotched with stinging iodine stains, as though he were suffering from some horrible skin disease.

Thick clusters of black and gray ticks, their squashy bodies bloated to the size of dimes on his blood, had collected in his armpits and crotch. Only the stinging splash of iodine could make them drop off, one by one, like rotten nuts from a decaying tree. He knew if he tried to pull them off, the tiny black head would stay embedded in his skin and infect. He shivered with the sharp pain of the iodine stinging his armpits and crotch, but so far as he could tell, he had gotten all of them. He smeared a part of his precious supply of insect repellent all over him and once more pulled on his filthy clothing, which had already begun to mildew and rot, the cloth turning a vaguely greenish hue.

Life in the Amazon wasn't exactly like a Tarzan movie, he reflected, as he tore into the muddy-tasting piranha and faintly acrid purslane, washed down with the coppery water. Of course, when Tarzan had yodeled through the jungle tendrils, nobody ever mentioned the mosquito bites on his ass, he thought wryly. Maybe that's why Tarzan had yodeled. He allowed himself one of his precious candy bars, which had melted to a shapeless fudge, for dessert, to get the filthy taste of dinner out of his mouth. The only decent part of the meal was the crumpled cigarette he lit when he finished eating.

He threw a few pieces of green wood on the fire to send up a thick column of smoke to help drive off the mosquitoes. He knew the fire might alert the Achuals to his presence, but there wasn't much he could do about that. Unless he cooked his food and boiled his water, food poisoning and bacteria were bound to kill him anyway. Even so, he was just buying a little time and he spent a few cheerful minutes trying to calculate when the inevitable dysentery and malaria would hit him. Just thinking about it made his stomach rumble uncomfortably.

So he thought about the Starfish Conspiracy. He had to grudgingly admit that they had used him, that he had acted as their unwitting agent. Harris and Wasserman were involved for sure, not to mention the mysterious von Schiffen, whoever the hell he was. But they had obviously miscalculated, because they certainly hadn't expected him to get out of this alive. Once they found out, he'd have the lot of them, and maybe even the Company, still after him. What Cunningham had told him so long ago still held. He would have to watch his back. But he had foxed them, he thought exultantly. He was still alive.

"I'm still alive, you bastards!" he shouted into the inky darkness. The jungle seemed to echo with his cry and it was taken up by the chattering birds and a nearby colony of monkeys, their raucous shrieks filling the night with terror. He felt something silky brush his cheek and then it was gone with a faint stir of air. He shivered with disgust and huddled closer to the fire. It might have been anything: a spider or a vampire bat, most likely. God, he hated this sickening, living hell.

They had sent him on a one-way mission and that made it personal, he thought grimly. He had a score to settle with them because they had put him here. But why? Why after all these years had they wanted Mengele terminated? Von Schiffen and the Starfish Conspiracy, who were they?

He remembered something Mengele had said. Something about Müller. That Müller was one of the few *Kameraden* who refused to betray him. That meant that others *had* betrayed him. Others in ODESSA. There could have been a power struggle within ODESSA between Mengele and von Schiffen.

But then how could the Company have been involved? Those were pretty strange bedfellows. He began to get a vague feeling of dread. Whatever they were after, he knew it wasn't just beer and pretzels. He remembered Auschwitz and the old Gypsy and he began to shiver. He couldn't quite grasp it, but it smelled as rotten as this filthy jungle. Whatever the Starfish Conspiracy was, it was still running and there was the terrible feeling of being caught in a nightmare that you can't wake up from. Somewhere, like a snake oozing out of its old molted skin, the horror was stirring to life again. And he was the only one who knew about it. It was the Starfish or him—and it was more than personal. It was war.

* * *

He reached the edge of the mangrove swamp by the early morning of the third day. The steambath heat and the insect onslaught had badly weakened him and he was suffering from recurrent bouts of fever. The jungle was slowly devouring him whole, as an anaconda devours its prey.

A fetid odor of decay wafted from the brooding darkness of trees, garlanded with hanging moss and liana vines, their spaghetti tangles of roots exposed above the still, black surface of the water. A poisonous miasma of something evil seemed to hover in the gaseous air. A black water snake corkscrewed across the stagnant water, its head poised over the inky surface like a hook. Bubbles of foul-smelling marsh gas languidly widened and popped in the stillness. A thick branch trailing in the water was lush with obscenely pink and white and purple orchids. Their very prettiness seemed somehow macabre in this terrible place, like lilies in a corpse's hand.

Caine went into the swamp, jumping from root to root and grabbing at sticky vines to keep from landing in the shallow black water that might conceal patches of quicksand. But after a hundred yards or so he had to give it up. There was no telling how far the swamp extended. He hurriedly retraced his steps until he reached solid ground again. There was no help for it. He would have to try and go around the swamp.

Turning away from the Yarinacocha, he penetrated deeper into the jungle. Now the tall trees, hundreds of feet high, completely screened the sky and he was in a world of semidarkness. The air was loud with insect buzzing and they swarmed around him like a mist, despite the insect repellent. The foliage was as thick as a wall and he had to hack his way through with the machete.

Left and right, left and right, he slashed at the living green barrier before him until he thought his arm would drop off. His right arm grew numb and he switched to the clumsier left; then the right and then the left, then the right again, until the blade slipped from his lifeless fingers. He turned and looked back to see how far he had come, then checked his watch in disbelief and horror. In over an hour of exhausting work he had managed to cover barely a hundred yards! He sank to the ground with a sense of complete despair, of the utter futility of it. He would never be able to make it!

The forest stirred ominously around him, like a fermenting brew. It was a malevolent, seething mass—shapeless and alive. A hairy black tarantula, the size of a dinnerplate, ran along a vine, inches from his face. The trees were crawling with sickly green and rust-colored fungus and grotesque insect shapes. Pale white grubs clustered on the sticky undersides of leaves. Bloated black beetles and roaches scurried restlessly along the ground. The rotted remains of a lizard stirred with movement as maggots and fat red worms fed off it. Everything fed off everything else in this cannibalistic universe, he thought with horror. He felt it was impossible to go on. The jungle had won, he thought dully, as he felt his will to live ooze away, like everything else here. It was as though his body had turned to liquid.

Aren't you something, some part of him jeered. Sitting there and feeling sorry for yourself, with injuries that any hospital emergency room would laugh at. Remember Chong and Lim. Remember the old Gypsy and the camp. Those millions of inmates would have swapped places with you in a second and thrown in their eyeteeth into the bargain.

He had to survive. He had to. He was the only one who could get to the bottom of the Starfish, the only one who could stop the horror. He couldn't shake a sense of foreboding about the Starfish. He didn't know how he knew it, he just knew it.

You have to make it, he told himself. Because you're the only one who can do anything about it. There is no one else.

He got to his feet, electrified. With a sense of purpose he had never felt before, Caine picked up the machete and began hacking viciously at the green wall in front of him.

The canteen was empty and he desperately needed water. He looked around at the thick ropes of vines and slashed at a vine as thick as his forearm, as high up as he could reach. Always make the first cut on top, he remembered. Then he severed the vine down low and let the clear, warm water, tasting of vegetation, drip into his mouth until he was full. He cut another vine and used it to refill the canteen.

About an hour later the first attack of dysentery hit him, the cramps doubling him over with sharp surges of pain, like a knife slowly twisting in his intestines. Soon the cramps were forcing him to relieve himself every twenty minutes or so. He pulled down his grimy pants and squatted where he stood, his bowels twisting with pain. After the sixth or seventh time nothing came out except a slight trickle of foul brown liquid. He had nothing to wipe himself with and the crack between his buttocks was soon chafed and raw.

On and on, he hacked away at the jungle. Without

the coca leaves that he chewed constantly, he would have collapsed a long time ago. By midday the swamp that had loomed like a black cloud on his right, began to peter out and he could head in an easterly direction once more.

It was late afternoon when he forded a wide brown stream, using a pole on the upstream side to break the current. After crossing, he carefully dried the carbine with his shirt. Then he washed his clothing in the stream and spread them on the sand to dry. He lit a cigarette from the last pack in the knapsack, rolling the smoke sensuously across his mouth and deep into his lungs. A scarlet macaw chattered merrily, high atop a fat *paxiuba* palm. The cigarette was delicious and he sat there, quietly smoking. Later he used the glowing cigarette butt to clean off the leeches and ticks, and then daubed his wounds with iodine.

When his clothes were dry, he dressed and he had barely started again when he saw and shot a parrot. After about half a mile he found the tiny clearing by the giant spiderweb and set up camp. He made a camp bed, collected deadwood for kindling, and plucked and cut up the bird.

He chopped down a nearby plantain tree with the machete, cutting it off about three inches above the ground. Using the curved edge of the machete, he scooped a bowl in the portion of the trunk still protruding from the ground. The bowl quickly filled with clear water drawn up from the roots, but it was far too bitter to drink. He splashed the water out of the bowl with his hands and waited for it to refill. By the fifth bowlful the water was fresh and drinkable. He filled his canteen and covered the stump with broad plantain leaves, to keep off the insects. The stump could provide water for days, if necessary.

The tough bananalike plantain fruits could not be eaten raw. He threw a dozen of them into the fire to roast, next to the parrot. Of course, the plantains wouldn't do his dysentery any good, but he was very weak and needed nourishment desperately.

Night fell like an ax over the jungle, and as always, the darkness echoed with the shrieks of hunter and prey. A few furtive stars could be seen blinking over the clearing, like the glowing eyes of stalking predators.

"My compliments to the chef," Caine announced and pushed away the remnants of the parrot. The charred bird tasted like gamy chicken; the hot plantains were coarse, grainy, and slightly sweet. All in all, it was a pretty good meal. He was about to light a cigarette, when the dysentery grabbed him again. He staggered into the darkness and painfully relieved himself. When he finished, he huddled closer to the fire as a protection against the unseen predators and insects. Every day in the Amazon is a victory, he thought.

A full day of rest in camp would do him a world of good, he decided before turning in. He spent the next day resting under the mosquito net on the camp bed, in the shade of a palm tree. He passed restlessly from strange, confused dreams to waking, his clothing soaked with sweat. He had dreamed about a giant starfish living like some mythological creature in the flames of the Auschwitz ovens, tearing the skeletal bodies to pieces with its slimy arms and devouring them one after the other. He lay sweating under the mosquito net and tried to sort it all out, but he couldn't. Somehow it had all melted into a jumbled kaleidoscope of images: Wasserman and Mengele, Lim and C.J. and Inger, the Amazon and Laos and Paraguay. They were all part of the same, confused pattern.

The tropic sun pounded down on the clearing as on an anvil. Caine tossed and turned throughout the afternoon. Twice he walked down to the stream and bathed. Now, huddled by the fire like some primitive ape, he felt sane for the first time in days. A low growl came out of the darkness and he superstitiously touched the carbine. Probably a jaguar, he thought, and felt the hairs on the back of his neck bristle.

Nature had nothing to do with good and evil, he felt. Nature just was, that's all. And it didn't care. It was neither friendly, nor hostile, simply indifferent. And man was just another life form scrambling for existence. If there was any truth in the world, that was it, like the fire in front of him, which obeyed the same laws of combustion whether it was used to roast a parrot or burn the Temple of Zeus at Ephesus. All the rest was human invention, words told around a campfire to charm away the specters of the night.

"I'll drink to that," he toasted loudly and took a long sip of plantain water. Overhead the stars glittered brightly, like holes poked in the fabric of night, to reveal the light of another, brighter universe.

He resumed the weary march shortly after dawn, in a torrential downpour that plastered his clothes and the mosquito netting to him like a tattered outer skin. The monotonous chop-chop of the machete sounded dull and squashy amid the dank, dripping leaves. The leeches clung to him in clusters, like slimy grapes. He had to stop every fifteen minutes to burn them off with a precious cigarette, cupping his hand over it, to keep it from getting soaked. He was beginning to worry about how much blood he could lose to the leeches before they bled him white.

Shortly after the rain stopped, he used half of his last cigarette to burn away the leeches again, then smoked the rest. He glanced ruefully at the butt before flicking it away. Something told him, he was about to give up smoking.

The dense foliage began to thin out a little and soon he was able to slip through it and he hung the machete at his belt. The high trees formed a dark tunnel, dense with insects and heat and he drank frequently from the canteen. The ground felt loamy and dank underfoot and black pools of water were everywhere. The bush was loud with the croaking of frogs and the whine of the mosquitoes.

Sweat blinded his eyes and he moved like a machine through the endless chain of black pools and foul, squashy mud. And then he almost pitched forward because his feet couldn't move against the suction of the soft mud. He tried to wrench free and sank up to his thighs before he realized that he was caught in quicksand.

Don't struggle, his mind urged him desperately. But the thought of such a horrible death panicked him; to disappear forever without a trace in this horrible muck was more than he could bear. Drop the pack and rifle, damn it! You have to lighten up, he screamed at himself. He dropped the rifle and wriggled out of the pack. They sank without a trace into the few inches of murky water that floated on the quicksand. That's it, he thought as he lay back, his arms spread wide to spread the weight. The black water was almost up to his nostrils. But at least he had stopped sinking. So far, so good. Was there anything he could grab? A slender liana vine hung just a few feet out of reach. Close, but not close enough. If he could only reach it. Then he remembered the machete.

With infinite care, he slid his hand down to his waist and slowly pulled the blade free. Holding it in a death grip by the tip of the handle, he stretched out his arm till he thought he would dislocate his shoulder and just managed to touch the vine. He poked it tenderly with the hooked point of the machete and managed to hook it. He pulled the vine toward him until he could just reach it with his fingers. Clamping the machete blade between his teeth, he pulled the vine gently with his fingers till it was taut. He grabbed it tightly, wrapping the vine around his wrist, and with a sudden heave he pulled with all his strength, kicking out both legs at once.

His legs came free to the knees with a loud sucking noise, and he scrambled up the vine like a monkey till he was on solid ground. It took a while before he realized that he had done it. He was free! An incredible sense of joy took hold of him and he began to laugh wildly till the tears came to his eyes.

He finally managed to calm down, except that every once in a while, without quite knowing why, he would break into a little snort of laughter. All right, he thought. What did he have left? There was the machete and the almost empty plastic canteen attached to his belt. He had been lucky that it was almost empty. No doubt its buoyancy had helped him. All he had in his pants pockets were a few coins. His left shirt pocket contained the soaked Payne passport and a wet, smelly wad of money. In his right shirt pocket was the vial with the tip of Mengele's thumb floating in the formaldehyde, like a piece of discolored wood.

He cut a pole to poke the ground ahead of him and some vines for water. When he started again, he felt lighter and stronger than he had in a long time. But after a few hours the euphoria passed and it was all he could do to just stumble on. All he wanted to do was just sleep, just lie down and close his eyes. Why go on suffering? he wondered. He didn't know why anymore. He didn't know anything, except that he was nearing the end.

He scarcely felt the insects or the heat. There wasn't anything to feel. C.J., the money, the Starfish, how impossibly remote it all seemed. There was only the dark, slimy shade of the trees and his own plodding steps. He no longer watched where he put his feet to avoid the snakes, scorpions, and quicksand. What difference did it make, he thought dully. His machete slashes grew weaker and he was wondering what it was that still drove him on when he stumbled to the edge of the clearing. His eyes opened wide in astonishment. He had never seen anything like it.

The clearing was huge, bigger than a football field, and it was filled with millions and billions and trillions of butterflies. There were giant bright blue and iridescent violet morphos butterflies with wingspreads of over half a foot, scarlet butterflies, golden pierid butterflies, butterflies of every possible shade, in the brightest, richest blues and reds and whites and yellows he had ever seen. They filled the clearing from the ground to the sky, as though the air had turned into brilliant, swirling, ever-changing patterns of color. There were colors that he had never seen before, that he hadn't even known existed. The sun burned behind a dazzling cloud edge and poured shafts of pure white light down into the clearing, the rays shining through the jeweled wings, like light through stained glass.

Caine stood there, transfixed. The clearing was a living rainbow of riotous color that changed its pattern moment by moment. He wondered if he had ever seen color before, in all its heartbreaking purity. It was the most beautiful thing he had ever seen—and it was his alone.

He was certain that he was the first white man ever to see this incredible place, perhaps the first human being ever. It was like a gift from God, a reward for having come so far, for having endured so much. He wished C.J. were here so that he could share this with her. He had been so wrong; there was redemption. It was there before him.

It was with the greatest reluctance that he finally left the clearing, looking longingly back over his shoulder at those endlessly swarming, living jewels. He wanted to stay longer, but the desire to live, to go on, surged up in him as never before. He wanted to see C.J., to blow the Starfish wide open, to do everything. He wanted to live forever.

Gradually the ground grew firmer and he had to use the machete less. Orchids of every kind and color flourished on rotting, fallen trees, which he stepped over with great care. They usually harbored snakes and scorpions and—even more troublesome—savage wasps and bees. Nets of lianas and thorny creepers hung from the trees in profuse tangles. He came face to face with a monkey, who peered curiously at him as though he recognized his distant kinship with the man, and then scampered easily up the vines. Caine regretted the loss of the carbine. He was getting very hungry.

Several hours after he had left the clearing he came upon what was unmistakably a trail. The narrow foot-worn path had beaten a tunnel through the dense foliage and Caine gratefully hung the machete at his belt. He was on the trail for barely an hour and had begun to look around for a place to camp, when he saw a fetish tied to a branch that hung over the trail about shoulder height.

It was a monkey skull, decorated with bright red macaw feathers and the teeth of some large animal dangling on a vine necklace from the hollow eye sockets. Caine sighed and shook his head with a wry smile. He didn't understand the symbolism of the fetish, but he could recognize a No Trespassing sign when he saw one. He carefully examined the trail around the object for traps, or any other sign of human hands, but there was nothing. The black shadows of the dead monkey's eye sockets seemed to stare at him, and he couldn't repress a shudder as he stooped over to pass under the branch.

CHAPTER 16

He was a short, ugly man, naked except for a loincloth and a braided crown of red and yellow toucan feathers. His face was tattooed red and black with horizontal strings of inverted triangles and he wore carved bamboo plugs in his ears. He was holding a bow, the long reed arrow aimed at Caine, as they faced each other on the trail. The barb was black-tipped with curare. The Indian was looking at Caine's head as if he were visualizing how it would look shrunken to size and added to his collection.

For a long moment they regarded each other silently, neither of them daring to move. Then the Indian was joined by two more Achuals, who materialized like wraiths out of the shadows of the trees. One of them carried a blowgun and the other, garbed in a tattered shirt and trousers, carried a rusty twelve-gauge shotgun. The rush of blood pounded at Caine's temples and in his mind he could hear the distant echo of Hudson's warning: "In the jungle the penalty for a mistake is death."

With slow deliberation he raised his palms to them to show them that he was unarmed. Stony-faced, the Indians watched him and did nothing. He had to do something to win them over, and fast, he realized. But what? He was all out of tricks. Of course! Tricks! As a kid, he had practiced the patter and the thumb-palm from a magic book he had got for six cereal box-tops for weeks. It was worth a shot, he thought.

He carefully reached into his pocket and plucked out a ten-sol coin, which glittered in the waning sunlight as he flourished it before them. The Indians watched the coin intently, their eyes wide in fascination. Caine held the coin in his right hand, tried the thumb-palm as he closed both hands with a flourish, blew on his hands, and opened them empty. He pointed his left index finger into his left ear and pulled the coin from his right ear. Then he smiled broadly, the one universal human gesture.

The wide-eyed Achuals clicked their tongues appreciatively and one of them ventured an astonished, "hoo-hoo," which he later learned was their version of applause. The Indian with the shotgun cracked open the barrel, pulled out the cartridge, and stuck it through the hole in his earlobe. Reversing the gun, he placed the muzzle to his mouth and blew an ear-shattering trumpet blast through the bore. The other Indians smiled and clicked their tongues, "hoo-hooing" appreciatively.

They led Caine in triumph to their village, the Indian with the shotgun tooting every few paces to announce their arrival. Huey, the Indian with the gun, spoke a few words of broken Spanish and he appeared to be the only one who had ever had contact with white men. Huey wasn't his real name, of course. But when Caine had asked them their names, their eyes had turned sullen and suspicious. Evidently, there was some sort of taboo against revealing their names, so he simply pointed to them in turn, and said, "Huey, Dewey, and Louie." They appeared delighted with their new names and every so often, one of them would say his new name aloud and then burst into laughter.

The Achuals moved swiftly and confidently down the trail, sidestepping around and bending under unseen obstacles. At first Caine simply followed them, thinking that this was their normal way of movement. Then he began to notice that they were sidestepping cleverly concealed traps and snares. Dewey stopped him and gestured for him to bend over. It was only as he did so that he caught a glimpse of a slender, almost invisible neck-high strand of thorny vine strung across the trail. It came to him with a rush that these were not animal snares, but mantraps. That stupid coin trick had saved his life. He remembered what Father José had said about the savagery of the Amazona Indian. Despite their apparent friendliness, his life was hanging by a thread.

As they marched, the Indians kept glancing at him curiously. He wondered if they were trying to figure out how long it would take them to shrink his head. Each of them in turn came up to Caine and touched him as unselfconsciously as a child, as if to assure themselves of his reality. When they felt his groin, there was a lot of hoo-hooing and tongue-clicking. All in all, Caine thought they made a merry group as they approached the village in the evanescent orange light of dusk.

The village consisted of four huts in a clearing, surrounded by a fence of palm fronds and thorny vines. The huts were simply raised wooden platforms covered with palm thatched roofs and open to the air. Summoned by the trumpeting of Huey's shotgun, the entire village had gathered in front of the largest hut.

There were about thirty of them, mostly women and children, their bare bodies glowing with a bronze sheen in the twilight. Most of the women wore only short, intricately patterned cotton skirts and dozens of strands of beads around their necks. Their faces were tattooed in bright lines with *urucú* dye. Their generally flabby breasts were naked, the nipples large and copper colored. Most of them carried sullen, black-haired infants. The children were completely naked.

One little girl about eight years old cradled a gray-and-white *paca* in her arms. The furry rodent must have been at least two feet long. Yellowish mongrel dogs roamed the clearing, barking incessantly. With a muffled grunt a taller Achual brave, who wore Western trousers and a torn straw hat incongruously perched on his head, kicked a yapping dog in the side. The animal let out a wild squeal and the Indians all laughed as he scrambled away.

The Achuals looked expectantly at Caine and this time he knew what to do. He repeated the coin trick, the coin glowing like a ruby in the last rays of the sun. This time he finished the trick by fishing the coin out of the tall brave's ear and presented the coin to him. Their mouths hung wide in astonishment and then there was lots of tongue-clicking and hoo-hooing.

The chief, for that's who Caine took the tall Achual to be, stared for several long minutes into Caine's eyes, as though examining his soul. Caine returned the stare with his own unblinking gaze. His life was on the line and he knew it. At last the unsmiling chief placed his hand around the back of Caine's neck and touched his forehead to Caine's and Caine was immediately swamped by noisy, giggling Indians anxious to touch him.

They seemed particularly fascinated by his week-long growth of beard and the hair on his chest. Caine winced as one after another of them tugged at his hair. The thick stench of their unwashed bodies almost suffocated him. Several of the women slyly touched his groin and there was more tongue-clicking. One of the men shouted something at the women and suddenly everything was still.

Trouble over the women was the last thing he could afford, Caine realized. To distract them, he handed all his coins over to the chief. They gathered in a dense crowd around the chief, who examined the coins carefully before taking two of the largest for himself and then distributing the rest to the others. There weren't enough coins to go around and a noisy quarrel broke out between Dewey and Louie over a ten-centavo piece.

The two men shouted angrily at each other, slapping their chests and shoving as they grappled for the coin. Surprisingly, no one, not even the chief, paid the slightest attention to them. After a brief scuffle, Dewey grabbed the coin and swallowed it, leaving Louie blinking stupidly. The quarrel ended as quickly as it had begun, and as the darkness fell, the Indians began to disperse to their fires.

Caine followed the chief into the main hut. Ducking to avoid the main beams, he almost bumped into a half-dozen round objects hanging from a beam near the fire. Then he recoiled in horror and swallowed hard. They were human heads, the lips and eyelids sewn shut, shrunken to the size and shape of ducks' eggs, hanging by long black strands of hair. The skin had the color and patina of beaten copper and each head's features were distinct and clearly recognizable.

At a gesture from the chief, Caine sat beside him by the glowing fire. The fire was built of three logs, touching at the center and radiating outward. As the logs burned down, one or another of the chief's wives would push the remaining stumps toward the center. The chief passed Caine a gourd of *masato*. Caine drank deeply of the clear, fiery liquor and passed the gourd back to the chief, who took a long swallow. The warmth of the liquor flooded Caine's body and he was almost immediately light-headed. He hadn't eaten since a brief lunch of sticky, boiled bracken stalks on the trail, before he had hit the quicksand. You had to be careful when eating bracken, to be sure that they were true ferns and not hemlock or some other poisonous plant. The only sure way to identify edible ferns was by the lines of brownish dots, which were really spores, on the undersides of the leaves.

Two handsome brown women with long inky black hair, whom he took to be the chief's wives, served them a meal of fried plantains, gritty *mandioca* gruel, and stewed monkey. Caine knew that the meat was monkey because clumps of fur were still attached to the chunks. He thought of the monkey he had encountered on the trail and he began to feel queasy. It was like being a cannibal. He forced himself to swallow the bile that rose to the back of his throat and accepted another piece of meat from the chief's fingers. He wolfed it down. In spite of his nausea he was ravenously hungry and in truth, it didn't taste that bad.

The chief passed him the gourd again and Caine took another swig of *masato*. Then he began to sputter and laugh at his own finicky food taboos. The Achuals weren't that different from anybody else, he realized. We are all apes in clothing and no matter how we dress it up, we all eat plants and dead animals, just like any other ape. The image of hairy apes dressed in suits and dresses and making a ceremony out of eating animal corpses at some fancy restaurant struck him as wildly funny and soon the chief and the women were laughing at his hilarity. He was drunk he realized, and then the dysentery grabbed at his intestines, like a powerful hand.

Caine bolted from the hut and ran to the deep shadows near the fence, where he vomited and painfully relieved himself at the same time. After what seemed like hours, he weakly pulled up his pants and returned to the hut on unsteady legs. He was sweating profusely and he held out his hands to the chief in what he hoped was a gesture of apology. Then his legs gave way and he collapsed on the wooden floor of the hut.

The chief gently placed his hand on Caine's brow. It felt cool to Caine and his feverish eyes watched helplessly as the chief and his women pulled off his filthy clothes and examined him. Caine glanced down in fear and loathing. He scarcely recognized his own body. His sunburned skin was mottled and swollen with countless insect bites and he winced at the lightest touch. His ribs were clearly visible. He must have lost at least twenty pounds after barely a week in the jungle. Lying naked on the hut floor, surrounded by savage Achuals, he realized that he had lost the last traces of civilization. He had nothing more to lose. Father José had been right: to enter the darkness of the Amazona was to enter the midnight of the soul.

The chief said something to one of the women and she soon returned with an old man who wore tattered trousers and long earplugs decorated with toucan

feathers. His face and chest were hideously tattooed.
My God, Caine thought desperately. They had called
in a *brujo* to treat him. He tried to struggle up, but
the chief pushed him forcefully down to the floor
again. A feeling of lethargy invaded him and he
closed his eyes.

When he opened them, he found himself staring up
at the row of shrunken heads, swaying slightly in the
faint breeze, the flickering shadows from the firelight
bringing their features back to evil life. The *brujo* was
sitting cross-legged by the fire and chanting. Caine
wondered vaguely whether his head was about to join
those hanging above him. The red firelight, the chanting, the tattooed savages and naked women, made the
whole scene seem dreamlike. He could hardly believe
that it was real, that it was actually happening to him.

The *brujo*, his tattooed face a demonic red mask as
he crouched by the fire, rolled green tobacco leaves
into a fat, crude cigar and lit it. He took long deep
puffs and the smoke twisted and rose in the updraft
of the fire. He passed the cigar to the chief, who took
several puffs and then placed the cigar between
Caine's lips, gesturing for him to smoke it. Caine
deeply inhaled the strong, acrid smoke. It burned his
throat and he launched into a bout of coughing.

Still chanting, the *brujo* stirred a dark liquid in a
small gourd with a bone-white knife carved from a
jaguar's tooth. He placed the gourd to Caine's lips and
said something, gesturing for him to drink. Caine hesitated. The brew smelled bitter and poisonous. The
brujo's eyes gleamed maniacally in the firelight and
Caine feared that he was being given poison. The
chief and his wives clustered around his naked body,

their faces solemn and impossible to read. The chief gestured for him to drink.

"*Ayahuasca*," the chief muttered solemnly, pointing at the gourd.

Should he drink it? he wondered. If it was poison, the Starfish would win, and he somehow knew that it was more evil than anything in this jungle. In an instant brief as a heartbeat Caine regretted that he might never see C.J. again, that he might never return to tell anyone about the butterflies, that he would never get to the bottom of the Starfish Conspiracy. He longed for the shush of snow and the crystalline purity of the mountain air, the giddy feel of his descent as he and C.J. skied down an Alpine slope towards the warm comfort of a lodge. He opened his mouth and tossed the bitter black *ayahuasca* down in a single gulp.

The *brujo* placed some dry brown leaves on the fire and began to inhale the thick cloud of smoke they sent up. Then he stood up and began to sway and dance as he chanted, his eyes closed, but still appearing open, because he had painted eyes on his eyelids. Caine grew very dizzy and the hut began to spin. It was as though he had become conscious of the earth's rotation and he clung to the floor to keep from being spun off into space.

With a sudden cry the *brujo* sprang at Caine and buried his face in Caine's belly. The *brujo* sucked harshly and loudly at Caine's navel, then sat up and spat into the fire. The spittle seemed to Caine to be a stream of blood, but when he looked down at his navel, there was no wound. Then it came to him that the *ayahuasca* was a hallucinogenic drug and they were trying to help him! The *brujo* was trying to suck out

the invisible poison dart that the Achuals believe
causes illness. The chief stretched out his hand and
touched Caine's forehead and as he did so, the fingers
sprouted into branches and the branches into leaves
that rustled against his face.

A wind sprang up and stirred the palm fronds into
life. The fronds kept whispering and whispering in an
unknown tongue. Then the hut was filled with Indians, grinning like gargoyles, their naked bodies swaying in the red glow of the fire and Caine no longer
knew what was real and what wasn't. The chanting
went on and on to the rhythm of the whispering
palms. Beads of sweat rolled down his face and he felt
himself floating on a burning stream of molten lava,
down the countless miles of the Amazon to the distant
darkness of the sea.

He was swimming in the dark ocean, riding the
roller-coaster waves. Then he sank into the green
depths and a giant starfish wrapped its arms around
him, pulling him into its mouth. Caine struggled desperately against the suction of the arms. He cut off
the tip of one of the arms with his machete and then
he was free. He rose through the water for a long
time, and when he finally broke the surface, he was
back in the fetid darkness of the mangrove swamp.
He began to wade through the still, black water.

Then he was caught in the quicksand again and
above him was a wildly screaming chorus of giant spider monkeys, each of them with a human face and he
knew them all. There were so many of them. He
hadn't realized that his life had touched so many. He
Lim, pleading for her unborn son, and Dao, screaming
about the war. His mother with her green eyes. Wasserman telling him about his father's accounting firm

in Leipzig. Chong, his bleeding, mutilated monkey face looking as it had when Caine had straightened his body at Nong Het. The old Gypsy at Auschwitz. Müller screaming "Peru." And Cunningham and Koenig and Hudson. Harris saying something about how oil is the only thing that counts these days. Inger, drooling, and Pepé, still pierced by the arrow. Mengele screamed, "Is there no redemption?" Father José said nothing, but only stared at him with sad, black eyes. A monkey with sleek blond fur and C.J.'s face swung from a vine and repeated, "you never came back" over and over, until Caine couldn't stand it and he cried out, "I'm coming back, you bastards! I'm coming back!"

He sank into the quicksand, down to an underground river, and then somehow he was floating on a raft down the Amazon. A lithe, naked Achual maiden ran her hands along his body, a sly smile on her brown face in the flickering firelight and then she straddled him, her belly rippling in slow, sinuous curves, like a snake. She uttered a cry of pleasure and moved faster as he entered her, her sweat dripping onto his belly. From inside her he could feel her entire body surging around his penis, beating like a giant heart, with the timeless rhythm of the surf. He came with a shuddering groan and the woman bathed his body with cool water from the river. He could see the stars, like distant campfires in the night. The rustling wind blew them out one by one, like candles, and then it was dark at last.

He awoke to the sound of retching. The morning was hot and clear and all around the village the

Achuals were matter-of-factly vomiting. A slim, young woman brought him a large gourd of bark tea to drink. She smiled slyly at him and he wondered if she had been the woman in his dream and whether any of it had been real. He drank the medicinal-smelling tea, which she called *wayus,* and he quickly toddled on rubbery legs to the edge of the hut and threw up. The *wayus* is a violent emetic. Apparently it was the Achuals' normal practice to start the day by clearing their stomachs and surprisingly enough after retching he felt much better.

The woman brought him a breakfast of fried plantain and a number of *characins,* a kind of freshwater sardine, which she had broiled over the fire. He felt stronger than he had in days. His fever had broken and his skin was no longer so tender. Even his stomach had stopped rumbling. That *brujo* could make a fortune in southern California, he mused.

They had dressed him in his filthy clothes once more. The woman took a thin strip of saw-toothed grass and stretched it taut. She rubbed the grass strip along his face and he was surprised to find that it took off his beard as cleanly as a steel razor. She had nearly completed shaving him when the chief entered the hut.

Caine got to his feet and regarded the chief for a long moment. Then he took off his watch, wound it, and gave it to the chief. The chief examined the watch curiously, then held it to his ear. A delighted smile broke over his face.

"Tick-tick-tick-tick," he said, and clicked his tongue appreciatively. Caine hoo-hooed and placed the watch on the chief's wrist. The chief swaggered out of the hut and soon he was surrounded by Achuals, who clicked their tongues and hoo-hooed in admiration. Caine smiled broadly. The watch was a complete success.

Later Caine called Huey over and asked him about the Ucayali. At first Huey seemed embarrassed.

"Where is the river?" Caine asked in Spanish. Huey shrugged.

"Where?" Caine repeated, and pointed in various directions. The Achual laughed and pointed toward the rising sun.

"Is it far?"

"*Sí, sí,*" Huey laughed.

"How many days?"

"*Sí, sí,*" the Indian said amiably.

It was frustrating and Caine tried to think of another way besides Spanish to communicate. Then he pointed to the sun and described an arc across the sky from east to west. He repeated the gesture until Huey laughed, holding his stomach with merriment. Then he shook his head at Caine and made a single arc from east to west, with a cutting gesture when his finger reached halfway across the sky. Caine laughed and shook his head. It was only a half-day's march to the river!

The Indian began tugging at his arm, as though wanting to show Caine. Caine brought his thumb to his first two fingers in the Spanish gesture that means *wait*. He walked back to the hut and got his machete. The chief glanced curiously at him. Caine put his hand around the chief's neck and touched his forehead to the chief's. The chief smiled. As he walked away to join Huey, Caine thought that the savage Achuals were really no different from anybody else.

Then he followed Huey on down the relatively easy trail.

They reached the broad expanse of the Ucayali by midmorning. Huey cavorted and pointed excitedly at the brown water and the two men embraced and touched foreheads. Caine began searching along the bank and Huey followed him curiously. It took Caine more than an hour before he found a grove of suitable balsa trees. He began to chop at the soft, porous wood with the machete and Huey immediately understood what Caine wanted and enthusiastically pitched in.

The soft wood was easy to work with, and in an hour Caine had half-a-dozen logs trimmed and laid side by side on the riverbank. Each log was about ten feet long and close to a foot in diameter. About a foot from each end, Caine cut a triangular notch for the crosspieces on the top and bottom side of every log. Each notch had the apex of the triangle on top and the baseline about two inches deep in the wood. When all the notches were cut, four to a log, two at each end, top and bottom, Caine cut four relatively straight branches and began fashioning triangular-shaped crosspieces with the machete.

Huey watched with fascination as Caine worked, nodding excitedly every so often. The Indian intuitively grasped the superiority of using the triangular-shaped crosspieces. When the crosspieces were wet and began to swell with water, they would bind the logs securely together, even without lashing. While Caine smoothed and shaped the crosspieces, Huey found green coconuts for drinking and mature nuts for eating, and they stopped for lunch. Then while Caine worked at fitting the crosspieces into the notches, Huey pounded the white coconut meat with a shell and left the pounded meat in the shell to heat in the sun.

Once the crosspieces were slotted across the logs, the two men lashed the ends of the crosspieces with liana vines. Then Caine cut two long branches, trimming one for a pole, and the second, broader branch he fashioned into a paddle-shaped sweep. The raft was ready to go.

Huey handed Caine the shell of heated coconut meat. It was brimming with oil and he gestured for Caine to smear on the oil. Caine stripped and smeared the oil all over his body till he glistened in the sun. The oil would help protect him against sunburn and insects. Then he pulled on his grimy rags once more.

The two men looked at each other. Caine didn't know what to say or do. These people had saved his life. He had nothing left to give them. Then he remembered his Meo bracelet, the one Dao had given him. He pulled it off his wrist and handed it to Huey, who blinked his eyes self-consciously. Then with great reluctance he handed Caine his precious shotgun in return. Caine pushed the gun away emphatically, but the Indian stubbornly resisted. Caine knew he couldn't shame the Indian, so he looked around for something else. He pointed at the toucan feather headdress and the Achual gratefully took it off his head and adjusted it on Caine's head.

Caine took off his shirt and the two men loaded coconuts on it and tied it into a bag. They pushed the raft into the warm brown water, and without any further ceremony Caine hopped on and he was off. He poled away from the shore, the Indian watching him with his impassive gaze. When Caine reached the middle of the river, where the current was stronger, he sat down and began to use the sweep. He glanced back at the shore, but the Indian was gone, as though he had never been.

The tropic sun glinted cruelly off the surface of the water. The raft bobbed gently downstream, the balsa logs riding buoyantly on the placid surface. Caine wondered how long he had before the porous wood became water-logged and sank. He hoped to hit a village and get a boat before then. All he could do was trust to luck. After all, with a raft one doesn't have much choice.

A sense of peace enfolded him as he drifted downstream. He was heading back into the world. Once again the brooding green hedge of the jungle slipped by. Along the near bank he could see what seemed like an endless carpet of giant Victoria water lilies. The pads were thick with bullfrogs croaking a loud chorus that could be heard for miles. He began to feel drowsy in the steaming heat as the current carried him ever downstream. He was on a journey without end. He remembered a lyric from a Janis Joplin song: "Honey, the road don't even end in Khatmandu."

CHAPTER 17

"Did you find Dr. Mendoza?" Father José asked.

"I found him," Caine said.

"How is he?"

"How should I know? I'm not his damned keeper," Caine snapped. The priest looked at Caine with his sad eyes, then he looked at the river. Violet and gray clouds covered the sky over the river with a thick woolly blanket. The large *lancha* trembled with the throb of the engine. A light wind stirred ripples on the surface, where the deep current ran. Soon it would rain.

"You murdered him, didn't you?" Father José said, and looked back at Caine. It was not a question. Caine didn't say anything.

"My God, did you think that sort of thing can be kept quiet? The word has spread like wildfire through the jungle," Father José said.

"Has the news reached Iquitos yet?"

"Not yet," the priest admitted. He struck a match and lit his pipe. The smoke wreathed his face like a halo.

"Why did you wait till now, before bringing it up?" Caine asked. After all, they had been together on the river since Flor de Punga two days ago. The priest shrugged wearily, resting his chin on his chest. His thick black beard covered the grayish cassock over his chest like a bib.

"I thought you were too weak. Besides, who am I to judge you? Judgment belongs to God. Besides, I didn't want to know."

"No," Caine said quietly. "You don't want to know."

"How could you do such a thing?" Father José said suddenly, his face reddening, as though he were embarrassed.

"How could I not do it?" Caine retorted. "Dr. Mendoza's real name was Josef Mengele. Does that mean anything to you? Yes, I can see that even here in the middle of nowhere you've heard of the Angel of Death of Auschwitz," Caine said, his green eyes glittering. "He was responsible for more human suffering and death than any man in the world. What's one death amid all that carnage?"

"One death is what it's all about," the priest said.

"It doesn't do any good to talk about it. I've seen Auschwitz and I tell you Mengele wasn't fit to walk the earth. I'm not sorry about any of it."

"But who nominated you to do it?" Father José asked. Caine shrugged and spat over the gunnel. His spittle was touched with pink. His gums still bled a little from where Rolf had knocked out one of his teeth.

"It just happened that way. Besides, I was the right man for the job. You said it yourself. I'm a hunter. God didn't create the jaguar to be a vegetarian," Caine said.

"I should turn you over to the authorities when we reach Iquitos," the priest said unhappily.

"Are you going to?"

Drops of rain with the size and force of marbles began to fall into the river. The surface of the river looked like a vast field of water flowers splashed up by the raindrops. A small waterfall cascaded over the edge of the canvas sunscreen under which the two men sat. Father José stretched his bony frame and sighed.

"'He that is without sin among you, let him cast the first stone,'" the priest said, staring into the gray wall of rain. "No, I won't betray you to the authorities. But when we dock in Iquitos, let's just pretend we never met."

"In a way we never did," Caine said, getting up. He walked to the prow of the *lancha* and just stood there in the rain. The raindrops smashed like bullets, soaking Caine's new clothes and molding them to his body. He had bought the cheap slacks and shirt for a few soles at the one tin-roofed general store in Flor de Punga, a tiny riverfront village. He had landed the raft there and caught a lift back to Iquitos with Father José, who was taking the mission *lancha* downriver to straighten out a delayed shipment of medical supplies, which were being held up by the customs office in Iquitos. Father José told him that it would take a lot of palaver and a judicious bribe before he would be able to get the shipment released.

The *lancha* was piloted by a young *caboclo* seminarian, who drove the boat day and night with the reckless audacity, if not the skill, of a Grand Prix driver. By the afternoon of the fourth day they were approaching Iquitos, about a half-day's journey downriver from the junction of the two great rivers, the Marañon and the Ucayali, which join to form the Amazon River. And Father José had waited all that time before confronting him.

The rain felt cool and refreshing to Caine. He was feeling much better. Maybe that was why Father José had held off talking about it. Out of a rare sense of delicacy, not wanting to confront Caine while he was still weak and shivering with fever. Well, at least it was out in the open between them, Caine thought with a sense of relief. Now he no longer had to pretend to be the oilman McClure for the priest. One of the real hardships for a spy is often trying to pretend to be less interesting than he really is. In fact, Koenig had once warned them about agents who deliberately courted danger out of pure boredom with their cover roles.

The priest had treated him with Lomotil, chloroquine, and penicillin. The medicine combined with canned food and lazy days of rest on the boat to bring Caine back into relatively good condition. At long last he felt that the nightmare was ending. Except for the Starfish. That was still running. For the rest all he wanted was to collect his money and C.J. from Wasserman and take off for Zurich. He wanted to make his dream about skiing in the Alps with her come true.

Father José came over and stood beside him in the rain. The priest's head was bowed and his hands were clasped behind him in the posture of a penitent, submitting himself to the flagellation of the raindrops. They stood like carved figures, rocking slightly with the motion of the boat. Rainwater ran down their faces in tiny rivulets.

"I lied just now about not judging you. I'm still judging you—I can't help it," Father José said.

"I guess you're as human as the rest of us, Padre," Caine said.

"Just tell me this, was it truly necessary to kill him?" Father José asked, his earnest gaze searching Caine's face.

"I don't know," Caine said softly, his voice almost lost in the hiss of the rain. For an instant their glances touched and they both looked away.

"I think you found the darkness I warned you about, didn't you?" Father José asked.

"Yes, you were right, but there's something else. I think it's possible that killing Mengele was the first decent thing I've ever done in my life," Caine said. "Maybe it makes up for . . . well, maybe it makes up for some of the other things I've done. I don't know. But when and if the time ever comes for God to judge me, I've got a few questions of my own to put to Him," he added.

"We all do," Father José murmured sadly.

The two men stood side by side for a long time in the cooling rain, each of them locked into his own private world of darkness and light. Finally the rain began to slacken and Father José suggested a cup of coffee, which they brewed on the little Primus stove under the sunscreen. They shared one cup between them as though it were a kind of communion.

They docked at Belén, a floating slum of small boats and shacks on stilts which formed the port section of Iquitos. Belén was built on a long, narrow mud flat joined by a ramshackle wooden bridge to the town built on a bluff overlooking the river. It was late afternoon, the tropic sun caught in the distant treetops like a giant yellow balloon.

Caine helped Father José tie the *lancha* to a rotting
wooden pier that balanced precariously over the river.
The air was pungent with the smells of mud and garbage and decaying fish. *Caboclos* swarmed along the
wharf, laden with heavy reed baskets and clay water
jugs. Day laborers were loading bananas and animal
skins onto a rusty Booth Line freighter. Scores of
pirogues and *lanchas* were beached on the mud flat
and the air was alive with the cries of Indians and
traders hawking goods. After the isolation of the jungle the sudden return to the world startled Caine. All
the noise and vitality stunned him, and he felt more
than ever an alien in the crowd.

Father José and Caine parted without *abrazo,* or
even a handshake. They glanced briefly at each other
and then the priest kind of nodded. Caine hopped
onto the pier and walked toward the narrow wooden
footbridge that joined the port to the town, without
turning back. Yet as the Indians jostled and shoved
around him while he crossed the bridge, Caine could
feel the priest's dark-eyed gaze burning into his back.

Caine climbed up the muddy street to the Malécon,
the old-fashioned promenade that ran along the bluff
overlooking the river. At a number of places he had to
walk around barricades of crumbled cement, where
the rise and fall of the river had taken giant mouthfuls
out of the walkway. Young couples and tradesmen
strolled arm-in-arm along the Malécon, past Victorian
buildings fronted with white tiles decorated with blue
floral patterns, relics of the rubber boom around the
turn of the century when Iquitos had been a thriving
city instead of a sleepy jungle town. The air was redo-
lent with the scent of decay from the port, characteris-

tic of a city with a past more alive than its present. Caine turned off the Malécon and went into a large sidewalk café called the Caravelle.

Caine sat at the bar and ordered a pisco sour from the sweating Indian barman. The café was filled with the smell of cigarette smoke and the vinegar scent of *ceviche*. *Anticuchos*, skewered chunks of seasoned beef heart, were roasting over a nearby charcoal brazier. It was incredible how keen his sense of smell had become in the jungle, Caine thought as he stared at his reflection in the tarnished mirror behind the bar. He scarcely recognized the gaunt face in the mirror as his own. The sun had burned it to a reddish mahogany, covered by a coppery-blond stubble of whiskers. His skin was stretched taut over his cheekbones and his tangled hair badly needed cutting. Only his eyes hadn't changed. They were as cold and green as ever, only now they seemed larger somehow. He drank the pisco sour and ordered another.

A bright green-and-red parrot squawked from a cage at the other end of the bar. A stuffed monkey snarled at him from atop a branch nailed to a wall, next to a poster advertising Cristal beer. The monkey, the parrot, and him—they were all out of place here. For a second the taste of monkey meat was in his mouth again and he almost gagged. Maybe they should stuff and mount me on the wall too, he mused, and tried to avoid the monkey's glass eyes.

Overhead a ceiling fan slowly stirred the heavy air. The tables were filled with local tradesmen dawdling over their liquor, plus a few wide-eyed tourists. At a nearby table a red-faced dealer in animal skins, with an accent rich in the vowels of London's Chelsea district, was regaling the tourists with some story about how he had single-handedly captured a boa constrictor.

"The bugger must have run thirty feet, by God. Had a fair time wrestling him into the bag, I don't mind telling you. When he wrapped himself around my chest, I thought sure he was going to put 'paid' to me. Fearsome thing, an anaconda. Tackle anything in the jungle, even a jaguar. I've seen 'em swallow a two-hundred pound *capybara* whole, I have. You wrestle a boa, you'll find out what the jungle's all about."

"Weren't you afraid?" a well-dressed American woman asked, her voice tremulous with an appropriate note of awe.

"Not a bit of it," the Englishman said. "You've got to treat 'em like a woman, show 'em who's boss. That's what I say." He winked.

I'll bet that's what you say, Caine thought, and grimly drained his drink, the foam leaving a frothy mustache on his lip. At another table several perspiring Peruvian businessmen in dark, shiny suits morosely discussed the falling price of raw rubber. At the other end of the bar a local grower was bargaining with an American trader over a consignment of chicle. The Englishman tried to convince the American woman that there was a fortune to be made in shipping parrots to the States.

"Top dollar. Absolutely top dollar," he guaranteed, paternally patting her knee and giving it a sly squeeze. Caine began to wonder why he had been in such a hurry to get back to civilization.

He spotted two long-haired American hippies in faded, patched blue jeans and T-shirts, morosely sipping from brown bottles of Cristal at a corner table. He ordered three cold bottles of Cristal and carried them over to the hippies. He placed the bottles on the table, as though he were paying an entrance fee, and sat down to join them.

"What's happening, man?" Caine said. One of the hippies looked disdainfully up at Caine, then he shrugged and grabbed one of the bottles.

"Ain't nothing happened in Iquitos since the rubber boom, Jack," he said, and took a long pull at the bottle. The other hippie twitched nervously and regarded Caine with wide, vacant eyes. His nostrils were red and partially eaten away from cocaine. He sniffed a dribble of snot back into his nose and languidly reached for the third bottle, staring through Caine as if he were transparent.

"You guys hang out in Belén?" Caine asked.

"Who wants to know?" the first hippie said, thrusting his lip out belligerently.

"Just asking." Caine shrugged.

"Just telling," the hippie retorted with a self-satisfied grin.

"Suppose I wanted to move something and didn't want the local pigs to know about it, who would I talk to?" Caine said, and put a couple of hundred-sol bills on the table next to the beer.

"Talk to the Chinaman," the hollow-eyed hippie said, reaching for the money with the same languid gesture. Caine planted his bottle on the bills and held it there.

"Where do I find him?" he asked.

"Import-export office, at the end of the Malécon near the old Clube Iquitos. The big iron building wit the fancy colonnade. Shit, man. Everybody knows the Chinaman," the first hippie said.

Caine left them sitting there, arguing about the money, and stopped off at a nearby barbershop for a haircut and shave. He left the barbershop feeling pounds lighter and cleaner, his skin and hair gleaming like burnished copper in the brief tropic sunset. Insects swarmed around the ornate streetlights on the Malécon as darkness fell over the river. A waxy yellow moon hung over the jungle with the haunting face of a primeval deathmask. He found the building with the faded sign above the doorway, that read: A. FONG. IMPORT-EXPORT.

Import-export was the classic cover for a smuggling operation in river ports around the world. There was sure to be a lucrative trade in smuggling illegal animals, gold, and, most of all, raw cocaine out of Iquitos on the run to Bogotá, the so-called "Colombian connection," Caine thought as he mounted the rickety stairs and knocked on the office door. Even though he had the Payne passport, it was essential that he get to Lima without risking an encounter with the Peruvian authorities.

Ah Fong was a short fat Chinese man with a smiling, perspiring Buddha face. He was wearing a neat white linen suit and he bowed several times as he led Caine into his private office. The office was as hot as a greenhouse and lush with orchids and other jungle flowers. But Fong's pride and joy was a purplish Venus flytrap, and his face shone with sweaty pleasure as he invited Caine to watch him feed it.

Fong's short fingers plucked a live fly from a swarming glass jar and he held it delicately, then shook it like a thermometer. He dropped the dizzy fly into the brightly colored open pistil. The fly staggered drunkenly among the down-pointing hairs of the petals as it slipped downward. Fong smiled happily as the petals suddenly closed over the fly. Caine wondered if he, too, was walking into a trap again.

"I fear you do not take pleasure in the Venus plant, señor," Fong said, gently touching his fingertips together over his bulging belly as they sat across from each other at Fong's lacquered black desk.

"I'm afraid my sympathies are all with the fly, but *por favor*, don't let my opinions interfere with your pleasure," Caine said.

"My pleasure is in your presence here," Fong said, bobbing his sweating face in a little bow.

"Your house reveals the presence of a man of exquisite taste and sympathy," Caine replied.

Fong leaned back and brought out a lacquered Chinese cigar box. He offered the box to Caine, then took a cigar for himself. He sniffed the cigar appreciatively and the two men lit up.

"How may I be of service to you, señor?"

"I need to return to Lima as soon as possible, but I wish to avoid the inconvenience of the Peruvian authorities, especially the *aduaneros* at Customs. I was told that 'El Chino' is a man of considerable influence in such matters. *Naturalmente*, I came to seek your advice."

"Will you be carrying *contrabando*?" Fong inquired shrewdly.

"Neither *contrabondo*, nor coca, nor anything else. Only myself. Your men can search me if you wish. *Naturalmente*, I wish to compensate you for your kindness."

"I can see that you are a serious man, señor, so I will be frank. I have a plane leaving this evening for Lima. I am shipping a quantity of animals for trans-shipment to the U.S. There will be no problem with the *aduaneros* at either end. If a man of your . . ." Fong paused, searching for the right word. ". . . delicacy does not mind sharing cargo space with our little jungle friends, I would be honored with your patronage."

Caine smiled. That was funny, he thought. After what he had gone through in the jungle, that was funny.

"How much?" Caine asked.

"Will you be returning to Iquitos, señor?"

"Not unless there's a slipup," Caine said, and smiled coldly. Fong glanced at his smile and shifted uncomfortably in his chair.

"I see," Fong said, pensively tapping his fingertips together. "In that case, señor, the fare will be five hundred dollars."

"Two hundred. I'm not a *millonario*."

"As you wish, señor. For two hundred, I recommend the Satco or the Lansa airline offices in the Hotel Turista. But for a man of your stature, I would be honored to have your patronage for four hundred and fifty, in advance."

"Four hundred and no questions asked," Caine said and stood up. Fong stood up and extended his hand, palm upward. Caine counted out four hundred dollars and gave it to him. Fong smiled like a sweating Buddha and bowed.

"There will be no *problemas,* señor. You have the word of 'El Chino.' Be at the *aeropuerto* at eight tonight. Just tell the *aduanero* you are going on El Chino's plane."

"It's a pleasure doing business with a serious man," Caine said and bowed.

"*Buen viaje,* señor," Fong said.

When Caine left him, he was standing with the glass fly jar in his hand, indulgently contemplating his Venus flytrap.

Caine spent the next hour shopping at the brightly lit shops around the small town plaza. He bought a lightweight overnight suitcase, toiletries, an inexpensive white linen suit, and a new pair of shoes. He changed into the new clothes, leaving the old ones in the store's dressing room. He stopped at the telegraph office and sent a telegram to the classified section of the L.A. *Times* to place an ad in the Personals column, which read: "C.J. Don't be mean, Lima bean. Stop. Bring bread and paper soonest. Stop Hot *signed* Crillon Stop."

He gave Wasserman's Hollywood address for billing and hoped that she would readily decipher the message that he wanted her to meet him at the Hotel Crillon in Lima with money and a new passport from Wasserman. Then he found a dilapidated Chevy with a hand-painted taxi sign stuck in the window and went out to the airport.

The airport terminal was little more than a large, dilapidated shed. It was almost deserted except for a few *caboclos* and a young Indian boy who tried to sell him a fan made of parrot feathers. When Caine shrugged him off, he pressed Caine to buy some carved Yagua arrows. Caine walked up to the *aduanero,* a sleepy Peruvian in an ill-fitting brown uniform, his face slick with the humid heat. Behind the *aduanero* a centipede crawled along the wall and disappeared into a large, jagged crack. Fong was as good as his word. Caine simply mentioned the plane of El Chino and the *aduanero* lethargically waved him through the gate.

An ancient twin-prop DC-3 was being loaded with wire-mesh crates packed with parrots and spider monkeys. The silver plane gleamed in the harsh light of naked bulbs that lit the tarmac as the Indian laborers manhandled the heavy crates into the cargo bay. Many of the animals were worth more than a thousand dollars apiece, duty-free, to pet fanciers and medical laboratories. If this shipment was any indication, Fong was indeed a serious man, Caine thought.

A lanky American in faded jeans, T-shirt, and wearing a Yankee baseball cap stood in the doorway of the plane, cupping his hands around his mouth, so that his shouts could be heard over the screeching animals. When he saw Caine, he waved and motioned him to a steel ladder. Caine climbed up and the American, whom he took to be the pilot, pulled him in.

"Where you heading, Sam?" the American said.

"Lima. You the pilot?" Caine asked.

"Nobody but. El Chino send you?"

"Nobody but, Sam." Caine grinned.

"That's the ticket." Sam winked, then he leaned out the doorway and shouted at one of the workmen.

"*Arriba, arriba,* you fucking turkey! Right side up! *Los animales arriba!* Hey you, Sam! *Sí, sí, usted,* you shithead. Move it, *arriba!*" he shouted, then turned to Caine and said conversationally, "Did you see that, Sam? Those dumb bastards were loading a crate of monkeys upside down. Christ! Hey, hand me a beer, will you? They're in a crate behind the seat up front."

Caine went up to the cabin and found the beer. He opened two bottles with an opener attached by a cord to the pilot's seat and brought them back, handing one to Sam. They grinned and took long gulps.

"Do you call everybody Sam?" Caine asked.

"Sure. In this business nobody has any name anyway, right?" Sam asked, his blue eyes twinkling. "Besides, it makes it easy to remember," he said.

After about an hour the plane was loaded and fueled. Sam leaned out of the cabin window and yelled something at the tower as Caine strapped himself into the copilot's seat. The plane began to taxi even before the runway lights switched on and then they were hurtling down the runway and they were up. The plane climbed in a slow arc over the scattered lights of Iquitos, reflecting off the tin roofs of the town. Then they were over the jungle that stretched as dark and endless as the ocean all the way to the moonlit horizon.

The sound of the engines was deafening, drowning the shrieks of the terrified animals as the plane rattled and bucked its way through the cloud cover up to the starlit night. It felt and sounded as though the old DC-3 were shaking itself to pieces, and Caine wondered what were the odds on surviving a night crash in the jungle. But Sam nonchalantly ignored the noise and popped open another bottle of Cristal.

Caine found himself dozing off, until he was roused by the high-pitched scream of the engines as they fought for higher altitude in the thin air. They were approaching the massive barrier of the Cordillera. The instrument panel gleamed like stars in the cabin darkness and around them the night was filled with stars, like a distant city in the black sky. Sam told him that they would reach Lima in about an hour. Caine opened another beer and they shared it between them.

"Hey, Sam, you got a lady?" Sam shouted over the roar of the engines. Flames shot out of the prop exhausts, and it looked as though the wings were on fire. Snow gleamed a pale blue on the peaks of the Cordillera, so close beneath them that Caine felt he could reach out and scoop up a handful.

"Yeah, I'm meeting her in Lima in a few days. What about you?" Caine said.

"Are you kidding? This country spoils a man. For five bucks you can get the most beautiful young thing you ever saw, plus a room for a couple of hours. That's about what I figure it's worth. Five bucks and you can walk away, as easy as you please. Not like some of those American dames who act like they're giving you the crown jewels of England. And then they expect you to give them bed and board just because you made them a few times. Shit, there ain't nothing they're giving you, you can't have for five bucks."

"What about love?" Caine asked.

"Listen, Sam. When most American women say, 'I love you,' the operative word is *I*. Now you take the Latin women. They know how to treat a man."

"Sounds like you had a rough time," Caine put in.

"I flew F-fours in Nam. When I got back, I found my wife had been fucking everything on two legs. It cost me all my separation pay just to get rid of her. Now you figure it. She fucks her brains out while I'm off risking my life and the courts give her all my money," Sam said, shaking his head in wonder at the injustices of the world. "I figured, piss on the whole thing," he concluded.

"Well, maybe I've got a good one," Caine said.

"Don't bet on it," Sam said darkly, his face livid in the glow from the dashboard dials. "You find me a woman who ain't looking out for Number One and I'll show you a ding-a-ling broad."

"Yeah, well we do it, too. We're no saints."

Sam laughed and slapped the dash with delight.

"Now that's the fucking truth, Sam," he exclaimed and turned with a wide grin to Caine. "Hey, you been in Nam?"

"I was there," Caine said.

"That's what I figured. Funny, you can always tell. I don't know what it is. The way a guy moves, or something. But you can always tell, can't you?"

"Sure, we're the ones who look like born suckers," Caine said.

"Fucking A, Sam!" Sam exclaimed delightedly and happily slapped at the dashboard. "Hey, are you on the run?"

Caine hesitated, wondering just how far he could trust the pilot.

"I might have to lay low for a while," he admitted.

"Well, if you're looking for a place where they don't ask for papers or anything else, try the Pension Adolfo. It's in the *zona roja,* off La Colmena. Just tell them Sam sent you. After all, us shitheads have got to stick together. And don't worry about Fong or me. We're making *mucho* money off of these dumb animals, so we don't give a shit about anything. It's the only way, Sam. The only way."

The walking wounded, Caine thought. Is there anyone who isn't a secret casualty? he wondered. He leaned back and stretched restlessly. Directly ahead he could just make out the distant sky glow from the lights of Lima, brightening the horizon like a moonrise.

Sam brought the DC-3 down in an easy three-point landing and taxied over to the cargo area. As Caine started down the ladder, Sam flipped him a casual salute, readjusted the baseball cap to a jauntier angle, and began loudly cursing the cargo handlers for being a bunch of incompetent Sams. Caine's stomach tensed as he approached the *aduaneros*. They were armed with automatic rifles, but they merely looked at him curiously and waved him through the gate. He walked through the crowded terminal and out to the taxi stand. He told the driver to take him to the Pension Adolfo in the *zona roja*, which is what the red-light district is always called throughout Latin America.

The taxi drove through the heavy traffic on Avenida Nicholas de Piérola, called "La Colmena" by the Limeños. The broad avenue was noisy with horns and dazzling bright with electric and neon signs. All the noise and people jangled his nerves with a gnawing persistence, like the ringing of an unanswered telephone. It's just culture shock, he told himself. The transition had been too abrupt. That very afternoon he had still been gliding down the trackless Amazon with Father José. The world was going to take getting used to again, he mused.

He checked into the Pension Adolfo and went directly to his room. As Sam had indicated, they hadn't asked for his passport and registered him as a Señor

Smith. It was better to play it safe and keep his presence in Lima quiet for a few days until he could connect with C.J. and get back to L.A. under a new cover name, he decided. Just in case, he made all the usual checks on the room before locking the door and wedging a chair under the handle. Then he took a long hot shower, his first in weeks, and went to bed.

She was sitting by herself at a corner table next to the panoramic window that overlooked the bright moving lights along La Colmena, twenty stories below. She wore a simple navy-blue dress, her golden arms and shoulders gleaming in the candlelight. Her shining flaxen hair was pinned up to highlight her long slender neck, encircled by a single strand of pearls, and women around the room nudged their husbands with annoyance because there wasn't a man in the restaurant who could take his eyes off her. If she was aware of the effect she was having, she gave no sign of it as she nervously toyed with the pearl necklace. After all that had happened, Caine could scarcely bring himself to approach her. She was the loveliest woman he had ever seen.

He had staked out the lobby of the Crillon for three days, using standard surveillance techniques to avoid the appearance of loitering. He hadn't approached her when she checked in that afternoon because he wanted to be certain she wasn't being tailed. When he was sure she was clean, he waited till the evening, when he spotted her in the lobby, heading for the elevator. She was dressed for dinner and he figured she was going to the Sky Room restaurant on the top floor. She was absentmindedly looking out the window at the lights of the city below as he approached her table. He waited till she spotted his reflection in the shiny glass and turned to him with a start.

"Hello, C.J.," Caine said.

"It's you, Johnny. It's really you," she said, her eyes wide and watery.

"It's been too long," he said.

"For God's sake, sit down. You've got me all jumpy," she said brightly and nervously touched her hand to her hair. He sat down and leaned forward, clumsily kissing her on the mouth. He cursed himself. It wasn't at all the way he had planned it.

"My God, what have they done to you?" she said, her eyes brimming as she stared at him. She bit her lower lip to keep it from trembling. He shook his head with a wry grimace.

"It's okay. It's all over now. From now on it's just you and me," he said, and took her hand. For a moment she looked away.

"You don't know what it's been like, these past weeks. Couldn't you have called or written, or something? I didn't know if you were dead or alive or what."

"No, I couldn't," he said simply.

"Jesus, Johnny. What's happening?"

"I told you. It's all over now. You and I are going back to L.A. tomorrow. Wasserman owes me a lot of money. Then we're off to Switzerland and we're both through with the life back there for good. That's what you want too, isn't it?"

"Oh, yes, more than you know," she replied happily, and taking his hand in hers, she bent forward and gently kissed his hand.

The waiter came over and Caine ordered two pisco

sours. She looked away again, then turned to him and began gaily.

"Karl gave me a passport for you and ten thousand dollars. Is it all right?"

Caine nodded. Maybe it was just that she was nervous at seeing him again, but there was something wrong and he couldn't put his finger on it. He couldn't help remembering something Koenig had said, that women were an agent's Achilles' heel. It was bad if you needed one, and worse if you loved her.

"You don't know how glad I was to see your message in the *Times*. 'Don't be mean, Lima bean,' indeed. Although it took me a while to figure that 'Hot Crillon' was the Hotel Crillon in Lima. Cute, mister, very cute," she chattered brightly and his sense of her forced gaiety was beginning to get to him. What the hell is it? he wondered.

"What's the matter, C.J.? Has Karl or anybody been pressuring you?"

Tears began to roll down her cheeks, leaving a thin black trail of mascara. She sniffed, trying to choke them back.

"It's been awful," she said. "I was followed everywhere in L.A. And I think the phone is being tapped. Then last week a man from the FBI showed up at the beach house, wanting to know if I had heard from you. He asked me all kinds of questions about something called 'the Starfish.' Over and over. It was terrifying, Johnny. My God, what are you mixed up in?"

"I don't know all the pieces. Maybe I never will. But you have to believe me. Our part in all this is over; but the sooner we get out of the States, the better for both of us. Now for God's sake, stop crying.

Anyone would think you weren't happy to see me," he said.

She forced a smile and muttered, "Oh, shit. I must be a mess"—wiping her eyes with a handkerchief.

"You're the prettiest mess I ever saw," he said.

"Talk like that can get a man into trouble, mister," she said, a silly grin painted on her face, as though on a doll's face. Things were going wrong and he didn't know why it was happening or how to stop it. Their love was trickling through his hands like water.

"Damn," she said. "Look, give me a minute to go to the powder room and pull myself together. Then let's start again, like we're just meeting. Please, Johnny," she pleaded, and he knew that whatever it was, it was important to her. He nodded and she got up and walked shakily toward the ladies' room.

He lit a cigarette, his first since the jungle, and waited for her to come back. He waited a long time. He was about to go after her when he saw her coming back, looking more composed. She might have pulled it off except that her color was high and her eyes were bright and feverish. She put her hand on the back of his neck, bent down, and kissed him.

"Forget the food, handsome. Let's go down to my room and get reacquainted," she whispered in his ear.

"Don't get cute with me, sailor. I'm cheap, but I'm not easy," he said and finally won a smile from her.

She kept his hand clenched tightly in hers as they made their way to the elevator and down to her room. As soon as she closed the door, she threw her arms around him and hugged him desperately for what seemed like hours.

"Don't talk. For God's sake, don't say anything? Just

take off your clothes and make love to me. Make it matter," she whispered and kissed him tremulously on the mouth.

She unzipped her dress and wriggled out of it. Then she stripped off her bra and panty hose and hugged herself for an instant before diving under the bed-cover. Her eyes, which were bluer than the Mediterranean, never left him as he sat down on the edge of the bed and began to undress. As he pulled off his shirt, he vowed to get to the bottom of this. He wasn't going to lose her because of the Starfish, or Wasserman, or the Company, or any damn thing else.

He was just pulling off his shoes when suddenly the door crashed open and five uniformed Peruvian security policemen rushed in, their guns drawn. As they clamped the handcuffs on Caine, his gaze desperately sought C.J.'s face. She was cowering under the bedcover, drawn up to her chin, her eyes wild and anguished, like those of a trapped animal.

PART III

STARFISH and sea star are names given to radially symmetrical, more or less star-shaped, bottom-dwelling animals found on the margins of almost all seas. They constitute the class Asteroidea of the phylum Echinodermata. . . . The body is more or less flattened, with the mouth located centrally on the underside. From the body project a number of radially arranged arms, usually 5. . . . Their power to regenerate missing arms is spectacular, some sea stars being able to re-form completely from as little original tissue as the mouth framework (*see* Regeneration). Where fishnets are left untended for any length of time, sea stars may move in and devour a large amount of the catch; they are also known to enter lobster pots and eat the bait. Sea stars are acceptable as food only to a few animals. For man they are utterly useless. . . .

—*Encyclopaedia Britannica*

CHAPTER 18

For a long while Caine couldn't tell whether he was awake or not. Normally it isn't very difficult to distinguish between sleep and waking. There is a sensation of returning consciousness, sounds begin to filter in, you start to stretch, open your eyes, and there you are, back in the world again. But when Caine felt consciousness returning, there was no sound, and when he opened his eyes, nothing happened. It was still pitch dark. He had no idea where he was.

So he tried it again, stretching and opening his eyes, but still there was nothing. He began to panic. Suppose he couldn't wake up. Suppose he was dead, or in a coma. His body ached unmercifully, yet he felt the pain strangely comforting. I feel pain, therefore I am, he remembered. He couldn't be dead. The dead feel nothing, the old Gypsy had told him, and after what the Gypsy had been through, he surely knew.

Then he began to remember. They had taken him directly to the old city prison and had begun to question him about Mendoza. He wasn't sure what had infuriated them the most, his refusal to talk, or their anger when they found the vial with Mengele's thumb in his pocket. Whatever it was, they had set to work with the rubber truncheons with a vengeance. His last memory was of being curled on the floor, his arms covering his head to protect it, while they flailed at him. But why couldn't he see? My God, suppose he was blind! he thought, terror-stricken.

He touched his eyes with trembling fingers, but there was no physical damage he could feel. Then he began to explore his body carefully. He was lying on a concrete floor of what had to be a solitary cell. That could explain the darkness. His body felt like a mass of bruises, but there were no broken bones so far as he could tell. He staggered to his hands and knees and began to crawl around, exploring the darkness with one hand extended before him. His fingertips soon touched a smooth stone wall and he painfully stood up. He felt his way along the wall, counting his steps carefully, until he reached a corner. He felt along that wall, his hands caressing the coolness of a solid steel door, which provided the only opening to the cell. There was a small hinge on the bottom of the door, which he assumed was for food. He managed to lift it slightly and a barely discernible shaft of light crawled a few inches along the floor. Well, at least he wasn't blind, he comforted himself.

He continued his circuit around the cell. Besides the door there was absolutely nothing else of note, except for a small, foul hole in the center of the floor, which was obviously supposed to be used for a toilet. Tiny scurrying sounds came from the hole and he really didn't feel like investigating it further. The smell was nauseating and he wondered if anybody ever got used to it. By the time he completed his circuit, he had a fairly good idea of his prison.

He was in a rectangular cell, about six by eight feet, with stone and concrete walls and floor. He had no idea how high the ceiling was, but it was too high for him to reach. Except for the hole, the cell was completely empty, and the only way in or out was the steel door. They had taken his belt and shoelaces and everything he had had in his pockets. He had no idea how long he had been in there and absolutely no way of judging time. The darkness had a completely disorienting effect that way. It could have been hours—or days. There was no way to know. Still, it could be worse, much worse, he thought. Like the tiger cages Smiley Gallagher had taken him to see outside Hué. That was worse, all right.

There were hundreds of them, mostly captured VC, according to Smiley; but then he never entirely trusted anything Smiley ever said. From a distance it looked like a giant monkey cage at the zoo, but when he got closer, he realized that these prisoners would have sold their souls to get into a monkey cage.

The "tiger cages" were rectangular pits dug into the ground and covered by heavy wooden bars. *Pits* was the term Smiley used, but they were more like vertical graves. It was impossible to lie down or sit in them and they were too short to stand up in. The ground at the bottom was marshy and filled with snakes, scorpions, and centipedes, so that you couldn't even stand squatting on it. Most of the prisoners tried to hang by their arms from the bars for as long as they could. That's why it looked, at first, like a big monkey cage. The cages were open to the sun and the heat was intense. The air was filled with insane screaming and moaning. Most of them were covered with blood from head wounds, caused when they tried to kill themselves by pounding their heads against the wooden bars. It was like nothing Caine had ever seen. It was hell on earth.

"Why don't you at least give the poor devils some water?" Caine had asked Smiley.

"Why bother? Most of them will be dead in twenty-four to forty-eight hours. Nobody ever lasts longer than that in a tiger cage, anyway," Smiley said.

"Forty-eight hours! Jesus Christ!" Caine exploded.

"Now, wait a minute! These are VC in there. Besides, we have nothing to do with it. It's under ARVN control. We're just advisers, remember?" Smiley said defensively, a hurt expression in his piggy eyes.

"Well, why don't you advise our gooks to give their gooks some goddamn water, Smiley? Why don't you just do that?" Caine said carefully, trying to control his voice.

"I can't do that, Johnny. It's out of my hands. Besides, these are VC, goddamnit!"

"You bastard," Caine hissed. "You fucking degenerate bastard!"

Smiley stood there in the hot sun, blinking unhappily.

"I'm afraid you just don't understand what this war is all about, Johnny. That's your trouble," Smiley said.

It was still there, he thought. The war would never go away for any of them. "You never came back," C.J. had told him. And then she betrayed him. Well, he was coming back, all right, Caine thought grimly. He had a few scores to settle.

The thought that it had been C.J. who had betrayed him gnawed at him like a cancer. There wasn't even a shadow of a doubt that it had been her. There was no way to connect the oilman McClure in Pucallpa, with the mysterious Señor Smith in Lima. The only ones who could have fingered him were Father José, Fong, and Sam and he doubted that any one of them would have informed the authorities. And even if they had, they had no idea where he was in Lima or what name he was using. Besides, he had been clean as a whistle in Lima. He was sure of it. There was no one else. It had to be C.J. She must have made a call when she went to the ladies' room. That was why she had been so nervous. She needed practice, Caine thought grimly. Well, give her time and she'd get better at it, he thought.

So C.J. was part of the Starfish Conspiracy and that meant Wasserman was too, right from the beginning. They had played him for a sucker all along. No, you allowed them to do it to you, he amended, and a terrible anger flooded his veins. It was time to stop being a pawn of the mysterious von Schiffen, he decided. It was time to strike back.

He sat down on the floor and leaned his back against the wall. The stone was cold and damp, soaking the back of his shirt. He shivered. Jesus, he thought. First it's too hot, then it's too cold. You're never satisfied. He wondered when they would feed him. Then his anger took hold. You're a man, not an animal waiting at an empty trough, he told himself. So be a man, goddamnit! You've got a mind. Use it! That's what it's for. Because unless you kill the Starfish, it's going to kill you.

But there isn't enough data, he objected. Oh, bullshit, there's never enough data. Figure it out anyway. After all, you've got plenty of time. You're not going anywhere, he told himself.

What did he know about the Starfish, anyway? he wondered. They were all in on it somehow. C.J.,

Wasserman, Harris—that meant the Company—and
ODESSA. Mengele had known about it too. The Starfish had wanted Mengele killed and had picked him
to do the job. Why him? Obviously because they
couldn't do it themselves. Why not somebody from the
Company? Of course, because it was a dirty business
and the Company wanted to disclaim any involvement
if it all came out. That was probably why they
wanted Mengele out of the way in the first place. Because something was about to come out and they
didn't want the infamous Mengele to be associated
with it. The Peruvian government was obviously involved, because they had landed on him like a duck
on a June bug as soon as C.J. picked up the telephone.

How many did that make? he wondered. There was
Wasserman, the Company, ODESSA, and the Peruvians. That made four. How many arms did a starfish
have? Five, he thought. Unless von Schiffen was the
fifth. What's in a name, anyway? Starfish was a funny
name for an operation. So was von Schiffen, come to
that, he mused. He stirred restlessly. He was getting
close, he thought with a growing excitement. His shirt
was soaking wet from the damp wall and he moved
away from it, uncomfortably. Fucking water, he
thought. And then he had it. Water!

Jesus, he thought with a sense of awe. Names mattered. Those fucking krauts! *Der Seestern* was a water
animal! He thought back to his first interview with
Wasserman, because there was something there that
had bothered him right from the beginning. Something Wasserman had said. Then he remembered his
confused dream in the jungle, after he drank the *ayahuasca*. The Wasserman monkey had said something
from that first meeting. His subconscious mind had

been trying to tell him something. Of course! Leipzig! Now he had it all, he thought darkly. He had thought there was something phony about the accent right from the beginning. The trouble was that he had been thinking in English and yet he had been dealing with Germans all along. He should have been thinking in German. The German names all had something to do with water. And as Koenig used to say, there are no coincidences in this business. Names mattered, all right. He had the what and the how. The only thing missing was the why, and he would get to the bottom of that soon enough.

The betrayal was complete. It was incredible! The Americans and the Peruvians and the Nazis were all in it together. How could the Company do it? he wondered. How could they do it after what happened in Vietnam? And then he remembered Talleyrand's line about the Bourbons. "They have learned nothing and forgotten nothing." Well, the Bourbons were still running the show. Principles are mankind's most expendable baggage, he thought grimly. And they had used him to further their evil scheme and then tossed him on the garbage heap as soon as he was no longer needed. But they had made one mistake. He was still alive. And he wasn't playing their game anymore. He was on his own now. And it was very personal.

It was happening again, he thought with horror. It was Germany and Laos and Cambodia and Nam all over again. And he was the only one who could still stop it. They had made a mistake—he was still alive. And he was going to stop them just as he had stopped Mengele, he vowed. The job wasn't over yet. And nothing on earth was going to stop him. Nothing! He got up and began to pound on the steel door in a fury.

"I'm alive, you bastards! I'm still alive!" he shouted again and again. At last he slumped to the floor, exhausted.

Nothing happened. There was only the darkness and the terrible silence. He began to pace up and back, up and back, carefully counting his steps hour after hour, until he got into the rhythm of it. He had to plan his escape.

Sounds of muffled footsteps reached him through the steel door. There was a grating sound as the hinge opened and a tin plate slid in. Then the footsteps receded. He examined the plate by the dim light of the hinge, which he held open. The plate held a small portion of watery fish soup. It smelled disgusting and he almost dropped it as his stomach turned. There was something floating in it. He touched it and it turned over and stared back at him. It was a fish eye. But he would have to keep up his strength if he was to escape, he thought, and forced himself to slurp it all down.

He resumed pacing, hour after hour in the darkness. He no longer noticed the stench, or gagged when he swallowed the fishy water, which seemed to be the only item on the menu. They had to come for him soon, he thought. The darkness and the silence were getting to him. And he was getting weaker all the time. Judging by the stubble of beard on his face, he had been there several days already and it seemed that they fed him the watery plate only twice a day. He didn't know how much longer he could last.

He tried and rejected one plan after another, counting out each move in rhythm to his endlessly shuffling steps. No matter what he did, conditioning would matter and he forced himself to do push-ups till he collapsed. Then he did sit-ups until his stomach hurt so much he could scarcely breathe. Then he went back to push-ups. He began to evolve a regular routine. One hour of push-ups and sit-ups, one hour of pacing up and back, then back to the exercises. He estimated the time by counting twenty breaths to the minute, twelve hundred breaths to the hour.

He was constantly hungry. Thoughts of elaborate meals tantalized him and he spent hours planning the meals he would have if he ever got out. He could almost taste a big steak and fries, but the thought only made him hungrier. He couldn't shake it. Hunger was a dull, gnawing ache that never went away. He could feel it even while he slept. The whole thing was impossible, he thought. He was getting weaker all the time. Besides, what could one man, alone, unarmed, and in solitary confinement, do to stop the powerful forces that were gathering like storm clouds. Don't think that way, he told himself, warming himself on the fire of his anger. One man can do anything if he's willing to die for it.

By the end of what he estimated was the third day, he had a plan worked out. It wasn't much of a plan, but it was all he had. It depended on the notion that they apparently wanted to keep him alive, probably for a murder trial. That was the heart of it, that they wanted to keep him alive and he was now willing to die.

He would have to make his move in court, at a hearing or trial or whatever their procedure was. It would be the one place where he probably wouldn't be handcuffed or under heavy guard. He would have to get near a guard, disarm him, and shoot it out, or grab the judge or someone important as a hostage.

They'd probably never agree to let him escape. If he could get out, he could go to ground, contact Sam, and arrange a clandestine flight to the States. But that was probably a pipe dream. More likely he could hold them off for a while and try to get his message through to reporters, to try and blow the Starfish wide open. It probably wouldn't help, but it was the best he could do. He ought to be able to hold off the security police long enough for that, he thought.

They'd kill him in the end, of course. And then try to hush it up by claiming he was some kind of a lunatic, or a political terrorist. But somebody might believe him. Feinberg would know the truth. And maybe Amnon and a few others. That was all he could hope for. They'd kill him anyway—the Bourbons would see to that. They always did. But at least this way he would have chosen his death. It wasn't much, he admitted. But at least it was something.

Now that he had a plan, he felt a certain sense of relief. The die was cast and all that remained was the acting out. When the time came, he would be ready. He remembered how Koenig always used to quote his favorite line, slapping his ruler against the poster of it that he'd had made up and tacked to the blackboard. It was something that Louis Pasteur had said: "Chance only favors the mind that is prepared."

He was in the middle of a push-up when he heard the sounds of approaching footsteps. It sounded like a number of men. He leaped to his feet, his heart beating with the frenzied rhythm of a voodoo drum. The footsteps paused outside the door and he backed against the wall. Sweat dripped into his eyes and he could hardly catch his breath.

The steel door opened with a loud clang and the

cell was filled with blinding light. He threw his arms over his eyes to shield them against the agonizing brightness. He heard someone step into the cell and there was a murmur of voices. Squinting his eyes open the tiniest crack, he could just make out the dim figure of a man silhouetted against the white, smoky light flooding the doorway. Gradually his eyes began to focus and then he could begin painfully to see. Except that they had come for him too late, because he knew he must be crazy. He simply couldn't be seeing what he was seeing, he thought despairingly.

Bob Harris was standing there in the doorway.

Harris was elegant as ever, in a gray three-piece tropical worsted suit, smoking a cigarette as though he were posing for a magazine layout. Harris wrinkled his nose with distaste at the stench in the cell.

"Jesus, Johnny. Whatever you're wearing, it isn't exactly Chanel Number Five," Harris said.

CHAPTER 19

"Oil," Caine said finally and glanced out the window at the shiny blue surface of the Pacific, far below.

"What the world needs now is oil, sweet oil," Harris crooned off-key to the tune of an old love song. He reached up and pressed the button for the pretty blond flight attendant in the modish yellow Braniff uniform that made her look like an extra on the *Star Trek* set. When she came over, Harris ordered another round of martinis. As she walked back to the first-class cabin bar, Harris contemplated her cute behind with a dreamy smile of pleasure.

"So that was the why behind the Starfish," Caine mused.

"Biggest damn strike since the North Slope in Alaska. That's what started all the balls bouncing. It was first brought to our attention by Sobil National, a consortium of American companies headed by Sobil Oil, the company who made the first strike on the Santiago River, a tributary of the Marañon. You were closer than you knew with that Petrotex cover, Johnny. You almost blew it right then and there," Harris said, glancing around to make sure they weren't overheard.

The flight attendant returned with the drinks and a couple of extra bags of peanuts. She almost spilled the drinks, because she couldn't take her eyes off Caine. That was hardly surprising, considering the fact that his picture had been plastered across the front page of every major newspaper in the world for the past two days. Caine smiled absentmindedly at her and she responded with an inviting grin. Caine sipped moodily at his drink and she turned away with a shrug. The martini had that vaguely metallic taste that he always associated with pressurized cabin air.

"Then Sobil Oil was the fifth arm of the Starfish," Caine said. Harris nodded.

"How did von Schiffen and ODESSA get involved?" Caine asked.

Harris lit two cigarettes and handed one to Caine, as if he were Paul Henreid about to tell Bette Davis that the affair was over.

"That was the funny part," Harris admitted. "Nobody knows who or where von Schiffen is. All we know for sure is that von Schiffen heads ODESSA. Von Schiffen acquired the mineral and oil rights to almost the entire Peruvian Amazon about twenty years ago as a perfectly legitimate business investment, using some of ODESSA's vast funds. At the time most of his *Kameraden* probably thought he was crazy, but ODESSA isn't exactly run in a democratic fashion. Anyway, von Schiffen owned it all.

"Sobil had information indicating that the left-wing military junta that runs the Peruvian government planned to nationalize the Amazon oil fields and that's when we got involved. If the Peruvians took over the fields, the American consumer would have never seen a drop of that oil. The biggest oil strike in history, right in our own backyard, found by us and they were going to lock us out of it.

"It went right to the top, Johnny. The DCI himself took it to the National Security Council and they gave us our marching orders: The energy crisis is the moral equivalent of war and we were to secure the Peruvian oil for the U.S. no matter what the cost. Out of that came the Starfish Conspiracy."

Caine angrily stubbed out his cigarette and stared out of the window at the endless ocean. Somewhere in the shadowed depths of the sea thousands of starfish were undoubtedly crawling. They always came back, he though grimly. The Bourbons. The Nazis. Like starfish, they could regenerate themselves from the tiniest fragment. A starfish cannot be killed, only exterminated, he thought.

"So we decided to overthrow the legitimate Peruvian government and replace it with a Nazi regime who agreed to sell us the oil. Congratulations, Bob. You've risen to a new low," Caine said, realizing how stupid he sounded. Insulting Harris was like pouring water on a duck.

"Not a Nazi regime, Johnny," Harris said mildly, bringing out his sincere smile as though it were a gift. "A coalition government of right-wing Peruvian Army officers and certain acceptable representatives from ODESSA. Shit, ever since the leftist General Velasco was forced out in '75, the junta has been moving to the right, thanks to a few key ODESSA appointments in the right spots—and a little help from us. And why the hell shouldn't we pursue our own interests? We were well within our rights. Monroe Doctrine and all that. Besides, we're the ones who found the oil in the first place."

"Monroe Doctrine my ass! If you're going to be a pirate, at least fly the skull and crossbones. What we're talking about are Nazis, for Christ's sake! That means Peru would be a Nazi enclave, just as Paraguay is already. Chile is further to the right than Genghis Khan and if the Nazis make common cause with the Perónistas and their own fascists in Argentina, then most of South America, with all its potential riches, falls into ODESSA's hands. And we'll have done it! Us! The good guys!" Caine retorted angrily.

"We've always known about your somewhat 'liberal tendencies,' Johnny," Harris said, as if he were describing the symptoms of a disease. "Don't you think it's about time you grew up? The Company's job is to protect American interests. And if getting rid of a leftist Peruvian regime and securing oil for the U.S. in the middle of an energy crisis isn't in America's national interest, then what the hell is? You've had your head up your ass since Laos. Believe me, if this damned Mendoza business hadn't cropped up, we would have never pulled you in. You're a wild card, Johnny. We don't know which way you'll jump, that's why you were marked lousy in the Company. Unfortunately for us, you were the perfect man for the job. So we had to run you blind, without you knowing about it."

"Did you know that Mendoza was Mengele?" Caine asked.

"No. That was a brilliant piece of work," Harris admitted. "All we knew was what Sobil passed along from von Schiffen, that Mengele was somewhere in the Amazon. Naturally he had to be brought around the corner. With people crawling all over the Amazon in the middle of an oil boom, it was inevitable that someone would spot him. It wouldn't look good, us playing ball with a team that had Mengele on their side. If it had been almost anybody else, we might have tried another ploy. But the infamous Angel of Death of Auschwitz was a little too hot for us. You know how it is, Johnny. The public might get the wrong idea about what we were up to."

"I can't imagine why," Caine put in archly.

Harris ignored him. He drained his martini and signaled for another.

"His existence endangered the entire op. That's when we decided to run a mission. As soon as we knew Mengele was involved, we knew the Jews would be interested. That's how we connected with Wasserman. He agreed to act as the cover and to finance the Mengele phase. But nobody knew where Mengele was or how to get at him. We needed a specialist. You," Harris said.

"Why didn't Mengele go to ground again?" Caine asked.

"Who the hell knows?" Harris shrugged. "He may have actually begun to believe in the role he was playing—the saintly Dr. Mendoza, the Albert Schweitzer of the Amazon. Maybe it was his way of expiating the guilt. Who knows? All we knew for sure was that he was adamant and that his refusal to leave his Amazon sanctuary caused a major power struggle within ODESSA. That's where you came in," Harris said.

The flight attendant brought them another round. She stared at Caine like a kid with her nose pressed against the toy-store window. Harris glanced at her with annoyance and she moved away. Harris punched Caine's arm playfully. The martinis were starting to get to him. Any minute now he would be breaking into a sentimental song, Caine thought irritably.

"It really was a sensational op, Johnny," Harris enthused, exhaling a miasma of gin at Caine. "Just sensational. You weren't officially connected to the Company anymore. You had the right languages and skills for the job. We baited the hook with money and a chance for you to be the knight in shining armor against a real, live dragon. There was even the beautiful damsel for you to play with. We thought of everything. That's why I was in Berlin. To make sure you got on the right track. It was a sensational op. We took every detail into account."

"Except one," Caine put in.

"Except one," Harris admitted grudgingly. "We never figured you to get out of the jungle alive. Nobody knows how you did it, kiddo," Harris said, and playfully punched Caine's arm again. Caine looked at Harris with his icy green eyes.

"Don't ever touch me again, Bob," he said softly.

Harris looked away, then turned back to Caine with a truculent expression that gave him the cute-ugly appearance of a bulldog puppy.

"Let me tell you, when we spotted your ad in the *Times*, we all went into a state of shock. But you gotta believe me, Johnny, that was the one part of it that I didn't like. Sending you on a one-way mission. But I'm glad you made it, you son of a gun. That was the one part that bothered me."

"How did you spring me?" Caine asked. Maybe it had bothered Harris to send him around the corner. Harris was a little too fastidious to enjoy wet work. It really wasn't his field. Harris fancied the role of the *éminence gris*, the man behind the throne with clean hands and a Colgate smile.

Harris raised his glass in a silent toast to himself, then drained the martini with a flourish. He popped the olive in his mouth and chewed it, obviously pleased with himself.

"It's been a rough two days, Johnny. You don't know what I've had to go through to get hold of you."

"Remind me to cry when you get to the sad parts, Bob," Caine said. Harris grimaced, his expression implying that field agents never did appreciate what a senior case officer had to go through.

"We did a deal with Presidente Diaz. It was the only way. The Peruvians were planning a big show trial for you. It was quite a scenario: CIA spy kills the good Dr. Mendoza, the saint of the Amazon, as a part of an American imperialist plot. The Commies and the Third World press would have had a field day with it! By the time I got to Lima to try and plug the dike, you were front-page news all over the world," Harris said.

That was true enough, Caine thought. They had escorted him from his cell under heavy guard and with great care, as though he were a shipment of delicate porcelain. They returned his belongings to him in the warden's office, where he put on his linen suit. They returned everything to him, except the vial with Mengele's thumb. When Caine asked about it, Harris nudged him. That was obviously part of the deal. But that didn't matter anymore. All that mattered to him was that they returned his keys intact. Most of the keys were phonies, but two were critical; the safety-deposit keys to boxes in L.A. and New York. He was going to need them if he was ever going to stop the Starfish and get out of this alive.

There hadn't been enough time to wash up before he left the prison. The Peruvians were clearly anxious to get him off their hands. They drove Harris and

Caine to the airport in a giant motorcade, flanked by hundreds of soldiers and security police. The police kept a swarm of shouting newsmen and photographers away from him as they ushered him through the terminal and onto the Braniff jet to Los Angeles which Harris had arranged to have standing by. It wasn't until they were safely aboard in the first-class cabin and the plane had taken off that Caine was able to head for the lavatory. He ignored the curious stares of the few first-class passengers as he made his way back to the lavatory, where he shaved and washed. His white linen suit was smudged and wrinkled, giving him the appearance of one of the seedier characters in a Humphrey Bogart movie and he tried to smooth it out as best he could. He felt almost human again by the time he made his way back to his seat.

"How did the Peruvians know that I had been with the Company?" Caine wondered aloud.

"They didn't at first," Harris remarked with a snort of derision. "For them the Company is simply a convenient scapegoat for anything that goes wrong. If a traffic light goes out in Lima, they're liable to blame it on CIA agents. It was one of their standard propaganda ploys. This time it just happened to be true," Harris said with a shrug.

"Poor misunderstood CIA. What was the deal, anyway?"

"Obviously we couldn't let you stand up in court before the world press and blow the Starfish wide open. That would have made the beating we took on Chile from the Congress and the press look like a love-in. Anyway, I made a deal with Diaz and sweetened it with good old Yankee *dolares*.

"The deal is that we won't reveal that Mendoza was really Mengele. Diaz was very sensitive to charges that the Peruvian government was providing a haven for Nazi war criminals. In exchange they turned you over to us and let the CIA off the hook. It was all a mistake. Subsequent evidence now indicates that the saintly Dr. Mendoza died of snakebite. Flags are flying at half-mast in his honor all over Peru. The United Nations is thinking of issuing a commemorative plaque," Harris said, his voice unctuous with mock sympathy.

Caine pressed the seat button and leaned back, closing his eyes for a moment. He was feeling tired and knew that soon he would need all the energy he could get. The irony of it, he thought. Honoring Mengele's memory. And yet in this topsy-turvy world it made a curious kind of sense. In the army the brass often covered up a fiasco by handing the culprit a medal. But then the whole damned op had been an exercise in irony from start to finish.

"It's ironic," he muttered.

"What is?" Harris asked.

"Mengele wasn't killed for the Jews at all. He was killed to help the Nazis," he said disgustedly.

"You're in the big leagues now, kiddo. You can't tell the players without a scoreboard these days," Harris said.

Caine massaged his closed eyelids with his fingertips. Blue and yellow spots floated across the darkness, and for a second he was reminded of the butterflies. He opened his eyes and he was back in the cabin, looking out the window at the pale blue sky. Far below could see a small white cloud floating on the wind like a dandelion. He turned away from the tranquil skyscape and looked at Harris. Peace was just a dream, he reminded himself. The Starfish was still running.

"Tell me, Bob. Has it occurred to you planning geniuses that the ousted left might not take kindly to a Nazi regime?" Caine asked. Harris lit a cigarette with a gold Dunhill lighter and exhaled slowly and evenly. He picked a fleck of tobacco off his lower lip.

"You haven't been listening, Johnny," Harris began patiently, like a teacher with a not-very-bright pupil. "This is a first-class op. Everything has been taken into account. Everything. If the left wants to try something, we'll be ready."

"You realize you're talking about a guerrilla war. One that just might tear the whole South American continent apart," Caine said.

"Well, naturally we intend to keep the Russkies out of our backyard. I think we can safely assume that an ODESSA-backed government will be appropriately thorough in handling political extremists. Of course, there is a contingency plan just in case things do get out of hand."

"You mean advisers, Special Forces, Company men—that sort of thing," Caine prompted.

"Well, that would be the only logical way to handle it," Harris admitted.

"Sensational, Bob. Just sensational. It's just like Nam all over again, only this time we'll be fighting for the Nazis instead of Diem. I've got to hand it to you guys. You've come a long way, baby. There's just one thing—"

"What's that?" Harris said, looking speculatively at Caine, as though he were trying to guess his weight.

"What are you going to do about me? I'm the only

one who knows all about the Starfish and can prove it. You didn't haul me out of Peru so that I could come back and sell my memoirs to *The Washington Post*. So what are you going to do about me?" Caine said, his emerald eyes focused directly at Harris, as though he were peering at him over a gun barrel.

Harris sighed heavily. This was the touchy part, the question he had been waiting for. He trotted out his sincere smile, like a singer with a single tune.

"We've decided to put you on ice, Johnny. There's a Senate Intelligence Subcommittee investigation starting and we want to make sure you don't testify. So we're going to put you in cold storage for a while. Don't worry, kiddo. We'll take care of you," Harris said and winked, invoking the esprit de corps of the professional agent.

"What about C.J. and Wasserman?" Caine asked.

"Her, too. We'll keep Wasserman under surveillance, of course. Besides, he knows it's in his own interest to keep his mouth shut."

Caine stared at Harris and shook his head slowly. Harris really had him figured for an idiot, he thought. Not even the greenest recruit would fall for that two-bit bedtime story. There was only one way that they could ever be sure he wouldn't spill his guts.

"You'd be better off terminating me, Bob. Safer that way," Caine said quietly.

"Now, Johnny, don't talk that way. You're family. And you handled this Mendoza business just great," Harris said, shaking his head. "Don't go off the deep end on this, kiddo. Remember, I'm your friend."

"That's what Benedict Arnold told George Washington," Caine replied.

"Now just wait one damn minute, Johnny boy. You're the assassin, not me. You're the one who murdered Mengele for money—and the Nazis. So don't go all 'Holy Joe' on me, kiddo," Harris retorted angrily.

Caine turned away and stared out the window for a long while. When he turned back, Harris was grumpily sipping at another martini, an adolescent pout on his boyish face.

"We're all assassins, Bob. Don't you know that yet?" Caine inquired quietly. He didn't wait for an answer and pulled down the windowshade and pressed the seat button to a reclining position. He leaned back gingerly, as if entering a hot bathtub, and closed his eyes. The hum of the jets sounded in his ears like the constant roar of the surf on some distant shore.

"Ladies and gentlemen, we are on our final approach to LAX and will be landing in approximately ten minutes. Please fasten your seat belts and observe the No Smoking sign. The weather in Los Angeles is slightly overcast and a pleasant seventy-two degrees. On behalf of Captain Wilson and the flight crew, we want to thank you for flying Braniff and hope you'll fly with us again. Have a pleasant day," the flight attendant's metallic voice announced over the loudspeaker, with all the spontaneity of a tape recording.

Caine pressed the seat button and adjusted the seat to an upright position. Harris crushed out a cigarette and straightened his tie.

"Now listen. When we land, you are not to say anything to the reporters. Not a word, get it?" Harris said.

Caine nodded, but he scarcely heard him. His mind was busy with other plans. It was all a matter of timing, he thought. The only chance he had was to move so quickly that they wouldn't have the time to react. His best assets were that he was willing to die and they weren't and that their own secretiveness and bureaucracy would slow down their lines of communication. He would have to complete the job before they even knew what had happened.

The plane made a wide turn over Westchester, the single-family rooftops forming a neat Monopoly board pattern as the plane came in. Just below him he could see the oval green of the Hollywood Park racetrack. Sunlight glinted off the El Segundo oil refinery, looking somewhat unfinished, like the ruins of a vanished industrial civilisation. The air was hazy with smog that misted from the brown Santa Monica hills to the white-capped waves beyond the shore. There was a slight bounce and the rumble of the tires on the runway, his body lurching forward as the brakes were applied.

Caine and Harris were the first ones let off the plane. They walked side by side through the connecting tunnel to the terminal gate. At the mouth of the tunnel he could see a jumble of reporters and photographers, flashbulbs popping, behind a police cordon. Standing at the the foot of the gate to receive him were Chuck Powell, a southerner with a bland "good-ole-boy" expression and blow-dried hair, who was the Company's public spokesman; Smiley Gallagher, wearing a rumpled suit and a beatific smile on his pudgy face; and two unsmiling types with beefy torsos straining at their dark suits, who were obviously there for muscle.

"Make it look good, kiddo," Harris hissed and smiled at the crowd.

"What do I get if I do, Bob? A berth on the *Good Ship Dollipop*?" Caine remarked.

They were engulfed by Powell, Gallagher, and the Company men, who formed a ring around Caine, reinforced by a flying wedge of LAPD cops. They moved rapidly through the throng of newsmen and wide-eyed spectators that ran alongside the cortege. A noisy jumble of voices shouted questions about Mendoza and the CIA and Powell and Harris kept snapping, "No comment! No comment!" as they shoved their way through the melee. Caine glanced quickly around as they neared the down escalator to the street level. In all this crowd and with all the cameras he didn't think they would shoot. The escalator was his best shot, because it funneled the crowd and minimized the number of people in front of him. A cop and one of the shields got on in front of Caine, with Harris, Smiley, and Powell right behind.

Caine stepped onto the escalator and Harris moved onto the same step. As they glided down, Caine took a deep breath and shifted slightly, but something alerted Harris and he took hold of Caine's jacket lapel.

"Don't do anything stupid, Johnny," Harris whispered.

"I warned you—" Caine began and started his move. He locked Harris's hand to his jacket with his right hand and smashed the base of his left palm against the outside of Harris's elbow, breaking it. Harris screamed.

Caine slipped past the shield in front as the lead cop began to turn around. Caine's foot caught him in the chest, knocking him down into the crowd in front. They tumbled like bowling pins and the escalator was clogged with screaming people and tangled limbs.

Caine vaulted over the handrail and began sliding down the slick metal incline beside the escalator. A shot rang out near his ear and he was running and sliding down the incline amid the panicked shouts and popping flashbulbs.

He leaped to the ground and dodged through the crowd, knocking people aside. Someone was shouting "Stop him!" and he crashed into a businessman carrying a briefcase and a valise. They tumbled to the ground in a tangle, the businessman cursing loudly, and then Caine was up and running. He glanced briefly back over his shoulder. The second shield and one of the cops had reached the foot of the escalator and had snapped into a two-handed firing position, but people were in the way and they held their fire. Out of the corner of his eye he spotted one of the gray-uniformed airport security guards moving to head him off and he ran even harder, bursting through the open doorway to the street, crowded with double-parked cars unloading.

A middle-aged woman in a Chevy station wagon was seated behind the wheel, while another woman was getting out of the front seat. Caine shoved the woman behind the wheel over, leaped into the driver's seat, and slammed the car door.

"Don't move, lady, or I'll kill you," he snapped at the startled woman, his eyes glittering murderously as he started the car.

"Who are you?" she asked in a quavering voice, her eyes wide in terror.

"Shut up, goddamnit!" he growled urgently. He put the car into gear and pulled into the heavy traffic flow. He turned around and saw a couple of cops and the second shield running after them on the sidewalk.

Another cop jumped into a taxi, but it was momentarily blocked by the traffic.

"Take it easy, lady," Caine ordered, noting a movement out of the corner of his eye as he picked up speed. He knew he would have to switch cars as soon as possible. It was only a matter of seconds before they had an APB out on him and the vehicle. He took the turn off to Sepulveda Boulevard and raced through the light, nearly sideswiping a van. Then they were speeding down Lincoln Boulevard, weaving in and out of traffic, angry drivers blowing their horns and gesticulating obscenely at them.

He spotted a line of taxis outside the Airport Marina Hotel and suddenly pulled over with a screech of brakes. He leaped out, stuck his fist in his jacket pocket as though it were a gun, and told her to take off. She hardly needed urging, and with a last frightened glance at him she moved over to the driver's seat and pulled quickly away.

Caine ran across Lincoln Boulevard, just beating a wave of oncoming cars and jumped into the first cab. The Chicano driver started to move and leisurely flicked on the meter. Caine told him there was a C-note in it for him if he got him to Hollywood in fifteen minutes.

"You got it, *hombre*," the driver shouted happily and gunned the engine as if he were on the starting line at Indy.

The cab leaped forward and the driver stopped to turn onto Manchester, as a police car tore down Lincoln, its siren wailing like a voice of doom. The cab sped down Manchester and headed north on La Cienega, over Baldwin Hills. The oil pumps scattered over the brown hills relentlessly bobbed up and down like giant mechanical insects feeding on the vast corpse of the city. Oil and money, that's all it was ever about, Caine thought bitterly as the taxi came over the rise. The city spread out before him, swathed in a smoky white shroud of smog, as though the city were burning from an unseen fire.

As the taxi weaved through the heavy traffic on La Cienega, Caine checked his watch, trying to compute how much time he had before Wasserman and C.J. got the news. The taxi radio was tuned to hard rock music, and fearful of a news broadcast, Caine told the driver to shut it off and concentrate on his driving. The Chicano glanced reproachfully at Caine in the rearview mirror as he turned into the broad expanse of Wilshire Boulevard.

Caine told the driver to slow down on Wilshire and the driver nodded, as they drove past the expensive stores and office buildings. The last thing he needed now was to get stopped for speeding. He ordered the driver to pull over at the Bank of America branch and wait for him, jumping out of the cab before the Chicano had time to object.

He walked directly to the counter without glancing around at the moderately crowded bank and signed the safety-deposit slip. The attractive blond teller, barely out of her teens, verified his signature and buzzed him in. As they fitted the two keys into the locks, he thanked his lucky stars for the hunch that had prompted him to rent the box before he had gone down to Peru.

Carrying the metal box, he followed the teller to the small cubicle. As she turned away, he locked the door and sat down with a sigh of relief. In a way a safety-deposit cubicle is the last sanctuary left to Western man, the one remaining place where his privacy is inviolate, he thought. He opened the box and took out the big S&W .44 Magnum revolver and cracked open the cylinder. He loaded it with the large and lethal-looking Remington hollow-head bullets and placed a handful of cartridges in his sagging jacket pocket. He took the $2,000 he had left in the box and put it in his inside pocket and stuck the heavy gun in his belt, buttoning his jacket over the bulge. At last he was ready for the Starfish, he thought grimly. He signaled for the teller and they returned the box to his slot. She wished him a good day and he mechanically returned her smile as he headed for the door.

Through the glass door he spotted a black-and-white police car stopped by the taxi, and without breaking stride, he turned on his heel, snapping his fingers as though he had forgotten something, and walked calmly to the side door to the parking lot. He walked through the lot away from Wilshire and turned down a palm-lined sidestreet. He walked a long block, then turned up Western Avenue and stopped at a coin-operated newspaper box. His own face grinned up at him from the front page of the *Herald-Examiner*, under the banner headline:

CIA INVOLVED IN MENDOZA DEATH?

He didn't need to buy a paper to know that they were playing it cagey. The question mark at the end of the headline told him that the editors were worried about libel and security violation charges. They were probably relying on carefully worded innuendo to handle the story, he decided. He felt naked, standing there on a busy street with his face on the front page like that.

He walked away and went into the big Thrifty Drugstore on the corner.

He bought a pair of sunglasses, a silly-looking canvas porkpie hat, and a cheap blue blazer. It was essential that he alter the image now that the APB was obviously out on him. He walked into a nearby restaurant and headed directly for the men's room, where he put on the hat and sunglasses and changed jackets, putting the money and bullets into the blazer pockets. He left the white suit jacket hanging on the hook of the cubicle door. Whoever found it would assume that it had been left by an absentminded customer. He left the restaurant and mingled with the lunchtime crowd on Western until he was able to hail a taxi.

He had the leering driver drop him off about two blocks away from the massage parlor. As he strolled down Western, he kept checking the street. There was no problem in being open about it: furtive glances were normal in this seedy district. He hesitated as he neared the massage parlor. The beige Mercedes was parked in front and he could see Freddie's hulking outline behind the wheel. Wasserman must have been tipped and was planning to get out, he surmised. He had gotten there just in time, he thought as he approached the car, checking the street one last time. It looked okay and then he exhaled slowly. Freddie's nose was buried in a comic book. That was the break he needed, he thought, and walked up to the open window on the driver's side. Caine pulled the S&W from his belt and stuck the muzzle into Freddie's ear.

"Don't even blink, Freddie baby," Caine said.

Freddie started to turn his massive head. Caine jammed the muzzle harder into Freddie's ear and the big man froze.

"This is a .44 Magnum, Freddie baby, so don't even breathe. Now, reach very slowly over to the ignition with your left hand and, using just two fingers, pull out the key and carefully hold it out the window," Caine said.

Freddie did as he was told and Caine pocketed the keys. Then he ordered Freddie out of the car, keeping the gun aimed at Freddie's head and standing clear of the door, in case Freddie decided to try some heroics.

"Wasserman inside?" Caine asked.

"No, man. He's left for the day," Freddie said.

"You're a lousy liar, Freddie baby," Caine retorted, and jamming the muzzle against Freddie's spine, he marched him into the empty massage parlor. The reception room was still lined with the same photos and somehow this time they made Caine think of Fong and the Venus flytrap. They'd caught him twice with sex. There wouldn't be a third time, he vowed savagely.

"You're making a big mistake, man," Freddie's voice rumbled as they stepped through the side door into the dim corridor to Wasserman's office.

"Don't be stupid. This isn't one of your comic books," Caine whispered, easily hiding himself behind Freddie's giant bulk as they posed before the closed-circuit television camera. Caine prodded Freddie again with the gun.

"Open up. It's me," Freddie said.

For a long moment they stood there in the silent corridor, waiting. The steel door slid open with a faint hydraulic hiss. Caine prodded Freddie ahead of him as they walked into Wasserman's office.

CHAPTER 20

Wasserman was seated at the computer terminal as they entered. He was wearing an expensive blue blazer, white slacks, and an open-necked floral-print shirt. He looked like one of those Beverly Hills yachtsmen, who do most of their sailing by pushing their olives from one side of their martinis to the other. An open attaché case stuffed with papers lay on the big Chippendale desk. It was apparent to Caine that he had been tipped and was clearing out. Wasserman half turned with annoyance to look at Freddie and his eyes opened wide with shock to see Caine standing there. He trotted out his benign grin, but the smile faded when he saw the gun.

"You can stop dropping files now and log off," Caine said and was rewarded with a stupefied expression from Wasserman.

"I don't know what you're talking—" Wasserman began in a quavering old man's treble.

"Shut up and do as you're told," Caine snapped, gesturing with the gun. He ordered Freddie to lie facedown on the floor and told Wasserman to tie him up.

"With what?" Wasserman muttered, his florid sunburned face suddenly bleached white.

"Use the telephone cord and make it good and tight. I'm going to check the knots," Caine ordered.

Wasserman ripped the cord from the wall and tied Freddie's hands behind him with shaking fingers. Caine ordered him to sit on Freddie, who lay rigid with fear, and Wasserman complied. For a long moment the two men stared silently at each other.

"Please, John. You don't know what you're doing," Wasserman said.

"Shut up!" Caine shouted. He aimed the gun at the bridge of Wasserman's nose and was almost overcome by the temptation to squeeze the trigger. Then he thought about the stamp and exhaled slowly.

"First things first, Herr von Schiffen," Caine said conversationally. Beads of sweat formed on Wasserman's face and his eyes darted briefly around the room. Caine noticed the glance and smiled coldly.

"You made four mistakes," Caine began. "I should have caught it sooner, but I was so filled with blind greed that I didn't see what was right in front of my eyes"—gesturing with the gun at the room.

"You must be crazy—" Wasserman began anxiously.

"Don't bother to deny it. You're von Schiffen, all right. It took me a while to see it, that's all," Caine said.

"What were these so-called mistakes?" Wasserman asked quizzically, like a man who still has a few cards left to play. Caine smiled and calmly began to tick them off.

"First, that fairy tale you told me about your wife. You said that you came from Leipzig, but you have a Low German or Bavarian accent. They speak High German in Leipzig.

"Second, you filled this room with rare pre-

Columbian *huaco* figurines from the Andean cultures. So either you must have been in Peru, or you had strong Peruvian contacts, because these *huacos* come from Peru and it's illegal to take valuable archeological artifacts out of that country," Caine said, gesturing at the pottery displayed in the armoire.

"Von Schiffen must have important connections in Peru, otherwise he couldn't have bought the oil leases. You used those contacts when you had C.J. set me up for the fall in Lima. No one else knew where I was, so it had to be her and she was connected to you. It had to be you. There was no one else," Caine added.

"And third, you got too cute with the names. That was pure, stupid pride," Caine said contemptuously. Wasserman returned his stare with horrified fascination, as though Caine were a poisonous snake coiled to strike.

"Go on," Wasserman said breathlessly, almost in spite of himself.

"Water was the key. I expect that you have some kind of family connection to shipping, or perhaps the navy."

"My father was a U-boat captain and my grandfather was an admiral in the Imperial Navy," Wasserman stated proudly, drawing his chest up and looking contemptuously at Caine.

"It had to be something like that." Caine nodded. "*Schiff* means 'ship' in German, *Seestern* or 'starfish' is a five-armed aquatic animal, and Wasserman means 'water man.' And Sobil found the oil in the Santiago River. It was all 'water, water, everywhere.' What fools you must have thought us all. But you just couldn't resist that ridiculous German penchant for symbolic code names, just like the bad old days in the Wehrmacht. What were you in the war, anyway? Naval intelligence or the SS?"

"Nothing so trivial," Wasserman snapped, his eyes gleaming. His Beverly Hills Jewish mannerisms dropped away like a molted snakeskin. He surveyed Caine with a calm arrogance.

"I am General Karl von Schiffen of the Waffen SS and later, in the Gestapo, I was a senior aide to Himmler himself."

"You forgot to click your heels," Caine remarked.

"We have no quarrel, you and I. You'll get your stamp. You've earned it," von Schiffen said with a strained geniality.

"That's very generous of you."

"Not at all. I assume you have the thumb."

"I'm afraid I misplaced it in a Lima prison."

"Then how can I be sure Mengele is dead?"

"Read the newspapers."

"Fair enough. Besides, you have me at a certain disadvantage," von Schiffen said, tilting his head toward the gun.

"Satisfy my curiosity on one point. Was there ever really a Jew named Wasserman?" Caine asked.

"Oh, yes," von Schiffen responded, a wry smile dimpling his cheek. "I met him during an inspection tour of Dachau in January 1945. He had been a diamond merchant in—"

"Leipzig," Caine threw in.

"*Natürlich.*" Von Schiffen smiled. "He tried to bribe his way out of the camp with several handfuls of exquisite gems. I simply accepted the bribe and had him gassed anyway. But the similarity of our first names and the water symbolism struck me. I knew that the war would end in a few months and that I would have to assume a new identity and flee Germany. Wasserman was like an omen for me.

"I checked and discovered that his entire family had been wiped out, so there would be no one to ask any questions. I secretly arranged to have his number tattooed on my arm and saw to it that his name was never added to the lists of those who had been gassed. When the time came, I simply threw on some rags and wandered west till the Americans picked me up and brought me to a DP camp. It wasn't difficult. Refugees and deserters were wandering all over Europe in those days. I had almost never visited the camps—that one time in Dachau was a rare exception—so no one knew my face. When the time came, I immigrated to America and used the diamonds to begin my business empire."

"Brilliant," Caine admitted. "Who would have ever suspected an important Nazi to be masquerading as a Jew, the thing he most despised? Truly extraordinary."

"I created the plans for *der Seestern* years ago," von Schiffen went on. His face assumed the calm demeanor of a man accustomed to authority. "I knew it was only a matter of time. Western civilization is on its last legs. A recent American secretary of state once admitted as much. The European and American democracies are tottering on the brink of chaos. Only a single unifying force can ever stop the Communists and that force must unite behind a single mind. *Ja*, Hitler was right: the only alternative to moral bankruptcy is the *Führerprinzip*, the Leadership Principle.

"All the elements for a Fourth Reich that will dominate the world are in place, beginning with Peru. South America is fertile ground for revolution, with a large and docile population and a tradition of machismo and violence. We Nazis know how to put such elements to use. We already have Peruvian fascists and ODESSA *Kameraden* in key positions in the army and the police. Now that Mengele is out of the way, we can begin to move at last. At the right moment we will overthrow the weak leftist junta and take over, just as in Chile. And we don't have to worry about the Americans, because the CIA is helping us to overthrow the leftist regime. Victory is inevitable," von Schiffen sneered.

"So you take over Peru. So what?" Caine said.

"First Peru and Paraguay, then Chile and Argentina with their large German populations and military dictatorships, until finally the entire continent, with all its natural resources, will be in our hands for us to mold into a weapon.

"The only thing lacking was the catalyst. Then Sobil struck oil and it all belonged to me! And my oil would be coming on line in the last decades of the century, just when the Arab oil begins to run dry. Imagine how irresistible all our wealth and power will be! Think of it, Caine. Unnoticed in the backwaters of the Third World, the Fourth Reich is being born," von Schiffen rhapsodized.

"ODESSA, Sobil, the Peruvian fascists, and the Company," Caine ticked off. "Who was the fifth arm of the Starfish?"

Von Schiffen smiled.

"I don't think I'll tell you," he said.

With a wide swing of his arm Caine swept the terra cotta *huacos* off the armoire shelf and smashed them across the room, littering the floor with broken crockery.

"Who was the fifth arm?" he shouted.

"Those were priceless works of art. You are a barbarian," von Schiffen declared contemptuously.

"And don't you forget it," Caine said, and calmly cocked the hammer of the revolver. "For the last time, who was the fifth arm?"

Von Schiffen seemed to shrink inside his clothes and he couldn't tear his eyes from the gaping muzzle aimed at his head.

"A secret committee of right-wing elements from neighboring countries—Chile, Paraguay, and Argentina. It's called the *Kameradenwerk,* the 'Comrades' Organization.' And nothing can stop it! No matter how you try to kill a starfish, it always regenerates itself," he said, his eyes gleaming.

"But Mengele got in the way," Caine prompted.

"Let's just say that Mengele was no longer an asset to the organization," von Schiffen remarked.

"Mengele wouldn't leave his Amazon sanctuary so you could bring in the oil crews, so he had to be terminated. But he had too many friends within ODESSA, so you needed someone from the outside. Someone like me," Caine said.

"We needed you because Mengele forgot what it means to be a German. There was a time when a good German knew what was expected of him. An officer was given an order and he would retire to a room with his Luger. Once Germans understood about such things as honor and duty," von Schiffen said contemptuously.

"We live in decadent times," Caine shrugged. "You said I made four mistakes. What was the fourth?"

"You misunderstood me. You should have had me killed in that Lima prison," Caine said.

"I assumed the Company would handle that. They bungled it, those pathetic amateurs with all their computers and gadgets," von Schiffen said, his voice thick with derision and disgust.

"You're the one who made all the mistakes," Caine said quietly.

"What now? Killing me in cold blood won't stop the Starfish."

"The stamp," Caine said, holding out his hand, palm up.

"*Natürlich*. It's in my safe, hidden in the armoire. If you'll allow me," von Schiffen said, a cynical smile flickering across his sweaty face. Caine nodded and moved to a position where he could cover both von Schiffen and Freddie.

Von Schiffen moved cautiously to the armoire and opened a panel in the back that concealed the safe. He twirled the combination dial and opened the safe with a loud click. Freddie stirred restlessly and Caine glanced at him for an instant. When he looked back at the safe, von Schiffen was whirling, something gleaming in his hand.

The S&W went off with a deafening explosion and von Schiffen's head flopped over like a rag, as the body collapsed. The massive .44 caliber slug had torn away most of his neck. The nearly headless torso spilled a bright stream of blood over the floor. Caine aimed at Freddie, who stared in horror at von Schiffen and the Walther PPK in von Schiffen's hand, now almost submerged in the widening pool of blood.

"I didn't know he was a Nazi, man. I swear it,"

Freddie whined. Caine nodded grimly and crossed to the open safe, stepping on the corpse to avoid staining his shoes with blood.

He quickly rummaged through the safe. He found some correspondence relating to the Starfish and a thick stack of hundred-dollar bills, but the stamp wasn't there. Now he knew C.J.'s price for the betrayal, he thought. He also found a sterling silver ring that bore a snarling Viking face, with a swastika carved on one side and the lightning flashes of the SS on the other. Caine wearily shook his head and tossed the ring into the pool of blood. He pocketed the papers and the money, and using a handkerchief to keep his hands from getting bloody, he picked up the Walther and locked it in the safe.

"Is C.J. at the beach house now?" he asked.

Freddie nodded, wide-eyed. He knew it was his turn now.

"Does she have the stamp?"

Freddie nodded again, his body curled into a quivering fetal position. The blood lapped silently at his shoes, like the tide. Caine stepped around the blood and kneeled by Freddie's head.

"I need about an hour's head start, so I'm going to knock you out. When you come to, I suggest you clear out, because everybody and his brother will be looking for you. I'm not going to kill you, because I don't think you knew what the old kraut was involved in. Got it?" Caine said conversationally. You must be getting soft in your old age, Caine told himself.

Freddie nodded and Caine clouted him behind the ear with the butt of the S&W. Freddie's head clunked against the floor and Caine slapped his face a few times to make sure he was out. He looked around at the office. Then he walked over to the big sunny painting and took it off the wall. He ripped the canvas from the frame and rolled it up. He decided to mail it anonymously to the Louvre, if he got the chance. The painting was probably part of the SS war booty and after all, Monet had been French. Maybe it would help square accounts a little, he thought.

He walked outside, putting the hat and sunglasses back on. He threw the painting in the trunk of the Mercedes and started the car. No one paid any attention to him, except for a blond street girl with wan, washed-out features, who stared hungrily at the Mercedes as it started up Western.

Caine turned west on Sunset and drove smoothly through the traffic, the S&W heavy against his belly. Large garish billboards along the Strip advertised the latest rock music albums. At the outdoor vegetarian restaurant white-togaed waitresses served organic nutburgers to patrons who stared dull-eyed at the endless stream of traffic. Maybe the gasoline fumes from the cars added something to the taste, Caine mused. A police car tore by, its lights flashing, but they weren't after him, and a minute later he saw the police talking to the bushy-haired teen-age driver of a dune buggy.

He followed the gentle curves through Beverly Hills, past grandiose rococo houses behind high gates and lawns that were manicured like putting greens. Maybe he couldn't kill the Starfish, Caine mused. But by killing von Schiffen and by mailing the papers he had taken from the safe to Presidente Diaz in Lima, he just might be putting a dent in it. That part felt all right, anyway.

After Bel-air, he drove through Brentwood and Pacific Palisades, where the houses weren't quite so grandiose and the curves were steeper. He reached the beach and turned north on Pacific Coast Highway. The blue-white disk of the sun retreated toward the blue line where the ocean touched the sky. Well offshore, he could see the distant silhouette of an oil tanker heading south toward San Pedro. As he approached Malibu, a highway sign warned of rockslides and he felt somehow that everything was falling apart.

Cantilevered houses tilted precariously along the bluff overlooking the highway and he wonderd if the people who lived in them ever felt like Humpty-Dumpty. All along the road stringy-haired, wet-suited surfers were loading their boards in the backseats of convertibles. Near the Malibu pier a restaurant sign proclaimed "Fresh Fish," as though it were a new species. He saw a dark Buick sedan parked near the beach house and cautiously parked on the shoulder. He checked the mirrors, but it looked all right.

He approached the house from the side and found a partially opened window. He listened breathlessly, but any sound from inside was swallowed by the insistent rumble of the surf. He eased the window open, drew out the S&W, and silently climbed over the sill. He was in an empty bedroom and then he heard a sound from the direction of the living room. He crept to the bedroom door and peered into the big living room. It was empty and he removed his shoes. He darted into the living room and saw Smiley Gallagher's massive back on the balcony. He was intently scanning the beach through a pair of binoculars. Caine crept carefully through the house, checking all the rooms. Smiley was alone.

He walked up to Smiley and stuck the muzzle into

Smiley's back. Smiley jerked and Caine poked him harder.

"Nice and easy, Smiley," Caine said.

"Is that you, Johnny?" Smiley said, without turning around.

"Take your gun out with two fingers of your left hand and hold it out by the muzzle."

Smiley tensed, then he slowly held out the gun.

"Now toss it behind you and don't get cute," Caine said.

Smiley flicked the gun backward and it bounced silently on the living-room carpet. The copper-colored sun hovered on the horizon like a new-minted penny, balanced on edge.

"Where's C.J.?" Caine demanded.

"On the beach. You can see her through the field glasses. Do you know what you're doing, Johnny boy?" Smiley said.

"Inside," Caine snapped and backed carefully away from Smiley. The two men faced each other in the dim shadows. The sky was slashed with red, as though it had been stabbed. The two men looked like burning figures in the dusk light.

"Where are your handcuffs, Smiley?"

Smiley shook his pudgy face and smiled to indicate he didn't have any. Caine cocked the hammer of the S&W.

"Would you rather I shoot you?" Caine asked, and Smiley hurriedly reached into his jacket pocket and brought out the cuffs and key. Caine cuffed Smiley's hands behind him and pocketed the key.

"We'll get you, Johnny. You know it as well as I do," Smiley said. Caine shrugged and yanked the phone from the wall.

"Give it up now. Maybe I can swing a deal for you," Smiley said.

Caine laughed. He bared his teeth and glared at Smiley, his eyes like burning coals in the dying light. Then he suddenly stepped forward and savagely kicked Smiley in the groin. Smiley pitched forward and rolled on the ground squealing in a high-pitched scream.

"Why, Johnny? Why?" Smiley managed to gasp.

"Because I don't have a tiger cage handy, you son-of-a-bitch," Caine retorted, and kicked Smiley again.

Smiley screamed. He went on screaming until Caine's cold-cocked him with the butt of the S&W. Smiley's unconscious body lay on the floor like a massive animal carcass, his breath sonorously whistling in his throat. Caine walked out to the balcony and spotted C.J. standing on the sand. She was wearing rolled up jeans and an oversized man's plaid flannel shirt, her long hair blowing in the wind and flickering like flame in the coppery light. Caine stuck the gun in his belt and walked down the balcony stairs to the beach.

At first she didn't see him approach. She was staring vaguely at the lights strung along the Malibu pier, her body tense and awkward, like a seagull poised for flight. She was waiting as only a woman can wait, straining with every molecule of her body, for the sound of a footstep. When she saw him, she hugged her arms, as though she were cold. The hiss of the ebbing surf sounded in his ears like a long sigh.

"I thought we had something, you and me," Caine said.

"So did I," she said, her voice sad and wistful.

"Wasserman is dead. Give me the stamp, or I'll kill

you, too," he said, unbuttoning his jacket so that she could see the butt of the S&W.

"I need it. Now that everything is busted wide open, it's my only chance to get away. So if you're going to kill me, do it now. They're going to get me anyway. If someone is going to do it, I want it to be you," she said breathlessly.

"Then you do have the stamp?"

C.J. nodded, her jaw set defiantly.

"Where is it?" Caine asked.

"I have it here," tapping her shirt pocket. "It shouldn't be too difficult for you to take it from me."

"All you ever cared about was the money! You had to be a whore about it, didn't you?" he said, anger rising like bile in the back of his throat, almost choking him.

"Wait," she snapped defiantly, her eyes gleaming. "Before you kill me because of some damn male code, let me say one thing. It was the only logical thing to do. Wasserman never told me anything about the Starfish until just before I left for Lima. You were alone and outnumbered, with the U.S. government, the damned CIA, the Nazis, the Peruvian Army, and God knows what against you. You didn't stand a chance. Wasserman threatened to kill me if I didn't do it and offered me the stamp if I did. I made the only logical choice. You'd have done exactly the same thing in my place. Tell the truth. Wouldn't you?"

And then Caine was laughing, helplessly, wonderfully, for what seemed like the first time in years. She was absolutely right, of course. He'd have done exactly the same thing in her place. He sat down on the sand and shook his head derisively. She squatted beside him and finally began to smile. For a long moment they gazed in silence at the sea turning to reddish rust in the sunset. She rested her hand on his knee as lightly as a butterfly.

"I did it, but I didn't like it, Johnny," she said softly.

"I wasn't too crazy about it myself," he said.

"What are we going to do now? They'll all be after us," she said finally. Her watery eyes were flames in the burning dusk. If she was a Venus flytrap, she was a good one, he thought wryly.

"Do you like to ski?" he brought out suddenly. A sandpiper ran along the water's edge, chasing a retreating wave, then plunged its long bill into the wet sand. A large wave, veined with foam, curled onto the beach and the sandpiper ran before it.

"It's even better than sex . . . almost," she said. She reached over and touched his cheek lightly, as if to brush away a dirt smudge. He glanced at her and then back at the ebbing tide.

"First, New York, to pick up new cover identities. Then Zurich, with the stamp. After that, the Alps. Okay?" he said.

He looked at her and could almost hear that little computer of a brain ticking away as she smiled at him and nodded yes. Caine smiled. It was going to be an interesting trip.

AFTERWORD

This is a work of fiction and, with the single exception of Dr. Josef Mengele, any resemblance to persons living or dead is purely coincidental. The description of Mengele's crimes and other activities up to 1973, in Part I of this work, is based on eyewitness accounts and published material. As of this writing, Josef Mengele is still alive and is living in Paraguay.

Both ODESSA and the *Kameradenwerk* still exist. These powerful Nazi organizations are often involved in intelligence and political activities and their influence is widespread.

There is a Schweitzer Medical Institute located near Pucallpa in the Peruvian Amazon. In addition the Mobil/Union Group, a consortium of American oil companies, has made an oil strike in the Amazon and is presently engaged in exploration and drilling activities. To the best of my knowledge, neither of these organizations has ever been involved in any way with the Nazis.

The Starfish Conspiracy is a complete fiction.

Andrew Kaplan
June 1979

ARENA

NORMAN BOGNER

"Another *Godfather!* It has virtually everything!"—*Abilene Reporter-News*

The spectacular new novel by the bestselling author of *Seventh Avenue*

Four families escaped the Nazi nightmare with dreams that could only come true in America.
For Alec Stone, the dream was a boxing arena.
For Sam West, it was a Catskill resort—a refuge for his beautiful, speechless daughter, Lenore.
For Victor Conte, it meant establishing a west-coast talent agency.
And for Paul Salica, it meant a lasting committment to another family—the Mafia.
But to young, gifted Jonathan Stone, no dream was big enough. Obsessed by love for Lenore, he would risk all they won—again and again.

A Dell Book   (10369-X) $3.25

Comes the Blind Fury

John Saul

**Bestselling author of
Cry for the Strangers
and *Suffer the Children***

More than a century ago, a gentle, blind child walked the paths of Paradise Point. Then other children came, teasing and taunting her until she lost her footing on the cliff and plunged into the drowning sea.

Now, 12-year-old Michelle and her family have come to live in that same house—to escape the city pressures, to have a better life.

But the sins of the past do not die. They reach out to embrace the living. Dreams will become nightmares.

Serenity will become terror. There will be no escape.

A Dell Book $2.75   (11428-4)

Dell BESTSELLERS